PRAISE FOR Y

Not What She Seems

"Jac's return to her hometown reveals lie after shocking lie. You're going to want to help her dig up every dirty secret. *Not What She Seems* is a must-read for thriller lovers."

—Melinda Leigh, #1 *Wall Street Journal* bestselling author

"In a small town, secrets collide with the grief and guilt of our fierce, feisty heroine, Jac Brodie. As her world is falling apart, Jac pieces together a mystery that could change her life as she knows it. With an expertly drawn setting, pulse-pounding pacing, and an explosive climax, *Not What She Seems* is a magnificent read. This twisty, high-octane thriller instantly hooked me and never let go. I'm now a forever fan of Yasmin Angoe's stunning writing."

—Samantha M. Bailey, *USA Today* and #1 international bestselling author of *A Friend in the Dark*

"Anthony award–nominated author Yasmin Angoe is an expert at blending fast-paced action, jaw-dropping plot twists, and flawed but likable characters. Her first standalone, *Not What She Seems*, is a must-read for domestic suspense fans. An excellent tale of cat and mouse, or should I say spider versus fly."

—Kellye Garrett, award-winning author of *Missing White Woman*

"Angoe not only creates believable characters, she crafts a layered mystery woven through with family secrets, sharp-edged revenge, and unexpected redemption. All that plus it has heart; the climactic scene brought tears to my eyes."

—Jess Lourey, Edgar-nominated author of *The Taken Ones*

"Jacinda Brodie, you have my sword. Never have I fallen deeper in love with characters than I did the Brodies of beautiful, troubled, small-town South Carolina. Yasmin Angoe's incredible blend of talents—her ability to deliver high-intensity blowups on par with the best action thrillers and her deep character work, which shines through her uniquely voicey prose—make *Not What She Seems* a total knockout. I laughed, I gasped, and—shockingly—I cried. In an astonishing feat, Angoe combines a dark-as-sin psychological suspense with a heartwarming tale of familial redemption, peppered with laugh-out-loud social commentary. Like me, readers will marvel at her virtuosity while eagerly awaiting her next."

—Ashley Winstead, critically acclaimed author of *Midnight Is the Darkest Hour*

It Ends with Knight

"Watch your back, Liam Neeson. This avenger is tough."

—*Kirkus Reviews*

"High-stakes action, intrigue, and a professional assassin . . . the thrilling conclusion to Yasmin Angoe's Nena Knight series has it all."

—*Woman's World*

"Nena Knight can cover Orphan X's six o'clock any day! Stolen from her village in Ghana, Knight reinvents herself as an elite assassin capable of all orders of badassery. One of thrillerdom's rising stars, Yasmin Angoe paints Knight with nuance, strength, and grace. These books burn hot and read fast."

—Gregg Hurwitz, *New York Times* bestselling author of the Orphan X series

"*It Ends with Knight* finishes this trilogy every bit as heart pounding, soul searching, and explosive as it started. Nena Knight now takes her place alongside crime fiction's most unforgettable heroines."

—Rachel Howzell Hall, *New York Times* bestselling author of *We Lie Here* and *These Toxic Things*

"Yasmin Angoe returns with both barrels blazing in *It Ends with Knight*. Nena Knight is such a well-crafted character, and Angoe's writing is an absolute joy. You need some pretty strong writer mojo to get readers to root for an assassin, and Angoe pulls it off. I truly hope *It Ends with Knight* is not the end of this wonderful series."

—Tracy Clark, bestselling author and winner of the Sue Grafton Memorial Award

They Come at Knight

An Amazon Best Book of the Month: Mystery, Thriller & Suspense

"There's nothing ho-hum about Nena Knight, the killer at the heart of Yasmin Angoe's *They Come at Knight* . . . In one blistering action scene after another, we get to see how good Nena is at what she does."

—New York Times Book Review

"A second round of action-packed, high-casualty intrigue for professional assassin Nena Knight. A lethal tale of an all-but-superhero whose author promises that 'in this story, there are no heroes.'"

—Kirkus Reviews

"This action-packed novel drives toward an explosive conclusion. Determined to survive devastating loss and mete out justice, Nena is a heroine readers will embrace."

—Publishers Weekly

Her Name Is Knight

"This stunning debut . . . deftly balances action, interpersonal relationships, issues of trauma, and profound human questions in an unforgettable novel."

—*Library Journal* (starred review)

"A parable of reclaiming personal and tribal identity by seizing power at all costs."

—*Kirkus Reviews*

"Angoe expertly builds tension by shifting between her lead's past and present lives. Thriller fans will cheer Aninyeh every step of the way."

—*Publishers Weekly*

"An action-packed thriller you can lose yourself in."

—PopSugar

"Memorable characters, drama, heart-pounding danger . . . this suspenseful novel has it all."

—*Woman's World*

"A crackerjack story with truly memorable characters. I can't wait to see what Yasmin Angoe comes up with next."

—David Baldacci, #1 *New York Times* bestselling author

"Yasmin Angoe's debut novel, *Her Name Is Knight*, is an amazing, action-packed international thriller full of suspense, danger, and even romance. It's like a John Wick prequel except John is a beautiful African woman with a particular set of skills."

—S. A. Cosby, *New York Times* bestselling author of *Razorblade Tears*

"It's hard to believe that *Her Name Is Knight* is Yasmin Angoe's debut novel. This dual-timeline story about a highly trained Miami-based assassin who learns to reclaim her power after having her entire life ripped from her as a teenager in Ghana is equal parts love story, social commentary, and action thriller. Nena Knight will stay with you long after you've read the last word, and this is a must-read for fans of Lee Child and S. A. Cosby. I found myself crying in one chapter and cheering in the next. I couldn't put it down!"
—Kellye Garrett, Anthony, Agatha, and Lefty Award–winning author

"This was a book I couldn't put down. Yasmin Angoe does a brilliant job of inviting you into a world of espionage and revenge while giving her characters depth and backstory that pull the reader in even more. This story has depth, excitement, and heartbreaking loss all intertwined into an awesome debut. The spy thriller genre has a new name to look out for!"

—Matthew Farrell, bestselling author of *Don't Ever Forget*

"This brave and profoundly gorgeous thriller takes readers to places they've never been, to challenges they've never faced, and to judgments that leave the strongest in tears. *Her Name Is Knight* is a stunning and important debut, and Yasmin Angoe is a fantastic new talent."
—Hank Phillippi Ryan, *USA Today* bestselling author of *Her Perfect Life*

"*Her Name Is Knight* is a roundhouse kick of a novel—intense, evocative, and loaded with character and international intrigue. Nena Knight is a protagonist for the ages and one readers will not soon forget. *Her Name Is Knight* isn't just thrills and action, either—the book lingers with you long after you've finished. More, please."
—Alex Segura, acclaimed author of *Star Wars Poe Dameron: Free Fall*, *Secret Identity*, and *Blackout*

NOT
WHAT
SHE
SEEMS

OTHER TITLES BY YASMIN ANGOE

It Ends with Knight

They Come at Knight

Her Name Is Knight

NOT WHAT SHE SEEMS

A Novel

YASMIN ANGOE

This is a work of fiction. Names, characters, organizations, places, events, and incidents are either products of the author's imagination or are used fictitiously. Otherwise, any resemblance to actual persons, living or dead, is purely coincidental.

Published by Thomas & Mercer, Seattle

www.apub.com

ISBN-13: 9781662508332 (hardcover)
ISBN-13: 9781662508318 (paperback)
ISBN-13: 9781662508325 (digital)

Cover design by Kimberly Glyder
Cover images: © Jon Lovette / Getty; © innovatedcaptures / Getty

Printed in the United States of America
First edition

To the McClinton family: I am endlessly inspired by your support, love, and incredible sense of family.

The road to hell is paved with good intentions.

—Unknown

PROLOGUE

Montavious Brodie Sr. clicked send on his Dell computer, the desktop over five years old that his eldest granddaughter had been begging him to let her upgrade to one of those Macs. He didn't need something skinny, fast, and flashy. He liked his clunky, heavy computer because it had just what he needed—the World Wide Web, where he could connect to his fellow Armchair Detectives, or Armchairs for short, on the latest unsolved crime they were working to crack.

He loved solving puzzles, or being what the young ones these days called an armchair detective. He didn't care. He had been a South Carolinian detective and investigator (depending on the agency) in his heyday before he'd retired and left the policing to his son.

Now, something new, something he'd heard when he probably shouldn't have, had put a bee in his bonnet. *Colleton.* The name jiggled something in the recesses of his mind. Something from decades ago, but he couldn't quite shake it loose.

Colleton. This was an old one. He could spend his time trying to track the name down to answer the question that was beginning to light a fire in his gut. But honestly, he hated the World Wide Web. There were too many searches. Too much bullshit clouding the truth. He left that kind of work to the younger Armchairs. They found some information, and he combed through it, teasing out the clues and the obscure bits of fact that the novices tended to gloss over. It was a good work model for the group. Everyone knew their lane. People from all points of the world came together in the name of helping to bring justice for victims and closure for families.

Montavious used his two pointer fingers to peck out the letters into his group forums—where he usually went to find new cold cases—to see if someone might recognize the name. Then, satisfied his message had gone through, he logged out and picked up his weathered iPhone. It ran so slow these days because the damn Apple people didn't send any more updates. Plus, he'd heard on the CNN that consumers were suing the company for forcing customers to upgrade to new phones by not sending updates for the old ones. Well, no damn Apple was gonna make him buy a new phone. He'd ride this one until the wheels fell off.

He looked over his half-moon-shaped readers. He only wore them to read the bright screens of his phone and computer. Maybe the newspaper, too, since the damn print seemed to be getting smaller these days.

He pulled up his recent-calls list, bypassing the first few: Chief Linwood's office (same office his boy used to head); the post office; Mrs. Barbara Harris (Barb let him take her out a time or two), who volunteered at the hospital and worked part time at the Manor overseeing the renovations with Ms. Arden; and his youngest granddaughter, Pen. He scrolled until his slightly crooked finger landed on the name of his favorite partner in crime, the one who humored his critical, never-trusting eye. Jac, the older grand who'd lost her way, and for years, he had prayed to the man upstairs that he'd be able to get her back home. Somehow. Whatever had happened out there on the bluff, Montavious knew the truth wasn't gonna be found in the town's gossip . . . or even in what *she* believed. What had driven Jac away from home.

Maybe this time she'd pick up the call instead of replying to his voicemail messages days later. Maybe this time she missed her old granddad enough to call back, and he could hear her voice one last time before the night was up.

Probably out with her college folks, he concluded as the automated message told him his granddaughter was unavailable. As usual—though the robot lady didn't say that part.

"Hey, JD." His knobby fingers rubbed absentmindedly at the area where his pacemaker was situated beneath his skin.

Junior Dick. The nickname between the two of them. One his daughter-in-law, Angela, hated with a passion, which made her daughter love it even more. Her junior dick to his senior. Partners in crime. Partners in this thing called life.

"'Member how I said way back then you can never run from your past?" He hesitated. Was this really how he wanted to begin? Did he really want to piss her off before he'd even gotten his message out? "Or rather, the past comes and finds you no matter what?"

Maybe this time he'd been asking for the past to find him. He'd willed and hoped that someday the one that got away would come knocking. And they had.

"Junior, this ole man might have played his hand a little too soon. I think . . . think I screwed up real bad." He swallowed nothing down his dry throat. "It'll make sense when I can show you. It's been years." He couldn't believe it. After all this time. To have another chance at this again. "Who would have thought?"

He was breathless, looking up to find he was facing his large whiteboard stand and staring at the word he'd just typed to the Armchairs. *Colleton*. It was as if the name had beckoned him to it, and he'd come running, twisting his chair around instinctively to face the past. The name had just been mentioned in passing. Probably didn't realize it had even been said. But a reckoning came with that name, *Colleton*. As in, Colleton *Girls*. He scribbled it on his whiteboard.

He was in his cabin in the woods, away from the house, where he could get his thoughts together without the constant distracting chatter from Pen and her mom, Angela. Back at the house with them, it was easy to get caught up in Angela's helicopter mothering and Pen's incessant doctoring, like he was some kind of invalid. It was just a little thing with his heart.

He cleared his throat and chased away the case of jitters that had suddenly sprouted. "Call me back this time, will ya—"

The snap of brittle branches crushed beneath weight stopped him cold. He ended the call.

Out here, the woods were always alive with sounds, but he knew them all, and they soon became background noise he barely said "boo" to. This wasn't a raccoon or a coyote, however. Not a bear (hadn't seen one in decades) or a gator (too far from the lakes and swamps). A tree limb falling? No. Heavy enough to be a deer, though.

The old man's heart was terrible. Eyesight wasn't like it used to be, but he thought it was better than that of most folks his age. But his hearing was damn near perfect and could suss out a racoon digging in the trash bins or a wandering deer out there. This was not either. There was no more noise after the snap, as if the trespasser had halted, worried the old man had heard them. Well, he had. And if they were worried about being heard, then that meant they weren't supposed to be there.

He ignored the protesting creaks from his bones as he eased out of his worn, wooden swivel chair, pulling his half-moon glasses from his face before setting them upside down on the oak desk he'd built from scratch. He cocked his ear, honing his hearing and waiting for more noise so he could determine its cause.

Snap. As sharp as a crack of thunder. So loud. So deliberate.

Not an animal or falling wood. Was closer this time.

His cabin—the home he, his dearly departed Mae, and their two sons had owned for over half a century—was made up of five small rooms. Two square bedrooms on opposite ends, with the living room in the middle and their kitchen at the top of it with a tiny bathroom beside it. A small half hall to the left of the kitchen ended at a single side door. If he went out that door, he'd be deposited into the dense woods and marshes surrounding his home. His land stretched out until it bumped into the sprawling Moor property that was made up of a good portion of these woods. The Manor, the winding trails that dumped into the clearing before eventually hitting the cliffs at the back of the mansion—all of that was Moor property.

Stacks of old papers, piles of books, corkboards stuck with push-pins where Montavious had mapped the cases that he and his folks followed with the stereotypical red yarn, all cluttered his living room. No one used the yarn anymore, but he liked it just the same, a nostalgic reminder of back in the day when a cop had to pound serious pavement to figure out the connection. It wasn't just practically at the tips of your fingers on the computer like it seemed to be these days. Maybe that was a good thing. Maybe not. He hadn't decided yet.

He thought of going to his bedroom and double-checking his hidden safe, which held two things. A case he'd die for. And a case he'd kill to solve. He'd been keeping watch on the first for nearly thirty years. It was the only case he never wanted solved.

Lord forgive him.

The half hall and the side door were where the noise came from. He moved toward them, pulling his handgun from the top bookshelf, where he kept it locked and loaded. If he was anyone else, Montavious would have given the unannounced visitor a second thought before opening the door. But this was his home, his property, his neck of the woods.

Hell, in his career, Detective Brodie had gone up against the likes of murderers, bank robbers, abusers, organized crime syndicates (yes, even in the good ole South), traffickers, and even a serial killer or two.

Not to mention that, as modern and accepting as people claimed to be now, this was still the South. He was still a Black man living in a small house, alone, deep in the woods. He was not far removed—not removed at all—from those times of his life when his advancement in the military, then in the police academy, then through the ranks to detective, then to a job as an agent at SLED, South Carolina's State Law Enforcement Division, was hindered and nearly made nonexistent because of the color of his skin.

That kind of hell would never be forgotten, no matter how much he and his family were known and respected throughout South Carolina, especially in the Lowcountry, by both Black and white folks. He'd seen the worst of society because of skin color. He'd seen the worst of humanity because of what Cain did to Abel way back when. Murder.

He'd seen plenty of terrifying things. Yet, alone in the pitch black with nothing but the spotlights surrounding his property to stave off the night, and despite his aged body and slowed reflexes, Montavious Brodie Sr. refused to ever be scared.

Despite what he'd endured in his lifetime, some clown in the woods wasn't about to make Montavious Brodie Sr. lose his religion. Not then. Not now.

Still, his mama didn't raise no fool, either, and the old man could never be too careful. He had his gun. When he opened the door to the warm autumn night, the leaves rustling in the wind, he saw nothing but dark. The light of the cabin shone behind him, making it harder for his eyes to adjust. He should have remembered his police training instead of assuming nothing could touch him here. He should have cut the lights in the house so he could have made out the figure coming close in the dark. Montavious should have done a lot of things differently. But he didn't.

Recognition washed over him as his visitor approached, and his once-defensive stance with gun at the ready relaxed. Shouldn't have done that either.

"Well now," he said. "It's damn late to be calling." Surprise, annoyance, and a tiny bit of curiosity overpowered what should have been suspicion and mistrust. "Had time to think it through?"

The Taser lashed out quicker than his numbed reflexes could react. Montavious stumbled back from the impact, surprised at the force with which the contraption was shoved into his chest, right on top of the area where the pacemaker kept his rhythm in check. His gun clattered to the ground, going off in a sharp crack that rendered one ear useless. But the suddenly muted sounds didn't faze him.

It was the electricity. The volts surging through his body over and over. Paralyzing him. Making his teeth come down hard on his tongue. His mouth flooded with the warm gush filling his throat, spilling through his bared teeth as he ground in. His hands clawed and couldn't help to break his fall. The Taser was one thing. He'd been hit with one before, though not over and over.

It was his heart. The volts seized the muscle, making it beat faster and faster—too fast. Frighteningly fast. Until it stopped entirely.

As his body lay half in, half out of the tiny cabin where he'd lived with the love of his life (now gone), where he'd raised his two boys (both gone too), where his granddaughters had played, his last thoughts settled in his mind. This had been a happy home. He was glad to die here.

His last thoughts—before the blood from his heart stopped pumping to his brain, until the room went hot and bright and then his sight began to dim—were that now his partner in crime, his JD, would be able to find her way back home to Brook Haven. He was finally bringing her home.

1

There's a scene in the movie *Waiting to Exhale* when Angela Bassett's character, Bernadine, lights her husband's BMW on fire because he left her for another woman after years of marriage. She packs all his expensive-ass stuff in his car and douses it with gas. She lights a cigarette, making a choice right then to no longer be a doormat for him, to not go down without a fight. With a flick of her wrist, the match is soaring through the air and hits the pile of clothes peeking out of the sunroof in a spray of orange sparks and *whoosh*! The car, the clothes, her hope for their marriage, her grief go up in that raging inferno. She walks away from it all, fierce like she's walking the runway, rising like a phoenix from the ashes of that burning car.

It didn't work that way for me when, that afternoon, I found out I'd been betrayed. I didn't pile all of Conrad Meckleson's belongings in his car and torch it. There would be no cleansing burn, and I wouldn't be rising from the ashes, like a phoenix, of what Conrad had done. I would remain the same old Jacinda Brodie, only now likely unemployed and without my research fellowship. But as I stood in the darkened study of Conrad's empty condo—the box of what he stole from me tucked securely under my arm, murderous thoughts in my head of waiting for him to return home so I could gut him with one of his cherished knives—I thought that, even though I might have blown up my career and would likely get charged for breaking and entering, I was taking back what was mine. I was taking from him the thing he wanted the most, something he never should've had.

The second-worst day of my life had started right after lunch, with me at work, where I was a teaching and research assistant in the Programs and Grants Office of the College of Arts and Letters at Capitol University. At the desk in my cubicle, I sat buzzing with excitement about what I knew was going to be my acceptance into the university's highly competitive Fellows Program.

I fired up my department-issued laptop, signed in to my school account, pulled up my email, and scanned the short list of unread messages for the one that would determine my professional career for the next year. I ran through a series of calming breaths. My right hand landed on the mouse and eased the pointer to the email, hovering there while I psyched myself up. I didn't know why I was going through all this drama because I just knew I was a shoo-in for the position. I was the most qualified, had submitted my best writing curated from my time at the university as a grad student and then as a teaching assistant and assistant to the writer in residence. I had done the work, and now I'd be rewarded with this prestigious position. And then, I'd go overseas and be a writer abroad, leaving the darkness of my past behind me.

I just knew I was a shoo-in. Did I say that already?

I clicked the mouse, opening up the email that would tell me what I wanted to hear. My eyes scanned the first line, going through all the initial greetings and pleasantries and their hope to find me well.

> We regret to inform you . . .

My mouth began to dry.

> . . . that you were not selected . . .

My stomach lurched and fell to the bottoms of my feet.

> . . . as this year's Research Fellow.

The eventual Capitol University tenure, subsequent government appointments, and prestige oozing out of my pores disintegrated into smoke, and all my plans and dreams with them.

I read the email twice more. I must have misread. Or maybe they'd sent it to the wrong applicant. Then reality began to sink in. I was not a research fellow. I didn't get in. And I had nothing left. I sat, wondering where I'd gone wrong. What in my portfolio had gotten me rejected? Where did I go from here?

The first person I thought to ask was my roommate and closest friend at the university. She'd tell me why the judging committee had rejected me. She'd help me understand how I could have failed so miserably when I was supposed to be the best. I'd worked so hard for this.

"Jac, you know I can't," Maura Singh said, her brown eyes wide and worried behind her oversize teal-colored glasses. "I can't give you special treatment just because I worked on this. I'm not going to do it for any of the other candidates."

I clasped my hands together in a plea, hoping that my being near tears would show her how important this was. "There's nothing special about telling me why I'm a colossal fuckup," I said to her. "Again."

"You're not a colossal fuckup. You're not even a minor one."

"Then why didn't I get this? This was a done deal. I was the top prospect, everyone said," I complained, plopping down backward on her desk beside her chair. I clamped my hands together. "Please, just tell me. You don't have to show me anything. And I won't approach any of the committee members. You know I won't. I just need to know why so I know how to do better next time."

Maura sighed, throwing herself into her chair so hard that it pushed back a couple of centimeters from the force. "You didn't do anything wrong, Jac."

I was confused. "What do you mean?"

"I mean, you were a go. But then the chair voiced concerns and got the committee to revote. Those 'concerns'"—she used air quotes here—"made the vote a fifty-fifty split."

My stomach dropped as the realization hit me. "With the chair as the deciding vote."

Maura nodded, and her mouth twisted to reflect her displeasure. "Exactly."

"That asshole." I seethed. My mind still didn't want to believe that what was mine had been snatched away like that.

"What concerns?" I asked.

Maura shrugged. "Bullshit. Lies. But he's convincing. And he has an axe to grind, and you know why." She looked at me pointedly.

I looked back. I'm sure my eyes were wide as saucers. I did know, but I didn't want to believe it. No, I couldn't believe it. To believe it meant accepting that my rejection was planned. Was me being singled out. Was payback.

"That rat bastard," I fumed. This was my life. My career. Be mad at me, sure, but take away an opportunity like this? And for what?

"I told you not to screw with that man," Maura whispered hurriedly. "I said he was a snake and a dirtbag flirt and that you'd regret getting involved with your boss."

My mind searched for excuses, justifications as to why having a relationship with Conrad Meckleson was no big deal and would have no impact on my future in the collegiate world.

"But what does our affair have to do with this? He wouldn't." I couldn't finish.

"Sure he would," Maura confirmed like she was psychic.

She answered my question like it was the most assured piece of knowledge she had. She said it with a conviction that scared me, because if he'd do that, then what else would he do? But he couldn't be that cruel, could he?

"He absolutely can be that cruel." Maura scooched her chair closer to me, pulling my hands from my face, her face displaying all the embarrassing pity I didn't want her to have. "I told you to be careful, not to get sucked in, because that third-rate has-been bestselling author was our new writer in residence. I told you he was a lothario."

I didn't have enough energy or brain capacity. Only Maura would speak in language from a different century.

"I said he was only here to screw anyone who was young, willing, and worshipped him. I always said he's just waiting for his next big break."

"Okay, but we broke up."

"You mean you dumped him, Jac," she corrected. Maura blew out an exasperated breath, as if I should have known the rules of dating your boss. "You weren't supposed to be the one who cut things off. He'd want you to be crying and acting all lovesick so that he could lord his authority over you and gaslight you into believing it was you and not him. Then he'd tell you not to tell anyone so that your career wouldn't be ruined, when it was really his career he was trying to protect. Me Too movement and all." Maura emphasized her philosophizing with a point of her finger.

"He's not thinking about me. He's gotta be dating someone else now."

She nodded sagely, the well of collegiate gossip. "Oh, he is. Trust me. Erin hangs around his office all the time. They have long advisory sessions a couple times a week. Long." She mouthed the last word.

Even more reason for him to forget about me and let me do my thing. It wasn't like we were in love. It wasn't like it was anything more than decent sex and good conversation. He was a way for me to lose myself in something other than thoughts of my past. Nothing serious enough to kill my dreams like this.

"You know how men can be about their pride." She rolled her eyes again. "Who said 'Hell hath no fury like a woman scorned'?"

"William Congreve," I muttered, barely listening, pulling out my phone and finding his number in the contacts list.

"How do you know this shit?" Maura snorted. "Well, clearly William Congreve hadn't met Conrad Meckleson yet. And of course the other committee members would believe him because he worked the closest with you. You were his assistant."

Regardless of our intimate relationship, I'd done the work. I deserved this.

"We didn't even discuss me applying for the Fellows," I muttered, staring at his name on my phone's screen. "He had nothing to do with it."

"He's got everything to do with it now, huh?" Maura's eyebrows rose. "But how would anyone know that you actually put in the work despite the fact you were boning your professor?"

It wasn't like that.

"They won't know that this is a scorned-lover plot twist and that he's the villain. They'll think you did it to get favors from him. All they know is that the world-renowned Conrad Meckleson, *New York Times* bestselling author, National Book Award and PEN finalist, said he had concerns. His literary résumé was enough for him to pull rank and affect the vote."

More like his narcissism, entitlement, and obscene case of pettiness that no amount of therapy would ever rid him of.

Maura's expression cracked into concern. "I'm really sorry, Jac. It's not fair. That's what these guys in power do, you know? Wield it over our heads, and make us think we have to give in to their advances or kiss their asses for a referral, even though they're pieces of subhuman shit."

Her voice had risen a couple of octaves, fueled by her righteous indignation. Someone in the next cubicle over coughed, seeming to remind Maura of where she was, and she regulated herself. "And what's fucked up is that you can't expose him without exposing yourself. It's not worth it. You can apply again. I heard he's been bragging about some huge deal he got on a true crime thriller, so maybe he'll leave before his time is up."

True crime thriller. The words pricked at me. For as long as we'd been together, Conrad had suffered from a severe bout of writer's block. Every idea he had was knocked down by his agent—and rightfully so. They were horrible. Now, he had an idea worthy of a major-league book deal and never mentioned it, when he'd once told me every little thing. My hands dampened. He wouldn't have. Would he?

I stood up quickly, startling Maura from her endless stream of dialogue about the evils of men with power. Any other time, I would have humored her, but now, there was a spark of something stirring that I hoped to hell I was wrong about.

"I need to . . . go back to my desk." It was the first thing I could think of.

Maura looked skeptically at my phone. "Promise me you won't contact him. Don't give him the satisfaction of seeing you down."

I didn't answer her. There were no promises I could make.

Maura looked at me in a way that said she didn't like my silence. She was blocking the entrance to her cubicle, but I edged past, my next steps already forming in my mind. I needed to get to my cubicle. There would be no more work for me today.

She called after me, "Whatever you're thinking about doing, Jac, don't. Think it through first, okay? About what it will mean for you."

Thinking about what it would mean for me was exactly what I was doing when I went to his condo, parked up the street, and opened a blank email on my phone.

My eyes, once trusting, prickled with the sting of betrayal. Conrad had been my mentor, my getaway from the real world, my confidant. Now, he was the architect of my failure. I summoned the strength to record what I felt in words that would echo through the academic corridors of the College of Arts and Letters. The evidence of incriminating messages, dates and times of our meetups and trips, and when and why I'd ended our relationship. The cursor blinked angrily, waiting for me to expose the man who had not only cheated me out of my fellowship, but might have also stolen the very essence of my being. My story.

I imagined Conrad sitting at the head of the table, telling the other committee members how I wasn't good enough for the prestigious research program that would have set me up for my career, knowing the only reason he was sabotaging me was because I'd cut him off before he was ready.

My fingers trembled as I held the phone. I began typing, the words a concerto of feelings I'd held on to for six years. Six years of suppressing how angry, hurt, and betrayed I felt, not only by him but by everyone back home. I unleashed it there. The email unfolded like a manifesto, detailing the affair, the professional sabotage. How hard I had worked on my portfolio. How I hadn't told anyone, not even him, that I was applying because I didn't want him to influence my work. How he had spoken against me during the committee's decision when he realized I was one of the candidates, and how that had affected the committee's decision, his vote being the deciding factor when he should have recused himself. I kept his theft of my personal tragedy to myself. I had another idea about how to deal with that.

As I laid bare the pain inflicted by Conrad's actions, I felt a strange sense of liberation. The truth, no matter how painful, demanded acknowledgment. I wished I'd realized that back then, back at home, when I'd run from what I'd done instead of confronting it.

The muted taps on my screen became a cathartic rhythm—a sort of cadence of defiance against the injustices I had suffered at his hands and at my own. Before I hit the arrow to send, I made a call.

"Is this about the decision on the Fellows?" Conrad's smooth voice said through my phone's speaker. Soon, everyone would put it all together . . . why I had run out . . . my losing the fellowship . . . my relationship with Conrad. I didn't need to be there for that.

I could hear the smile in his voice. He was loving the fact that I'd called. I imagined him leaning back in his chair, propping one leg over the other knee as he relished my defeat.

"Are you there?" he asked when I said nothing. "Why are you calling me?"

Why was I calling? I hadn't planned to confront him or ask him why he'd sabotaged me. That I already knew. I didn't know how to ask him what I really wanted to know without becoming more fodder for his story.

"It's nothing personal, Jac," he continued, apparently not needing my response. "It was a hard choice, really."

"That's bullshit," I spit out, no longer holding myself back. "What you did was very purposeful and personal."

Something rustled on his end, as if he was shifting in his chair. His voice lowered, the easiness slipping away. "Personal," he repeated, a tinge of anger slipping through. "Who would know that? Huh, Jac?"

"You sabotaged me. This is payback for me breaking up with you." My anger had subsided as I wrote the email that I wasn't sure I'd send, but hearing his cockiness—his dare—refueled the dwindling fire.

"Who's going to believe you over me? They'll fire you before they remove me. I bring the students, the funding, and the prestige. What do you bring? Paper and pen to meetings? Notes on whatever research project they throw at you like breadcrumbs? Come on."

He laughed at me.

I hated to be laughed at.

"Fuck you."

"Been there, done that," he said easily. "You know, I should actually thank you, Jac. Not sure if I mentioned . . . probably not, since we haven't communicated for some time, but I'm publishing a new thriller soon. Just signed the deal. Big Five publisher, six-figure, two-book. I mean, I have to finish the manuscript—got the deal on spec because of my history. But this will be my finest work. This will be the Pulitzer."

"What is the story about?" I forced out. My eyes were on the unsent email, the words blurring from the intensity with which I stared. "You haven't had anything good in over a year. You've been mining ideas from your students, and I know because you kept talking about them."

"Yeah, but I also had you, my muse, my inspiration. Theirs was made-up shit that couldn't hold water. You . . . you are the real deal."

Muse . . . inspiration . . . words he'd said often to me in the last few months of our relationship. But I'd never put too much thought into them. They were just the lines of an ego-inflated man who thought he had a naive girl under his thumb. All that time I had been using him for a warm body, as a pill to chase away the nightmares and make me finally feel good about something in my life after that one night.

My heart pounded as I waited for confirmation of what I feared the most. "How did I inspire you, Conrad?"

He toyed with me, taking his time to finally answer. "I think it's about time the world knew about a small-town police chief who mysteriously fell off a cliff, and the only person there when it happened was his daughter. Don't you think so, Jac?"

His words dropped down on me like mini explosions.

"You can't . . ." My words failed me. My mind couldn't fire fast enough to turn jumbled thoughts into coherent words. "That's my . . ."

Before, I only had a whisper of suspicion. But I never truly believed he'd use something I'd told him during our most intimate moments. But this was irrefutable confirmation.

"I told you that in confidence. You can't. That can't be your book! You don't have permission."

It couldn't come out . . . what had happened that night, not in any version that wasn't mine. Not when even I couldn't remember it all. So what truth had he come up with?

"Jac, Jac, Jac," he said in condescending placation. "Don't worry too much. I won't make you come across as totally deplorable, even though you committed patricide."

Patricide. The word was an electric shock.

"You can't write this." I hated the way my voice sounded. Weak and useless. Dread growing. What would Mama say if this came out? What would the folks of Brook Haven say?

"Why can't I write this story? Huh? Because I'm not Black?" He spit the last word out like it was a sudden contagious disease, the attitude a fallback defensive reaction to the eternally privileged finally being denied. "Is this about to be a woke thing? Appropriation and shit? Most of those writers who write about leaping from planes have barely ridden an elevator."

"It's not the same thing." The way he was twisting words made my head spin.

"I'll change her race. How about that? Doesn't matter anyway, right? I'll make her white. Maybe Kate Hudson can play her. Or Margot Robbie. Studios are already sniffing for my story, even though the book's not even done yet. A pretty blonde will draw in more for the box office numbers anyway. If the issue is because I'm white, then I'll make it a nonissue."

He said it so simply, the erasure of the best thing about me. My Blackness.

I whispered, "No." Reflex, years of my own conditioning to make them feel better, at ease, to pull back, even though they were in the wrong. And yet I was always trying to appease. I cleared my throat.

"No," I said again, firmer this time. "You can't, because it's my story. I'm still here."

"Yeah? But who's going to listen to you? Hmm? I'm about to make you infamous. Thank me for it. Class now."

He ended the call.

I refused to let the tears welling up fall. I wouldn't give him the satisfaction. I looked in my rearview at his condo, empty and waiting, and then again at the email.

With a final, determined tap of my finger, I hit the blue send button, detonating the bomb that would destroy my professional career at the university, where my truth waited to be acknowledged in the inboxes of Dean Higgins, the president of the university, Human Resources, and every faculty and staff member of the College of Arts and Letters. Then I pulled out my copy of Conrad's key, which I'd honestly forgotten to return when I ended things, and exited the car, my brain asking all the while if I was really about to do this.

2

People live by some sort of routine, a process they follow religiously. They rarely stray from the traditions that bring them success by their standards. Sometimes, their methods sound crazy. Athletes may wear the same dirty jersey for the entire winning season. Some people play the same "lucky" numbers in the lotto, no matter how many times they lose. Others can't begin their day until they've had a cup of coffee. They have superstitions. They have rituals. They have their way of doing things.

Conrad was no different. Even though he was only fifty-three, he was old school when it came to writing. He once said in a lecture I'd attended, and had said often in interviews, that he wrote longhand. His story outline, his notes, his first draft—everything—was by hand. Not even a typewriter. Only once it was completely penned would he begin to type the next draft and revise as he went. He'd make his students print their work so he could write out his notes—damn the trees and the environment.

Once I was in his darkening home, I looked around. He'd mentioned getting his deal on spec. That meant he hadn't sent an entire manuscript. Only a few chapters and a synopsis. Whatever he'd typed up, it wasn't the whole thing. The handwritten pages would be in his study, along with any notes he'd taken. I went there first. Because we hadn't been together in a month, he could've kept his work out freely.

Everything was there—the one good thing to happen to me that day. He must have forgotten that I'd never returned his key.

Grateful for small favors.

His desk was as messy as I remembered, with half-filled pages of loose-leaf strewed all over. Beneath them was a leather-bound notebook. I paged through it, my heart flipping with each scrawled note about me.

—cold, windy January

I swallowed hard, my eyes glossing over the words describing a night I really didn't want to relive.

—night of the cotillion . . . something occurred . . . what???

—he chased her

—Can't recall, or is she lying?

My hands curled into fists, mouth clamped in a firm line.

—She says they argued over??? (hazy—push her for more . . . argued about????)

My racing heart reverberated against my rib cage.

—she shoved him

My eyes shut, the last line seared in my mind.

—and he fell

I took a beat, slowly reopening my eyes with laser focus. I pushed all the free pages of notes together, shoving them into the leather-bound notebook beneath them. The notebook held pages and pages of Conrad's story about me—definitely a sample's worth. I didn't bother reading it. I'd figure it out later. I stuffed it all in a box. Then I saw the publishing contract. Proudly displayed because, of course, he'd want to see it all the time. I took the top page with me. When I was sure I had the most important things he'd need to complete the manuscript, I left the study, hesitating slightly. What if he'd been different this time and typed it up? What if there were more notes he could use? What if he started all over from memory? No, the notes had dates. Dates of when he'd gotten the information from me. He'd notated everything I'd said, recorded my words every moment I wasn't around, before he forgot. Conrad wrote notes about notes . . . his routine.

I should have been suspicious when Conrad had started in with the questions. First, they were innocent and infrequent; then his curiosity seemed to grow like a snowball rolling down a mountain, gaining traction and heft, coming at me in moments when I wasn't expecting it. Then he would use sex and distractions and feigned confusion to calm any prickles of suspicion I had. The seemingly innocuous questions began after one night spent grading term papers—and maybe after drinking one too many bottles of Corona to celebrate the end to the seemingly endless grading—when I'd made two declarations. The first was that I hadn't been back home to Brook Haven, South Carolina, in six years. The second was about a night I never talked about. About what transpired that murky night, a night of shadows and screams and secrets and rage. I could never pick apart that night to put it back together in a complete picture that could explain what had happened to me, to my mother and sister, to Brook Haven. Answers that might one day allow me to go back home.

The one therapist I'd gone to after I left said it was common to have repressed memories. They were the brain's way of protecting you from a traumatic experience. I should be thankful my brain was looking out for me, because it couldn't get any more traumatic than knowing you'd killed your own father.

3

I spent two years of my life, first as his assistant and then in the past year as his lover, losing myself in Conrad, because anything was better than thinking about home and what I'd done. I thought he was trying to help me, even when I knew that wasn't in his nature. Just like he did to his students' stories, he'd helped himself to my life, my pain, and had gotten himself a damn book deal for it.

God, I really wanted to burn down everything in Conrad's place, just like Bernadine. Firing off that email to Dean Higgins and the entire department hadn't been satisfying enough. Tomorrow, I'd regret blowing up my job, but truth be told, I wanted a little payback.

Conrad's teaching career at the university was a start. And I couldn't just let him use my past. Taking all his meticulous notes and his partially finished manuscript, taking back what was mine from someone who could not tell my story—that I would never regret.

I took one last inspection of the condo, making sure there wasn't anything else I needed to take. Nothing I could see. I stopped in the kitchen on my way out. The page from his contract for the manuscript *Deadly Daughter: A Lowcountry Killing*—the bastard—rested on top of the box I held.

In the hallway outside, I stood in front of his closed door. I locked it, then bent down to pick up the page from where I'd put it on the floor beside his door.

Don't ever be a fool over love. Or anything, come to think of it. That is what my granddad would have said. *Don't be a fool over nobody.*

I'd been a fool over Conrad. It wasn't going to happen again.

I placed the first page of Conrad's contract in the middle of his front door and stabbed his kitchen knife though it, holding it there.

My shoulders sagged, reality settling in. Maybe the email was a mistake. What was I supposed to do for work now? No other college would hire me, because who at the university would recommend me? My southern saint of a mother would never let me live it down if she had to drive up from South Carolina to bail me out of jail. I couldn't bear the look Granddad would give me, letting me know that, once again, I wasn't making the best choices.

I jumped when something moved behind me. I spun around, expecting that Conrad and the cops had caught me. My hand went automatically to my heart when I saw it was Mrs. Dixon, the nice old lady in the condo across from Conrad's, with hair so white it was nearly blue. My small-town upbringing didn't allow me not to know a neighbor's name, even if the neighbor wasn't mine. Conrad wouldn't know her.

We said nothing as the seconds stretched while she took in the whole scene. I watched as her clear blue eyes looked me over from head to toe, then danced over the box at my feet with the notebooks protruding from it, finally resting on the knife embedded in Conrad's door.

My body deflated. The jig was up. The knife might have been overkill.

Her voice came out wobbly and thin as she looked up at me. "Haven't seen you in a while," she said. "You aren't back, are you?"

What was that supposed to mean? Past triggers of being Black in not-so-Black spaces bubbled to the surface, making me pull on my armor, readying myself to do the daily battle of fighting for my right to just be. Until I remembered she had just caught me squared up in front of my ex-boyfriend's door, playing darts with his contract and chef's knives.

"No, ma'am," I said, my southern manners slipping through in a complete clash with the wobbling knife handle and the paper. "I, um . . ."

Had she already called it in? Was DC Metro on her speed dial and careening here to take me in?

"I was just leaving him a note, Mrs. Dixon." Should I say more? "I stopped by to . . . grab the last of my stuff."

Her eyes lit up with a satisfied glint. "Well, good. He's an ass anyway. I was just telling my daughter about him the other day, although she thinks I'm being a busybody. He's so rude and pompous, like those privileged male chauvinists I used to admin for back in the day who thought women were just around for their pleasure." Mrs. Dixon harrumphed. "You're better off without the likes of him. You aren't the only young thing he entertains in there, you know."

I dropped my head, feeling not a little embarrassed. "I know."

The woman tutted disapprovingly. Probably for the pitiful young women these days who weren't built like they used to be. She tightened the belt of her flowered terry robe, giving the knife a long look. There was a glint in her eye as she decided on solidarity, an unspoken multigenerational girl code passing between us.

She jutted her chin toward the staircase. "You should probably get going. And don't come back."

I bent down, scooping up the box in a fluid motion. "I won't, don't worry!"

Then, I ran for my life.

Mama's name lit up on my phone screen as I slipped back in my car, the box in the passenger seat next to me. I hesitated, debating whether I was up for her call. If I didn't answer, there would be a voicemail. I hated checking voicemail. The 237 unheard messages were an indication of my aversion to them—let alone ones from my mother. The texts would follow, each making me feel guiltier than the last for not answering.

I accepted the call.

"Hi, Mama," I said brightly, mustering up all the cheer I could, even though my mind was filled with murderous thoughts. The things I could do to the bastard. Bash his head in, watch him bleed. Relieve him of his pitiful, deceitful, thieving ass. Maybe Conrad was karma for what I did back home and for running from it.

Mama's voice was thick with emotion as she struggled to speak. "Jac, baby?"

The sound of her sobered me up, my mind switching from murder and burglary to apprehension. Dread coiled tightly in the pit of my stomach. Only one topic could make my mother sound like this. Death.

I put all thoughts of Conrad in my rearview, pulling out quick in case Mrs. Dixon had a change of heart and was peeking outside her window, or Conrad turned up.

"Who is it?" My mind scrolled down a list of names her call could be about, ignoring one because it better not be. Not him.

"Granddad."

Not. Him.

My mouth became cottony, and only one word made it out. "How?"

"There was an accident," Mama said. "He was—he fell and had a massive heart attack, and he's . . ."

"Dead," I finished, wanting to say it first and quick because then maybe it wouldn't hurt as bad. The word sounded alien to me, like it wasn't even me saying it, though my lips moved.

"The doctors have him heavily sedated to stop any further strains on the heart or any more attacks while they stabilize him." She hesitated, working her way to the point of the matter. "I know it's been some time since you've been back, Jac, but you need to come home before . . ." A sob robbed her of the rest of her words, forcing my little sister to pick up where she'd left off.

Pen asked if I'd come. What could I say?

"Shit," I moaned after we'd finally hung up. This news was the cherry on top of a truly fucked-up day. My love life. My job. My future. And now . . .

Six years ago, when I was chased away by the town's angry whispers and accusations that I'd killed my father, I hadn't stopped or corrected them. I hadn't felt the need to clear my name.

It had just been him and me out there, arguing over . . . didn't seem worth it now. Was stupid. Then Daddy was gone, and I was there. His death was a noose around my neck, cinching tighter while my toes struggled for purchase on wobbly ground. Despite that, I couldn't tell any of them all of what had happened that night. All the unglued bits and pieces were too fractured and confusing and fluttering in the wind.

Couldn't even explain it to myself. And did they really matter, the details, when the only thing that mattered was that I'd done it?

Guilt and shame had made me swear I would never step foot in Brook Haven again, and I hadn't for over six years.

Now here was Granddad making an absolute liar out of me.

4

I was on the road as soon as I could be, not wanting to be in town when Conrad got home and saw what I'd done. But I had to be a different kind of Jac, one who thought things through. Plus, everything was happening too fast, and I needed to slow things down just a little.

I went back to my place and grabbed what I could, with no intention of returning. I hit the bank, taking out as much cash as I dared for the next few days in case the cops decided to track my spending through my cards, like on TV. I was probably doing too much. If the local cops wanted me, they'd know in a heartbeat where I was from and would be in Brook Haven in a flash to grab me.

Some kind of criminal I made. I cleared the intruding thoughts from my mind. I watched way too many movies. Going home for Granddad bought me a couple of days. But what about after? Couldn't think of that. I planned for just right now. By the time I'd sorted out my immediate needs and fought with traffic in and around the Beltway, it was pretty late. I didn't hit the road until around eleven o'clock, ignoring the beginning pings and chimes of missed calls and messages, and planned to drive through the night.

I also didn't want to face Maura, who'd been my roommate since I'd finished grad school and we realized living alone in DC was not economically feasible on teaching assistant salaries. She'd been repeatedly calling my cell . . . she, along with others, whose many calls, texts, and voicemails I wouldn't check anytime soon. I hoped the note I'd left her about why I was suddenly gone would be sufficient, as if a few scribbled lines on the back of an old envelope from a credit card offer would absolve me of ditching her and leaving her in the middle of my mess.

The drive down I-95 South to Brook Haven was going to take eight hours if traffic was on my side. Volatile feelings chased me all the way down the highway. Made me press the gas, pushing my small car to eighty-five when the speed limit indicated seventy. I didn't bother with the speed trap apps to check for state troopers. I think part of me wanted to get to Granddad as fast as my Beetle could get me there. But my mind and fatigue wouldn't let me be great, and my eyes became heavy with sleep. Sleep was easier than thinking about what was behind me, and what was ahead.

My tires rumbled over the grooved sides of the road, shocking me back to temporary wakefulness. I pressed the volume button on my steering wheel so the song from my iTunes would rise from background noise to a bellow, filling the car with enough sound to hopefully drive away sleep and all the thoughts invading my mind.

An infestation of thoughts poured like a deluge over the security gates that protected my mind—mostly of my grandfather, lying in the hospital, attached to tubes and wires and deeply sedated until I got there. Only a week ago, he'd been inundating me with emails and voice-mail messages, talking about his online forum of armchair detectives. He'd resorted to texting when I didn't return his call fast enough. He was always so impatient and never took care of himself well enough. "This is bullshit," I mumbled.

I bet Granddad hadn't been taking his meds. I bet he hadn't been going to Dr. Winters on the regular to have his pacemaker checked. I bet he hadn't been eating well, or sleeping enough, or exercising. Just sitting at his computer or in his recliner, reading the endless stream of tips on whatever case he and his online friends were currently working on. I bet he hid his not taking care of himself so well that Mama and Pen didn't notice. If I placed all those bets at a blackjack table in Vegas, I figured I'd be a millionaire.

"Dammit."

Who was I to complain about any of them not doing what they were supposed to be doing, when I hadn't been there? I was going to have to keep myself in check.

Keep your head down, Jac. And watch that mouth of yours too.

Famous words—easier said than done.

Granddad was a celebrity within those cold case and true crime groups because, while most members were novices, learning the art of investigation through true crime programs and *48 Hours* on the Investigation Discovery channel, Granddad had been the real thing. He'd been a police officer and a detective with the local police departments, then an agent with SLED, where he'd finally retired fifteen years ago.

I was terrified I wouldn't make it to him in time, that he'd spend his last moments without his junior detective there.

You need to come home before . . .

He dies. Mama couldn't say it, and I couldn't think it.

My chest tightened. Mama was too deeply rooted in her superstition that what was spoken out loud often became real. Unfortunately, I had taken it to another level—I was afraid that even allowing the thought would make it true.

But feelings about my family weren't the only ones in the car with me. Fear was right up there with the others. Fear of facing the people of the town who had always thought I wasn't good enough and now thought I was a killer. And rightfully so. What would they think when they saw me rolling through?

It was déjà vu. Shame was chasing me out of DC, just as it had Brook Haven. The new city that had been my refuge was now one of embarrassment. I had made a fool of myself at work and would probably lose my job. Lost the fellowship. Betrayed twice: slandered in front of the Fellows application committee, manipulated into talking about Daddy's death to be used as content for a manuscript I had no idea was being written.

My plan was to use this time in Brook Haven to lie low, figure out what to do about Conrad's manuscript and about my life, now that I was probably unemployed. Oh, and the knife in his door. There was that to consider, as well as the possibility of a charge or two waiting for me from the DC Metro police.

Four hours in, I pulled into a rest stop. I parked near the entrance, beneath as much light as possible, just in case, and double-checked the locks. I eased my seat back, lowering Cardi B and Megan Thee Stallion enough so I could drift off to sleep. If Mama knew what I was doing, she probably would have pitched a fit. No way should a woman stop at a rest stop in the middle of the night by herself, and any other time I would have agreed, but exhaustion and the thoughts plaguing me were winning this battle.

My eyes cracked open, and I fumbled to tap my phone screen: 4:45 a.m. I sat upright in a panic, cursing myself for having been asleep for nearly two hours, longer than I'd intended. I looked around, thankful my rest was uneventful, and hurried to get back on the road. I focused on nothing else as I crossed into South Carolina, moving farther south and toward the coast, until the sign that indicated the town of Brook Haven was a few miles out made my palms dampen. I turned down the music, swallowing the surge of panic at the thought of being closer to home than I'd been in years.

I turned onto the state highways and routes and then took the crisscrossing network of tree-lined, one- and two-way roads that carried me toward my childhood home near Charleston. Brook Haven was surrounded by woods and wetlands, and right on the outskirts of Brook Haven's town limits was the entrance to the Moor Manor property. I slowed, taking in the plush greenery of dense trees. The winding road that cut deep into the woods to the vast estate, which sat on a steep incline, and beyond, at the peak of the hill, was Moor Bluff. The entrance to the estate was clear, not overgrown like I'd imagined it would be after all these years of being deserted and left to nature and the elements. Someone had been maintaining the property, and the realization made me slow my car to a stop in the middle of the empty road.

Moor Manor Country Inn and Events

Murder Manor . . . the tales wrapped up in that place. I shuddered.

I tried to peer through the bank of trees lining the road for a better view, knowing I wouldn't be able to see the house of horrors from the road. It was at least a mile in and up. Beyond it, at the large manor's back, was the high jagged bluff, beneath which the Santee River ran and eventually flowed into the Atlantic. Moor Bluff was the highest point among the typically low-lying terrain, making it unique. At the bluff, the heavy fog and mists could render the entire area leading up to the bluff's edge practically invisible and deadly.

The bluff was Jekyll and Hyde. One moment, beautiful, serene, and idyllic, with a breath-catching view of the river that seemed to stretch endlessly before dumping into the ocean. The next, ugly and cold, with jagged, slippery edges and quick drop-offs and fog and mist so thick that you'd never know you were out of earth until the ground was no longer beneath your feet.

A car horn blew, making me jump and slam my knee against the steering wheel. I let out a small scream, trying to get my bearings until I remembered where I was—in the middle of the road. My eyes flew to the rearview mirror, which revealed a blue older-model pickup truck that had pulled up right behind me. It was idling, waiting for me to move on or move aside. I waved my hand in apology, hoping to ease any nerves, before pulling out of the truck's way.

Through my rearview, I watched as the truck cut to the left from behind me, holding my breath as if that would make me invisible as it slowly passed by. It was too high up for me to get a good look at who was in the driver's seat, jacked up on oversize tires. I hoped it was the same for whoever was in the cab, that they couldn't see me, either, recognize me, and remember way back when. It wasn't until the truck had accelerated once it cleared me, slid back over to the lane I was blocking, and driven off that I released my breath and turned my attention back up the road to the estate.

Since when had that old and decrepit place become an inn? I didn't recall anyone in my family telling me someone had bought it and made it into a vacation destination. I shuddered involuntarily, thinking about staying the night in the place from which most Brook Haven kids' terrors were born.

It was a setting that made horrors seem real: stories of witches, the Caretaker—our version of the bogeyman—and angry ghosts of former patients confined during Murder Manor's shady iterations as medical and mental facilities throughout its centuries of existence. The former mansion turned makeshift hospital after the Union had taken it over turned many other sinister things was going to be a country inn?

If those walls could talk. I shook my head at the thought. The Manor and its grounds were manifestations of my childhood and adult nightmares. Finally, I pulled myself from Murder Manor, checking both sides of the road for oncoming traffic before easing onto it and heading back to the past that I thought had been left behind.

5

As I drove through downtown Brook Haven, the sense of familiarity hit me. It felt as if I'd been here just yesterday instead of six years back. Though some things had changed—there were two Starbucks instead of the one, and a Dunkin'—everything else was the same. There were still the rows of bright- and pastel-colored storefronts with angled parking in front of them. There were still people ambling by. Still old-timey trucks with beds filled with hay or other produce heading toward the farmers' market. Downtown already bustled, even though it was early, as most quiet southern towns did.

I was able to forget about my nerves for a bit while driving through town, feeling the nostalgic recalls to my youth, when I saw things that I thought would've been long gone by now. I noticed the advertisements of an upcoming art auction and wondered if my mother was involved in facilitating it. If anything charitable or social went down in Brook Haven, Angela Brodie probably had a hand in it, the eternal socialite that she was.

I studied a looming brick structure, a fairly new addition. In there was my granddad. The man who'd brought me back to the world of the living, simply by being himself, after Daddy died. Knowing Granddad might not be walking back out of this place was more than I could handle.

Despite my fears, I managed to get out of the car. I locked it, as living in the city had quickly taught me to do. But there was little you could get away with in the middle of downtown Brook Haven without everyone, their mama, and their ancestors catching you and whooping you afterward.

I surveyed the lot warily as the realization soaked in that I was back in Brook Haven and that people would recognize me. Not that I was famous, but there was no face in this town that a local wouldn't know, no matter how many years had passed. Was I ready for that? The stares and whispers? The judgment and suspicions about what hell I was going to bring on their heads this time around? I decided I was not ready. I took in a deep, settling breath. It was go time, and shit was about to get started.

~

Inside the cool, pristine lobby of sparkling white and shades of gray, I cleared my throat. "Looking for Montavious Brodie Sr.'s room," I announced, leaning lightly against the information kiosk and speaking low. The floor was busy, with visitors littered throughout the waiting room and hospital personnel going back and forth. "Please."

The receptionist on the other side of the desk glanced up from her computer. She took me in over her half-moon wire spectacles with two chains of tiny white beads hanging on either side of her face. She would've looked more at home in a library figuring out the card catalog than here doling out room numbers, but there we were. I tried for a sweet smile to usher her along toward a faster reply.

There was no rushing a southern woman. She took her time, considering me longer than was polite, the unease of possibly being recognized making the back of my neck tingle. I scratched it, still trying to look as innocent as possible, wishing this was the one time my face would be totally forgettable.

She blinked, and the millisecond of apprehensive recognition evaporated from her washed-out blue eyes. "Visiting's not until eight o'clock. You can wait over there with everyone else if you like." She nodded toward the U-shaped row of seating I knew was behind me.

My eyes flicked to the red block numbers on the digital clock: 7:40 a.m. Air trickled out of my lungs, deflating my body like a balloon. I met her gaze, hoping my expression was readable. Seriously?

My grandfather could kick at any moment now, and I had no time to be playing southern hospitality with this old lady from the pre–Dust Bowl era. A curse pressed the backs of my lips, and I closed my eyes to count out my inner peace.

I reopened my eyes and widened my smile. I softened my tone, slipping in a bit of my accent I'd worked these past years to tamp down. I wanted her to know I was one of them.

Be full of sugar, no spice, and only the nice. One of Mama's incessant life lessons. Only I could never. The spice was always in me. Maybe too much. No, definitely too much.

Right now, I needed to fake it until I made it and be that southern belle who was only worried about her poor granddaddy.

I gave a chaste nod. Widened my eyes so I looked young and innocent, like I could never do any harm. And as if any other time, I would never break the no-visitors-till-eight rule.

"Ma'am, yes, ma'am. I understand. 'Cept Granddad is . . . they say he could . . ." My voice caught. Real, not fake. How could I say it? "He's real bad. Ma'am." I remembered my manners.

I added, "I came all this way to get here before he got worse." A minute had already ticked by. Would she actually make me wait the nineteen remaining minutes before releasing the information to me and giving me a guest badge? "My family is already up there waiting with him."

"Montavious, you say? Why, all his family is—"

The moment. I held my breath when it came as I watched the dots connect and the light of recognition flip on behind her eyes. She looked up at me sharply now, sitting up a little straighter.

I tried to keep my face clear of any reflexive emotion, but my hidden fingers curled, and I ground them against each other. Was this how it was going to be? When, one by two, people started to recognize me as that prodigal Brodie girl returned, praise the Lord. Or maybe the sign of the devil walking.

She averted her eyes, as if she'd been caught with her hand in the cookie jar and was ashamed I'd caught her staring at me and that I was staring back like a store mannequin, unreadable.

"Yes, well," she demurred, suddenly interested in a sheet of paper she'd been ignoring seconds before. "Quite a shock. Very sad. He is a good man. Good family."

She caught herself, as if she'd said something damning, and sneaked a look up at me before shifting her gaze back to the paper and then to her computer screen. If the situation wasn't so miserable, I'd have laughed at this old lady acting like a schoolgirl in the presence of one of the greats from back in her day, like Nat King Cole or some shit.

When you don't have nothing nice to say, say nothing at all. A lesson from the book of Mrs. Angela Brodie.

I didn't have anything nice to say, so I kept my lips pressed tightly together.

Less than a half hour in town, and already Mama's damn lessons were plunking down into my brain like a *Tetris* game.

"Name?"

Okay, now she was just fucking with me. It was 7:45 a.m. She knew exactly who I was. This was how it was gonna be.

I swallowed. "Jacinda Brodie." I was relieved that it came out smooth and like there was no problem I knew of, other than my grandfather being upstairs. Now, I needed to do it just like this for the subsequent thousands of times I'd be forced to say my name to people who already knew who the hell I was.

She pursed her lips, her eyes working me over. Then they hopped to the screen, and with a few strokes of the keys, she had seconds' worth of information that it had taken five minutes to pull out of her.

On the counter of the kiosk was the white IdenT-FyMe machine with the round black camera positioned to take my photo. My name tag printed out like a large receipt, and I tore it off at the perforated cut. My face was a grainy, digitized, dark fuzzy mass against a white backdrop, and I couldn't help wondering how this was a sufficient method of security.

Maybe I'd luck out and spend the rest of my time here as an unidentifiable pixelization, passing through the town quietly and taking care of my familial obligations. I focused on pulling off the wax paper and placing the sticky name tag on the upper part of my T-shirt just right, purposely wasting time.

"You should be on your way, then," she said—not rudely, but not politely either.

Only then did I notice a line had formed behind me of people wanting to be on their own sticky labels that didn't confirm shit.

"Third floor. Room 305. It's a private room. Real nice."

As if this were a hotel and not a hospital where my grandfather lay in a coma with no expectations of coming out of it. But then I realized that's what she meant. Granddad was in a nice private room—"real nice." Nice enough to wait out his final moments. I pulled my shirt over my hips, channeling into that motion my urge to scream at everyone not to be so quick to call him gone. He wasn't gone. Not yet. Not now. He'd outlive me.

Then she had the nerve to add "Go on up, Jacinda girl. They're expecting you."

My attention snapped to, and I nearly blurted out "Then why the hell did you keep me here, playing with me, if you knew they were waiting?"

But a glance at the clock on the wall above her, and my mama's voice in my head reminded me to chill out. She was letting me up a whole thirteen minutes early. I swallowed down any nasty retort I was on the cusp of spitting out.

When a person came from a place like mine, they grew up knowing everybody. Every day was a receiving line of *hello*s and *how are you*s, and I prayed no one would come up saying, "Do you remember me?" It was the line of death. Even though I'd been gone, I should probably know this woman, because we were never supposed to forget a local face. But I didn't know her.

I forgot plenty. On purpose. By accident. Who knew? And I did not remember her. It was as if I had erased people and large swatches of my life. I had created black holes in my memory of things and people that were important, and I would now have one more thing to be ashamed of.

6

The intensive care unit was on the third floor, and normally only one or two family members were allowed in the room with the patient at any given time. But I guess since we three were all Granddad had, we were allowed in. At least, that's what the doctor told me. She was a younger white lady who looked like she was still on the cheer squad at Richmond Regional High and thankfully didn't recognize me.

When I asked if room 305 was to the right or left, she barely acknowledged my tag—so much for increased security, but I was thankful for one less person to deal with. She pointed to the right. I turned on my heel quick so she wouldn't catch the name, just in case. On my way down the hall, I heard them.

"Catie, who's that heading down the hall?"

The doctor who'd directed me answered: "I don't know, a Jacqueline something, maybe. Last name was Brodie."

So, she had caught some of my ID. Joke was on me. I was one door from Granddad's, still able to hear their voices, which carried down the empty hall.

The nurse she was talking to was older and her accent very much like that of a child of the Lowcountry. "You mean Jacinda? Jacinda Brodie." She let out a gasp, and I imagined her hand flying to her décolletage for those nonexistent pearls. I bet her neck craned around Catie to get a better look at my retreating figure. "Nooooo, she's here? She's actually come back?"

My stride slowed just outside room 305, and I stared at the numbers, listening to the women, relishing the last bits of my life as I knew it, because on the other side of the cream-colored door, my world was going to change forever. Maybe to a reality I didn't want a part of.

Catie was asking, sounding peeved at not being in the know, "What, is she on TikTok, or an actress, or something? What's the big deal?"

No, I wasn't like the late, great Chadwick Boseman or other small-town South Carolinians who'd made it big. Catie would soon learn all about me and my infamy.

I envisioned the game of telephone. Next, the other nurses at the station, the doctors, the rest of the hospital staff would receive the hot gossip of the day. Downstairs, the kiosk lady was on the phone letting her girlfriends know, and on and on, the news zinging around the pinball machine that was Brook Haven. The town would soon be on notice: "That wild Brodie girl has returned. You remember, the one who killed her daddy? She finally come back home." Or "The way Jac left and stayed gone was likely what caused her granddaddy's heart to go. Heartbreak. That's what this is. His own son taken from this world by his granddaughter. Bless their hearts."

Bless your heart. The southerner's kiss of death.

I pushed all those crowding thoughts away. Granddad was behind this door. And he was waiting for me.

I felt that—that Granddad had been waiting for me. When I entered the cool room with the monitors beeping in the background, it was bright, the blinds opened so the natural light could shine in. Three people stood talking—the attending doctor, Pen, and Mama—while a nurse off to the side was recording readings from the computer screens.

I hesitated at the door, feeling like an intruder, but then pushed that away, too, and let the door swing closed behind me, alerting them to my arrival. Four sets of eyes stared at me. The doctor with mild interest at the newcomer. The nurse with curiosity. My sister with relief and joy at seeing me. And my mother with reserved trepidation and relief that I had made it.

I looked over at the figure in the bed with covers wrapped tightly around him, up to his chest. His arms were out and on either side of him.

My little sister, Penelope, rushed me, launching herself at me like she was five and I was nine and still bigger than her.

"Jac!" She hiccuped, burying her face in my neck, even though she beat my five foot six by three inches. I was older, but she was taller and better at adulting than I ever was. She had a whole fiancé and everything.

The Brodie girls, back together again. Slowly, I gave in to her affection, as I've always done, my arms slowly encircling her torso as I melted into her. I held her tightly, taking in the scent of her. The one moment of happiness and the warmest welcome I could have possibly imagined nearly broke me. Why had I been gone so long when I could have had this whenever I wanted?

Seeing my little sister without her usually cheerful and relaxed demeanor felt unnatural. I was used to the eternally upbeat disposition she had during our many video chats where we talked about her classes at USC School of Medicine in Charleston, where she was in her third year of med school. The idea that she'd be sitting across from where her grandfather lay sedated in the very hospital where she'd spent summers and holidays volunteering since she was sixteen (and now job shadowed as part of her studies) was a cruel twist of fate.

"What's up, kid?" I said, patting her back so she'd let me go.

When Pen let go, I approached Mama, who was waiting her turn at me. It had been about six months since the three of them had last come up to DC, knowing their visits were the only way my family was going to see me, since I wasn't stepping foot back here. They claimed their visits were to check that I was alive and eating enough, despite how often we communicated, but Mama and Granddad had to see me to believe it. I tamped down the thoughts that Granddad wouldn't be jiggling my locks or grilling the guard downstairs, testing my apartment building's security or trying to convince me to come back home.

"How am I supposed to solve the cold cases without you?"

I'd give him side-eye, wondering how an old man could pout like a little boy. "How'd you solve 'em before I was born?"

He didn't have an answer for that one.

"Then come back for your mama, then. She needs you. And so does Pen."

I'd watched Mama giggling with Pen, just as relaxed as could be, the only temporary worry that I might have been too thin. Or what my boss might think about the septum piercing I'd just gotten. Or my sudden hankering for the hookah. Once I was out of her line of vision, all her worries would abate.

"Ahhh." I stalled for the easiest reply. "Mama doesn't have to worry as much with me up here."

Then, I'd pretend to ignore the pained expression that washed over Granddad as he smothered his disappointment and gave up until the next time, when we'd rinse and repeat.

Mama hugged me tightly. I inhaled her familiar scent, too, feeling my defenses beginning to crack. "Hi, Mama," I said softly so my voice wouldn't tremble.

"Thank you." She ran her hand the length of my back like she'd done since I was a child. "Thank you for coming back for him."

The cracks widened.

There was a lot of meaning in those seven little words. None of which I could parcel out and analyze now, even if I wanted to. I wanted to enjoy this rare moment when she held me, and it was because I had finally done something right.

My face warmed, and my eyes burned. Her seven words, a balm a moment ago, became a torment. I couldn't take the reminders right now that I'd caused so much, too much, pain to my family and that they'd suffered, literally and figuratively, because of my selfishness. And now I hated myself because this was what had brought me home—Granddad in that bed.

Maybe this time things would be different, and we both had changed enough to be cool.

But Mama pulled back from me, taking in the sight of me with a critical eye. Her gaze started with my hair, naturally out in loose waves down to my shoulders, held back from my face by a colorful scarf with palm trees. It then trailed down—probably noting the bags under my sleep-deprived eyes—before finally resting on my nose. Her eyes narrowed, and my nose suddenly itched where the thin gold ring rested nearly flush against the base of my septum. Her lips puckered slightly, but she kept her disdain in check, probably reserving comment for a more appropriate time.

Mama touched my cheeks, twisting my head this way and that. "You're still looking too thin. You're not eating up there? Probably a lot of junk. And Jac, you want the doctor's first impression of you to be in wrinkled jeans and a plaid shirt? You didn't stop by the house first to change when you got into town? Freshen up a little?" She managed a tight smile. "First impressions and all." She leaned in toward my ear. "He's single, you know."

Here was the Mama I knew. The one who always had something to say, well meaning or not, and always at the worst time. I pulled away, my face burning hot. Not here. Not when Granddad was in the bed right behind her. I cast a quick look at the doctor, hoping Mama's rundown of me had been too fast for him to register. The way he averted his eyes, the tips of his ears reddening, told me he was clocking the whole thing. My embarrassment grew exponentially.

I shimmied out of her grasp, biting back the urge to say something improper. My focus shifted as I turned to the doctor. I gestured toward the bed. "How is he?" All was quiet in the room. The lull before the storm.

Still unaware that she ever did wrong, as usual, Mama placed her hand lightly on my back, and I beat the urge to flinch, my annoyance not yet abated. "This is my eldest, Jacinda."

Dr. Weigert was young, tall, red haired, and at any other time someone I would have taken a second, third, and probably fourth glance at. I thought that he might have felt the same because he offered a slight smile that went beyond doctor–family member courtesy. His eyes searched me, lingering on the curves hidden beneath my T-shirt and plaid. He looked as if he had x-ray vision and could see through my travel-worn attire.

He seemed to remember himself, offering his hand, which I took, returning his hint of a smile and promise of *If times were different . . .* Did I feel ashamed for the little flirting when my granddad was lying there and I was supposed to be brokenhearted over Conrad's infidelity and stealing? Wasn't I the bad Brodie girl? This was my brand. Salacious and wild. Plus, I appreciated that Dr. Weigert was another person who didn't know me right off the bat. I had a few moments before he walked into the hallway to learn all about me through the grapevine and be told to keep his distance.

"Glad to meet you. It's been touch and go since Mr. Brodie has been with us." His accent suggested he wasn't from around here.

Been with us, as if he were a guest at a resort. *Be our guest.*

"Was he not taking care of himself? Was the pacemaker off, or what brought on the heart attack?"

Dr. Weigert cast a look at his patient, deciding how best to explain, likely switching his doctor lingo to regular speak like I'd watched Pen do countless times. "Your grandfather did everything correctly. He followed his doctor's instructions and went to every appointment religiously. But he is what we call 'pacer dependent.'"

I looked at Pen.

"Means he would have had another heart attack if it wasn't for the pacemaker. He was relying on it," Pen translated.

"But when did he become"—I searched for what Weigert had said—"pacer dependent? When did that happen? I never knew things were this serious."

"Had you come home once in a whi—"

"You know how Granddad can be." Pen cut Mama off, shifting closer to me as if to be the buffer between us. Pen, always the shield. "He doesn't like us fussing over him, so he went to the cabin."

"The pacemaker failed and therefore couldn't prevent the massive heart attack. When the attack came on, he fell and must have hit his head, which caused a contusion and a concussion. The sedatives given were to stabilize his heart and so we could check for any injuries to his brain."

Mama added, "He might have been alone at the cabin like that for hours if it wasn't for Patrick going out there to check on him!"

Pen offered, "Patrick was on patrol and knew I was worried about him being at the cabin for so long that he did a drive-by, getting to Granddad not long after he fell. The paramedics say he was barely alive, nearly coding." Pen blew out a breath. "Honestly, I don't know how he made it long enough for Patrick to get there."

He's a Brodie, I thought, looking at his unmoving body, so small when he was supposed to be larger than life. *Toughest guy I know.*

Dr. Weigert nodded. "Mr. Brodie was very lucky." Then, more doc talk. "When the paramedics arrived, your grandfather had a baseline heart rate of ten. Officer Stanton's CPR when he first arrived on the scene might have saved your grandfather's life. He coded in the bus and then again here."

Not lucky enough. I sneaked a look from the doctor to my mother.

Mama dabbed at her eyes. "He was in the doorway, and the door was open. Any animal could have come in. A gator . . . a bear . . . coyote. All the elements."

I swallowed a snort. *Elements.* Only Mama would think about bugs or rain coming through a door left open.

Pen said, "Mama, no one's seen a bear in years."

"That we know of," Mama returned. "The point is, he was out in the elements."

"Was he up or down?" My question came from nowhere. Even I was confused, mimicking the faces blinking back at me. I didn't know why that was important. It wasn't what I should've been thinking of at the moment. But if Granddad was awake, he'd be asking the same thing.

"What?"

"Was he lying face up? Or down?"

"You'd have to ask Patrick," Pen said. "I can text and ask him." She pulled out her phone.

"As I was saying, Mr. Brodie had a little hemorrhaging because of the intensity of the heart attack and not having immediate care. He coded on the way here and once he got here. Due to the severity of his injuries and his advanced age—"

I half expected Granddad to jump up and kick Weigert's ass for referring to his "advanced age," but he remained unmoving, the monitors in orchestra with one another: the heart rate and rhythm monitor, the one checking oxygen levels, the blood pressure cuff whirring as it took its readings.

"Sedation was the best way to stabilize him while we figured out the next best course of care. We tried to make him comfortable."

I moved around Mama and Dr. Weigert. The nurse had left us. "What happens if you shut off all of this stuff?" I motioned to the machines.

"The machines are keeping him stabilized right now. Without them, I'm afraid there would be too much strain on his heart, causing another failure. Even though he seems to be doing slightly better than last night, with his vitals as they are, I'm afraid if we take him off completely . . ." Dr. Weigert trailed off.

"So, he can't wake up at all," I surmised. "Can't talk to us?" Or see that I'd finally come home?

Mama squeezed my shoulder. "I think he can hear you. His pulse is stronger now. Isn't it, Doctor?"

He could hear us. I gravitated toward the bed.

"It is slightly stronger," the doctor said carefully. "And I eased back the sedatives to see how he'd do now and because your mother said you were on your way. If there's an opportunity for Mr. Brodie to wake up, we can monitor how his heart is taking the stress. If he can handle it at all. He may or may not come to enough to be lucid. He may need to be put right back under if it all proves to be too much." Weigert looked at my mother. "Just want to prepare you to manage your expectations here."

Dr. Weigert excused himself with one last appreciative look my way, claiming he needed to continue his rounds.

Pen and Mom melted into the background, giving Granddad and me space.

I crept up to the side of the bed. The chair in the room was too large to move since it was a fold-out futon-type deal, one that Mama had slept in as she and Pen kept vigil. The other chair was too short, and I wanted to be able to see Granddad clearly. I took his hand in mine, careful not to jostle the IV sticking from it.

"Granddad, it's me." I sneaked a look at Mama. "It's Junior Dick." I whispered the last word.

Mama sucked her teeth. "So uncouth. I hate when y'all call each other that. You are a lady."

The monitors beeped his response.

I smirked, sharing a pleased look with Pen as she fluffed Granddad's blankets. Her phone on the bed buzzed. "You have to wake up so you can update me on your latest cases. Can't do that with you lazing around in bed. What would all your fellow Armchairs chatters think about you wasting valuable time like this?"

Mama fussed, but with a smile. "The child's trying to harass him back awake."

But Granddad wasn't doing much of anything. He looked so fragile and frail. His skin, ashen and already gaunt. It was hard to believe he was the same fiery grandfather who chased down criminals by day and ran the woods with me at night. Same one who was a bad loser at Spades and dominoes, whose baritone laugh could rattle the room, and whose voice thundered when he was angry.

I asked, "Did Patrick ever reply?"

Pen looked up from her phone. "Hmm? What? Oh." She swiped through. "Uh, yeah. He said Granddad was facing up."

"Hmm." I tucked that away for further contemplation.

"Patrick asked why. And what everyone wants for breakfast. He's doing a food run before his shift at the station."

No one ever had a chance to answer, the questions pushed to the back burner by the monitors' beeping ticking up. The hand that I had once considered the size of a bear's but had shrunk in Granddad's sickly state jerked, tightening the loose fingers I held in my hand.

The noise was confusing. It didn't register at first that the fingers were moving, slowly, as if underwater. Realization hit. I looked up. My eyes met the rheumy, blinking, confused eyes of Montavious Brodie Sr.

His arm flopped limply, his fingers groping at the oxygen tube in his nose.

I stayed by Granddad's side while Mama and Pen rushed to him, the monitors gaining momentum. Mama offered him some water, and he took a tiny sip from the straw. He coughed something raspy and full of phlegm, which Pen explained was from the trach tube they'd put down his throat last night but removed once his breathing had stabilized. He coughed again, the bed shaking. Then he stilled, training his eyes on me, focusing until I recognized the sharpness that was Granddad.

I told him to hold on. Dr. Weigert was coming, and we'd be walking out of here soon, all four of us.

"You look good, old man," I told him.

Granddad cracked a smile, nodding slowly as he fiddled with the oxygen around his nose again.

His head lolled toward Pen's and Mama's side, watching them for a bit, like he was searing their images in his mind. I bit my bottom lip, wanting to scold him for being up in this bed . . . something very Mama-esque. But I couldn't bring myself to do it. Instead, I held on tightly to his cold, weakened hand.

Then he turned to me, resolve set firmly in his face. He pulled down the oxygen, going against all our demands for him to leave it alone. He held out his hand, bent and clawlike, and I took it.

He licked his lips, still chapped even though Pen had taken a wet washcloth to them and I had fished out the ChapStick from my pocket to apply to them. Plain, because I hated the flavored kinds. He tugged at me, and I leaned in close. Pen's eyes constantly flickered to the monitors, steady in the background.

Granddad wheezed, "I—I—I . . . got you back." It was barely a whisper, barely audible above the noise of the monitors and the roaring in my ears. Dread coalesced in my chest, sitting there heavy and unyielding.

All I could do was nod, too afraid anything else would make me break down into a complete mess.

"You. Belong. Here," he said between pants, the exertion making each word heavier than the last.

I looked to Mama, but she remained a statue, like his words were paralytic.

"Sure, Granddad," I said, rubbing the back of his hand. "I got it."

His breathing was becoming labored. "Granddad, don't overdo it." Pen spoke up, eyeing the monitors with concern, her forehead a board of wrinkles.

He ignored her, huffing out the words. "Need to be careful." His swallow was hard. He waved away the cup of water and the feeble attempts to silence him.

He looked at me straight. Tugged me even closer. It took everything for him to speak. "Need to . . . tell you . . . Brodie. Always."

"Of course I am, Granddad." I looked at Mama, but she wasn't looking at me. She wasn't looking at him, either, but down at her feet. I raised an eyebrow at Pen, but she shrugged, as much in the dark as I was. The ramblings of an incoherent man massively hopped up on drugs. Pen pressed the button for the nurses to come. The beeps ticked up.

My internal alarm heightened in time with the beeps. The nurses weren't coming fast enough. "Granddad, please," I begged. Of all the times for him to be stubborn.

Sweat beaded his face, but his expression remained ice cold while heat bloomed from his damp skin. He winced, gnashing his teeth, breathing through what I knew was the coming of another heart attack. I tried to shush him. I tried to dial this all back. To get him where he was when I'd gotten there. Again. Something was happening. Something bad. Because I was here.

"Fight to be here, Jac."

His head hit back against the pillow as he seized. The pain cut off his speech. His hands clawed; teeth bared. The monitors, their steady rhythm having lulled me into a false sense of security, went haywire. The jagged lines Etch-A-Sketched across the screen in dark, furious sharp lines mashed together to make one long block of blur.

The door burst open, and Weigert and his team rushed in, pushing a crash cart with a defibrillator. They shoved us back, the room flooding with bodies. How was I again witnessing the death of someone I loved, watching as Granddad's body betrayed him, locking him in a petrification of angles and bends?

Didn't matter how hard the medical team tried. How loud the incessant beeping became, how erratic and rapid. It was like we were all role-playing in a prime-time medical show, with too many people and machines wailing and family standing around uselessly in horror, hoping not to get kicked out.

The once-quiet room was chaos with barks of instruction: someone trying to administer CPR, someone charging the defibrillator, someone yelling for everyone else to clear the bed. The sound of the pads on Granddad, a buzzing shock of electricity. His body lifted, then fell when the charge released him. Pain was etched into every crease in his face, his teeth set in a grimace.

The screeching switched from a cacophony of shrill beeps to one long threaded tone that echoed on and on in the room, ricocheting in my head, even after the doctor called time.

Even after someone cut the monitors off.

Even after Granddad was dead.

7

We were kicked out of Granddad's room so the nurses could ready the body for transport, and I spent a little time in the family waiting room, twisting in the uncomfortable chairs with Mama in between Pen and me. Hospital personnel filtered in and out with endless questions and paperwork. When the service department was supposed to go get him, I went back to his room and leaned against the wall in the hall.

One minute, I could still pretend he was alive. The next, I was walking by the side of my dead grandfather. When the door opened, the orderly wheeled Granddad's sheet-covered body out of the room, passing me by. I was waiting there on purpose, wanting to see him off as far as they'd allow me. I didn't want him to be alone. I trailed behind them as they made their way to the elevators. Slivers of memories of Granddad and me laughing together in his truck mingling with those of his last moments—contorted in pain, his eyes fearful of his impending death.

Pen stopped me just as the elevator doors were closing, shutting me away from Granddad's body.

"He wouldn't want you doing this," she said softly, leaning her forehead against my temple like we'd always done, ever since she'd shot past me in height. Not sure who found it more comforting, her or me. But it stopped me and infused me with a sort of calm I didn't know I'd needed. "Granddad would say to let him be."

She was right. Sometimes I forgot I wasn't the only grandchild and that Pen had had her own special bond with him. She wasn't his junior detective like me, but she was his baby girl, his princess. And she knew that he'd always wanted to do the protecting; he'd always wanted to go out with his strength and not be seen weak and dead, beneath a sheet. He wouldn't want those images to be the last ones we saw.

There were other things I could do in Granddad's memory. I just had to figure out what.

Sometime after they'd called Granddad's death and gotten the paperwork started for the autopsy and preparation to release the body to the family, Mama insisted I head to the house to get settled and rest.

"You just got here," she said, "and have already been through a lot. I'll be home soon."

I stopped fighting. All of it drained from me the moment the nurses shut off the monitors, throwing us into a blanket of silence that was louder than all the medical alerts combined.

I slipped out of the hospital unnoticed. I walked through the same front doors I'd entered and caught a whiff of expensive perfume, reminding me of the wealth that surrounded me in and around DC. My chest panged from recalling what was left there, the little piece of life I'd managed to scrape together, and Maura and that pitiful note citing a family emergency, with no mention of the bomb I'd detonated and left in her lap for her to get the blowback in my absence. Just like I'd done to Mama, Pen, and Granddad years ago.

I was in the process of leaving when the fragranced mass bumped into me, encroaching on my space in the breezeway between one sliding door and the other, as we passed each other. I faltered, surprised at the impact, and while the collision was not my fault—she was way beyond the assumed right side she should have stayed in, like with driving—I nearly deferred.

"Ooh, hon, watch your step!"

An automatic apology nearly slipped out from me, but her words made it die a quick death in my throat.

First, she came off all affronted, like she wasn't the one who had clearly strayed from *her* path and into mine. The way she effortlessly transferred blame over something so trivial struck a deep, resonating chord of exhausting familiarity in me.

Second, she'd called me *hon*, which I hated with a passion. It was so condescending and patronizing. I wasn't her honey. This woman did not know me.

She waited a beat. "Hello?" she sang when I didn't answer fast enough. Her eyebrows rose, and her neck swayed to catch my attention.

I was sizing her up—cataloging her pink heels, her pink-and-white tweed suit that ended several inches above her knees, and her flawless, tanned (for October) complexion—when she turned to me. She was stylish and striking and older—maybe late thirties. While figuring out ages and remembering names weren't my superpowers, if this lady had been here way back when, I'd have remembered her. She wasn't easily forgettable.

When she glanced at me, it was like she was looking right through me. Any other time, I'd have chalked up her incorrect assessment of events as an accidental take. I often experienced that seeing-but-unseeing look when I was in spaces occupied mostly by people who didn't look or live like me—a.k.a. white or wealthy folks. They didn't see others who weren't the norm in their lives.

But with Ms. Tweed, the look was different. Her unseeing was a dismissal, like she'd sized me up and determined I didn't register on her worthiness meter, all in a matter of seconds.

It wasn't the first time and wouldn't be the last. That wasn't what rankled me. It was her audacity. Her audacity to be pissed at me, look down on me, for having the nerve to disrupt her life.

Not fine. It might sound insignificant, like I was starting a fire where there was no smoke. But when you've had a lifetime of being apologetic and deferential when it wasn't your bag to hold, and when you've experienced that dismissiveness, even the most minuscule display riles you the hell up.

Plus, my grandfather had just died. So, maybe I was being overly sensitive at the moment. Or maybe I was spot on. At any rate, I was pissed and had time that day.

I swallowed my apology like a vitamin, using it to energize me as it worked its way down, and offered my own fake two-second smile. "Apology is accepted."

Her mouth opened and closed. Her wheat-colored eyes were the same shade as her voluminous honey-wheat hair. She huffed out a sound as if to say "Well, I never."

Had she ever been called out on the fact that she was in the wrong? Probably not.

She considered me for a moment longer—taking me in, sizing me up—and I did the same to her. She took a step back, breaking out a wide smile. "Okay," she said, amused. "I do apologize."

I nodded firmly. "Good," I said.

I pulled my shoulders back, refusing to allow any self-doubt to weasel its way in. We went our opposite ways. Her voice carried as she entered the hospital—singsongy, ultra sweet, like the grande dame of a ball—before the closing doors cut off the rest of her words.

8

The news about Granddad spread like wildfire, and if anyone recognized me now that it was afternoon and the town was lively and packed, they kept their distance, respecting the death in the family . . . at least for now. I was able to get to my car without further incident. I followed Mama's advice. Get home. Get settled. Get some rest until she and Pen returned home. Maybe then it wouldn't feel like I was living in some state of déjà vu.

Navigating the network of tiny country highway roads that webbed out from downtown to where we lived—not in one of the older neighborhoods, where there was a bit more space for privacy between houses—was easy. I didn't have to think about where I was going. I just went. I pulled my Beetle into the farthest space to the right of the drive, unsure who parked where and not wanting to block access to the garage. In the passenger seat next to me was the box of notebooks that weren't mine. Had Conrad noticed yet?

I gathered everything else—suitcase, backpack with my computer, and the other backpack (the one where I kept all my hookah gear)—and headed up to the house of my youth.

Up until this point—from the drama with Conrad to Mama's call to racing down here to Granddad's death—everything had occurred in rapid fire, and there hadn't been much time to digest what any of it meant for me. I'd been running on adrenaline, and the moment I stepped into the house I'd grown up in, its familiarity made me feel as if everything was frozen in time. Nothing had changed except for an added piece of art, a new flower arrangement, and two new flat-screen TVs—one in the living room and a smaller one in the kitchen—and I wondered whether Pen's fiancé, Patrick, had somehow gotten Mama's approval for them.

Thoughts, memories, decisions I didn't want to deal with crowded my mind, and without warning, the adrenaline that had kept me going since the day before whooshed out, making me almost collapse where I stood.

Photos of our family at various stages of our lives decorated the walls and every surface I could see as I strolled through to acclimate myself. It was like time traveling. Pen and me as little kids in Myrtle Beach, helping Daddy build a castle. Mom and us in matching attire, posing in front of the family Christmas tree. Dad in his US Marines sergeant's uniform with Mama, way back before I was born.

It was one of my favorite photos—they looked so young and in love. Daddy held on to her small frame like he'd never let her go or allow anything bad to happen. And she couldn't take her eyes off him. She worshipped him. They were like that every time I saw them. At times, it could be gross.

I moved on to the other photos: Mama and Daddy on a Vegas vacation for one of their anniversaries. Me, Daddy, and Granddad posing on the shores of the Saluda River after they'd caught a largemouth bass. Daddy and Granddad at Daddy's ceremony when he was sworn in as chief of the Brook Haven Police Department. All of us together on Daddy's final birthday, December 2017. A month later, a photo of the five of us again, dressed in tails and ball gowns at Penelope's cotillion, the same night Daddy died.

I took time reacclimating to my childhood home, winding through halls and around corners, recalling vivid memories of each of my family members running, walking, dodging in and out of rooms like they were right there with me. Then I'd blink and they'd be gone, and I was alone again. I didn't realize where I was until I was in front of the closed door to Daddy's study. It was tucked away in the back of the house next to the mudroom. He'd liked it there because it had a great view of our large backyard and was where the rest of us hung around the least. I hadn't been in this room in so long.

My fingertips gingerly tapped the doorknob as if it was going to burn like a hot stove eye. Of course it was cool to the touch, but I jumped just the same. I paused, vacillating between whether I was ready to do this or not. Pen had said Mama had left the room exactly as he'd had it the night he died and that Mama went in every other day to dust. I wasn't sure if that was dedication or pining away. Probably a bit of both.

I pulled out my phone. The screen was dark, phone off. I knew I should probably turn it on in case Mama or Pen needed to reach me. When I did, the pings of messages started coming in. One. And then a deluge.

I moved away from Daddy's office, the phone alive and yelling, reminding me of other matters to deal with.

Best to leave his room for another time.

Avoidance had always been my best friend, so I didn't need to read any of the texts or listen to voicemail or check email—I already knew they were filled with angry, threatening messages from Conrad, worried ones from Maura, and fishing ones from everyone else who wanted in on the drama I'd laid at their feet. I imagined the order of reveals as Conrad went through the day before and this morning: Got the email I sent the department. Saw the door. Realized his big comeback work was gone. He and Maura would have the same question I was asking myself. Same question I was asked six years ago, the night my father died.

Jac, what the hell have you done?

9

Granddad's funeral took place on Saturday, three days later. There was no need to wait because his instructions were clear. He wanted to be buried quickly and his homegoing to be a celebration of his life. He'd had the conversation with Mama years ago, and she followed his instructions to a tee. Quick funeral. No fuss. Call the cavalry of his military and law enforcement colleagues and round up the family. Whoever could make it made it. Whoever couldn't, he'd catch them on the other side.

Granddad's send-off was a true celebration of his life because, though everyone who eulogized him said he'd died too soon, Granddad had lived a good, long life, dying at seventy-five. Daddy's funeral had been one of incredulity and grief and, for me, guilt. Daddy died at forty-four, "much too young, gone too soon, and under tragic circumstances."

At least that's what everyone said in public. But the whispers said what wasn't going to be said out loud: that those tragic circumstances were my fault.

Those comparisons ran through my mind as I sat in the first row of Richmond Regional's gymnasium with my mother between Pen and me. Same comparisons as the night before, when we'd watched Granddad's college frat conduct their special ceremony to send him off, just as Daddy's had for him years prior. Same comparisons as when we'd stood in front of our family plot at Caldwell Memorial, where Granddad's body was buried next to Grandma, Daddy, and Daddy's younger brother, Uncle Jack. They ran over and over, through my mind on repeat, even now, as I suffered through the repast at the community center.

"It's a good thing the repast was here instead of at your house," said Sawyer Okoye, one of my best friends since first grade, when I traded my ham and cheese for the rice-and-spinach stew (complete with boiled egg) that her mother often packed. Sawyer was embarrassed by the other kids' teasing because her lunch was deemed "weird" by the arrogant American youths. It was the best lunch I ever had.

Even at an early age, I was a rebel, and after telling Bobby Thornton I'd make my daddy arrest his daddy for Bobby being an asshole, I asked Sawyer if she'd be my best friend, and the rest was history. Today, Sawyer plopped down next to me at the table in the corner, farthest away from the well-wishers, curious secret stares, and ears hustling for gossip—where I could safely tuck away without any accusations of being totally antisocial.

"Who wants a bazillion people running in and out of your house with an up-close-and-personal view of you? They'd never leave, and you wouldn't be able to get away from them," she concluded.

I surveyed the wide-open room, adjusting myself in the metal chair. "Can't get away from them here either."

Touché. She pursed her lips and made herself comfortable in her own chair, settling in because she wasn't going anywhere. "But you can fake a headache and go home. Or meet Nick and me at the diner for drinks and shooting the shit. I mean, it's been a hundred years since you split." Her hand shot to her mouth, her eyes as wide as small saucers. "I mean . . ."

I waved her off. "It's fine." If I got pissed at all the references to and reminders of my past, I wouldn't be able to make it out of bed.

I took the plunge to clear the air right away. Besides, this had been gnawing at me for a while. Another layer of my guilt was about me not reaching out to my friends. But as time passed, guilt had turned to humiliation, and then I just thought maybe it was too late to say sorry.

"It's never too late to say sorry," Sawyer said blithely. "Not that you would have needed to. We get it. The situation was . . . intense, to put it lightly."

"Yeah, but I shouldn't have dropped off the face of the earth like that. Not from you and Nick."

"Hey, look now, it's tough being here after what happened to the chief. And we all know how petty and shady Brook Haven can be—hell, all of these small towns."

She rotated in her chair, facing me. I obliged and followed suit, thinking, Okay, we were gonna do this here over a barely eaten plate of congealing mac and cheese, greens, brown sugar–crusted ham, and fried chicken. Oh, and a Hawaiian sweet roll because those were the best.

"I guess I just feel like I could have done more for you, you know? We could have gone with your mom and sis to visit you. I kept tabs with them. But I guess I felt it wasn't our place. Nick and I didn't want to intrude."

Wasn't possible. Sawyer and Nick could never be an intrusion. I should have seen beyond myself and articulated that. I should have done a lot of things differently.

"You couldn't do more than I'd let you do," I told her, irritated at the lump rising in my throat. I rubbed at it.

So far, so good. No public breakdowns. No added drama. I had been the proper, well-behaved Brodie girl with a magnifying glass on me, knowing all eyes were waiting for the slightest slipup. Not Sawyer, though. Or Nick either. Still, I stuffed them in the same box where I'd put the rest of Brook Haven and shoved them under the bed, relegating them to oblivion, only answering their occasional texts and social media messages.

"I'm just thrilled the team's back together again," Sawyer said and then fanned her hand over her eyes. "I never thought we'd be together like this ever again. I mean, he left for the military soon after you left—I think his dad had something to do with convincing him. Looks good for future politicians to have served, and Mayor Tate has always wanted

Nick to follow in his footsteps. When Nick returned from his deployment in Afghanistan a couple years back, he suggested we go up to DC to see you. You know how Nick is with you . . . your mom gave us her blessing, and I think she was hoping we could get you to come back."

I rolled my eyes in disbelief, wishing Sawyer didn't feel the need to explain why she hadn't come to see me.

"Stop," I said softly. "I didn't expect anyone to come up and see me. I wouldn't expect that." I looked over at Mama, bouncing around like a server in a busy diner, then at Pen, tucked into Patrick's protective arms.

Not to be derailed from her train of edification, Sawyer continued. "Contrary to what you believe, Jac, your mom really did want you back. But I didn't know if it was a good idea to intrude on you after all these years. You stayed away for a reason, and it felt, I don't know, unfair to guilt-trip you back home. So I stayed put, and Mayor Tate kept his boy busy, being the big political force here that our illustrious mayor is. Plus, everybody knows I am the most valuable player at the Brook Haven Police Department, so . . ."

Sawyer held her hands up to accept all the adulation from her adoring fan of one.

I couldn't picture it. "Yeah, how's that going? I never imagined you working at the very establishment you swore was always out to get you during high school and college. The police department? Really?"

She grinned. "I mean, we can't all take after you and be fuckups for the rest of our lives."

Had it been anyone else, I would have been pissed. But I laughed, drawing sour expressions from people at nearby tables who thought I wasn't grief stricken enough. They weren't saying the same of Pen, who was smiling and chatting quietly with the blockheaded Patrick by her side. Every now and then, she'd dab at her eyes with the handkerchief her fiancé had provided for her.

Maybe that's what I needed to do to appease these people. Shed some damn tears.

I went back to Sawyer. I'd missed this, missed her—the yin to my yang, as cheesy as it sounded.

"The whole department would go up in flames without me. They tell me this all the time."

I side-eyed her. "Do they?"

"Well, they tell me I should stick to my admin work and leave the detecting to the detectives. I like to be in the know, is all. I am a wealth of knowledge. I have opinions, you know."

I shook my head, feeling her struggle. "Always have. So, let me get this straight," I rationalized. "I'm the fuckup, but you still live with your parents at the big age of two-eight. Explain that to me."

Sawyer guffawed. "Girl, did you forget during your descent into hermithood? I am half Ghanaian and half Nigerian. It is my double God-given right and duty to live with my parents until I'm old and gray." She thought about it, tapping her bottom lip with a pointy-tipped French manicure. "Or until my betrothed bestows a hefty dowry worthy of my hand in marriage." She leaned in, her voice dropping. "There's no betrothed, by the way. This fucking town is dryyyyyy." Her voice faded as she raised her hand to her neck to emphasize her point.

"Speaking of your parents, have they forgiven me yet for convincing you to go to USC?"

Her father's family had immigrated to the US, and he met Sawyer's Ghanaian mother while they were attending Clemson University. It was a running joke between the Okoyes and me—off whom Sawyer still mooched, or *lived* (another running joke Sawyer was actually proud of)—that I had ruined Sawyer's life by enticing her away to attend Clemson's biggest rival, the University of South Carolina (the real USC, not the one in California).

I countered, "Not entirely my fault. Nick also had a hand in your defection and disloyalty, but no one ever blames him."

"Well"—she fell back into her seat in a dramatic flair—"I couldn't break up the team, could I? What would y'all have done in Columbia without me? Hmm?"

"The Three Amigos being back together again?" The last of our trio dropped into a seat opposite us. "Are you proud of us, holding out three days before pouncing on you?" Nick cracked a smile.

"Appreciate it," I answered, suddenly hyperaware of how sexy Nick's smile was and how it was generously directed toward me, like there was no one else in the room.

It was the worst possible time, but my goodness. The years had been very good to Nicolas Tate, town golden boy and only son of the current Mayor Tate. Nick had filled out in all the right places, had muscles in all the right places. I'd always had the biggest crush on Superman, and Nick developed into a picture-perfect Christopher Reeve blended with southern gentlemanly charm that never hit my radar until late in high school, to the irritation of my father. His reasoning was never quite clear, only that I was his daughter and therefore too good for those Tates, who "always had an agenda." I took that to mean that there would never be a man good enough in my father's eyes.

However, Nick's appeal was blipping on my screen again, and apparently also on the screens of several other women in this room, even the grandmas.

It was as if Nick exuded a hormone that made all the ladies want to drop their panties and all the guys want to be him. One of the more noticeable features was the swoop-like scar etched in the right side of his jawline, ending on his chin, just below his lip.

The scar gave Nick an edge, roughing up his perfect southern-boy face that I had suddenly found sexy as hell the day it had happened, during a Gamecocks football game our senior year, where he'd played defensive end. He had a hard hit. The budding scar hadn't been a big deal then, but now . . . the scar had me remembering that one time, before my world ended. It might not have been an entirely alcohol-induced fluke after all.

Get it together, Jac, now is so not the time. Plus, Nick was my best friend. Sex ended best friendships. Proven fact. I thought.

Nick leaned in, and I leaned back so I wouldn't fall to his powers of seduction. "What are we talking about?" he asked conspiratorially.

We really shouldn't have been friends, the three of us. We were from different walks of life. Sawyer and I were Black in the South. There was no escaping that. And we shouldn't have been close friends with a guy like Nick Tate, who came from the richer area of the county, the lakefront properties and gated communities of very old money and long-reaching pull throughout the state. Though Nick was from a world different from Sawyer's and mine, he never acted like it.

Nick wasn't supposed to have spent his high school and college years hanging with the kids who didn't look like him or his ancestors. He was all-American, a legacy, a politician's son. He wasn't supposed to have anything in common with two Black girls who liked to just chill and dream of when they could leave Brook Haven, one as a writer and the other a world traveler (because Sawyer said her job was going to be "traversing the lands").

He should have stuck around the groups of students at our high school who'd grown up like him—rich, southern, and white, with the safety net of generational wealth to sustain his lifestyle. But Nick seemed to feel more at ease with our diverse group, and especially with Sawyer and me. But who was going to say anything about the son of the town's mayor, with aspirations of becoming the governor or a state senator?

He wasn't supposed to connect with us, and we definitely weren't supposed to let our guard down and let him in. And yet Nick did. And we did, seeing something in him that was different from the rest of them. There was another side to Nick. A deeper one. An edgier, more enlightened and accepting one. He managed his own beliefs with his loyalty to his father and their long-standing, respectable family name in South Carolina. Maybe one day he'd break free of the chains of generational expectations. Maybe one day I would too.

10

"Karaoke at Park Diner later? Or drinks at Cog's?" Sawyer asked, referring to the best family restaurant in all of Richmond County and our old stomping ground at the local bar. She jiggled her shoulders in a sultry dance. Then, as if she'd just remembered where we were, her face fell and she suddenly became solemn, which was a feat for her. "I mean, when you feel up to it. I know you're grieving."

She tried to be serious, but it didn't last long. Seriousness wasn't Sawyer's style or what I needed. What I needed was her levity. I felt a sudden pang, missing my cousin from farther down south, wishing we'd had a chance to meet up before he left on his quick turnaround.

"Maybe just drinks at the house and chill. Something I can't do around my mother."

"Can't do it at mine either. Mrs. Okoye would even fuss at Jesus for making all that wine, okay?" Sawyer said to my vain attempts at covering my laughter. "So the only person who has their own place is Nick."

"How'd Tate end up the responsible one?" I asked. Out of the three of us, Nick had been the least ambitious. He wanted to do absolutely nothing.

"Rich white daddy," Sawyer returned. "You carry them around in your back pocket like an Amex card. Whip it out when you need a leg up."

Nick chimed in, "No, it's called being an adult."

On the other side of the community room, my mother elegantly played the one role she shouldn't have on a day like today—hostess. She should have been seated and letting everyone else cater to her. Instead, she was bustling around, greeting and thanking, ensuring everyone's plates and glasses were full, putting herself and her care last . . . as usual.

I landed on a face I'd seen only momentarily three days ago entering the hall like she was at a campaign rally and needed a few babies to kiss.

"What's that noise for?" Sawyer asked.

I hadn't realized I'd said anything.

"Yeah, the *hmm* you make when you've got something rattling around in your head."

"The *hmm* that means trouble. Usually for me," Nick chimed in.

"Oh, it's nothing much. That woman over there in the pink dress. I don't remember seeing her around before."

They followed where my head inclined toward Ms. Tweed, who was offering her condolences to my mom. Mama returned her own matching smile, not to be outdone. She motioned for the impeccably dressed woman, her hand secured around Mayor Tate's arm like she was staking claim, to follow Mama to one of the tables up front. Guess the good mayor and his companion were at one of the tables reserved for special guests and family.

Nick let out a low chuckle and looked at Sawyer. "What I tell you? Trouble for me."

Sawyer laughed.

"What? You know her? Why's she hanging on your dad like she's afraid someone's going to snatch him up?" I asked, pursing my lips. "She's afraid of losing her bankroll?"

"Come on now, Jac," Nick said sheepishly, his ears reddening as his gaze swept across Mayor Tate and Ms. Tweed before returning back to me.

It was probably inappropriate on several levels, but being back in Brook Haven had me settling into old, roguish ways, and my sliver of patience for anyone made me unable to keep myself in check. I did feel just the slightest tinge of guilt at picking on my friend. Sawyer's lifted eyebrow let me know I was being ugly and took the twinge up two levels.

Nick rubbed at his scar absentmindedly as I watched his father pull a chair out for the woman—younger by twenty years—and then seat himself next to her.

Nick said, "Tell me first why you've got that look on you?"

"What look? I don't have a look," I said innocently, making a show of wiping my face clean of any expression until Sawyer cracked a smile, my earlier pettiness already forgotten.

The two of them shared one look that said I was full of bullshit.

Finally, I gave in. "It's really nothing," I said, deciding it wasn't a big deal and chalking it up to her not paying attention and me being overwhelmed with Granddad and being back in town. "We bumped into each other at the hospital the other day. I mean she bumped into me and . . . sounds like she's pretty popular."

Sawyer was all smiles. "The one and only Faye Arden." She gestured to Nick, who shifted and gave her a wary look. "She's gonna be our Nick's stepmom."

Nick snorted. "She's like fifteen years older than us. Or something."

"Your math ain't mathing, bud," Sawyer teased. "She's like twelve years older. I asked." Sawyer paused. "Will you still be calling her Mommy?" Sawyer blinked innocently, her smile growing wider as our friend became visibly uncomfortable, to our immense entertainment, his ears turning a deep plum. She dodged Nick when he pretended to lunge at her.

"She's had work done, I bet. Like one of the Housewives," I surmised like we were critiquing a piece of artwork. "Tits for sure."

"Come on." Nick sighed like an overwhelmed dad who'd lost control of all his rowdy kids. "I'm not calling her Mom. Stop joking around."

"Everyone loves dear Mommy Faye," Sawyer continued, as if Nick wasn't shooting daggers her way. "She's nearly done renovating Murder

Manor." Sawyer straightened, her voice becoming proper. "'They call it Moor Manor now, honey.'"

I huffed out a laugh. "Stop playing. But who'd want anything to do with that place? She knows what it used to be, right? The stories."

Nick said, "She's into real estate. That's how she and my dad met a couple years back at a conference in Myrtle Beach. Guess they hit it off, and she's been here ever since. She's cool. Does a lot for the town."

Sawyer held up her hands. "No lie. Murder Manor got its name honest and all, but Faye's worked on not only renovating the property but rebranding its name too. She's like revitalizing the town."

I remembered the sign I saw coming into town, the pieces falling into a picture for me. "What are you, her publicist?" I grumbled.

If Sawyer caught my shade, she ignored it. "Just saying. Everyone's always hitting her up for a new business venture, or to ask her to attend an event, or be a sponsor for some cause."

I nodded, my initial perception of her recalibrating to see Faye Arden renewed, my mind creating excuses. If my mom was serving her a plate heaped with food, if Sawyer was singing her praises, if Nick didn't seem put out about the woman who was going to be his stepmother—and the temperature of the room had seemed to warm up when she'd arrived on the mayor's arm—then maybe I'd read her wrong before. Maybe she'd been in a rush and really had thought I'd bumped into her. It was possible.

"You'll see when you meet her," Nick said, shredding a napkin on the table. "If she can tame my dad and get him to marry after all these years while creating something positive out of Moor Manor, that's pretty good. Plus, she really likes it here. She says it cocoons you away from the world."

"Not sure if you sound like a proper Republican lobbyist or a representative from the South Carolina Department of Parks, Rec, and Tourism," I teased, accepting Sawyer's high five of approval for a landing well done.

I relished the moment and how easy it was to slip back into our old ways, almost as if I'd never left. It reminded me of the days when the three of us clowned each other without being overly sensitive, like teasing Nick about being cool and still Republican, but not one of the scary ones.

Nick and Sawyer switched to other topics I wasn't up to date on—work at the police station and at the government offices. The gossip in the mayor's office that Nick was willing to share outside his cone of silence. Who got drunk at the diner last night and had to have the cops take them home to a pissed-off wife.

Faye Arden took delicate bites of the mac and cheese, collards, and fried chicken, not getting into it with gusto like Mayor Tate and everyone else. She talked more than ate, holding court with everyone around her. She hammed it up with Mama like they were lifelong friends and worked the room like a pro.

Across the room, Faye's eyes somehow found mine. It took a moment for recognition to hit and for her to remember me as the person in the hospital's entrance breezeway. When she connected her own dots, she dipped her head in acknowledgment, and I returned the effort, raising the open bottle of Granddad's favorite beer, a longneck bottle of cold Heineken, clearing the air between us.

I turned back to my chatting friends and she to her awaiting crowd. Tonight hadn't been as horrible as I'd thought, and maybe I'd overreacted the other day. I'd been itching for a fight when there was none to be had, waiting to be branded with a scarlet *K* for *killer* when instead I should've been focusing on keeping a low profile and being the exact opposite of what this town expected me to be.

~

I never made it to drinks with Nick and Sawyer at Cog's. The day of the funeral was exhausting, and I had to do it again the next day. Plus, when we arrived home and Mama caught me checking the clock on the stovetop, she raised her eyebrows at me, twisting her lips in complete judgment, and said, "You're not about to go back out, are you? If people see you out playing around after just burying your granddad . . ." She trailed off, letting the rest of the sentence secure itself like a collar and tether me to her side. Her eyebrow lifted and her face settled into a look of distaste, deflating any intention I had for a little bit of reprieve.

I sneaked an embarrassed look at Pen from beneath my lashes. "'Course not, Mama," I said with a sigh.

Mama smiled. "Good, then let's get comfortable, girls. Pop some popcorn and watch a bit of TV. What do you think? You pick." She walked off to the first-floor bedroom before I had a chance to respond. Didn't matter anyway. We were going to watch what Angela wanted . . . *The Housewives of Something* or Hallmark.

Not even *Another 48 Hrs.* or *Law & Order* in memory of the big man. She didn't "have the stomach for all of that murder and darkness."

11

The next morning, I managed to sit through half the service before getting up to use the restroom, an excuse to instead get a breath of fresh October air outside the church, beneath one of the many oak trees. The day was perfect, sunny and warm, but cool in the shade of the trees' long sprawling branches. I sat on one of the thick roots that was protruding from the ground as if the tree was about to pick up and walk off, and I could watch the front door of the church from where I sat. I closed my eyes to bask in the dappled shade.

The heat of the sun and the light behind my eyelids disappeared as a shadow crossed over me. I thought it might be a cloud, but instead of moving, it spoke.

"I hear you're the older sister," she said with a flat accent I couldn't place. It was like nothing and everything. "Jacinda Brodie."

My eyes peeked open, prepared to squint against the sun should she move, but she remained hovering over me and peering down. That rubbed me the wrong way. It was an intrusion on my personal space, and it seemed like she was trying to be intimidating by towering over me the way she was.

I leaned away from her to get a better and fuller view, taking in her black-with-gold-piping tweed dress. I briefly wondered if she thought tweed was the designated fabric for political wives or something.

I shielded my eyes from the sun's glare with a hand. "And you're the lady who nearly knocked me on my ass at the hospital and assumed I should apologize."

I said I was going to reset, right? Give her a break, since everyone else in town thought she was the hottest thing since sliced bread? Well, the best-laid plans and all that shit . . .

The sun was at her back, and I couldn't be sure, but it looked like her placid face twitched right around the eye. She corrected herself, wiping away any evidence of irritation. She was really good at that, I noted. Didn't think I'd ever seen a mood switch as quickly as hers had.

Hmm.

Her mouth stretched into a smile. "Jac, I think it was a bad day for the both of us, and we had a minor"—she pressed her thumb and pointer finger together—"minor misunderstanding due to the shocking death of your grandfather." Her voice was as dainty as ever, like a Stepford wife's.

She didn't seem to want to move on her way, and I wasn't about to let her lord over me as I sat beneath her. I pushed myself from the comfortable tree root and took time to dust off the back of my navy blue wrap dress, making her wait for me to give her my attention.

We were round about the same height, though she was more slender. Nick had mentioned her being fifteen years older, but Sawyer had bumped it down to twelve, making her about forty. But she was naturally youthful and could pass for younger if she eased up on the heavy makeup. We sized each other up, taking in what the other was offering. I waited for her to disprove the first impression I'd had of her.

She didn't wait for my answer. I bet she didn't like waiting on anything.

"What brings you out here? Needed a breather? I get it. Losing a loved one can be hard." She said it wistfully, and she looked away so I wouldn't see whatever emotion had popped up into her eyes. I stayed quiet.

Sometimes it's better to be quiet and just listen—a life lesson from Chief MJ Brodie.

To better learn who you're dealing with would have been Granddad's addition.

She tried to wait me out, but I hadn't yet decided what I wanted to say. I should have channeled my inner Angela Brodie: said who I was, thanked her for attending, and asked something about her life that I cared nothing about.

But she had intruded on my solitude. She'd inched into my personal space, and the vibe from her I still couldn't put my finger on. Like she was expectant. When we'd first met, she was dismissive. I was nothing more than an irritating bug who'd gotten in her way, forcing her to acknowledge me. Now, here she was seeking me out.

"You don't say much, huh?" she said. "Not even hello." She smiled widely, and it actually made me crack just a little.

"Hello," I said.

"There we go." She sighed contentedly, brushing away the strands of hair swirling in the escalating wind. "Progress. I hate to be on the wrong side of folks. I hate when there's a misunderstanding."

She was laying it on thick. It wasn't that serious, and I was already getting bored and thinking: Didn't she have someone else to schmooze? Who was I?

"Can I call you Jac?"

I lifted a shoulder. "Everyone else does."

Her lips twisted, and she nodded. "Yeah, about that. You're Nick's close friend from college."

So that's what this was. She was feeling me out because I was a friend to her soon-to-be stepson, which was unnecessary, seeing as how I'd been around longer than she had, even with my six-year absence. If anyone should be feeling anyone out, it should be me about her.

"Since high school, actually. There's only one huge high school for Brook Haven."

She was surprised. "Wow, you're so close that you even went to college together?"

I shrugged again, sitting back down on my root. I wasn't worried about her towering over me anymore. She was just a new lady who wanted everyone to like her and tried too hard.

"Happens a lot around here. We tend to all move along in life together. We tend to stay where we were born and raised too. No big deal. I think it happens in small towns all over." I looked pointedly at the other exposed roots around me. "Are you going to sit, or keep looming over me like that, or maybe give me a minute alone? It's the reason why I came out here."

Her mouth opened, and a sound came out like a cough and gasp. She couldn't keep it in, and her hand fluttered to her chest while something sizzled in her eyes, dying out as soon as it had flared. Short fuse. I looked away so she wouldn't catch my smile.

She regained control of herself. "It's hard to tell whether you're joking or serious, Jac. I'm not sure what to make of you. You aren't at all what I've heard about you."

Bingo. The reason why she'd ventured out here to talk to me, even though hardly anyone else had talked to me since I'd gotten to town, except to extend the necessary condolences. Faye wanted to meet the girl everyone said had killed her dad. Using Nick was just a lame excuse.

I lit up. "Now we're getting somewhere, because I feel the exact same way. You're the new lady, even though I hear you've been here a while. Engaged to Mayor Tate and living the life, investing in real estate and about to make Brook Haven the latest vacation destination." I shook my head. "But Moor Manor? Why that place?"

She looked perplexed, tilting her head. "Why not?"

"It has a bad history."

She smirked. "I guess I like the macabre." Her eyes took a snapshot of me.

"That's putting it lightly."

"Your grandfather used to come up to the Manor to see how the renovations were coming along. He liked offering his insight. I found him very"—she searched for the word—"intuitive."

Not sure what to reply, I kept silent and hoped she'd take that as a cue to leave me alone.

As if that wasn't enough, she added, "Resourceful."

I bristled. She spoke like being resourceful was a bad thing, beneath her or something. Her patronizing tone instantly rubbed me the wrong way, and that it was directed at Granddad only amplified my irritation.

"There a problem with being 'resourceful'?"

Suddenly I wasn't so tired anymore. My senses registered warning bells as they had four days ago, when our paths had initially crossed. For someone so well liked in this town, Faye had a horrible way with words. How was she able to make her money when she couldn't keep her five-inch-heeled foot out of her mouth? Something about her words gave me the impression she thought Granddad was nosy or a nuisance. She wouldn't just come out and say that, with his service going on just steps away. But I wasn't about to let her snipe at anyone in my family. Even just by her tone.

She seemed startled, genuinely surprised at my ferocity. I got to my feet, needing to make my point face to face.

"Excuse me?" Her eyes rounded, and she took a step back. "I was only saying that he was determined. He was good about"—she searched for her words—"collecting what he needed. I guess that was the detective in him. All the people he was trying to help. They'd appreciate his dedication." When she saw the fire extinguishing in me, she kept going, softening her tone. "I'm sorry. A bad choice of words, I guess. I apologize. I guess I keep screwing up when it comes to you, when all I want to do is get to know you."

Was I the asshole? Yes, I was—the only thing wrong with this lady was her screwed-up way of expressing herself. She just didn't know how to talk to people.

"Yeah," I agreed cautiously, still not entirely sure where she was going with this line of talk. "Granddad didn't let things go easily. Not until he found the answer."

She made a sound, her look introspective and serious, thinking about something she didn't care to share with me.

"Why do you think he came around Mur—Moor Manor so much? What piqued his interest?" I asked, studying her.

"Hmm?" she said automatically. Hearing but not listening to me. My eyes narrowed. Where was Faye Arden right now? Because it wasn't here with me. It might not have even been in Brook Haven.

The church doors opened, and people started spilling out, Mama and Pen among them, followed by Sawyer, Nick, and Mayor Tate. The noise of their exiting shook Faye Arden out of her reverie. She looked around like she'd forgotten where she was.

Wherever she'd gone, she'd taken my few moments of solitude with her. The rest of the day would be receiving condolences and everyone pretending the only thing on their minds was their grief over Granddad and not curiosity about me.

Faye seemed to make a decision. "I like you, Jac," she said suddenly. Why she thought I needed to know, or cared, I wouldn't find out.

"I like the way you think. Straight, no chaser."

I tried to follow along. Her switch from one mode to another was remarkable. "M'kay." I played along, following up with "I mean, living in the political hot spot of the world will make you realize it's best to cut to the chase."

"Well, then I hope to see you around. Maybe you'd like a tour of the Manor in all its true glory before we open to the public?" She gave me a conspiratorial grin. "It's less murdery now. But that'll be great fodder when we open up to the public. Everyone loves good local lore."

If local lore meant murderous truth, then I guessed people might be interested. But I doubted there was anything Faye Arden could do to make the place less "murdery."

"Plus, I've had a master maze designer build a beautiful hedge maze in the back. The whole county is excited about it. Should boost tourism twenty percent."

I wasn't sure about her numbers, but if she liked it, I loved it.

She started to back away, a small smile playing on her lips, like she'd tossed a grenade and no one was the wiser. I was more concerned about her walking backward in stilettos and how I'd be pulling her off the ground in a moment when she tripped over hidden roots or broken twigs. She made it back to the sidewalk without my having to save her, stopping when Mayor Tate emerged from the church with a mini entourage surrounding him and Nick by his side. He called to her to meet them at their car.

Her lips tightened, and after she'd taken a second to get over her irritation with a finger snap, she was back to normal. "I hope we can be friends. I'm the new girl on the block. And you're the—what do they call you?"

I wasn't going to help her out.

She chuckled. "The wild Brodie girl. I can relate to that. It must suck, huh? When everyone thinks you're something you're not and don't want to be. When they don't let you be you." She sighed. "When people you thought had your back turn out to be disloyal."

There, again, in her eyes, was that vacant jump to a time and place I didn't know.

She was getting deep for our official first meeting, too deep, and I didn't know how to respond. She wasn't even here when all that had happened, so what gave her the nerve?

The next second, the woman was right back on earth again, picking up where she'd left off. Like fucking whiplash.

She pointed to her chest; then her hand did an elegant sweep toward me. "We'd make quite a pair in this little town. We could help each other."

Help each other. Her words circled in my head like a vulture over a dead carcass.

She gave me a haughty look, like we were sisters in crime or some shit. "How about it?"

My first thought was to blow her off. I mean, who was this lady, acting like we were about to become besties? And why me, when she'd been here going on two years, had a rich husband-to-be, and had the town eating out of the palm of her hand? Who was I to Faye Arden?

Look at where I'd ended up that morning. Still on the outside while everyone else was attending service in there, even Sawyer and Nick. And I realized I didn't want to be alone anymore. I didn't want to be angry or find an argument in everything anyone said. I didn't always want to be on the defense. And if this lady was offering me friendship, why not?

Maybe she also found me macabre and wanted to revitalize something that everyone else had labeled a lost cause. Even me. And I thought, *Why the hell not?* I didn't need her to save me like the Manor. But what I did need was someone who could see through all the ugly to the potential inside. Like Murder Manor.

What I wasn't ready to admit was, despite my need to make a friend sans judgment and baggage, I couldn't deny the sliver of dread at her offer. Felt a vibe like the deal came with terms yet to be established and likely to be regretted.

In retrospect, I should have gone with my initial instinct and said hell no. I should have left well enough alone. But then again, if I had known then the true weight of Faye's words, I might have handled everything else much differently, and I and the people I cared about might have suffered much less.

12

Mama was at the kitchen table, a cup of coffee in front of her, her hands wrapped around the steaming mug. Fanned out on the table was Granddad's last will and all his business affairs that the lawyer handling his estate had brought by the house Tuesday morning. I was across from her, scanning the subject lines of my email and ignoring the endless requests to meet regarding my position at the university and the situation with Professor Meckleson. The university had asked for my statement as part of their investigation into my allegations of Conrad's behavior.

> *Maura: J, you left mayhem in your wake. I don't know whether to exalt or cancel you. LMK you're ok? I can at least let ppl know you're alive.*

There were even more voicemail messages that I hadn't gone through. Reading what they were thinking and what they wanted was easier to stomach than having to endure listening to them. Their judgment was much easier in text than in audio. The numbers on the notification badges for my missed calls, voicemail, and email steadily ticked up to numbers that only amplified my anxiety and fortified my avoidance. Except, Conrad's. I must have been a glutton for punishment because his messages I listened to.

The only texts I was checking were from my family and friends here and from Conrad, who was fluctuating between messages and voicemail. He vacillated between anger, remorse, and panic.

"How could you do this to me?" he'd asked the night before, during a lapse in judgment. One minute I was thinking about Granddad; the next I was remembering the last time Conrad and I were together, when things between us had been good. It was easy for us to be in the same room and in sync, or at least so I'd thought. I missed that closeness. I missed being able to be with my person and get lost in him.

Conrad picked up immediately. I said nothing, just breathed into the phone, and he did all the talking.

"Jac? Jac, thank God. Are you all right?" The noise from the TV faded in his background. "Are you there? Just tell me you're okay."

I continued in silence, the timbre of his voice eliciting emotion I'd thought was dead—should have been dead. This man had betrayed me. I shouldn't be sad and wanting to reverse the course of time. In this moment, I didn't know what I wanted. An explanation for the notebooks. An apology. A way back in. I shouldn't have wanted any of that. And yet there I was.

"I've been worried. I miss you."

It was the first time he'd said it. In all his texts and voicemails, he'd begged for me to tell the school how serious we were, that our relationship was consensual.

"I can come get you. Bring you home. We can talk about everything. I can explain."

What explanation would be enough for what he'd done? I muted the phone so he wouldn't hear me sob, my weakness.

He whispered, a touch of hope in his voice, "What about my notes? My work, Jac."

And there it was, slamming me back to earth. My fist balled. "You mean my life," I said through clenched teeth.

"Please don't do anything to it. If they let me go, Jac, if they release me from my contract, the only thing I'll have is that book deal. I've already spent the advance. I have nothing else, and I needed a story." He hesitated. "Are you still there?"

I unmuted myself so he could hear the crickets calling each other in the night. But I remained silent. I might have called him, but I still had a little dignity. I wouldn't betray myself and ask to come back. I wouldn't forgive him for what he'd done. I wouldn't believe the lies he was telling me.

His sigh was heavy, tired. "I should have asked you. I should have encouraged you to apply for the Fellows Program. Truthfully, it's because I loved you. I didn't want to lose you, and I knew when you got the fellowship, you'd move away and find someone else. I was being selfish."

I don't know what I expected when I called. I thought I wanted to hear his apology. I thought I wanted to hear why he'd done the things he'd done.

"This is what I get for trying to contain you and keep you with me. I can accept that. But please, Jac, the manuscript."

Is my story, I wanted to answer but didn't.

"They will sue me for breach of contract if I don't turn it in to them. I'm sorry I didn't ask you first. I'm sorry I took what you told me in confidence and pitched it. But if you don't let me have it, I will be ruined. I'll be losing my job and my book deal."

The audacity to think I should be concerned with his losses when he had never been with mine.

What did I want from this phone call? The proof that Conrad saw me as nothing more than a lay and fodder for a story. He didn't respect me or cherish me. He wasn't even really sorry. He wanted me to feel sorry for him, to put my pain aside for him.

"Jac, are you listening?"

My head lifted, and I refocused on my mother speaking to me. I'd slipped away in the middle of us talking, thinking about stuff and people I should have laid to rest.

"Ma'am?" I said, my southern coming out.

She shook her head, giving me a long look. "When do you need to get back to work? Everything is over here. It's just sorting through your grandfather's things and deciding what to do with all of it. You don't want to get into that, do you? It's not your thing."

What would she know about me and my thing? She was always too busy being disappointed to get to know who I was.

I focused on my phone. "I took a sabbatical," I lied. "And they know about Granddad, so, bereavement. So there's no rush for me." I considered ending things there, weighing whether to keep my next thought to myself or be a glutton for punishment. I chose gluttony.

"Unless you're in a rush for me to leave?"

Mama tossed me a baleful glare. She was fully dressed, in full force at eight o'clock, while I remained in my T-shirt and shorts. It was a miracle I was up at all this early after my night of hookahs and calling lousy ex-boyfriends. With Pen gone to Patrick's or doing whatever, and with Mama up, there was no sleeping late in the house of Brodie.

"Does your sabbatical only consist of you smoking from that genie bottle every night?" She eyed me critically. "Do we need a doctor? For your addiction, that is."

I scowled at the table, willing myself not to react. "Hookah is like smoking a cigarette or maybe a cigar."

"You can get addicted to cigarettes."

Fair point. "Pen doesn't say anything about it, and she's gonna be a doctor. Plus, I hookah because I like it, Mama. It relaxes me. Better that than alcohol or actual drugs," I said. "Also, it's called a vase. Not a genie bottle."

Mama pointed at a display of white and yellow roses in a crystal rectangle on the countertop, then at another bouquet of wildflowers in a red glass bowl on the coffee table. "Those are vases," she told me. "You put flowers in them. What you have is a genie bottle. Is it going to grant you three wishes?"

"The wish for you to leave me the hell alone," I muttered under my breath.

"Come again?"

"Nothing."

I rubbed my cheeks, frustrated. Stood up in my bare feet, readying to leave but not sure where to go that would be safe from Mama's nitpicking.

She tsked. "You don't even have house shoes on. You can catch a cold like that."

I was pretty sure that wasn't how colds worked. But I let her have it.

Mama set her reading glasses on the table, the action having a whole lot of meaning behind it. I felt her eyes on me, and I didn't want to meet them. Didn't want to see what they'd tell me this time around.

"You're not being productive, Jac. Pen will be back to her classes soon and still volunteers at Regional in her free time. Without pay."

"Yes, that's what 'volunteering' means." It came out before I had a chance to catch that sneaky bastard.

"You—" She stopped herself, and I concentrated everywhere else but in her general area.

If I was a petty sibling, I'd be jealous of Pen, given the clear favoritism and comparisons Mama always made, more now than before Daddy died. She'd be insufferable with Granddad gone, too, reigning over us unchecked.

"I have to run paperwork to Faye Arden for the charity she and I are cosponsoring to promote Moor Manor's grand opening and for the art society, but I have a slew of appointments today to plan the training for next year's set of cotillion participants. You remember the cotillion, don't you? The one you kicked and screamed to not be a part of back when you were in high school?"

I swallowed a groan. Not everyone wanted to walk around curtsying to everyone else in white, full-skirted dresses like it was their wedding day.

Mama was unmoved. "Sawyer and Nick are back to work. Life is moving, and you are . . ."

It was freaking Tuesday, two days after all of Granddad's funeral events had come to a close. It wasn't even nine o'clock, when the day was really supposed to start, according to Dolly Parton. I wanted to scream.

"It's okay to be still sometimes, Ma," I admitted. "I just need a moment to catch my breath. Is that okay?" My voice rose, and I could feel my chest tightening and my blood pressure building like it did whenever Mama started up. Mama was not only back to work but back to being . . . Mama. But this time it was different. It wasn't just me and Mama in this circular thing I still couldn't name. It was me not having anywhere to go. Couldn't go back to DC. Couldn't stay here. Life was going on, and I was stuck, like I'd been before. Only this time I didn't have grad school to hide behind.

My voice hitched. "I'll pack up my stuff and head back, since that's what you want. I'm sorry I disturbed your peace."

I sneaked a peek at Mama, who was rubbing her eyes, another sign I was a burden. She sighed like she was dealing with a willful child. "It's not about you leaving. I told you I don't want you to leave. I just want you to know what you're doing, Jac."

"I'm on sabbatical," I repeated, trying to convince myself.

"Sabbatical," she deadpanned, lips pursed and nostrils flared. "Mm-hmm."

I ran my hand over my shorts, trying to dry the sweaty palms, flicking tiny peeks at her to gauge her mood and see if she was looking at me. I read the TV screen, catching the scrolling headlines at the bottom. *North Brill, Texas: How soon could the mysterious body in the barrel, located in Lake Worth near Fort Worth, be identified?*

"I can help out here," I said, an idea sprouting forth and gaining traction before it hit my mouth. "Granddad left the cabin to me anyway, so let me go there and begin sorting things out. I won't throw anything away that's not real trash until you and Pen can get there." Two birds with one stone. I'd get out of Mama's hair and out of her line of vision. And I'd have an outlet where I could figure out my next steps without being pressured.

Mama dialed back her aggravation, softening to a more palatable version of herself. "You don't need to keep anything for us to look at. I trust you to do whatever is needed there. We'll be keeping it in the family, per his will. Did you know that—"

"House is nearly one hundred years old," I finished, placing the glass I'd used to drink my orange juice in the dishwasher. "Granddad's parents built the house, and Brodies have been in it ever since." It was family history I could recite on demand, thanks to my grandfather.

Mama smiled wistfully. "That home is his legacy, and you've spent more time there with him than either of us. You do with what's in there however you see fit."

She seemed to have another thought, hesitating. "Will you be okay going through these things, though? You and he were so close. You did that detective stuff together."

I nodded. "I think it'll help." I pushed my chair to the table. "I'll go get to it."

I was nearly out of the kitchen when Mama added, "Could you run some paperwork by Moor Manor sometime today? I need her signature on it, and she said she'll be working out there today."

That haunted place? Little me shivered, recalling firepit stories of secret rooms and passageways and patients who'd died from horrible and mysterious experiments under the care of medical staff wanting to find cures to diseases, the ghosts of both the patients and some staff walking the moonlit halls.

Or years later, stories of the Caretaker, who took over management of the grounds and manor. He became Brook Haven's own Norman Bates, or rather a more sadistic version of Roald Dahl's Landlady, offering rooms in the mansion under the guise of a lodge, when in reality, it was a house of horrors and he was luring unsuspecting guests to their deaths.

The lore was that anyone who checked into Moor Manor never checked out. Like the old roach-motel commercials from way back in the day.

Eventually, the Caretaker was arrested, found guilty, and hanged for multiple murders. The story goes that he lured them by pretending to be a hitchhiker, then offered them a place to stay. No one knew how many victims there were because people went missing in the Lowcountry swamps and woods all the time. The bodies were never found.

Except a finger, somehow left unburned in the kiln at the property where the Caretaker had been disposing of the bodies.

We scared ourselves with the belief that vengeful wronged ghosts walked the Manor's cursed halls and that the Caretaker, Norman Bates, or the Landlady, all demons, would rise from the depths of hell and throw us in the kiln.

Even the adults kept their distance. We'd go on the property. We'd hang at the bluff and imagine what it was like to go off it (which I later found out), but we never, never went into the Manor.

Adult me should have known better. The doctors and staff were gone. The murderous Caretaker was long gone. For over fifty years, and the big kiln that used to be on the premises where he was believed to have burned the bodies was long out of commission.

Or so they said.

Still, the story persisted: When you're driving at night and it's raining, you'll see a man standing by the side of the road wearing a black raincoat. He'll have his hand out, asking for a ride. And if you stop and give the Caretaker a ride, you'll end up at the Manor and eventually in his kiln.

Of course, it wasn't real. Still, who wanted to willingly go inside a death house? I was a Black woman, and I refused to die like so many of us did in stereotypical horror flicks. Matter of fact, I rebuked it in the name of all things Black culture, commonsensical, and holy.

I would have to be the Final Girl, except you couldn't be the Final Girl if you were the only girl walking knowingly into a house of horrors like my mother wanted me to do. And she was supposed to be a Christian, saved and sanctified.

Big me wondered if Mama remembered why being at the Manor might be problematic for me, superstitions and country lore aside. The bluff where it had happened with Daddy was there, too, and I hadn't been back since.

Instead of asking, I fell back on wit as a way to find my way out of my childhood terrors and superstition.

"What, you two never heard of DocuSign? Everything can be done electronically now."

She barely looked up from the scattered papers on the table. "What's that?" She'd already moved on to her next task, sipping her coffee, eyes now on the anchors delivering the national news.

Guess I was dismissed. "Never mind. I shall deliver your paperwork to Ms. Faye Arden." Nothing to worry about, since those stories were nothing more than made-up country lore fueled by a whole lot of superstition and even more liquor.

Right?

13

The cabin my father grew up in was built after the Manor had been up and running for some time, when the groundskeeper at the time had married and wanted to start a family, but he still needed to be close to the property for easier access. He was able to purchase the land, which he cultivated, eventually building the small six-room home for his family. Granddad bought the cabin back in '68 and was adamant that it never leave our family.

The house was nestled relatively deep in the woods, without a neighbor for at least a mile; it was a little farther to the nearest highway. The only way to get to it was along the back roads. It was located at the base of the Moor Manor property, about twenty minutes from our house on the outskirts of Brook Haven's city limits.

In the woods, cell signals and Wi-Fi were spotty on a good day and nonexistent during storms. The dense woods and swamps were bad enough, but when bad weather blew in from the Atlantic, the coastal towns were always the heaviest hit, the eroding man-made and natural seawalls sometimes serving their purpose and sometimes not. But that was coastal living. We were used to it. At least Brook Haven was a little more inland, suffering less than the many towns and cities right on the coast, like Charleston and Hilton Head.

I drove over the small bridge above the creek, and just before turning off the main road onto the single lane that would take me to the cabin, I sent off a text to Nick and Sawyer.

At my granddad's to start cleaning then to MM to take pprwk to N's new mama.

Nick replied with a middle finger emoji and Sawyer a thumbs-up.

See you later at the diner.

They agreed. Then my phone pinged with another incoming message.

Nick: Maybe we can talk later? One on one

I read it a couple of times, trying to glean deeper meaning from his few words. What did he want to discuss that couldn't involve Sawyer, and did I want to deal with it right now? That night back then? Faye? Maybe she'd complained about me at the church service, and Nick was going to get on me about it. Or maybe it was something else. My stomach somersaulted at the possibilities. Then, the anticipation upended, becoming worry at those same possibilities. I put the Beetle in park and pressed the ignition button to turn the car off.

I surveyed my surroundings. The empty cabin still looked like I remembered, warm and welcoming, even though Granddad would never again open the front door with a creak to watch me make my way to him, as if I'd trip or get hurt in the few yards it took to get there.

As I walked the property, familiarizing myself with my old stomping grounds, I noted the overgrown grass and weeds that would have to be tended to. Maybe Nick could suggest someone. The toolshed was still locked tight, and when I opened it with the large ring of keys Granddad's executor had given me, none of his equipment looked out of place. The large generator was there, ready for duty should the need arise. I hoped not. I might have grown up here, but I still didn't want to be stuck out here when a storm hit.

I saved the side door, the one where they said he'd been found, for last. Purposely taking my time, knowing eventually I'd have to face it and my imaginings of how scared he must have been and in how much pain, if what I'd seen him go through at the hospital was any indication.

The side door looked as it always had. I climbed the few steps to it and slid the key in the lock. The door swung inward, and my eyes immediately went down to the doorway. I imagined Granddad lying there, half in and half out.

Granddad was facing up.

Pen's voice slipped in, reading Patrick's response. I took a big step inside, careful to avoid the area where I thought he'd been. In the short square of space.

Facing up.

I wasn't sure why the words kept rattling around in my brain like that. Why they bothered me. I turned around, facing the open door. Grandma's side table, the one she'd built during her woodworking phase. My fingers ran along the corner of the table. Dr. Weigert said Granddad had sustained a contusion and a concussion from a fall on the back of his head. From where Patrick had found him, Granddad must have hit his head on this corner. Ice-cold fingers reached inside my chest and squeezed as I touched the spot. Granddad had suffered, alone. Afraid.

I looked at the open door. My mind drifted to that night, to the steps he'd taken, wondering what had made him head out at that time of night. It had to have been late, because he was still alive, albeit barely, when Patrick found him.

He'd headed toward the door for whatever reason.

"Sorry, Granddad," I mumbled, unable to avoid his spot anymore.

I stepped up to the door, leaning through and pulling it closed. Then I opened it again. Granddad was found half in, half out. That meant he'd had to step outside.

"And then what?" I said to the room. The room knew the answer. But it wasn't talking.

I walked onto the step, looking out into the woods. Wondering what Granddad had been looking at. This was when the heart attack happened. Maybe. And then this was how he might have fallen backward.

I tried it. I was five foot six, and Granddad had me by a few inches. I moved back what I thought was four inches, then leaned as if I were falling.

Before I could lose my balance, I stopped. Reassessed my movements and tried again. It didn't work.

The distance between being half in and half out of the doorway and the corner of the table where Granddad hit the back of his head was too far. My stomach tightened.

Maybe he'd been outside, and the heart attack hit, and then he staggered backward, hitting his head?

I shook my head. "No," I said into the air.

Because even if he staggered backward, his body still wouldn't have been half in and half out. And if he went backward into the house, he would have turned around to grab something to anchor him, something to help him. He wouldn't have been lying flat, face up.

I ticked through as many probabilities as I could think of, just like Granddad had taught me when we were hot on one of his cold cases from his forum. Maybe Patrick had it wrong, and he wasn't really half and half. Maybe he was farther inside, enough to be able to hit his head as he fell backward. Though Patrick was trained to pay attention to detail as a police officer, he wasn't expecting to see Granddad lying there like that and could have gotten the distance wrong.

His first instinct would have been to save, try to resuscitate him. Call for help. Stay by Granddad's side until EMS came. Not to check how far inside Granddad was. All he would know was that the door was open and Granddad appeared half in. Not partially. Not a little bit. It wasn't a murder scene, and Granddad hadn't been dead. There wouldn't have been an investigation because they would have thought it was just an old man suffering a pacemaker malfunction, resulting in a heart attack.

I was making more out of it than necessary. I closed the door and went into the cabin, turning on the light. The house looked the same. A bedroom on either side of the main living room. Through the front door was a good-size enclosed porch. The desk was cluttered with Granddad's books, notebooks, an empty plate of crumbs from when he'd had a sandwich. Just stuff. His computer was off but plugged in, just as Granddad had kept it all the time. I turned it on, and the sign-in screen came up.

I checked out the rest of the house, taking stock of the work I'd have to do. Not too much. Granddad was very tidy. And really, Pen should have been here . . . our cousin Kei too . . . to figure out what they wanted. For now, all our grandparents' stuff would remain as it was.

Something was off with the large whiteboard. It took me a minute to realize what was wrong. It was too clear. It was wiped almost clean, which was odd because the board was never clean. Granddad was a scribbler and wrote notes everywhere, especially on it. Sometimes the board would contain a quick grocery list, but mostly it held the names involved in whatever cold case had piqued his interest and he'd decided to work on. Most people played *Wordle* or sudoku. My grandfather solved cold cases and true crime cases with his Armchair Detectives forum group. It was as exciting to him as watching football.

But the whiteboard wasn't entirely clean. Someone had given it a quick swipe, leaving streaks of black marker around the edges. When Granddad was done with a case and about to start another, he would completely wipe down the board, leaving it spotless before he immediately started filling it up again.

Girl, if you're gonna be my junior dick, then you'd better go over that board again. How many times had I heard that?

I stepped in closer, turning on another light. I saw two words in the middle, with an oval drawn around them. Someone had mostly wiped them off, but Granddad was heavy handed and the wipe job was half-assed, leaving the imprint of the words still there.

Colleton Girls.

A band? Or a family?

There was nothing I could see on his desk about Colleton Girls. Was it a case he'd started, then DNR'd? Had he solved it? If so, the board would have been wiped clean, and a new crop of case info would've taken its place. It certainly wouldn't look as if the board had been cleaned in a rush.

I paused my physical search, sitting on the arm of the couch, checking my phone. Three bars. It was a good day. I wouldn't have time to fire up Granddad's computer for a deep dive because the thing was ancient and would take forever to load. Plus, I had to get those papers to Faye to sign, or Mama would have my head. My cell would have to do for now.

Colleton Girls.

A quick search of the term yielded a number of hits from Colleton County, South Carolina's, high school JV and varsity basketball teams. There was also a prep school by that name.

My eyes went back to the erased words. He couldn't have meant these schools. I scrolled down my screen, trying to see if there was a hit I could chase down. I tabled more thorough research for a later time.

Focus, Jac. I resumed my search, but for good measure, I traced the two words on the board.

The next place where he might have kept his open cases was in his cabinet. I tried several keys until one unlocked the black drawer. Nothing was there. I sat in Granddad's creaky chair. It swiveled in a half turn until I faced the fireplace and the mantel that was . . .

I approached the mantel. Confusion ballooning, shifting to mild unease. Had Mama or Pen grabbed it to use during the funeral? Had they *buried* Granddad with it because they, too, knew how important it was to him? I slid my hands along the flat top of the mantel as if somehow my hands would find the object that wasn't there and should have been. It was *always* there, for as long as I could remember. It was the ugliest, most ridiculous thing I'd ever seen in my life, but it was special to him.

"It's a reminder," he'd said when Pen had dared me to ask why he kept that stupid thing prominently displayed like it was fine china. "Of the one who got away."

There was more than one case that my grandfather didn't solve. Less than a handful. But for some reason, this one stood out to him the most. This one he'd held on to and kept a reminder of for all my life. Even Daddy had tried to get him to let it go.

"It's okay if you can't solve them all, Pops," Daddy had told him. "You can't get them all."

"Yeah, I know, boy. But this one, I really should have. This one was no good."

Even at Daddy's big old grown age—with two young girls, a wife, military service under his belt, and a career rising up the ranks at the police department—MJ was always "boy." And Daddy loved it.

"Keeps me grounded. I can get as big as the president," he'd said. "But I'll always be my dad's 'boy.'"

Whatever that case was that had haunted Granddad every day, he never told me about it, probably working it bit by bit throughout the years. There was no way that ridiculous memento would be gone. It was always here, a beacon sending out signals that hopefully one day would help the case be solved.

"There are two cases I always keep an eye on," Granddad mentioned, bending down in front of a hidden black safe, its heavy cast-iron-like door gaping open, in his bedroom. I sat on the bed, dutifully waiting for him to finish, my legs swinging happily. I was with him because my parents were at work, and I'd thrown a fit at my after-school dance classes during our preparation for a recital. I hated those classes with a passion. They were all methods of antiquated proper southern-girl training. I wanted no part of that.

The instructors had called my emergency contact when they couldn't reach my parents. Mama was with the doctor she worked for, on their rounds. Daddy was busy being a police chief. Granddad swooped in like the superhero he was and rescued me, bringing me here and putting me to work wiping down his board. Before he was to take me home, he was putting things in his safe.

"One of my two most important cases is the one attached to that reminder on that mantel. The other one's attached to a place I need to keep an eye on."

My legs swung back and forth, and I was hoping we'd get McDonald's on the way back home after picking up Pen at day care. "Why do you keep an eye on it?"

"Because that's the only case that should never get solved. And the one attached to my reminder is the one case that absolutely must get solved."

Granddad's safe. It was the last place his keepsake could be. I hurried to his bedroom, wedging myself between his bed and the wall with the cutaway hole where the safe had been built in. I stared down the dial on the combination lock. It took me back to my days at Richmond Regional, where I'd kick the locker doors, trying to remember the three numbers of Nick's or Sawyer's combinations. I needed my textbooks, and Nick's locker was the closest to my lit class. Who wanted to carry heavy literature textbooks throughout that massive school? Not this Brodie.

I flexed my fingers like I was the dude in *Mission: Impossible*, determined to crack the safe and see what was inside. The decision to come to Granddad's had reinvigorated me, giving me the purpose Mama had hinted earlier that I didn't have. What would Granddad's number be? The probabilities were endless, and the way my patience was set up . . .

The first four tries were a bust—birthdays for Daddy, his younger brother Jack, Pen, and me. Then I thought about who Granddad was and what was most important to him: family. I thought about who would have been the one to give him what was most important to him. Grandma. I put in her birthday. Another strike.

Then I thought, if she was the one to give him the most important thing to him, then their wedding anniversary would be the most important day to Montavious Brodie Sr. I spun the dial to the right—*12.* Went left for one full revolution, then again left—*30*, right . . .

I was stuck, my mind drawing a sudden blank at the year they were married. The month and day were easy. They were the same as Daddy's birthday. Granddad had said that year he got the best anniversary gift from Grandma. With no rhyme or reason, the year came to me. I twisted the dial around.

—*68*

The lock clicked, and I pulled the safe door open with a swoosh, peering in.

I was so shocked that it had worked and I'd managed to get the safe open that all I could do was stare into it for so long my vision blurred and I had to blink to refocus, looking at the top shelf, then the bottom. Two files were on the top shelf. One, written in Granddad's familiar script, was labeled *Colleton, Nevada.*

"Colleton, Nevada," I said like I should have known. So much for my random internet search that had turned up absolutely nothing.

The other folder read *Lake Worth*. I quickly flipped through its contents; the first item was a printed news article about the lake. I rolled my eyes. Who printed out articles these days? Then I remembered whom I was dealing with and was surprised there weren't multiple stacks of yellowed, cracking newspapers cluttering the house.

I wasn't 100 percent certain, but I thought I'd heard the name on the news cycles on and off for the last few months. It took another moment for the recall to complete itself as I skimmed the article. The lake was evaporating, and objects that people had thrown in the water were resurfacing, like a barrel with a body in it. I shuddered. Fucking creepy. Could this case have anything to do with the missing memento?

At the bottom of the article was the contact person for the article about the barrel.

Contact roberta.lyken@yahoo.com with any news, comments, or questions.

I sent off a quick email, ignoring the still growing number of unread messages, especially the one from Conrad. I wouldn't be surprised if his next communication attempt was by carrier pigeon.

The bottom shelf had rolls of rubber-banded money, which I knew Granddad had been siphoning away as emergency funds "just in case the banks go to hell." Birth and death certificates of his wife and sons were there—guess he'd had copies of Daddy's and Uncle Jack's made.

The item I was looking for—a plastic quartz clock shaped like a handgun the color of tarnished steel (complete with faux bullets as hands) that had sat as a stoic reminder on Granddad's fireplace mantel in his home since I was a little girl—was nowhere to be found. Granddad said this clock was given to him by the mother of a victim of what he said was an unsolved case that had haunted him for years. He said the clock was the key to cracking it, though he wasn't sure how yet. And he said that the clock, like him, was waiting for the right time to reveal the truth. Whatever that meant.

I picked up the Colleton folder. It was thicker than the Lake Worth one and filled with pages of case notes and grainy images, from maybe twenty or so years ago, of five girls who looked about high school age. The pictures didn't jump out at me. The girls looked like sweet all-American cheerleaders and track runners.

My mind swirled with my findings, too many things to pick through now because the main finding was that there was *no* finding . . . of the clock, that is. That was number one.

Number two: The two cases he'd held on to for decades. One from twenty years ago. The other even older—the barrel had surfaced a year ago, but the authorities guessed it could have been there for nearly thirty. Why these cases?

Number three: Granddad had said one case shouldn't get solved and the other had to be. So, which was which? I drummed my fingers on my knee from my position on the floor.

Where the hell was his effing clock? I searched everywhere for it.

When Granddad talked about the clock, I figured he was being dramatic to ramp up the suspense. Or maybe he was trying to hide his penchant for ugly clocks. Who knew? Whether it was the key to cracking a case or hideous taste, it was not in the safe or anywhere else to be found in the cabin. I even braved the spiders and other bugs and checked the shed. Nothing. I might not have known much, but one thing I did know was that Granddad would never in a million years part with it, which meant someone had to have taken it. And they would have had to pry it out of his cold, dead hands.

14

Murder Manor was fifteen minutes away from Granddad's house. After discovering that the clock was missing from his home, I could only think about getting back to town as quickly as possible to ask Mama, Pen, or Patrick if they'd seen it around or knew what had happened to it. I grabbed the two files that were in the safe, locked it, and left immediately. Maybe Nick and Sawyer could help me figure out where the thing had gotten to.

The drive up to the Manor wasn't as treacherous as it used to be, with the bowling-ball-size potholes and crumbling asphalt roads, and in the middle of the day, it was less creepy. The trees hanging overhead as I drove through looked like a leafy canopy rather than claws trying to squash me between them. The beauty of the mansion was unexpected when I rounded the bend, passing the tiny man-made lake at the bottom of the drive with ducks moving about lazily in it. If I didn't know the area and the infamy that came along with it, the place might have been picturesque.

I gazed up at the sprawling Manor, newly renovated and freshly painted, with its wide picture windows and lush green lawns and bushes.

"They weren't lying," I muttered, letting the scene sink in.

Murder Manor wasn't how I remembered it. It used to be gray and ashy, siding and rotting wood barely hanging on, with shattered windows because some kid had thrown a rock or two through them.

Murder Manor—Moor Manor—was now beautiful, restored to its original state from before the Civil War, when it had been purchased by the Moor family, then abandoned when they decided to move back to England. Now, the mansion had enhancements that would hold up to the needs of modern-day guests who still wanted an Old South sleeping experience in an antebellum home, complete with four prominent pillars out front, a walk-out porch and terrace, and a slate horse-carriage pull-up for ladies who didn't want to muddy their colorful hoopskirts.

The lawns were meticulously mowed and so green and lush you wanted to roll down the small hills that cascaded below one side of the home. At the back of the large mansion and estate, leading up to the bluff, was an intersecting network of sculptured shrubs and plants fashioned into a pretty impressive hedge maze, a new addition and likely to be a key tourist attraction. Who didn't love a good maze to get lost in, like in *The Shining*? At least it had replaced the evil Caretaker's old kiln.

Small trails and pathways lined with palmettos, live oaks with graying Spanish moss, and sweet-smelling magnolias crisscrossed the grounds and beyond, into the woods, if one wasn't careful. With the ghoulish and grisly dialed back to minus one, the Manor was exquisite, brought back to its original glory.

It was hard to believe that this beautiful place had been run down and ignored only a few years ago. The newly placed windowpanes, reflecting cerulean skies, were once jagged pieces of rock-shattered shards. The steps leading into the front yard were crumbling then but now shone with freshly packed stone and brick. Looking at this house of horrors with a fresh coat of paint gave me faith. If Murder Manor could be reinvented as Moor Manor, maybe there was hope for me yet. Faye had really done something here.

I asked one of the groundskeepers where I could find Faye. He pointed me in the direction of the house, saying she was likely in her office. Inside, the Manor was bright and airy. It looked nothing like I'd imagined. Not like a hospital or a sinister motel with ghouls lurking at every turn.

An older woman was walking by with an arrangement of flowers in her hands.

"Excuse me, do you . . . Mrs. Harris?" I broke into a smile when I recognized her. She was a widow now, but her husband was my high school math teacher and had died when I was in my senior year at Richmond. It had been hard on everyone because he was one of the cooler teachers. I'm sure it had been much harder on his wife.

"It's Jac Brodie. I was in Mr. Harris's geometry class." Along with everyone else under the age of thirty-five.

She stopped and politely allowed my walk down memory lane, humoring a random who wanted to believe that she'd know her from all the other students who claimed to have been taught by her husband. I caught myself, shutting up. Of course she'd know me. She probably thought the same as everyone else.

I repeated myself, more self-consciously. "I'm Jacinda."

She shifted the arrangement to the side so she could see me fully. "Of course I remember you, Jac! You gave my husband hell in class."

I grimaced, trying to recall what kind of student I'd been for him. I hated math. "He told you that about me?" I guess at my age, old teachers and their spouses could tell you what they'd really thought of you as a student without fear of angry parent calls or reprimands from administration.

She nodded. "But I also heard you were a hardworking student. While math may not have been your strong suit, Henry said you were an exceptional writer."

A quick thought to the fellowship I'd lost dulled whatever temporary happiness I was feeling.

"I am deeply sorry about your grandfather. Montavious was a great man. He and I got to know each other a little more the last year or so. And of course, your father. I never had a chance to tell you directly."

My chest clenched at the mentions, but my mind pulled out the parts I could mentally deal with at the moment.

Got to know each other a little more? As in dating? I nearly dared to ask. But Mrs. Harris was of a certain age, and there were things you just didn't ask your elders because it wasn't your business.

I gestured to the burden in her hands. "Can I help you with that, ma'am?" I inched my fingers around the vase, pulling it gently away from her and toward my body. "I'm here to see Ms. Arden."

Mrs. Harris's face clouded. Her eyes slid up the curved staircase leading upstairs. Her vibe went from sunny to stormy with just one line.

She lowered her voice. "What do you want with her?"

The question was a surprise. Up until now, I'd been the only one less than impressed with Faye Arden. Everyone else thought she could walk on water. But Mrs. Harris was a different story, and my interest was piqued.

I held up the manila envelope with the art charity paperwork. "My mother needs these documents signed for that."

I waved the envelope to the tripod sign detailing the upcoming Ladies of the Black Southern League Charity Dinner for the Arts. Mrs. Harris followed my direction and nodded. "Yes, she is involved in that, too, isn't she?" Then she mumbled, "Though I don't know why. Last time I checked, that is one thing Ms. Faye Arden is not."

I choked on spit. "Mrs. Harris! You don't have to be Black to want to advance Black art and support Black organizations." I looked around, worried our conversation could be overheard.

Mrs. Harris didn't seem to care if any of the workers wandering about, checking off their to-do lists, heard her. She definitely didn't seem to give a hoot if the boss heard her. "So I'm told," she spit out.

I followed Mrs. Harris up the staircase, in awe of the work done to this place in the amount of time Faye had been here.

"I'm not going to speak against the woman. I'm here helping to get the inn up and running because I like that Moor Manor may be remembered for more than a house where people died."

Murdered, maimed. Disappeared. Lots of *disappeared.* I kept those additions to myself.

"The property has been abandoned and wrapped up in infamy for much too long."

I kept my mouth shut. *Abandoned and wrapped up in infamy* was an understatement.

"I want our county to be known for more than Murder Manor."

My mouth formed an O. The old lady knew what we had been calling this place since elementary school.

Mrs. Harris slowed at a closed door, the nameplate on the wall saying it was Faye's office. "Here you go. Just knock, and she'll let you in if she's there."

"Let me in?" I made a face.

"If she's there. The door is always locked. She has some mechanism at her desk that unlocks it to let people in. Very high tech. Otherwise there's no getting in. Unless you come in through one of the secret passages."

She smiled, breaking her act. "I haven't found a secret passage yet. A room or two, but no passage. Anyway, no one goes in there unless she's there." She side-eyed the gold nameplate. "Very shady. But I'm just a lonely widow with trust issues; let everyone else tell it." She rolled her eyes, taking back the flower arrangement and hefting it like a baby on her hip.

"Right?" I cosigned, relating to her words more than I probably should have let on. Mrs. Harris was me. But, like, forty years older, grayer, and still looking cute.

Props to Granddad.

Mrs. Harris became serious. "Be careful, Jac, okay? There was something Montavious was into—"

The door opened, and there was Faye on the other side, a smile already on her face like she'd known we were there. Like she'd heard us speaking.

"My new friend Jac!"

Mrs. Harris gave her a long look as she said, "Well, I'll finish up these arrangements. Good to see you, Jac. Let's make sure to talk, okay?"

She locked on to me, holding my gaze, her expression speaking volumes. We needed to talk.

Then she broke the contact, her face melting into stony aloofness. "Ms. Arden." She nodded curtly and turned heel just as Faye opened her mouth to offer a goodbye.

"Thank you, Mrs. Harris . . ." Faye trailed off, staring hard at the back of the retreating woman. The smile, wide and perfectly red, was wiped clean, and there was nothing but contempt in her gaze. She stared until she couldn't see Mrs. Harris anymore. And then she kept on staring, her fists balling at her sides like she was restraining herself from going off. The temperature had cooled ten degrees. The switch was lightning quick.

"Faye," I said tepidly, trying to bring her back to the happy place where we needed to be. The other option was damn scary. I held up the envelope.

She spun around, forcing me to step back, suddenly defensive and wary of her. She blinked like she'd forgotten I was there, and when the fog cleared, she was smiling again and ushering me into her office.

"I am so excited for this charity dinner! It's going to be glorious." She plucked the envelope from my hands and headed to her desk, pulling the documents out.

I trailed behind her, absorbing the office. The dark mahogany bookshelf nearly filled with books that lined the entire length of the wall behind her desk. The beautifully accented armchairs opposite her desk where she motioned for me to sit. A tan globe in the corner, which I was automatically drawn to, my finger wanting to do what fingers do—touch and spin. I refrained. Mama would have been so proud.

"I'm signing these now and am giving them back to you so there won't be any delays." Faye's voice faded to the background.

My search continued, and I was unbothered about whether my actions would be considered innocent curiosity or bordered on rude inspection. "Where'd you come from?" It came out more bluntly than intended, but we all couldn't be linguistically eloquent.

"I'm sorry?" Startled as if thrown by my very normal question.

I glanced at her on my way to the big bay window overlooking the front lawn. "Before you came to Brook Haven. No one outside of SC knows it. Most people relocate to Charleston or Columbia. Greenville, even. Bigger cities, you know? Not tiny out-of-the-way towns like this one."

She shrugged, casually leaning against her desk like she was about to indulge me. She pursed her lips as she thought before finally speaking. "I'm from Nevada. I've traveled throughout the States, most recently in Connecticut and Delaware, where I . . ." She seemed to prepare herself. "I lost my husband sometime back."

Husband. How far back? I gave her a second look. Faye was young, not that it mattered. Death happened to both the old and the young. But I hadn't expected a dead husband, and guilt made me immediately dial back my interrogation.

"Wow," I muttered like the air had been let out of my balloon. "That's tough. I'm sorry."

She was too overcome to answer. She swallowed and looked away like she needed a moment, which I gave her.

She could have all the time she needed. I glanced over her desk. It was relatively neat, better than mine could ever be. If she'd been doing work prior to me showing up, I couldn't tell. She could have just been sitting here, twirling around in her chair.

Her desk had a black mat on it, I guessed to keep things from sliding about. Something caught my eye. It sat half on the pad and half off, blending into the black. I looked away, trying to give my eyes a reset. I might have seen wrong. But when I looked back, it was there. A black Taser.

Faye was oblivious to my seeing anything. This was Brook Haven, where the most serious thing that had happened the last time I was here—besides me, of course—was drunk and disorderly conduct after a late night tailgating or one too many at the bars.

Who are you? The words slid into my mind effortlessly, and I nearly said them out loud. I was about to ask her about the Taser—why she felt she might need it—when something else drew my attention. More specifically, the shelf directly behind her head.

Everything fell away as I zeroed in on the object that was there but shouldn't have been. Faye had started talking again, stuffing the papers back in the envelope, but I didn't catch a word of what she was saying.

I passed her, mildly aware that her talking had trailed off and now her eyes were on me. I felt the heat of them burning my back as I went straight to where Granddad's handgun clock lay on the shelf. The same missing clock that wasn't in his home was here.

"Where'd you get this?" I snapped, pointing. Without waiting for permission, I grabbed it, turning it over in my hands. My fingers gripped the familiar knicks and grooves formed over the years of handling it. This was surely the clock on the fireplace mantel I'd grown up looking at.

I repeated my question, tearing my attention from it and focusing on her.

She pursed her lips, not immediately answering. "I'm not sure," she said slowly, giving herself time. "What about it?"

"It's my grandfather's clock." I said it more to myself than to her as I stared at the object I'd seen about every day of my life up until six years ago—the tarnished silver paint, the bullet hands ticking around the face. *Handgun* etched in the hard plastic.

"Maybe he left it here and one of the workers put it in here? Come to think of it, he might have brought it to me as a token of his appreciation. He'd been visiting the Manor for a while, found the renovations and the inn interesting. We became close."

She looked exactly like she sounded, like she was floundering, scrounging around in her brain for any loose-change excuse that was gonna pay the bill.

I wasn't buying what this lady was selling. She was cute and all, and spoke like her words were made of honey, but she wasn't the Mrs. Harris kind of close to my grandfather. To anyone on the outside, the clock was a cheap, ridiculous plastic thing. But to Granddad, the clock was everything, and he never let it out of his sight, let alone out of his home.

So I knew he hadn't given this lady jack shit.

Clock securely in hand, I closed the space between us. "Are you saying my grandfather gave this to you as a gift?"

She made a play of looking at the ceiling as if recalling a memory, then returned to me. "Yeah. Yes, I think that's how it went."

"Bullshit." The word came out like a jack-in-the-box, startling the both of us. We looked at each other, wide eyed and unsure what was supposed to happen next. I was the first to recover, easing my tone and pulling from the book of Angela Brodie—you get more flies with honey than vinegar.

"My grandfather wouldn't have given this to anyone as a gift, let alone someone he barely knew. He wouldn't just leave it around, either, if that's the next thing you're about to say," I added when she'd opened her mouth to speak. "I don't know why you have something that is very special to him, but it's coming back with me."

Faye took a couple of beats before responding. Her bright wheat-colored eyes darkened as whatever conclusions had solidified themselves. A shiver ran up my back as the atmosphere grew frigid. She made me uneasy, but I couldn't place it.

Faye pursed her lips, straightening from where she'd been delicately perched on the edge of the desk, and smoothed the front of her outfit, then walked to her large bay window, which overlooked the expanse of the green front lawn gated by rows of thick, sweeping oaks, decades if not centuries old. She placed a hand lightly on a heavy-looking black sculpture the shape of a cinnamon-braid doughnut resting on the table in front of the window.

"What are we doing here, Jac? I thought we agreed to be friends." She turned to train her eyes on me, the earlier warmth gone. Her voice had changed, taken on a slower and more deliberate quality. The airy, annoying melodic speech—like she was living her life in a musical—had disintegrated.

"Why don't you tell me how you got this?" I held the thick plastic contraption out, using it to strengthen my resolve, even though the way she stared intensely at me had me near trembling.

She shifted from the clock in my hand to me and back to it again. "Are you accusing me of stealing that dollar store thing?"

"I'm not accusing you of anything." Not out loud, anyway. I was getting hot, the feeling that something wasn't right starting at the soles of my feet and working its way up. "But I am saying my grandfather wouldn't have given this clock to you." At least not without telling me.

A thought came to me, something I hoped would explain the inexplicable and toss her a bone because, surely, Faye Arden had things mixed up and needed some help straightening her memory out. "Maybe you've been by his cabin? It's just right down the mountain from you. His property backs right to the edge of the Manor's. When did you speak to him last?" It was like we were in an episode of *Columbo*. All I needed was an overcoat and a cigar. My hair was in a messy bun, and my clothes were disheveled, so I was already partway there.

"This sounds like an interrogation, and last time I checked, you aren't a cop. But I'll humor you," she said, moving away from the sculpture and window, back toward me. "I don't know how the clock got here. I haven't been to your grandfather's cabin. I couldn't even tell you where it's located. Like I said before, one of the workers could have put it in my office."

"Mm-hmm. Right. Because it's totally your decorative style," I scoffed. "And in the office you keep locked. They have the key to your office and can come in and out as they please?"

"Someone has to clean sometime, don't they?" she returned, cracking a smile.

"Then maybe we can ask around. See who might have brought it to your locked office," I said. "Ask them how they got their hands on the most important thing to him that he's had for years."

"Why was that thing so sentimental to him?"

I swallowed. What could I tell her? That it was part of a case? I didn't even know which one or how it could be a key to cracking it. I certainly wasn't about to relay all that information to Faye either.

She crossed her arms over her chest in what I recognized as an attempt at a reset. She wasn't used to someone questioning her. And from the way the corners of her mouth had tightened, she didn't like it. She'd probably gone through life calling all the shots and was used to everyone around her clamoring for her approval.

She countered, "How do you know this clock is his? It's a little presumptuous of you, don't you think? Is his name on it?"

I gave her a straight face, finding her attempt to flip the script unimpressive. Like with her response about where she came from, she wasn't giving anything up. Playing like she didn't know every speck of dust in this expensively decorated office. She'd know if someone had put a thrift-store clock on prominent display behind her.

Her voice remained low, reminding me of the warning growl a dog gave to back off when cornered. "What are you trying to do here, Jac?"

It was a question within a question, not just asking what I was getting at, but like she was asking if I dared to go there with her. Her tone quiet and damn near deadly. Her eyes darkened and focused unnervingly on me, watching my every move. She took a step toward me, and I forced myself to hold my ground.

"Okay, Faye." I stalled, unsure of where the conversation was going.

If she'd gone to visit him and swiped the damn thing, she should have just copped to it. I was sure being a klepto was a struggle she could seek help for. They had great programs for that. Giving me all this static like she was about to cut my throat was overkill.

I mustered up my courage. "How'd you get my grandfather's clock, Faye? The truth. No bull."

"Jac Brodie, what the hell is going on?" The bellow came from the doorway.

I jumped back like I'd been caught with my hand in the cookie jar.

And just like that, I watched as the curtain fell on the menacing Faye and then rose back up to reveal the angelic one. The way she could flip personae gave me whiplash.

I spun to face Chief Linwood, Mayor Tate, Patrick, and Nick, who had suddenly appeared at the open door, all of them clustered there and looking at me like I'd grown three more heads.

"I . . ." I didn't know what to say. The clock became an anvil in my hands.

Each of their faces registered something different. Chief Linwood was dumbfounded. The mayor was distracted, always thinking about the next stop, never really present. Patrick was simmering (nothing new there). Nick was the only one who showed any concern. He looked from me to Faye and back to me, assessing the situation.

His jaw tensed as he took in the scene and stepped toward me while the chief and mayor met Faye in the middle of the room. Not only did she flip personalities like a light switch, but she moved quick, too, hopping up from where she'd been perched at the window toward her desk as if she were some kind of frazzled, delicate soul, and then finally to them, greeting them with a narrative ready on her lips.

I clamped my lips together, holding the clock tighter, watching the whole scene unfold.

"What are you doing here, Jac?" my soon-to-be brother-in-law asked, hovering between me and Faye's group.

"Why were you raising your voice at Ms. Arden?" the chief asked once he'd assured himself that she wasn't traumatized by me. I hadn't been yelling, but that's what they were going to call it.

"I'd like to know myself," Mayor Tate said with a tight smile, while Nick stared down intently at me as if he were afraid I'd disappear.

He moved in closer until we were just barely touching. He bent his head toward me. "You okay?" he whispered. I looked up at him appreciatively for a second before I was brought back to reality.

"Jac was here to get some paperwork signed for the gala dinner." Faye spoke up from the mayor's side, her arm intertwined with his. She wasted no time latching on anytime he was in the vicinity. I guess proximity solidified the wifey status, but Mayor Tate looked unsure, as if he didn't know whether to step in or out of the matter. His gaze landed on me, then Nick beside me, displeasure evident on the mayor's face.

I added, "I came as a favor to my mom. Then I saw my grandfather's clock on her shelf, and I was just about to find out how she got it."

All sets of eyes, except mine and Faye's, zeroed in on my hands and the item they held, recognition hitting three out of the four as I watched them. Mayor Tate's face was blank. He'd probably never been out to the cabin and thus had never seen it.

Chief Linwood gestured toward me. "That sure does look like Montavious's clock. Ugly as sin, that thing." He chuckled ruefully.

Patrick studied the clock. I could practically see the wheels turning in his head, likely trying to determine how it would have gotten here. Nick was also quiet, shifting closer to me in a way that made me both thankful and comforted.

Faye pouted. "She thinks I stole the thing. Can you believe it? Does it even look like my style? How would I have even gotten it?" Her voice had gone back high. Her face smoothed into cute innocence as she faked the victim for the audience.

"It's not your style, and yet here is where I found it. Right in the middle of your shelf."

She blushed, blinking way too many times. "I told you I don't know how it got there." She looked at the mayor, then at the chief, appealing for help. And they were eating it all up too.

I asked, "So you're saying you've not been to my grandfather's house, where you might have accidentally dropped it into that big Coach purse of yours?"

If anyone saw the snarl she directed at me, they didn't show it.

She turned to the mayor, implored the chief. "I really don't know how it got here. I was explaining to Jac that one of the workers or groundskeepers must have found it and put it in my office."

The office she kept locked, and no one had the keys. Probably because she was hiding a whole bunch of lifted shit in here. I looked around again.

Patrick said, "Ma'am, please excuse my sister—"

"Not yet," I snapped. "There's still time for you to fuck up."

"Oh my," Faye gasped, her dainty hands flying to the base of her dainty neck, where she actually found pearls to clutch.

There was no way I was going to allow Pen's fiancé to apologize for me to Faye of all people.

"How do we even know it's the same one?" Mayor Tate asked. Didn't he have some mayoring to do? Babies to kiss? He was turning out to be the most unbusy politician I'd ever known.

"It is," Nick, Patrick, and I said in unison. Patrick agreeing with me was a first.

Chief Linwood said, "Now, Jac, I know you're still adjusting to being back after all this time, and with your granddad recently dying, you should take it easy. See to your mother and sister. Don't run around all half-cocked, shooting accusations."

"They're not half-cocked," I said.

The chief colored, snarling at me on top of it. "Well, be that as it may, maybe it's best for you to head home now. Take the clock. Right, Ms. Arden?"

"Please do," she poured in her worked-up, overexaggerated, aggrieved state that made me feel I'd been dumped in slime. "I am so sorry if I've done anything to offend you."

This was the second time Faye Arden had apologized to me. And, like the first, it was complete and utter bullshit.

"I don't want any trouble," she said, looking wide eyed and innocent. Next, her lips would be quivering from her being near tears.

I completed a half circle where I stood, my eyes bouncing over the desk for the Taser I'd seen before. It was gone, or rather pushed beneath some papers. I could see its faint outline beneath them. I could say something. Could ask her now why she had a Taser out. And for whom.

She watched me with acute interest. Like a lion right before it was about to pounce, playing with its food before it took the first bite. Watching. Waiting. Tracking. She was nestled safely between the two men who could make life hard for me if they wanted to.

That the chief was so easily taken in by a smile and crocodile tears was surprising. I'd always known him to be a reasonable man, and he'd known me forever. While I might have been that wild Brodie girl, I didn't go around falsely accusing people. I knew better than that. I was a cop's kid, a cop's grandkid. I was from a community that had a history of being wrongly accused and lynched for it. I would never launch accusations and suspicions wildly.

I wouldn't put on an act like Faye was doing. I had only one face, rarely as I wanted to show it, but for the third time I observed that Faye had many. She switched between them at will. She could feign innocence with ease, and when she thought no one was looking, the real Faye Arden slipped through the cracks. Not the one who was a bubbly and magnanimous town benefactor and investor putting Brook Haven back on the map with a newly renovated Murder Manor country inn. But the real one, down beneath her perfectly structured surface. The one who most people in this town didn't see.

But I did.

15

Patrick and Nick trapped my body between them as they hustled me out of Faye's office and down the stairs, away from Faye and her lies, past a startled Mrs. Harris, and out the front doors. The clock was tucked firmly against my chest. I held on to it like it was a football on the last play of a game in overtime.

"Let me go." I snatched myself from their grasp once we were out on the front lawn. I spun on them. I glared, first at Nick until he wilted and looked away. I was hurt by him the most. More than anyone around, I thought Nick would stand up for me, not drag me out like trash. I leveled my glare at Patrick, who matched me with one of his own, daring me to say or do something else. In the little interaction we'd had since I'd been back, Patrick had barely acknowledged I existed.

"You know why everyone shuns you here?" Patrick began. "It's not because of what happened with your dad. It's because you're a wrecking ball, Jac. You demolish everything in your path."

Nick said, "Hey, man, it's not that serious. Faye will get over it. Trust me. She can be a drama queen and probably said something to piss Jac off."

The same irritation from Faye's office reappeared, though Nick remained even keeled, keeping his emotions right below the surface as usual. He should've been more like me and let them fly. It was freeing.

"That's not the point," Patrick said.

Although I thought it, I surely wouldn't admit Patrick was right. Didn't matter if Faye was a drama queen. She had Granddad's clock, and that was weird with a capital *What-the-fuck*.

Patrick glared at me, nostrils flaring like he was some raging bull about to attack. I matched him, refusing to back down and let someone else get the drop on me like Faye had. The air between my soon-to-be brother-in-hell and me was volcanic and hostile. I couldn't stand the prick and wondered for the thousandth time what Pen saw in this blockhead. I nearly said it, but I cherished my peace and kept those thoughts to myself. But the man was so rigid he could crack in half or burst a blood vessel.

Patrick shook his head, chuffing an incredulous laugh. He tugged the collar of his bulletproof vest below his uniform shirt, away from his thick neck. He went to the gym way too much, and his head was way too little for his too-big body. The prick.

He said, "I don't get what you're trying to do here. I've been patient for the longest time, trying to understand you and why you never came home—regardless of what happened six years ago. I've been trying extra hard for Pen because, for some fucking reason, the sun rises and sets with your loser ass."

Ouch.

"She loves you, and she would choose you over anything else, but you keep doing shit to blow things up for her and your mom. Let's not even start on what your shit does to Ms. Angela. She always has to make excuses for you. Why you left. Why you never came home. Why you're standoffish. Why you don't go to church."

Patrick also didn't go to church. Did Mama make excuses for him too?

"When did you become the spokesperson for my mama?" Patrick was taking us to places I didn't want to go.

"Everything you do affects and reflects on your family. It's always been that way, and now it's even more so, now that you're back."

Nick held out a hand in Patrick's general area. "Ease up, man. This isn't the place for this conversation."

"He's doing too much," I added, wary of Patrick but holding the clock tightly in my little troublemaking hands.

Patrick scoffed. "Well, yeah. Life was easier for your mother and Pen when you were being a hermit in DC. Do you even care about them?"

"Again, what's it got to do with you?" I said, challenging his audacity.

"I mean, I've been here. But you . . . you don't care about what you're doing to them."

That stopped my flow. "What I'm doing?" It was a genuine question, something I'd never considered. "I'm doing something *to* them? I'm doing this for them," I said, holding up the clock like an offering to the gods. "I'm doing what Granddad would have wanted. He wouldn't want his clock with that—that—" I had to be careful. She was still sort of family to Nick. "Not to them. You wouldn't understand."

"I don't." Patrick implored Nick, "If you really cared about Jac, you wouldn't humor her like this. You'd be telling her what's what." Patrick pointed to the Manor. "That's your father in there. And his fiancée, your future stepmom. How the hell are you gonna navigate that minefield if you're following up behind the person causing her trouble? Huh? Because that's what Jac is. Trouble."

I didn't have a chance to reply because Patrick was back to me. "He's your best friend, and Sawyer too. The three of you, thick as thieves since high school. Well, this isn't high school or college anymore. He works with his dad, and Sawyer works at the department. Don't you care about jeopardizing her job because you pissed her boss off?"

"Come on now. That's a stretch. Chief Linwood's capable of separating the two. Hell, his best friend is the town gambler. Or was. Is Mr. Joe still alive?" I turned to Nick, who blew me off with a quick headshake. *Not the right time, Jac.*

"You might decide to go back home tomorrow with your multiple degrees, fancy teaching job, and that life you made for yourself, but everyone else still has to live here. Don't make them have to clean up the shit you leave behind. Again."

If only Patrick knew there was no life to go back to. I'd burned that down too.

Broad shouldered and probably imposing on the beat, Patrick wanted me to feel his authority, like I was one of the suspects he'd arrested or drivers he'd pulled over. I felt myself shrinking beneath his malevolent glare. I could read his thoughts. I hadn't just taken Daddy from Mama and Pen; I'd taken him from Patrick as well. I'd taken Daddy from everyone, and thus the reason I stood here, getting a verbal dressing-down from a guy.

My father had pushed Patrick to get his degree while working at the police department. But I hadn't just taken his boss from him; I'd taken his potential father-in-law, too, his mentor and hero ever since Patrick was in high school. So now here Patrick was—standing in front of me, the new man of the house now that Granddad was gone—handling me like I was the enemy.

I wanted to chuck the clock at his goddamn face. Instead, I clutched it tighter. "I'm so sorry the death of my grandfather has been an imposition on you. It's thrown a kink in your plans, right? His dying and me having to be here because of it?"

"Jac." Nick reached for me. I twisted away.

"Don't." I ignored the hurt that bloomed in his eyes. The last thing I wanted was for a man to console me.

Nick refused to give up trying to defuse the situation. "Patrick, man, let's just chill out for a minute, okay? Take a breath. Emotions are too high right now."

I tried to play everything off like what Patrick had said didn't bother me, like he didn't matter, when he really did.

I stared him down, wishing my looks could kill and he'd be dead meat, another vengeful ghost added to the ones already haunting the halls of Murder Manor. I thought Patrick couldn't go any lower.

"Wonder what your dad would think of how you ended up?"

Apparently, he could go lower. It was as if Patrick knew which match would burn everything down around me. My father.

"Pen and your mom, this town, no one owes you a goddamn thing, Jac. Stop walking around like they do." He stormed off, leaving me pissed at myself for letting him speak to me that way, knowing I'd done it because I deserved every word.

Patrick's words pulled the plug on me, everything swirling around the drain and down into a cesspool.

That's right. No one owed me one goddamn thing.

16

Days later, the situation at Faye's office was still weighing on my mind, taking up way too much space. I would vacillate between fear about when it would get back to my mother and anger that that woman had bested me in a competition of wills that I hadn't prepared for. The way Patrick came for me afterward hit harder than it should have. My sister's fiancé thought I was a loser and had made it perfectly clear he'd rather I not be in their lives. What was I supposed to do with that? I'd come back home thinking at least my family wanted me, but now I was more alone than before. Patrick had only reaffirmed the belief that I didn't belong here.

What I wanted to do was prove him wrong. I didn't have anything going for me at the moment. No job. Boyfriend. Fellowship. Now apparently my dignity was gone too. This place was waiting for me to fail epically. But those weren't the expectations I wanted to live up, or down, to.

All I had was Granddad's cabin and these two folders that were so important he'd locked them up in his safe.

It was like Granddad was giving me purpose.

I didn't know why Faye Arden had lied about how she'd gotten the clock, but it was suspicious that she'd have an item Granddad had specifically said was from an important case. An item that had been gifted to him. Of everything she could have had, why the clock?

The threads connecting Faye to anything concrete were spiderweb thin but strong enough to make me think again and shuffle through the thicker of the two folders, *Colleton*, and read through a sidenote written on the inside of the folder.

Why's this clock so important to Daphne?

Faye had to be lying, and the lie woke something in me. It got me wondering. Why had she lied? "Pen, had you heard anything . . ." I trailed off as I walked into Pen's room and found her trying on a floor-length dress. The color complemented her light-brown skin, bringing out the reddish undertones. The dress hugged her curves in all the right places, reminding me there was a body beneath the uniform of brightly colored scrubs she wore on the regular.

I leaned against the doorframe.

Watching Pen reminded me that my little sister wasn't so little anymore, and I was hit with a sudden nostalgia that made my eyes run hot. That had been happening quite a bit as of late. Soon—in less than a year—Penelope Brodie would become Penelope Stanton, someone's wife and eventually someone's mother.

The idea of being someone's auntie wasn't entirely terrifying.

"I'm sorry," I said. "I'm interrupting."

She turned from the mirror, motioning for me to come in. I did, taking a seat in one of her chairs instead of on her bed like she did when she came to my room, or like I used to do before I left.

Pen moved to her vanity, looking through her jewelry chest to select a pair of earrings. Her large-rock engagement ring glinted as it caught the light, blinding me in the process. It mocked me, just like the person who'd bought it for my sister.

"It's for the charity dinner," she said. "What do you think?"

"Pretty."

"Patrick and I were going to have a date night, but let's make it a family hangout instead. It's been a few days, and I'm thrilled that you're not rushing back home. I miss my little big sis making me laugh at our inside jokes. Plus, you can be a palate-cleansing break from all these wedding plans. Patrick's been after me to finalize some things. Between him and Mama . . ." Her nostrils flared. "You'd think he was the bride, and you know how Mama can be."

I huffed out a laugh. "Oh yeah, *I* know how Mama can be because she's always that way with me." I shook my head. "But with you? Doubt it."

Pen blanched, wide eyed and in disbelief. Her ponytail bounced in time with "Are you kidding? You have it easier. Mama's so worried about losing you that she ends up pushing too hard. With me, I'm so boring she doesn't even bother. I'm a yes-child."

I agreed.

Pen shrugged. "I'm a people pleaser. I can't help it."

We were joking. But what Pen had said struck a nerve. How could Mama be afraid to lose me when she pushed me away every chance she got? "Losing me to what?" It was like a whisper.

My sister snorted. "Only Mama knows in that bougie world of hers. Don't overthink it, okay? By the way"—she switched things up—"when do we get to . . ." She pinched two fingers together, held them to her lips, and pretended to inhale.

"What? No. There's no way I'm getting in more trouble with Mama and with Patrick." I searched around behind me in case either of them had magically appeared at the doorway. "And third-year med student on your way to becoming a big-time doctor? Girl, you're really trying to get me run out of this town." I nearly said *again*, but smartly kept it to myself.

Pen had the best laugh. She was always so carefree and happy. She'd never caused any trouble for anyone. They said the second kid was always the hard one and the first was like cake. Hadn't been the case for us.

"It's not like we're talking about coke or hard drugs. I go to the cigar lounge with Patrick in Charleston sometimes when we want to chill away from folks around here."

I huffed a laugh. "Well, aren't you badass?" More like *old ass*. It was official—Pen and Patrick were like old-ass people, which explained why Patrick was such an ass to me. He gave off old-man vibes, even though he only had me by two years.

She was looking at me with her big brown eyes, hands pressed together in a mock plea, her face crumpling in a pout.

This woman was going to be somebody's doctor.

It was rare I could tell Pen no. She'd always been able to get anything out of me when she wanted. All she had to do was bat her baby browns. I loved her to absolute death. Breaking down, I nodded, and she squealed like I'd just said we were going to Disney World. One more thing to add to my list of offenses. Drug dealer.

Penelope Brodie crackled with electricity. "Now? I'm off tomorrow."

Now?

She nodded, reading my lips.

There was no time like the present, and Mama was out running errands. It was the old days, when the Brodie sisters were alone and getting into some shit. Well, I would get into shit. Pen just followed along, as was the requirement for younger siblings.

I grabbed my bag from my room while Pen changed into more appropriate wear. I moved through the house, grabbing a bottle of cold water along the way, to the screened-in sunroom overlooking the backyard. I was setting up on the table when Pen joined me and eagerly watched. Pouring the water in the vase-not-vase (according to Mama), I glanced at her. "I stopped by your room earlier to ask if you'd heard anything about Granddad's autopsy. Or anything else?"

Pen frowned, trying to recollect as she perched daintily and watched the hookah shaft go into the glass base. Pressing against the silicone piece to make sure it was secure and nothing would come out, I connected the hoses. "I don't know that we asked for it."

"Don't you want to know? What caused his heart attack?" I pulled out several silver sealed packages from my bag, spreading them over the top of the glass table between us. Pen chose strawberry.

She shot me a look. "Heart disease?" She sounded like it was common knowledge.

I waved that notion away, opening the pouch to stir the contents in it, the sweet strawberry scent hitting my nose. I held it out at Pen for her to take a whiff, pulling it back when she smiled contentedly.

"You're a bag of laughs," I said. "I mean the pacemaker. Like why it didn't work." I broke the stuff up in the small bowl, lightly pressing it down and covering the bowl with a piece of aluminum foil before placing it on top of the shaft.

"I can ask." Pen pulled her phone from the pocket of the athleisure wear she'd changed into, apparently ready to have some fun.

She gave off young-and-upcoming vibes, while I lounged in baggy sweats and a New Edition crop top, my hair the same messy pineapple bun atop my head from when I'd gone to bed the night before.

"We can call Dr. Weigert. See if anything came in." Pen's face brightened, and her eyebrow lifted. "Or maybe you can call him."

I pointed to myself. "What? Me?" I shook my hands. "No, no. That's not right."

My face flushed, thinking of the cute doctor in my grandfather's hospital room and the way his eyes had moved over my body. That felt like eons ago. And then there was Nick, who was . . . well, I didn't know what he was just yet. We hadn't talked about it. I busied myself with lighting the coals and waiting for them to get hot enough before I placed them atop the foil with fresh holes poked in it. I spread them around.

Pen laughed, and I was filled with instant warmth—from being here, hanging out again, or her teasing, I wasn't sure. "Okay. You're so scary."

"I'm not." I waved her off. "Call him." I ducked my head, hoping she wouldn't see my awkwardness. "He's probably busy anyway."

Surprisingly, Dr. Weigert answered Pen's call right away. I always thought doctors were so busy that it took them days to answer, but I guess Pen's time at Regional got her an immediate response.

"Weigert," Pen said easily, not sounding like my giggly kid sister anymore but all authoritative and businesslike. She put him on speaker while I checked that the bowl was warming.

"Hey, Brodie." His voice came through a lot of background noise behind him. He was in the car or something.

"Did we get you at a bad time? You sound like you're in the middle of something."

"I was on my way to the lake to get on the pontoon. What's up?" He waited a beat, then said, "How's your sister? Jac, right?"

Heat that didn't come from fastidiously watching the coals moved from my scalp to my toes. I felt like I was in high school all over again. Pen and I had rarely done this, giggled over boys and been silly. She'd always been too young, and I'd always been too busy to pay deeper attention. Besides, Mama had her wrapped up so tight that I'd chalked her up to a lost cause, loving her from afar.

A slow smile crept onto Pen's face, reminding me of the Grinch right before he was about to get into a mess. "Actually, Weigert, she's right here. You're on speaker, so be nice. Say hello, Jac."

"Hello, Jac."

Pen shot me the bird, and I passed her the hard rubber tip, showing her how to place it on the hose so she could take a toke.

Weigert chuckled. "A smart-ass. I like that."

I don't know why, but the good doc saying that was . . . sexy, and my cheeks warmed. I refused to look at my sister, opting to model what she needed to do. I mouthed *Inhale, hold a sec, release*.

She held up a finger to wait. Now was business. "So, look, not trying to keep you too long, but circling back on our grandfather's autopsy. What brought on the heart attack? Or did you learn anything about the pacemaker? Did it malfunction? Was it faulty?"

"Uhh, yeah," he said as he switched to work mode. "I actually left a message with your mother to discuss. But I can run it down with you real quick. Let me pull over."

"We're not trying to keep you from your decompress," I said, jumping in. "We can wait until you speak with our mother about the results if it's easier for you."

"No, it's fine." The rush of air that had been in his background reduced, indicating he had pulled over. "Give me a sec to pull them up."

In the meantime, I passed the hose to Pen. She mimicked my moves, putting her cap on, putting it to her lips with all caution to the wind for her first time. She took a deep inhale, and I braced myself for what would come next. A bout of newbie coughing. There was nothing. There were only ringlets of smoke as she puffed them out, a smile growing when she shifted her gaze to me.

Newbie my ass.

"What the hell, Pen!" I squawked.

"I said I didn't know how to put it together. I didn't say I never smoked before."

Weigert gave a little cheer from the phone, reminding me he was still there. At first, I worried Pen had said something that could get her in trouble, but as he spoke, I relaxed, realizing he'd found the results.

"Basically, your grandfather had a massive heart attack due to his advanced-stage heart disease, but it seems the pacemaker did stop working prior to the attack. When that happens, we send the device out for further testing. The company doesn't want to get sued for faulty devices, right? So they will do their due diligence to make sure they weren't at fault, that there were outside factors that triggered the malfunction and the resulting heart attack."

All information I already knew. The heart disease was no secret. That the pacemaker could have malfunctioned wasn't either.

Weigert continued, "The company that makes the pacemaker has been running more tests, but preliminary findings show that there was a significant electrical event that occurred prior to system and device failure."

My mouth ran dry. "A significant electrical event?" I repeated, abandoning any more attempts to hookah. I'd lost all taste for it. I drew my knees closer to the table and the phone on it as if the proximity would help my hearing. Pen held the hose in her hand, her medical mind likely whirring as my layperson's one was also doing.

I asked, "What could cause a surge like that?"

"Could be a number of things. The pacemaker could have just malfunctioned. Electric devices do that sometimes, but, of course, no company wants that to be the answer. Puts them on the hook, and opens them up for a lawsuit. We—his physicians, I mean—of course want to absolve ourselves of any missteps, wanting to make sure we didn't miss anything in the course of our treatment. According to your grandfather's doctor, he had been monitoring it regularly at your grandfather's appointments. Mr. Brodie never missed an appointment."

I exhaled, relieved. At least Granddad was doing what he was supposed to be doing.

"Could be worn-out batteries, loose wires, circuitry failure," Pen added. She shrugged when I looked at her. "I was curious and looked it up when Granddad was in the hospital. I needed something to do. Something to focus on."

I reached out, touching her knee lightly. "Of course, sis." I was an asshole. All of this had been hard on my sister. And I was here, making her deal with it on her own, worried more about myself, the clock, and those two cases than about her.

"I'm sorry," I whispered.

"There's also high potassium in the blood. I checked for it when he came in too," Weigert said. "Another cause is the least likely, unless you're going through metal detectors and stuff like that. They call it electromagnetic interference."

I lost my balance, falling over to my side. Pen leaned over to grab me. Different plot points were dropping into place, nearly making a complete row that would explode like in *Candy Crush*.

"Something like a Taser?" I asked, my throat tightening.

Weigert made a sound like he was dubious. "Ehh, maybe? I mean, the Taser would have to be high grade with a high voltage. And maybe if it were applied multiple times without letup to create the level of failure that occurred with your grandfather's pacemaker to create that kind of event, maybe. But again, that's highly unlikely because a Taser would need to be engaged. Your grandfather couldn't just fall on one and have it start up and stay on in the same location enough to spark heart failure."

Weigert's words cancelled out all other noise. A Taser needed to be engaged. As in someone needed to turn it on and press it on his chest over and over. Someone who knew he had a pacemaker. It was no big secret. He walked around talking about it and rubbing it all the time because he could feel it right below his skin. He always used to complain that the doctor said he'd get used to having it in his body.

"What do those doctors know?" Granddad would grumble, rubbing away. "You don't get used to having something like that in your body."

Which begged the question, Who would tase my grandfather? And why?

17

"We're gonna let you go, Dr. Weigert," I said, tearing myself away from questions too terrible to consider and answers that couldn't be ignored. Who would attack my grandfather? Someone with something to hide who was willing to go to extremes to keep her secrets buried deep. But how did Granddad's clock fit in?

"Thank you."

"Sure thing. And Jac," he called before Pen could click the red circle. "Maybe we could go out sometime? Grab drinks. Whatever."

"Absolutely," Pen answered for me. "When you get back. Tomorrow night."

I shook my head, lips tight in an emphatic no. I didn't need anyone forcing a date on me or the good doctor.

Weigert laughed. "But am I going out with you or your sister? Not sure your fiancé would approve."

"Ow!" I grabbed the spot on my arm where Pen pinched me. She made a face, her eyes widening and flicking to the connected call.

"Yeah, sure," I mumbled, not sure what I was agreeing to.

I barely registered his ask and Pen's soundless squeal. She drummed her feet on the floor gleefully when the call disconnected, but I couldn't join in her joy over my prospective love life.

"Jac's gonna get some!" Pen sang loudly. She picked the hose back up, preparing to take another hit. "I should get a side gig as a matchmaker. That's a thing, you know."

I could only offer a tight-lipped smile, my mind far removed from the call. The flirting and play long forgotten.

My sister wouldn't be thinking the same thoughts that were running through my mind. She had no reason to. She wouldn't be suspicious. Because she hadn't seen what I saw in Faye's office. A Taser. She didn't know what I knew. That Faye had Granddad's clock in her possession and lied about how it had ended up there. So Pen wouldn't be crying foul right now like I was. She'd be happily picking up the hookah hose to smoke like the pro I now learned she was, not the innocent sister I'd believed.

I waved away my turn at the hookah, moving back to my side of the table and sliding into the lounge chair.

Who would tase my grandfather? Maybe the person who conveniently had a Taser on her desk one moment, gone the next. Maybe Faye. But that was a stretch. Tasers around here were a dime a dozen, just like guns. This was a carry state. I needed more proof than a hunch or intuition, even for myself.

If Granddad's clock had ended up in Faye's office, then he must have had a hunch about her, too, for some reason. That reason was serious: serious enough for her to prevent Granddad from digging into her past, serious enough for her to take back the clock that might link her to it, serious enough for her to kill.

My mind was preoccupied, firing too many synapses at once, so I didn't hear Mama coming up to the doorway, where she stood watching her cherished little girl smoking up the place with her eldest.

"What is going on here? What are you doing, Penelope? Put that down." She stepped out into the sunroom, the aura around her dark with a storm gathering. I shot to my feet, looking around frantically at all the hookah paraphernalia. Pen was less afraid, the privilege of being the blessed child allowing her to see Mama for what she really was being, overblown and overly dramatic. But it wasn't just that. My fear was real. I was corrupting her daughter.

Mama stomped to the table, gazing at the vase and smoking coal, the sweet strawberry scent wafting in the air a stark contrast to the hell about to rain down on my head.

"Is this what you've finally come back for? It's one thing to be out here at night doing this—this—" She couldn't find the words. "But it's another to bring Pen into it. She's gonna be a doctor!"

"Oh, Mama, stop it. If only you knew what really goes on at college and in med school," Pen said breezily. Pen was still holding the tip of the hose where it hovered at her lips. Taunting, testing. My eyes saucered, and I shook my head frantically. *Please, don't,* I said in a silent scream. *Don't!*

Pen was blissfully unaware of the impact her actions would have on me. She thought she was doing me a favor, showing Mama that she was just as "wild" and audacious as Mama thought. But Pen was only making it worse. Making Mama worse.

"She has a fiancé and is getting married next year," Mama tried next, her hands fingering the collar of her blouse.

"I lost my virginity in ninth grade," Pen deadpanned.

Mama swooned as if she was about to faint. My hands shot out to catch her, tossing a wide-eyed plea Pen's way to stop. Mama was right. I shouldn't have set it up in her house, in the middle of the day, even though Pen had asked.

Mama avoided me as if I were the plague. She must have thought I was. I'd come back after all these years and was already infecting her daughter, infecting the town, with my wildness, my obstinance, my inability to be the daughter I was supposed to be. I was an utter disappointment.

"Mama, leave her alone. I made Jac do it. If you're going to be pissed, then be pissed at me. Me," Pen said firmly.

She finally put the hose down, and my hand flew to my chest in relief. I gawked at my sister, then at our mother, terrified.

Mama leveled her gaze at me. "You don't know what you're talking about, Pen. I just came from Moor Manor, and guess what I was told?

That my own daughter had stormed in there accusing Faye Arden of stealing your grandfather's clock."

Pen said, "Faye had Granddad's clock?"

"I didn't storm in there," I blustered. "I—I . . . she invited me at church last Sunday. You told me to go."

"I told you to take papers for her to sign," Mama snapped. "Not accuse the woman of theft and cause a goddamn scene, embarrassing me like that. I have to work with her. I have to see these folks around town!"

Her words silenced both Pen and me. It cleared out the birds from the backyard. Even the insects didn't move. I'd never heard Mama curse. Never seen her so angry and that anger directed at me. Scratch that. I had seen this anger once before. The night of Pen's cotillion during her senior year in high school and my senior year at USC, when Mama and I argued over what I wanted to do with my life and how I was causing a scene, embarrassing our family, ruining our family's good name.

Me.

Mama's eyes were fevered. She gripped my arms, squeezing tight, seeing me but not.

Pen yelled in the background, "Mama, no! Let go of her."

"What are you still doing here? I thought you were gone. What are you? How are you still here?"

There was nothing in the world that could have cut me deeper. My knees buckled, but Mama's strong hands, stronger than I guessed, held me up.

"How can you be like him?" she screeched, shaking me so hard my head rattled. But I wouldn't fight back. She was my mother, and she didn't know what she was saying, what she was thinking. "I worked so hard. You don't know what I've done to save you. But you are—"

Pen pleaded, tugging at Mama's arms: "Mama, let go. You're hurting her."

It did hurt. Mama's nails dug into me, gripping me so tight I thought she'd lift me up. But when I looked in her eyes, she still wasn't seeing me. She was seeing through me. She was seeing someone else. It made no sense.

"Let go of me!" I said, pushing her away without thinking as Pen pried us apart. My arms stung from where her nails had dug in. My heart was bursting into pieces. My breath heaved, and Mama mimicked my every move, her fevered, unseeing eyes focusing, refocusing, settling on me, and realizing what she had done.

"Oh, Jac," she breathed, looking down at her hands that she'd just put on me for the second time in my life. She looked up at me through a curtain of tears. "Jac, I'm . . . Jac."

I'd spent my life watching my mother's eyes. They were the indications of how the day would go. If we'd be friends or enemies. Mother and daughter or warring opponents. That sense of walking on eggshells, wondering how I'd disappoint her today. She stayed in an eternal state of anxiety when it came to me, and I'd learned that anxiousness from her. I struggled when I was a kid to ease that trepidation, to show her I would behave and be an easy child. But nothing seemed to work.

I wasn't being honest when I said the town's whispers and accusations chased me away, and the guilt. It wasn't that. I could have withstood all of that. I could have dealt with the guilt and maybe figured out what it was I was missing from that night. But I couldn't do any of it because of Angela Brodie.

If anyone asked about my childhood and my mother, I would say that Mama was the kindest, most soft-spoken, doting mother a kid could ask for. Pen and I never wanted for anything, and she was the model for how to be a present mom. But what was hidden beneath was the weight of unachievable expectation. She feared that I would somehow not live up to what she wanted me to be. She wouldn't outright say I was a disappointment to her, that I was crass and worrisome when I should be delicate and reliable. Her feelings were reflected in fleeting looks, in a twist of the corner of her mouth, in a slight shake of her head, in the way her shoulders drooped.

Mama had always looked at me with apprehension. Like she was always waiting for the other shoe to drop. She was always searching for something deep within me, something she would recognize and affirm her fears and maybe she could cut it out or smother it. She waited for the devil to become unleashed from within me and lay waste to all of us. She held me back with that look, made me doubt myself and second-guess everything I did, whether I was being good. I wanted so badly to be good for my mother, to finally have her look at me, to finally *see me*—not through me, searching for the bad to cut out. To see me and be satisfied that what she saw was enough for her to be content and take a breath.

But there was always that look, that waiting for the shit to hit the fan. It drove me crazy. It made me love her, fight to satisfy her, and hate her for making me feel nothing I did was enough to wipe that look away. I could never understand it. Could never articulate my question well enough to ask. Or maybe I was too afraid to know the answer. To avoid that look, I stayed out of Mama's line of vision as much as possible. I'd be out of the house with my best friends. I'd involve myself in running track and field at school. I'd buck against anything Mama wanted me to do. I stayed with Daddy and Granddad as much as humanly possible. All to avoid the way she looked at me.

Then one night, that look was gone. Just like I'd wanted. The apprehensive fear was gone, but in its place was something much worse. A look that told me I'd achieved what Mama had been looking for all my life. A look that said *Ah, there it is. Just like I thought.* Like a hidden tic finally uncovered. Not disappointment. Not grief or anger. Not concern or tenderness. It was expectation reached.

She watched me that night on the bluff—with the aluminum and wool blankets covering my shivering body, unable to take the icy cold away—the accusation in her glance saying exactly what was on her mind. "I knew you were always in there, and here you finally are."

It was as if she'd spoken the words out loud, and they'd carried on the wind to where I sat in the ambulance. It was all in the one look she gave me before she caught herself and tried to wipe it clean, replacing it with genuine love and concern for me. The emotions she should have felt from the very start.

All too late. I'd already seen it. The glint of satisfaction that her expectation was justified and the sliver of guilt that maybe I'd seen her true feelings. That the years of her waiting for the unspoken thing in me to make itself known had been realized. Back then, that was the moment when I knew I couldn't be here any longer.

Today, we stood face to face.

"If your daddy were still here," she cried. "If he were here, everything would be okay. He would make things okay. He always did right by us. I—I always make the mistakes, though I don't mean to." Mama's voice hitched. She pushed Pen's hand from her mouth when my sister tried to physically shut her up. "You'll never understand what your daddy did so you could live."

If only she knew what he had done to her.

18

January 2018

That night was filled with tuxedos, gowns, and revelry. All the rightfully proud Black people of Brook Haven, South Carolina, had come out that cold January evening in 2018 to celebrate a time-honored tradition recorded from as far back as the 1700s, most notably in 1895 in Louisiana, when the free and upwardly mobile Black people of New Orleans had their first official African American debutante ball.

Recordkeeping reflects that these balls began not just with Black people but with white ones as well, when King George wanted to honor his wife. But to Black people, the debutante ball meant more than a mere nod to a wife.

It was a time for families to formally introduce their young sons and daughters to the world in the form of a cotillion. It was an evening when they "curtsied with pride" and displayed the results of the months of studying and rehearsals they had undergone. It was their first step into adulthood.

It was lavish. It was special. It was tradition. In the *New York Times* article "The Cotillion," a curator at the California African American Museum said that Black cotillions were a way to "dismiss the idea of Black people not being smart enough, or good enough, or worthy enough." Let that one sit with you.

The balls of yesterday meant something. If I'd been in one then, I would have twirled in my white silk and lace with pride for our Black excellence and culture.

But in 2018, to me, *cotillion* meant putting on pretenses, just pomp and circumstance. It was peacocking. And I hated every bit of it. I'd suffered it when my mother made me do it at eighteen. And now, tucked and plucked in this evening gown I'd had to starve all day to fit into and still couldn't move in, I was suffering through it again for my younger sister Penelope's cotillion.

Penelope loved it. She was just like Mrs. Angela Brodie in every way. She was prim and proper. She was going to be a doctor, something tangible and respectable. While I, the oldest and should-have-been wisest, wanted to be a writer.

But being a writer meant not having money or a good house. It meant being flighty and dreamy and always having my head in the clouds. It wasn't a degree Mama could boast about to her Eastern Stars or talk about when the Ladies Auxiliary got together to plan charity events for the underserved or for education. I was the thorn in our mama's side because I wasn't perfect like she needed me to be. I wanted to take another way.

I had been simmering for a long time, all through college, where I'd majored in English, minoring in creative writing and education. While I was in the top percentage of my class and earned internships, fellowships, and all the things that came with studying hard and doing good work, the fact that I wanted to put all that knowledge into writing—or whatever creative outlet I'd want to take—burned through my mother.

Maybe it was because she did not have family, and her own life had detoured from her original dreams. She'd fallen deeply in love, married, and had me. She was the military wife of her marine officer husband, following him internationally and stateside and making life as easy and as uncomplicated for him as possible. And he provided everything she needed. He'd protected her, saved her, loved her like no one else had. His was a real love, and she gave everything to him and their two daughters. She would become the pillar of society. And join every club and organization she could. She'd go to night school and eventually get her college degree. She loved her daughters, but my mother *lived* for my father.

He was a great man and an even better father. He had become one of the youngest Black men to be appointed chief of police. He'd managed to heal the racial divides within the department as best he could. He'd worked tirelessly to serve the county of Richmond. He had a perfect wife and one and a half perfect daughters. Everything he did was a success. He was above reproach and could do no wrong.

Through her daughters, she would live her dream that she'd had for herself. With one, it worked. With the other . . . not so much.

I don't know why I decided to tell Mama the night of Pen's cotillion that I was leaving South Carolina for grad school and wouldn't stay home. All Mama could answer was "To do what?" She'd never understand. It wasn't for her to figure out. It was supposed to be for me.

"It doesn't matter what," I argued as we stood outside in the cold air, dressed so elegantly and beautifully. "But I'm going."

She shook her perfectly coiffed head. "You'll grow up old and alone. Is that what you want? What's wrong with being something you can be proud of? What's wrong with finding a good man to take care of you and love you?"

I balked. The thought of diminishing myself so I could be with a man was like death to me. "I don't want to be like you," I told her. "I want to *be* something."

She was taken aback. The hurt showed so clearly in her face that I instantly regretted my words. "What's wrong with me?" she asked.

It killed me to hear her say it.

I hadn't meant it like that, but I'd said it, and I had to stand by my words. If I backed down tonight, Mama would win, and I'd never leave this state or do what I wanted, whatever that was. I didn't care if I had to work three jobs and live paycheck to paycheck or be alone, if I was happy being me. It should have been enough for Mama for me to be me. But it wasn't. I could see it in her eyes every time I did something the opposite of what she wanted.

"What about your dreams?" I asked. "What is it you wanted to be and do? Not just marry Daddy and support him and have his kids and sit on every board known to man?"

I said all that while orchestral music played inside. While Pen waltzed and smiled and curtsied, I was berating her mother.

"I am proud to be your father's wife. Without him I wouldn't be alive."

I didn't understand. How could someone put so much love and faith in one person? How could she set herself aside, even for a man as great as my dad, who was, indeed, a great man?

I said, "Daddy is a man. He's not God."

I continued to spew my blasphemy, telling Mama to have Daddy, since she lived for him.

"I absolutely hate you." The last part I screeched so loud that everyone around, once minding their business, was working double duty minding ours now too.

Mama slapped me. She never had before, no matter how much it had seemed she wanted to. But I'd pushed her too far. Embarrassed her, broke the perfect mother facade of always having everything together—self, husband, children . . . I had gone too far. She was so horrified over the scene I was making at her sacred cotillion and my ruining the night for Pen, who didn't even know anything was happening. I was making a mockery of our family.

But all I could feel was the sting from where she'd slapped me and how the heat from it was flowing through me, devastating me. My mother had slapped me.

And I ran.

I ignored Mama's calls for me to come back.

An old storage shed was not far from the municipal building where the cotillion was being held. The weather had turned nasty, misty rain coming in and out, but I didn't care. My hair, rolled into an exquisite

French bun, immediately began to frizz at the edges. My dress was muddied and becoming dirtier. My makeup ran like the Ashley River. I didn't care.

I ran to the storage shed, careful to keep quiet in case anyone was around. I tucked myself behind a riding lawn mower. I sent Nick a message to come get me, because Sawyer was inside with her family for her sister, and I had the foresight not to ruin her night. Even if Nick couldn't come, I would wait out the night and freeze to death before I'd go home to my mother.

Noises alerted me that I wasn't alone. I heard two voices, a man's and a woman's. They were whispering. I scrunched down lower, hoping they wouldn't see me. I pulled the skirt of my dress around my ankles, hoping they'd leave. But then other sounds started coming. Moaning, whispering, kissing sounds. A steady thumping of something hitting up against something else, rattling the chains and equipment hanging from the hooks. Their muffled voices called each other by name, but only one rang clear.

His title over and over. *Chief. Chief.* In panting breaths.

"Shhh, they'll hear us."

Slowly, I started to stand, not believing I'd heard correctly. Not wanting to verify what I knew I would see. With each inch I rose, the world that I knew, the people I knew, began to fall away.

He was there, his back to me, in between two legs that I knew weren't my mother's. The hiked-up dress was the wrong color. The legs were the wrong color. His pants were down just below his rear, and he moved in sync with her as she gripped his arms and made guttural moans that were not hers to make as she had sex with my father.

I gasped, stepping backward into some metal chairs propped up against the wall. I lost my footing, falling into them hard, losing sight of the two of them. The woman screeched, and I heard shuffling and rustling as I struggled to get up from the tangle of chairs, which only made more noise. And I tried to be quiet because I didn't want anyone to hear. I didn't want Mama to come and see . . . my father betraying her.

Without him I wouldn't be alive.

Daddy's head appeared, looking down at me as I looked up and right into his eyes. They widened as he recognized who I was and realized what I'd seen. His bow tie was undone, both ends hanging over as he reached out a hand to me.

"Jac, gimme your hand."

I didn't. My daddy was the best man in the world, and he'd betrayed the one person who loved him the best, who'd given up herself for him, who'd said she wouldn't be alive without him. And he'd spit in it, in her love, for legs that didn't belong to him.

I slapped his hand away, scurrying up, tripping over the hem of my skirt.

"Don't touch me," I said. "Leave me alone. I never want to see you again."

He pleaded; he tried to come around the half wall that separated us, but I moved farther and farther away from him.

"Let me explain!" he said. "Your mother . . . you can't . . . you can't . . ."

He couldn't bring himself to say that I should never tell her what I'd seen because we both knew that telling her might be the end of her. Without him, she wouldn't be alive.

I kept backing away, farther and farther away from him, until I was out the door and back in the mist and cold. The woman, whoever she was, was nowhere to be seen. I'd never know who she was. I hoped to never know.

I ran from Daddy as I'd run from Mama, with him calling from behind me, probably torn between chasing me and letting me go. I ran as Nick's Dodge pickup pulled up like he'd been reading my mind and knew when I'd need him the most, like always.

"Jac, don't!" I could hear Daddy yell behind me.

I climbed in, ignoring Nick gawking at me as I stuffed the long skirt of my evening gown into the truck's cab and slammed the door behind me. Nick winced but kept his mouth shut.

"Drive," I demanded, staring straight ahead, determined, confused, angry. "I don't care where. Just the hell away from here."

That night, I learned what Mama could never learn. I would never tell her.

That her husband was neither infallible nor invincible, and that he was just a man.

19

After the sunroom fight with Mama, with Pen trying to keep us apart, I had every intention of going to Granddad's, my refuge. I went to Nick's instead; my need to be in a judgment-free zone was so great that I sped the whole way there. He lived in one of the newly developed neighborhoods in town, a four-bedroom home all to himself. He was surprised when I arrived, having only ten minutes' notice that I wanted to see him. But he said yes immediately. I parked my car on the curb in front of his house. It was midday, and even in my emotional state, I knew well enough not to pull into his driveway like I lived there or was his girlfriend. And I wasn't coming there for girlfriend status. I was at Nick's for something else.

He opened the front door in a pale-blue button-down and suit pants. He looked like he was about to leave for work or like I'd interrupted him, and . . .

I eyed him. "You didn't rush home to meet me, did you?"

He was breathless, face flushed, but he cracked a slow smile that made his scar extra cute. "Nope. Was here the entire time."

I pulled a face.

"I was on the way home anyway." He stepped back to let me in, peering at my car in front of his mailbox.

"Why'd you park on the street?" He closed the door behind me. The house smelled of freshly sprayed cologne.

I sighed, taking in his very bachelor-ish home with its minimalist styling and brown leather furniture. I noted accents, color, and artwork that Nick likely wouldn't have purchased. It screamed of a woman's touch.

"Driveways are reserved for girlfriends, family, and wives." I turned to him, letting my eyes roll over the curves of his all-American face, reminding me of the new Jack Reacher. I let out a breath, stepping close. "Which do you want me to be?"

"Whatever you want to be." His voice grew husky on my approach, electrifying my senses. I loved that he caught what I was throwing his way.

I wanted to forget everything that had happened earlier. The drama with Faye. Granddad's autopsy. Mama. My life. I wanted to get lost in someone like I'd done years ago. Would he let me?

He stared deeply into my eyes, a hurricane of questions and confusion and want building behind his gaze like he had so many things to say and didn't know where to start. I wasn't here for talking.

"Now that you're back, I'm never letting you go again."

I walked into his arms, which immediately circled my waist, pulling me against his wall of a body. His thumbs made circles on my exposed back, driving me wild—the good kind. I pulled at his shirt, undoing the buttons as I wrapped my hand around the back of his neck, relishing it as my fingers glided through the short bristles of his haircut and pulled him down to my level, where he kissed me like he would devour me whole.

Nick scooped me up, holding me against him as if I weighed barely anything. My legs wrapped around his waist, locking him in, and he walked us to his bedroom, never missing a beat, never breaking his stride, never breaking our ravenous kiss.

I liked that too.

Come to think of it, there were a lot of things I liked about that afternoon.

~

The day after Nick and I had our "reunion," I received a call from Mrs. Harris asking to meet and feed the birds at the park in the center of downtown. She was already seated on a bench with a bag of day-old bread, which she dipped into to feed the geese and other birds milling about. The park was nearly empty since most people were at church. The October weather was perfect. We only needed sweaters if we sat in the shade.

"I'm glad you were able to spend a little time with me today," Mrs. Harris said, offering me an open bag of breadcrumbs.

I reached in and grabbed a fistful of hardened, broken bread and began scattering it, bit by bit, on the ground in front of us.

"Your granddad was very proud of what you'd made of yourself since your daddy died. He understood why you felt you couldn't come home. Believe it or not, your mama and sister do too."

I sighed, watching the birds approach with caution and peck at the ground. "In my mind I know you're right."

"And in your heart?"

I didn't answer. My throat wouldn't let me.

"You need to let go of that night, Jac. My Henry always said you were a bright light and bullheaded. But you had the biggest heart in the world. You take responsibility for things that aren't meant for you to take on. Things like not letting go of what happened to your daddy that night."

I shook my head. "Oh, I don't talk about it."

"You hold it in, it eats away at you."

"I know."

"You don't need to take on what happened to him all by yourself. Let it out."

I did that, and look where it had gotten me. Conrad's notebooks called to me from Granddad's safe, where I'd stashed them.

Mrs. Harris couldn't hide her surprise. "You don't talk to anyone about it? A therapist? A group?"

I shook my head. I wondered if the birds could really get full off a few crumbs of bread scattered everywhere. The pieces were minuscule. How could they be enough?

"You should go talk to someone."

I finally looked at her, and looking at her suddenly made me miss my grandmother, even though she'd been dead since I was five.

"You should, Jac. You're holding too much in, and we don't say it enough that it's okay to ask for help."

"If I speak about it," I said, "it means having to relive that night."

"And maybe forgiving yourself in the process."

Except I didn't want to forgive myself. Every day, I looked at my mother and how she missed Daddy or thought about how he wouldn't be there to walk Pen down the aisle. That was my fault. The only person who should continue to suffer was me. "Is that what you wanted to talk to me about, Mrs. Harris?" I asked. "Going to talk to a shrink?"

"I want you to be careful."

"You've said that before."

"Yes, but . . . I feel it's my duty now because Montavious isn't here to tell you. He wouldn't want you going head to head with Faye Arden. She's a different kind."

"A different kind?"

"Mm-hmm," Mrs. Harris affirmed. "She's a different kind of person. She's like one of those . . ." The woman put her hands up like she was clutching a ball between them, opening and closing her fingers together.

I was horrible at board games, Pictionary especially. "I'm sorry, Mrs. Harris, I'm not following."

"You know, one of those plants like in that movie *Little Shop of Horrors*."

"Oh! A Venus flytrap."

She clapped her hands together. "Yes!"

It felt like I'd won a grand prize—I was that proud of myself.

"She's like one of them. All fancy on the outside but sinister on the in. Girl, Faye Arden ain't worth a pot to piss in."

She said it with such vitriol that my hand flew to my mouth to stop the snort that came back anyway.

"Mrs. Harris!"

"Well, she isn't!" the old woman said.

The two of us made a pair, the widow and the wild child sitting on a bench, comparing Faye Arden to Venus flytraps and pots of piss.

Mrs. Harris seemed to sense that she was losing her audience. "What I mean is that you seem to know that she's not what she puts out there. I know that because I've worked for her for at least a year now. At first I thought, like the rest of the town, that she was this young socialite, a little too big for her britches, but who isn't these days? A white lady with too much money to spend, and she wanted to take root here. She'd met Mayor Tate in Charlotte or somewhere more north."

I was pretty sure Nick had said Myrtle Beach.

"And they got in with each other fast and hard. Nick is ambivalent. Maybe he's even relieved because it means Mayor Tate isn't suffocating him. He's a sweet boy, if a little intense, but who isn't these days? But little is known about her other than she came to town, fell in love with Moor Manor and all the lore around it, and figured out how to get the town to jump on her bandwagon. Talking about renovating and revitalizing the property and making it . . . oh, what did she call it . . ." She trailed off, thinking.

I waited her out, trying not to look at the time on my phone because I needed to head to my meetup with my sister and Dr. Weigert.

She perked up. "That's right. A vacation destination. Who doesn't want something steeped in misery to finally have a brighter future and to get the locals more money in their pockets while they're at it?"

Yeah, who wouldn't want that?

"The mayor's connections helped her get what she needed to make Moor Manor into the country inn it now is. She managed to get some big folks from around the Carolinas and Georgia to endorse it. She's made money, and Brook Haven's received good press from the anticipation of the inn alone."

"Truly wonderful lady," I said sarcastically, wondering where Mrs. Harris was going with this.

"She keeps everyone at arm's length. Never talks about herself. Or her family. And she's either all in with you, like you're the only thing in her world, or she's like you don't exist." The older woman's voice lowered, and I had to lean in to hear her. "That's when her true nature slips through. Not a lot of people see that. Except Montavious and me. She has things hidden in that office of hers. That's why she's the only one with the key. And the key is this little circular disk that she keeps on her person. She clicks it and can go in the office anytime she wants. Montavious saw it one day a few months back. And ever since then, he was on a tear to figure out who she was and why she rubbed him the wrong way."

Mrs. Harris emptied the rest of the bag of crumbs on the ground. "Right before your granddad had the heart attack, he told me she'd said something that rattled him something fierce, and he was itching to ask her about it."

"What was it?"

"Didn't say."

"Seems you two became close," I observed, wondering how it might have been to see the two of them together. It would have been nice. They deserved as much.

She nodded, a smile easing on her. "He did. We had gotten close. I never thought I'd find someone to turn my head again after Henry. But then Montavious was there. I loved how he talked about his Armchair Detective friends and what they were getting up to."

I smiled, thinking of the stories he'd shared with me too. "Yeah, he loved those folks. I told them he was gone. They knew me like I was one of them, so I've kinda been chatting them up every now and again. Little stuff Granddad was working on."

We sat silent for a moment before I thought to ask one last question. "I found Granddad's clock in Faye's office. The day you and I ran into each other at the Manor."

I had Mrs. Harris's undivided attention. "Her office, you say? But that old man never took that hideous thing out of his house."

I nodded in agreement. "That's what I was saying."

"And you're sure it's the same one?"

"How many of those monstrosities do you think are out there? Besides, what are the chances of two people ending up with the same clock? It's not like they both bought it at the state fair or something."

"What did she say when you asked?"

I snorted. "She said she didn't know how it got in there. She said one of the workers at the Manor might have put it there. Then she sicced the cops on me and played the victim."

Mrs. Harris rolled her eyes. "Lord. The age-old go-to. And they got it from whom? Montavious?" Mrs. Harris snorted. "Fat chance of that. She had to have taken it from him."

"Well, Faye said she'd never been to his house. He always came to see her when he was checking out the Manor's progress or about town."

I thought about how the whiteboard had been wiped in a hurry, the words *Colleton Girls* etched into it from Granddad's heavy-handed writing.

"Something she said triggered him, and he was determined to figure out the connection."

"And Granddad's pacemaker malfunctions, causing a heart attack. The clock is nowhere to be found." The words flowed out, and I could've kicked myself for not putting the sequence together faster.

"Then the clock ends up in an office that no one has access to except for her," Mrs. Harris finished, the clear plastic bag a scrunched-up mess in her grip.

Instead of looking surprised and terrified, Mrs. Harris was angry. I could tell by the way she clutched her purse straps and how her back had become ramrod straight. "What are you saying, Jac? That Faye Arden had a hand in Montavious's death because of a clock?"

"Sounds wild, right?" I asked. "Faye Arden can do no wrong here. She's hosting the charity gala and auction coming up. She's engaged to the most eligible bachelor and prominent figure in the county, and he's very likely to be governor one day. She is the epitome of a perfect socialite, even if she's not from the South. How could I ever dare to think she'd be a murderer?"

"Oh, cut the foolishness, girl." Mrs. Harris twisted her lips at my display. "If what you're alluding to is true . . . if Faye did something to harm Montavious . . . I need to—"

"Do nothing," I cut in gently. "Okay, Mrs. Harris? Say nothing."

She fussed with the bread bag in her hands. "I don't feel right about this, Jac. Remember you've only just returned, and that woman has made a name for herself in this town."

I dusted my hands off. If I heard that one more time. "So everyone keeps telling me."

Mrs. Harris looked at me pointedly. "Then you know. So maybe don't poke that bear."

I reached out, patting her hand so she could see that I had everything under control, even though inside I was working circumstantial guesses at best. "You're one of the few people here who don't think I'm a colossal screwup," I told her. "One of them is dead now. You just leave everything to me."

20

I went to the hospital, changing the previous date for drinks later with Weigert to lunch now with him and Pen. Granddad's autopsy results had come in, and he wanted to go over them with us. Pen wanted him and me to have a date. I wanted to make things as quick and easy as possible. Two birds with one stone.

"When you changed to lunch, I didn't expect we'd have a chaperone," Weigert said, amused, gesturing good naturedly at my sister, who was busily digging into her pecan-and-chicken salad.

Without lifting her head, she said casually, "Trust me. It's for your own safety."

"I have a habit of screwing on the first date," I said loftily, catching her drift.

I grinned as sweet tea nearly came out of his nose. "What?" Weigert said, using a napkin to wipe at his reddened nose. Cute.

Weigert low whistled. "You sisters are something. You nearly had me going." But he gave me a second, longer glance. Wanting danced in his eyes. Maybe if I hadn't just been with Nick and didn't want to use him as a casual lay. Maybe if my mind wasn't split in a million different directions.

Pen shrugged, shoveling a huge forkful in her mouth. I could only watch in astonishment.

"How are you even tasting what you're eating? You're inhaling."

"Gotta shove it in and get back to it," Pen said. "Welcome to what's going to be my life. Weigert knows the life."

Weigert huffed a laugh. "This is nothing. Wait until you're done with med school, and then you have residency."

Pen swallowed. "Anyway, the results?"

"Yeah." Weigert pulled out a folder and slid it to the center of the round table. Pen popped another forkful of salad in her mouth, pushed her container to the side, and reached for the folder to open it up. I leaned in to look and listen as they spoke, and Weigert summarized.

"It's what I told you when we spoke on the phone. Your grandfather was pacer dependent. That means without one, he would have a heart event, heart attack. The pacer prevented that until it shorted out. It can happen if the pacer malfunctioned, which is what the manufacturer is looking into."

I nodded while Pen munched her salad from the side. We were listening for different reasons. "That's pretty much the deal. A massive heart attack brought on by the malfunction of the pacemaker," he repeated for the layperson—that is, me.

"Did you find anything on his body?" I asked. "Like marks on his skin around the pacemaker area?"

Weigert's brows creased. "Now that you mention it . . ."

He shuffled the papers until he found one with a drawn figure and indicators around the upper area. "Yes, here." Weigert tapped the page. "Notes reflect four points, dark markings of unknown origin in the general area, where there's also significant bruising. But we don't know what that is, and the examiner didn't think it significant enough to go beyond us. Could be anything."

It could be anything without context, without knowing what I knew—that Faye had a Taser and those little point marks on his chest aligned with the prongs on it. I was putting things together.

I zeroed in on his autopsy report, allowing the images to become seared into my mind. The black circled areas of bruising around his skin near the pacemaker where the probes had made contact. A series of distinct contact points from when she kept hitting him with it, over and over.

All the proof I needed that Faye Arden had killed my grandfather.

21

Wheat bread, baking soda, self-rising flour, milk, eggs, shredded cheddar cheese, unsalted butter, two bunches collards, sweet onions, chicken stock, smoked neck bones . . .

The list of groceries went on.

The overhead lights hummed as I entered IGA, Mama's extensive list clutched in my hand like a badge of determination to be successful at this task. After the big blowout between Mama and me, when I eventually came back home late that night, I was more than happy to ignore what had transpired earlier and get back to a semblance of normalcy.

I knew Mama felt bad about our blowup and the things she'd said, how she'd grabbed and shaken me, but her words didn't die easy. Words could last forever. I might have been twenty-eight, but I still wanted to please my mother as if I were twenty years younger. Sometimes things were better left unsaid, and it wouldn't be the first time. Probably not the last, either, and I might have resented my mother for how she was with me, but she was still my mother. I needed to protect her, maybe even forgive her, even if it meant never living up to her expectation of me. For now, it was best to do as we'd always done: move on.

In this case, "moving on" was me glaring at Mama's loopy cursive and the flowers she'd drawn on the corners of her grocery list. They were always flowers, the doodles she traced when deep in thought—six-petaled bouquets with a stem and two leaves—as she listed out the items we needed to restock.

I grabbed a shopping cart and dumped my bag in the kid basket, cushioning the note and my phone for easy viewing and convenience. At the funeral, the air had carried the weight of condolences and hushed tones. The locals gave me a wide berth, cautious and curious. But the realization that Granddad was truly gone, the idea that I'd have to get used to his absence, was too great then for me to notice anything else. A town as close knit as mine knew that, and, respecting not me but Granddad, they held their tongues.

But now, as I read the overhead numbered signs telling me where to find the baking items and tried to determine which bunch of vibrant collard greens would garner Mama's approval, eyes that "accidentally" met mine and faux whispers that traveled the air into my ears were filled with something more than sympathy.

My cart filled with all the items from Mama's list—double-checked for accuracy, thank you. I had one more stop to make in produce for the navel oranges Mama wanted. I was doing that when snatches of conversation found their way to me.

At first, I ignored them, swatting them away like annoying buzzing flies. But then the words began to land and take shape. *Chief Brodie*, *pushed him*, and *barged into her office*, and *poor Faye Arden, such a lovely woman to be put through all that* followed me wherever I turned. I dried my hand on the back of my jeans, trying to shrug off my growing unease.

It's nothing, I kept telling myself. *No big deal. They're just talking shit.* But none of that pep talk worked. Their rumors, speculations, and accusations kept buzzing around me, invisible phantoms haunting me as if I were in Murder Manor. I believed it was time to leave.

I couldn't shake the feeling of eyes on me as I wheeled the cart from produce and headed toward checkout. It was before twelve, and I'd thought the store wouldn't have too much traffic. It didn't, for the most part. But I'd forgotten that while the traffic was lighter, here, the grocery store was a place of gathering. And gossiping.

I quickened my pace, my face warm from the heat crawling up my back and neck, armpits getting damp under my T-shirt with my building anxiety. I had to get out without causing a scene. I chanced a look back and saw them, young and old, male and female, even some store workers looking at me, heads together, talking and motioning toward me. They didn't even care to hide it—that's how much contempt they had for me. That one hurt. A lot.

I scanned the lanes, looking for the shortest line, and finally pulled into the one for twenty items or less. The guest at the register had to have more than twenty. Of all the times to be a rule breaker. I considered ditching the groceries—eighteen; I counted—and leaving. Pen could grab them on her way home. But then I thought about my earlier resolve to be more helpful, so I stuck myself in the nearest lane and prayed for a speedy checkout.

"Can I ask you something?" the young mother in front of me asked from nowhere. She had a newborn bound to her chest in one of those baby-swaddling things. She said it loud, or maybe I thought she sounded loud and that everyone could hear us in this suddenly too-quiet store.

She didn't waste any time with fluff questions, going straight for the jugular. I didn't even think she'd been paying attention to all the commotion behind me, but whispers traveled fast. They even hopped over me to the people at the front, apparently.

I hadn't noticed she had turned to me, or that we'd moved up in the line and her groceries were being scanned. I didn't look around, feeling the eyes on me. The checkout beeps went off in the background, making me think of Granddad's monitors, as the woman's items were scanned.

Slowly, to give me something to focus on, I began placing my items on the conveyor belt as space opened up. "Excuse me?" I hated how timid I sounded.

She patted her sleeping baby's back. *Pat. Pat. Pat.* Eyebrow raised and looking at me with distaste.

"Is it true that you pushed your dad?" She pulled no punches. Was willing to take one for the team and ask big bad Jac what everyone was dying to know.

My movements slowed to a stop, the conveyor belt still going with no new items added on it.

"Well?" Her eyebrow went up higher, her face hungry to get the dirt.

"Fuck off."

That's what I wanted to say, but I didn't. Instead, trying to gather myself when all eyes were on me, I opened my mouth to speak as we moved up the line. The cashier smacked loudly on her gum, her blue hair obscuring her face as she bagged the mother's groceries. There were lots of canisters of formula.

I made eye contact with the cashier, surprised that instead of accusation and anger, I saw care there; here is an ally, I thought. That appeared to be the case as she began to scan the rest of the items faster. Definitely more than twenty for this lady, too, with her rude ass.

"Well, if it isn't Jac Brodie. I am sorry again for the recent loss of your grandfather," Mrs. Harris said, coming up to the register, where the bags were ready to go back in the mother's cart for departure. She spoke loud enough for others to hear. Mrs. Harris's own bag hung from her hands as her eyes switched from me to the woman. "Samantha."

The newly named mother, Samantha, greeted the older woman.

I mustered the best smile I could. It was tight and probably looked weird as I threw the rest of the items on the belt. I should have thanked Mrs. Harris for her condolences. I wasn't sure why she was offering them again. She'd done so at Murder Manor already, and we'd had that long chat in the park. I still should have said something, but the atmosphere was suffocating, and everyone was still watching and waiting, pressing closer. I was trapped from the front and behind.

Mrs. Harris continued to study me, her eyes boring in. Samantha inserted her card in the reader, and again I considered abandoning everything and squeezing between Samantha's cart and the candy rack with the gossip magazines. I half expected one of them to have my face plastered on the cover.

A murmur rippled through the small crowd. Samantha's question still hanging in the air; Mrs. Harris still looking at me. Both of them—everyone—waiting for a response from me.

I nodded, hoping she'd see that as acknowledgment and thanks. She just stared. The cashier stared. Everyone stared, waiting for what was coming next. They could wait without me because I refused to stay and be fodder for more gossip and judgment.

I was just about to make my escape when Mrs. Harris raised her voice, breaking through the unbearable silence. She sounded like my math teacher, Mr. Harris. "John, chapter eight, verse seven, says, 'So when they continued asking him, he lifted himself up and said unto them, *He that is without sin among you, let him first cast a stone at her*.'"

"Amen," the cashier said under her breath in a cosign.

There was complete silence. Even the register stopped its beeping. The front door opened to let in another customer, pushing away the volcanic heat of my embarrassment and letting in a whoosh of air so I could breathe again.

Mrs. Harris glared at the crowd, her eyes moving from person to person, ending on Samantha, who *pat, pat, patted* her child but with less enthusiasm than she had before.

Mrs. Harris said, "I do believe Jac has been through enough, don't you think?"

Samantha's face flushed red. She cleared her throat, bouncing the baby, kissing its head, as if doing that would remind everyone there was a baby there so they should be gentle, even though she was not. You couldn't yell at a new mother, could you?

"Whatever we think we know, baseless gossip is unbecoming and beneath us. Don't you agree?"

A few heads reluctantly nodded, and the cashier, with her blue-colored hair and sparkling blue eyes, snapped her gum and offered a victorious smile.

"Have yourself a better day, Ms. Baker," she said to Samantha as the new mother shoved her bags in the cart and wheeled it away at practically a run. The rest of the customers, those who were too invested in me, scattered like roaches when the light cuts on. No one wanted any more from Mrs. Damn-You-to-Hell-with-Her-Bible-Quotes-and-Shame Harris.

Mrs. Harris asked, "Are you working at the Manor today, Mia?"

The cashier nodded. "Gimme a sec," she said quickly to me. She stepped away from her register to say something privately to the older woman. I tried to give them privacy by fumbling around in my purse for my wallet. But it was still awkward. Mrs. Harris gave me a quick look and a goodbye and left.

Mia returned to me when Mrs. Harris was gone. "Sorry about that mess," she said as I inserted my card. "It's not fair what they did. It's like high school and the mean kids picking on the newbie, even though you're not a newbie. Are you okay?"

I wasn't, but I wasn't going to lay that on Mia. She'd been nice to me, and we were going to leave it at that. "I'm good."

"Liar."

"Wow." I chuckled, plopping a bag in my cart. "Don't hold back."

Mia flipped the switch to her register light, and her numbered marquee went off. The people behind me groaned. "Sorry, it's my five," she told them, not sorry at all. She said to me, "Help you take your bags to your car?"

I didn't have a chance to tell her no. She grabbed the end of my cart and pulled her way through the sliding doors, with me following behind.

"Are you allowed to leave your register like that, without doing a count or with people still in line?"

Mia shrugged. "They'll be fine for five minutes. Plus, no one's working my register, so it'll still be my count."

Clearly Mia wanted something. It could have been to ask in private what Samantha the mom had asked in public. I steeled myself for it while also wondering how Mia would lead me to my car if she didn't know it. She surveyed the parking lot, slowing down. She looked back at me curiously.

"Over there." I pointed to the baby blue Beetle.

"No eyelashes on it?"

My mouth opened and closed. I pulled a face. "I am an actual adult."

Mia smirked. "Okay, adult. Listen, I know you had drama with Ms. Arden about something your granddad owned. I think maybe I can help."

This was what Mia wanted. Thinking, I opened the car, trying to seem nonchalant in case anyone else was paying attention. We were having small talk.

"What is it you do at the Manor?"

"I clean mostly. And whatever else if they're short. She's not fully staffed yet. Not until opening.

"Look, the woman's good at the smoke and mirrors thing, all right. You can't just go around thinking you're gonna catch her up, because you're not. I've seen when she thinks no one's watching. I swear she's hiding something in her office. It's why she has it locked up like Fort Knox."

"What do you mean?"

Mia shrugged. "Dead bodies probably." She laughed nervously. "You know how they say there are passageways and secret rooms that the doctors and the Caretaker locked their victims up in? I think she's got one."

"Why do you say that?"

Mia handed me the last bag. "Because there will be times when I knock on the door and she's not in there. And then a second later, she's coming out of her office. Then she either acts like I'm crazy, like she didn't hear the door—there's no way she can't hear it—or she gets mad."

Mia shivered, her nervousness intensifying. "I heard about the whole clock thing. Everyone's talking about it. I liked your grandfather.

He was a cool guy, and if she had his stuff in that locked-up vault of hers—"

"Vault?"

"Her office. She treats it like a vault," Mia said, rolling her eyes that I wasn't following fast enough. "I figured you might want in the vault. Take a look around and see if the secret room the stories say is in the house is in there. There's a reason why she locks that office up like a bank, you know. Maybe you can find evidence that she, I don't know, stole his stuff so you can be, like, vindicated and shit."

"But the room is locked. She always has the remote."

"She has a spare, and I can get it to you. I clean her personal room when she stays at the property. I know there's another remote she keeps in her curio cabinet as a backup. You just have to make sure you get it back to me, all right?" Mia looked at me with eyes that said they trusted me, and I couldn't let her down. Not when she was putting her neck on the line for me.

I waved like I was warding her off. "I can't ask you to do that."

"You're not asking. I'm offering."

My mother's words said *You're corrupting her.*

"But why?"

"My brother worked as a janitor at Richmond Regional. She got him fired, saying he took some money from a charity they had. He'd pissed her off somehow. I don't know, and he didn't give me the details. Then she begged Mayor Tate and the chief to let him off if he paid the money back. My brother had a debt that he worked off at the Manor. Then he left and said he wasn't coming back here again. So, I'm offering. If you can find something on that lying piece of shit, it would be my pleasure."

She began moving away, back to the store, throwing an anxious look over her shoulder. "I'll let you know when to meet. Your best time in is during the gala, when she'll be too preoccupied to notice anything, or anyone, is missing."

As Mia went back the way she came, I couldn't shake the feeling of being in over my head. I considered giving up and folding back into my quiet world of guilty acceptance. My thoughts turned back to Granddad's cabin, to the side door where Patrick found him, and about how he'd suffered in those moments. My resolve amplified.

Was I a step closer to figuring out the truth, that Granddad wasn't some bored retired cop with too much time who couldn't give up the glory of his heyday, and that I wasn't just the wild Brodie girl on some crazy quest for redemption?

22

The night of the gala, I sat in the back seat of Patrick's SUV feeling like a petulant child being forced to go to church, crammed in stuffy clothes and dreading the next four hours—minimum—of praise dances and calls to altar and Sunday school. Scratch that; that would have been better than where I was obliged to go now, the charity gala cochaired by my mother and Faye Arden for the Ladies of the Black Southern League.

We bumped along the road, heading to Moor Manor with many residents of Brook Haven, and as we neared the mansion, my mood darkened. Was I making the right play tonight, being here after what had happened between me and Faye last week? I wouldn't have that opportunity at this dinner Mama insisted I attend despite what happened.

Pen turned in the front passenger seat. "You really want to go to this? Mama will get over it if you decide not to."

I had an ulterior motive. I had to go. "I'll be okay."

"Will you?" Patrick asked gruffly, glancing at me in the rearview. "Because the last time—"

"Patrick," Pen said, snapping her head to him in a way that would have shut me up too.

The information from Weigert reinforced my drive. The confrontation with Mama emboldened me. While I didn't want to piss people off or start unnecessary drama, there was something about Faye I couldn't shake, and I needed to check for myself whether I was onto something or imagining it. The Taser was too much of a coincidence. The pacemaker findings and the marks on his chest aligning with the prongs were enough for me to put things together. Law enforcement would call it circumstantial, but if I got that circumstantial evidence to the police and they tested it, or matched it with the markings on Granddad, then they could connect Faye to Granddad.

Tonight, the plan was to play nice. The wireless key that Mia had slipped me was securely in my clutch, a bag big enough to carry a Taser if I managed to employ my emerging breaking-and-entering abilities with the same success I'd done at Conrad's. Only without the eyewitness in the end, I hoped.

Mia had wrapped her arms around herself as if she was cold and shifted from foot to foot on one of the trails we'd decided were private enough to serve as meeting places. She'd been on her way home from her shift cleaning rooms, sweat glistening from her trek down one of the many paths snaking along the mountain.

"Remember, I need this back immediately. Okay? Just in case." Mia's eyes were luminous in the dark, the threat of discovery heavy between us. "My shift starts at ten o'clock to help clean up after the gala."

I'd promised.

Hours later, I was still going over my plan. Get close to her office. Use the spare wireless remote Mia had taken for me. Get into Faye's office. Find the Taser. Prove she had something to do with my grandfather's heart attack.

Pen looked at me again, worry wrinkling up her gala-ready face. "Last chance?"

"I'm good," I said, feeling the exact opposite but planning to fake it until I made it.

Patrick scowled in the rearview mirror. Warning emanated from him like a beacon. I turned to the window, the blackness surrounding us, to ward it away. Better not to antagonize him.

Keep it together, Jac. Don't lose your nerve. You'll figure this out. You have to.

It was one thing for me to make accusations that Faye could easily bat away. In Brook Haven, I'd proved to be the unreliable one.

I was more of a stranger in Brook Haven than she was. But Granddad was a pillar of the community. He would have been listened to. There was a reason why Faye had chosen this small coastal town, and I could see why she'd stay. Southerners, while initially distrustful, could end up trusting completely, and once they did, it was hard to break their trust. And the things that earned it quickest were acts that were seemingly selfless and magnanimous. Something like restoring an eyesore, an infamous historical structure, and showering money on community interests.

The people of Brook Haven overlooked many things, even when they shouldn't. All because they didn't want scandal. They didn't want a mark on their good name. They didn't want outsiders judging them. Even if they knew someone bad was in their midst, they'd turn a blind eye. I could see why. Brook Haven was insulated, and what happened here mainly stayed here. No one wanted ugly secrets exposed that would throw the town back into the world of murderous infamy in the way Murder Manor had once done.

Faye enjoyed attention and admiration on her terms. She liked the idea of being Mrs. Tate and a big fish in a small pond. That is, until she got bored with the town and was done with it. I wouldn't have been surprised if she'd done this before. Faye, I thought, was like a swarm of locusts, ravaging crops and then moving on to the next field, leaving devastation in her wake.

Patrick's Navigator pulled to a stop in front of the brightly lit Manor. The valets, dressed in black-and-white button-downs, rushed to open the doors for us, take the keys from Patrick, and park. Somehow, I ended up between Pen and Patrick, like their good little girl.

"Hey," I said suddenly. Patrick looked down at me warily. "You look good. Handsome and shit. Thanks for the ride and, um, show my sis a good time." I popped out from in between them, making my way inside before Patrick could say anything to make me regret my attempt at an apology.

Those specially invited to attend the dinner portion of the gala were mostly there and listening to Faye as she discussed the renovations and gave them a tour of the new Moor Manor, especially the hedge maze. Neither Nick nor Sawyer were around that I could see. I saw my mother greeting guests and decided to be proactive and dutiful, since later I might be arrested for breaking and entering.

"Mama," I whispered in her ear, giving her a peck on her cheek from behind.

She startled, stopped midsentence, and turned to see who'd touched her. When she saw me, she showed at first delight, and then, when we both heard Faye over the din, the delight turned to anxiety.

I held both hands up. "Be not afraid," I said, quoting a famous religious song. "I come in peace," I finished, quoting a nonreligious movie.

She excused herself from the couple she'd been speaking to when I'd interrupted and took my arm, her deep-purple chiffon gown swishing alongside my simple black nonswishy one. She pulled us to a corner, looking around to make sure no one was in hearing distance. I braced myself, unsure what I could have done wrong in the two minutes I'd been here.

She looked flawless, like a movie star, and she eyed me. "How are you?"

"You look beautiful." It was something Daddy would have told her, had told her when she dressed like this. Her looking like this and my dad not being able to see it hit me in a way that was unexpected. I put a hand on my stomach to settle myself.

She smiled quickly, smoothing the front of her dress shyly, like the compliment had caught her off guard. "Thank you, baby. You do too." She swept me with a critical eye. "Where are your earrings?" She looked at my septum ring. "But that's still there." Her upper lip curled in a hint of disgust.

I touched my earlobes. I knew there was something I'd forgotten.

"Honey, you know you shouldn't leave without them. They complete the whole look." She touched several parts of my face and the top of my off-the-shoulder dress, adjusting things that were perfectly fine. I squirmed in her clutches.

"Just try, okay?"

"This *is* me trying." It was never enough. I forced a smile for the covert eyes on us. "I'm here, aren't I?"

She lowered her voice and leaned in closer. "Please, Jac, with Faye . . . just smile and nod, okay? Just like at cotillion studies. Smile, nod, and short and sugar replies. Or nothing at all if you can't. Let's get through the night with no added complications."

"Why'd you insist I come, then?" I asked, gesturing to the ornate decorations and the people in their evening best. "If you're so worried about how I'll act."

She leaned in. "I don't know what crazy notions you have about that woman, but even still, I won't give her or the public the satisfaction of thinking they got the best of a Brodie."

I was stunned. Mama didn't believe me but didn't want the other side thinking they'd won either. I was so busy trying to make the deductions that all I could do was utter a docile "Yes, ma'am" while thinking of when I'd get a chance to break into Faye's office, the remote burning a hole in my purse.

"Can you stick to Pen and Patrick?" She wanted my kid sister and her fiancé to babysit me. "For me? Please?" Her eyes pleaded. I swallowed down the hurt and how small I felt at her expectation that I might wreck her important night.

"Mama, I know how to act."

She rubbed my arm. "I know you do. It's just you know people are getting used to you being around again, and they may want to bring up things from the past."

Daddy was the "things from the past" she meant.

"I just don't want you to be triggered and"—she searched for the softest blow—"react." She could be Mayor Tate's second-in-command. She had the politician talk down pat.

I imagined the look on her face when I produced the evidence on Faye. Mama wouldn't be jumping to cosponsor anything else with a maybe murderer.

"Hey, ladies, stop looking so serious. Aren't we at a party?" My Ghanaian Nigerian bestie *Soul Train* danced toward us to music only she could hear. Sawyer was the only Black person I knew who could not dance but thought she could. "I have arrived."

"Lord," Mama muttered under her breath. "The girl has no rhythm. How's that possible when both her parents are from the motherland?"

I covered my mouth in a failed attempt at laughter suppression, an ugly giggle escaping through my fingers. The mood lightened exponentially, and finally I could breathe.

Thank God for Sawyer, who joined us sporting a deep-red velvet pantsuit, immediately dialing the building tension between Mama and me down several degrees. Sawyer dropped an arm over my shoulder. "We'll be on our best behavior, Mrs. B."

Mama's lips twisted as if to say both of us were full of shit.

I smiled and nodded, promising I wouldn't get into anything tonight, knowing I was lying through my teeth.

We parted ways with my mother. She returned to the foyer to continue her cohosting duties while Sawyer and I set out to do what we'd come to do. We integrated into the group Faye had gathered to take a tour of Moor Manor's restoration.

"I want a look at that maze." Sawyer grinned, linking arms with me. "I hear it's amazing."

I groaned. "She'll show upstairs, right?"

We followed along the outskirts, prepared to slip away the first chance we got. Sawyer looked around. "I'm sure she'll want to show the guest rooms. This place has more buzz than the Isle of Palms. Nothing beats quaint, with the opportunity to spend a night in the antebellum, minus all the ugly shit, of course, bless their hearts." She got southern there.

Ugly shit was an understatement.

Even I couldn't deny that Faye had done a remarkable job with the estate. The house, the grounds, the maze . . . the maze was going to bring everyone in. It was taking a slice of British lifestyle and setting it right in the backyard of *Southern Living*. It was really hard to believe how much had been done so quickly. And how different and full of life the Manor looked compared to all the years before, when it was busy living up to its nickname.

Ten minutes later, Sawyer leaned in again. "I still can't believe I agreed to this. I work with cops. I can't be an accessory to breaking and entering. I should have ignored your call," she muttered, smoothing the sides of her chic pantsuit. "You are freakishly calm about breaking into someone's locked office, come to think of it."

I pushed away an image of me in Conrad's condo, searching for his precious notebooks. "I saw it on *Law and Order*."

Sawyer shot me another dubious look. "Which one?"

"All of them." I gestured to the group. "Pay attention. The mermaid is speaking. There's a quiz after."

Sawyer snickered, the deep-red velvet pantsuit hugging the curves of her body. She looked awesome. Her natural hair bloomed above her like a halo, shimmering in the light from good moisturizing, with a thin gold chain pulling her coils up and away from her face like the regal African queen Sawyer was.

Faye, in her long, mermaid-like, shimmering emerald gown, walked us throughout the lighted grounds. Rows of lawn lights swirled beneath our feet, illuminating the network of pathways. Above, strings of white lights laced through tree branches, giving the premises an ethereal ambiance, the maze adding an extra touch. I guess this really was Murder Manor no more.

We finally had our chance when Faye guided us through her precious maze and the back doors heading back into the house to tour the upstairs. None of the guest rooms were occupied, the inn having not officially opened yet. Sawyer coughed, our signal for me to prepare to get inside the office. She moved on with the rest of the tour while

I remained behind, feigning the need to use the restroom. Not that anyone but Sawyer noticed. She flashed one hand at me. Five minutes. I acknowledged that I understood, feeling a little like 007 and liking it.

With the coast clear, I tried the door handle, just in case I lucked out and she'd left it open. No such luck. I pulled out a tiny black oval wireless remote from my purse, sending a silent thanks to Mia for coming through with the win.

I held the remote close to the knob and pressed the button, at first hearing nothing. The knob didn't give when I pushed down on it. I took a quick look around, checking if anyone was there. Down the hall, I could hear Sawyer asking questions, keeping the group occupied and the hall clear.

I shook the remote and pressed again, this time hearing a faint click. I twisted the knob quickly and slipped inside the dark office. I didn't dare turn on any lights. I waited until my eyes had adjusted to the darkness with only the moonlight to guide me, then went immediately to the desk. I wasn't going to be greedy, looking for more evidence than I'd come for. I had little time, not sure how long it would be before anyone noticed my absence.

The desk was clear, the Taser not on top as it had been the other day. I went around the back of it and opened the drawers. The drawer second from the bottom gave me what I wanted. I pulled the black plastic-and-metal object from the drawer and held it up in the moonlight. This might be the thing that had killed my granddad. Finally, something had gone right. I owed Mia and even Mrs. Harris big time. They'd believed me about Faye and had gotten me in here.

I was about to leave, but I remembered what Mia had mentioned about the office. She thought there was a secret room or passageway in here. Rumor had it the house was filled with them, and since I was here, why not see if what Mia and the rumors touted was true?

I moved closer, trying to see where there might be a false part of the wall. I picked a shelf at waist level and tugged. No give. I went as far as to knock in a few random areas like I'd seen on TV. Every sound was the same as the one before. I didn't have the first clue how to find the false door of a secret anything. I'd missed the 007 course back in college, and maybe Mia was wrong. The secret room was yet another rumor about Murder Manor. My phone buzzed.

Sawyer: 's up time to

I wish she used her words like a normal adult.

I made it out of the office, checking that I'd left it the way I'd found it—sans Taser, of course—and hurried downstairs as quickly as my heels would allow. I passed a well-dressed older Black man in a plum suit. I offered a small wave and remembered my Brodie manners. His reply was automatic; then he did a double take, which slowed my step. I just knew this old guy wasn't checking me out. The glint of what I thought at first was lust was instead recognition. I tensed, unsure where this was going to lead, my experience thus far putting me on high alert.

"Maybe you can help me," he said in a deep baritone, "but this is where MJ Brodie was chief of police?" There was an accent I couldn't place, southern, but not South Carolinian.

My guard ticked up. Strangers bringing up my dad made me wary.

He studied me, head cocked to the side and toward me, so I noticed the flesh-colored hearing aid wire coming out of his ear. "And his daddy just passed?" He said it as smooth as silk.

I relaxed. Okay, this was about Granddad.

"Granddad's funeral was over a week ago. Were you in the military with him? Or in SLED?" I smiled. "Or maybe you're from the Armchair Detectives?"

None of them had come, but they'd watched the live stream of the funeral.

He blinked, confused.

"Yeah. Chief Brodie," I said. "I mean, he's been dead for some time. And his dad—my granddad—just passed not too long ago." Emotion forced me to look away, and he gave me the time I needed to look back and continue.

He was looking at me oddly, like a light had switched on in his eyes, his earlier recognition confirmed. He let out a satisfied sigh, nodding his head like he'd achieved something. "And your mother . . ." He narrowed his eyes as he tried to recall. "Angie?"

I huffed a laugh. "Angie? Who's that? She'd lose her shit if someone called her that. Better call her Angela, if you value your life."

I almost missed the twitch of one of his eyebrows and how the corner of his mouth tightened ever so slightly. But then he erased all the tenseness, replacing it with a killer megawatt smile.

He was back to nodding. Tall, broad shouldered, rich mocha skin. In his hand was a cowboy hat with matching boots on his feet. Bet there was even a buckle on his belt. If I was a betting girl, I'd say Texas.

I half expected him to say *Want me to rustle up some grub, little lady?* And then dip his hat at me like they did in all the old westerns.

"I do value my life," he said introspectively, like he'd taken my warning seriously and made his decision.

"She's at a dinner now, or about to be at one," I said, glancing through the double doors into the formal dining room, where the dinner was beginning without me. "But I can introduce you to her if you're thinking of paying last respects to Granddad."

I made a move like we could go in together. I was sure Faye wouldn't mind. She was the ultimate hostess and wouldn't turn someone away, at least not with everyone watching.

He thought about it, tilting forward to look into the dining room full of chattering people. "No, I don't want to make a fuss. That's a private party, so I can catch her soon, I'm sure. I'll just look around a little at the artwork and maybe around the grounds."

"Sure, okay. There's a garden maze in the back that the new owner had put in. It's pretty unforgettable, if you don't mind being out there in the dark and alone. This place has a pretty sordid history."

He chuckled. "Murder Manor."

I was impressed. "You know it!"

"I can get around the internet," he said. "I'm not that old."

We stood for another awkward second. I had to go, but he seemed like he had more to say. Apparently I was wrong, because all he offered was "Thank you for your kindness . . ."

His lips pursed as he paused expectantly for me to finish what he'd started.

"Jacinda. J-Jac," I stammered. "I'm not like my mother. I don't mind nicknames."

He made a noise, nodding again, slow and sure, like he was waiting for me to catch up to something. It was a feeling I couldn't place and didn't have the time to figure out.

If I knew this town, I wouldn't have to do the work anyway. Word about a new guy in town, maybe a bachelor, would spread very quickly, as things normally did around here. Then we'd know all about the Texas cowboy in the casket-sharp plum suit.

He was gone, walking away to continue his exploration of the Manor before I had a chance to catch his name.

23

The opulent dining room shimmered with an air of influence and smelled of old money. Well, smelled of piped-in floral fragrances and roasted meats from the carving station at the corner of the room, but that was beside the point. Faye was already entertaining the long rectangular table of guests made up of South Carolina's elite. The who's who of not only Brook Haven but all around. The governor and his wife. A couple of senators and congressmen and women with their plus-ones. Mayor Tate at the head with Faye next to him and Nick on the other side of his father with a seat open next to him.

Nick's eyes were on me, but I avoided his gaze, suddenly shy—when not long ago I hadn't been—thinking everyone would know what he and I had been up to if they caught my expression. There was an empty spot beside Sawyer with my name likely on it. The double *P*s, Pen and Patrick, were on the other side of the empty chair next to Sawyer. Now I knew for sure Mama had positioned me there so I'd be monitored by my little sister. I rolled my eyes but made for the seat anyway.

"Jac."

I turned, coming face to face with a tuxedo shirt and black buttons. My head angled up to meet Nick's looking down at me, grinning too brightly for me to handle. How he'd sneaked up on me without my knowing and in those few seconds, I didn't know.

"Next to me," Nick said, slipping his hand into mine and tugging me toward the front of the gigantic table.

"My seat," I protested, glancing back at Sawyer, who peered at us knowingly over the rim of her wineglass, her eyes promising that there would be "'splaining" to do, as if I were Lucille Ball in hot water with her husband . . . again. My eyes jumped to Mama, who'd caught Nick's interception and sat rigidly in her seat, her gaze trailing us all the way to the head of the table, where I'd be too far from her and too close to Faye Arden. Mama's eyes warned me the entire way up.

Nick silenced my protests, pulling the empty seat out for me to sit in. I nodded a quick hello to Mayor Tate, who'd risen from his seat.

The Mayor offered me a cool assessment. He trained his steely eyes on his son, softening as they took in Nick, whose eyes I could feel on me.

"Son . . ." Like an appeal. It was only one word, but it held an ocean of meaning only the two of them were aware of. If I had to guess, the good mayor didn't want his son taking up with a woman with my history.

"Dad." Nick met his father's gaze with resolution. "Say hello to Jac."

Mayor Tate's shoulders sagged ever so slightly. But then he collected himself, returning to me with a different vibe. "Jac, it's good to see you." The mayor lied like a perfect politician.

I gave him a tight smile, wishing I was anywhere but here. "Mayor Tate."

Faye had trailed off in her conversation to coolly assess the newest addition to her section of prominent guests as we took our seats at the table.

I leaned toward Nick, tugging at his sleeve so he'd come close. "You must want my mother to lose her mind," I whispered. "Or your stepmother."

He smirked, casting a quick peek at Faye glaring at us, then returning to me. "Don't call her that," he whispered back, coming in so close his lips grazed my ear, and he kissed it.

I was unprepared for the contact. I sneaked an embarrassed glance around, hoping no one caught Nick being fresh. I thought we might have been in the clear until I spotted Faye with her death grip on the glass stem. It wasn't until one of her guests called her name that she pulled out of her trance, resetting the plastic smile on her face.

"I have my seat back there with Sawyer. I have nothing to do with Mur—Moor Manor and this charity thing."

Nick looked deep into my eyes as if we were the only two people in the room. "But I want you with me, Jac," he said.

My whole body flushed with heat. I pulled back a little to create more space between us.

He added, "We have years to make up for."

A nervous giggle escaped me, and I fluffed my napkin in a lame attempt to hide it. "Nick," I murmured, looking around again to make sure no one was watching.

"Let's leave right after dinner," he murmured.

I was calculating how much time spent at this gala would be considered respectable before we could leave.

"You two might need a room at the Manor if you keep that up." Faye laughed, grabbing the attention of more than the four of us at the head of the table.

It came off like an innocent joke, but there was an undertone I couldn't place—resentment? Jealousy, even? Couldn't be, but I wasn't sure.

I shot to the other edge of my seat, bumping into the person on the other side of me. "Sorry," I mumbled to the person I didn't recognize.

Nick took his time to move back to his personal space, casting an irritated flicker at Faye.

"Faye, I think you've had too much wine," Mayor Tate chided, making like he was going to slide her glass away. She held on tightly to it, not letting it budge.

She threw him a scathing look, probably not appreciating his reproach of her repugnant comment. The ugly was slipping through the cracks, but if anyone could really recognize it, I couldn't tell. She was a skilled actress, the hostess supreme, yet something about watching Nick and me was creating hairline fractures through her nearly impenetrable veneer. Nick paid neither of us any attention, sipping from his glass of bourbon on the rocks.

I sat at the huge table, scanning the room as I wrestled with the weight of the stolen Taser hidden in my purse. The charity dinner, an event orchestrated by Faye and my mother, unfolded in perfectly planned extravagance.

Faye continued to preen for Brook Haven's elite, Mayor Tate at the table's head doing his job to pump up the grand opening of Moor Manor Country Inn and Events. His attention flitted between the table and the watchful eyes of the town. Everything done in this room tonight would get back to everyone out there in town tomorrow. But Mayor Tate and Faye barely interacted. And when they did, tension crackled between them, nearly as much as what was bubbling between me and Faye. Subtle glances, strained smiles betrayed the facade of their happy engagement.

Faye said, "Jac, it's good to see you out tonight. I'm sure it's been hard dealing with the death of your grandfather. He was well respected. Loved by all." The pitying look and layered sweetness was a nice touch.

I sipped my wine, considering her words. "Hmm. Loved by all." My insides twisted. Not by everyone.

Nick implored his father. "Dad?"

His father sighed before finally directing his attention at his fiancée. "Faye, must we? Let's put all that unpleasantness behind us, shall we? Jac is Nick's guest. Angela Brodie's daughter. *Our* guest."

Guess Faye hadn't yet learned what we all knew growing up—Nick was the apple of Mayor Tate's eye, and if Nick was unhappy, so was the mayor.

She caught on quick, her eyes sliding to me, cold anger locked behind them. "Can we do that, Jac? Can we put the unpleasantness behind us and be friends?"

I seized the opportunity Faye presented. "You've really changed this place around," I said, looking at the high ceilings and elegance of a once-rotting estate. "It's nothing like how it was when I was growing up. There were rumors about hidden passages and secret rooms in the Manor. Any truth to those?"

Faye's expression tightened, the annoyance breaking through her composure. "Just rumors, hon. The Manor has been restored to its original glory. It'll be recorded as a historical site now. There's nothing sinister hidden within its walls."

No, just walking through it.

Out loud, I said, "Sure about that?" I leaned in. "No skeletons in the closet? No secrets tucked away tight? No more Murder Manor?"

"Is everything all right? Everyone enjoying themselves?"

Immediately my body locked up, and my shoulders rose to my earlobes. Our conversation broke, and my eyes lifted up the length of the familiar aubergine chiffon dress until they met my mother's anxious ones. She stood behind the deputy mayor and his wife. Her eyes were on me, and her hands were clasped together, wringing either in prayer for me to behave or in fear that I wouldn't.

My gaze traveled down the long table, finding Pen leaning over nearly in half, her head craned toward us, looking back and forth between Mama and me, her eyes a different kind of pleading from Mama's accusatory one. Two seats past her and Patrick, Sawyer was also looking at me with an eyebrow cocked up in warning. *Be cool,* she seemed to say. *Count it down.*

I broke away to the doorway, where the man in the plum-colored suit stood, leaning against the frame. When our eyes met, he raised his hand to the brim of his hat and tipped it to me, on his lips a ghost of a smile that wasn't weird but more like supportive.

Quickly I returned to my mother, fashioning my lips into a pleasant smile to counter her worry. *Everything's fine! Nothing to see here!* I gave Mama a happy nod of confirmation that all was well.

Nick slipped his arm casually over the back of my chair, his fingers grazing my shoulder. His thumb circled lazy O's against my bare skin. Mama saw this, and her body visibly relaxed, like Nick's arm was some sort of seat belt and I was buckled in for safety, unable to fall out and wreak havoc. I fought the urges to pull away—because the circling was annoying and too familiar—and to sit in his lap at the same time, my emotions at war. Keeping the peace won out.

Faye's smile now held a hint of a challenge. She swirled the remnants of her wine and cut her eyes toward Mayor Tate, who was engaged in a discussion with Nick about a property he'd found in the next town over. Nick's hand moved from the back of my chair down to my knee, inching to where the dress parted in a slit. He found the exposed skin of my knee, patted it twice as if to say *Be easy,* and left it there. I couldn't explain it, but the move made me uneasy. Felt proprietary, like he was staking his claim, when the only thing we were supposed to be having was noncommittal fun.

Faye didn't miss a beat, her sharp eyes clocking his movement, her face tightening in checked anger as she observed Nick's arm move from the chair as he conversed with his father. She met my eye, expecting a reaction.

When I gave her nothing, she laughed again, tinkling and drawing the attention of those closest to her, slipping back into her act of belle of the ball. She raised her glass to me in what I could describe as a challenge before putting it to her lips and downing the rest. She put the empty glass on the table just as one of the servers appeared from thin air to refill it.

As he poured, she finally said, "Jac, there are secrets everywhere. Moor Manor is no exception. But rest assured, I remain an open book."

24

Anticipation and a bad case of nerves drove me awake before sunrise, and I crept out of Nick's house and headed back home, where hopefully I'd avoid Mama's disapproving glare. Pen spent nights at Patrick's, but in the Book of Angela Brodie, that behavior was tolerable because Patrick had offered a down payment with a ring and wasn't getting the milk for free. I, on the other hand, was still in the milk aisle at the store.

Dressed and ready to go, I ran through my script, all I would say, as I paced my bedroom over and over, glad last night's event seemed to have forced Mama into sleeping in, if 6:00 a.m. could be considered sleeping in. When I heard sounds of movement from downstairs, I sprang from my room and made my way to the kitchen to wait for the right time to head to the station.

Mama was at the stove, scrambling up a pan of eggs while Pen pulled a pan of bacon out of the oven, our method of choice for the best results—not too crispy and not too limp. My job was the coffee. No one wanted me near a stove, but my cup of joe was unparalleled. A hookah-and-coffee bar—I could imagine it. As usual, the TV was on in the background. The *Today* show was on, and the hosts were running through the top news of the morning.

Mama put the wooden spatula she was using to scramble the eggs onto the spoon holder. "Thank you, Jac," she said without warning.

I tore my attention from the trickle of dark-brown liquid from the drip coffeepot—no Keurig here; I wanted to be like a true barista. "It's just coffee, Mama."

"For last night. It was lovely. And I think people are learning to be kinder to you now. Which is good. I don't like how it's been."

A bout of guilt washed over me, twisting my insides, because I knew what I was about to do. This gratitude, this rare moment when everything was just right between Mama and me, would die an ugly death the minute I stepped foot into the police station. But I had the best intentions. I always did. I hoped Mama would eventually come to realize that.

I swallowed down the guilt and plastered on a smile. "People are who they are, you know? It's not like I made it easy for them," I mumbled, finding the coffee easier to look at than my mother. She was gazing at me like she was two seconds away from crying with relief, and I didn't want that.

"The charity gala was very important to me. It was a way to honor your father with this scholarship in his name. The silent auction earned more money than I'd imagined, though Faye always said we'd knock it out of the park."

I broke a slice of bacon, passing half of it to Pen. "Oh, she did, huh?" I fought the urge to roll my eyes. She was going to get what was coming to her.

Mama nodded, dividing the eggs among three plates. "It meant a lot to me that everyone got to see you in a different light. I know it's been especially hard on you, with Granddad's death and you living away. You came back here, and things are different."

"And the same, in some aspects," Pen chimed in, rolling her eyes. She placed a plate of toast in the middle of the table. "They need to be worried about themselves instead of about Jac."

I shot her an appreciative glance.

"What you say is all true," Mama said, "but all we can do is pray for them and take the higher road, just like I've always taught you two."

I gave Pen a sly look. "That was one of Mama's lessons, huh? Take the higher road."

"We can't all be Michelle Obama or Angela Brodie," Pen returned, giving me a high five when I held my hand out.

"My girl," I said.

Mama sucked her teeth. "Anyway, you two keep up with your jokes. But all I've ever wanted was what was best for the both of you. Happiness. A good relationship with a good man taking care of you."

"Or us taking care of each other? Because times have changed, Mama. We don't have to be prim and proper anymore. We can be whatever. You can be whatever. You don't always have to take the high road, and you shouldn't."

"I just wish you understood me more. I wish you knew how deeply I love you girls, and your father. This family is everything to me. You have no idea. That's why I fought so hard to put you in all the things that would teach you the most, because you don't know what it's like when someone tells you that you can't and prevents you from doing so."

Her eyes welled, and the next thing, Mama's head was bent, her shoulders shaking.

"Mama," Pen said carefully, "who kept you from doing what you wanted?"

Pen's expression must have mirrored mine. We were freaked out. We'd gone from light thanks to something much deeper and more meaningful than either Pen or I were prepared for.

There were things Mama held on tightly to, like her obsession with being prepared for life. Having a good job. Being educated. Being well liked and respected. Being beyond reproach. Her beliefs were what had driven a wedge between us. Made me rebel and resent her. Drove me out into the darkness the night of Pen's debutante ball because the expectation of perfection was too much to bear. It was so suffocating that I ran to breathe while Pen decided the best course was to do exactly as Mama wanted.

"Yeah," I cosigned. "Who?"

It couldn't have been Daddy. He was the glue that held us together. He was the one who always told Mama to cut us some slack.

Mama shook her head, using the dishrag to wipe her damp face. She pressed the palm of her hand to her cheeks, patting herself back to presentability.

"I'm fine, girls. I'm sorry. Sorry. I just think about your daddy, and I get this way."

This wasn't about Daddy, though. This was about something else. I couldn't ignore a pebble of guilt blooming. We were having a good morning, which I would dismantle in an hour, when I went to the station. I thought about the cowboy from last night, how he'd asked about Daddy and Mama. Granddad, too, but he'd led with Daddy. So maybe that was his true focus. The pebble of guilt grew.

I swallowed, trying to decide if I should say something. Better to prepare Mama and Pen for whatever might come than have them be hit unaware.

I steeled myself. "I, um . . ." How to start?

They shifted their attention to me. There was no going back now unless I lied. I wasn't about to do that.

"You know how I've been organizing Granddad's house? And you know how we liked to talk about cold cases and try to solve them with his online groups?"

"Those horrid names you called each other," Mama grumbled.

Pen giggled. "I liked them. I wanted to be a dick."

My lips twisted. "There are plenty of times when you are a dick."

Pen mouthed *Bitch*.

I gave a small bow in thanks.

Mama rolled her hand, prompting me. "Go on."

"So, I found two hidden files in Granddad's safe."

"He had a safe?" Mama asked. She sent a questioning glance to Pen, who made a face and shrugged back.

I nodded. "Hidden in the wall in his and Grandma's bedroom. And there was a heck of a lot of rolled-up money in it, but I haven't counted or touched it, so Pen can do that part. Anyway," I said, because there was something more important than loads of unexpected money, "one of the files is about a case he helped out with in Colleton, Nevada, back in 2001. It's about the deaths of some high school girls and then the suicide of another they weren't sure was related."

"That's horrible!" Mama placed a hand on her chest, eyes widening. "The poor girls! Their poor parents."

"I'm trying to figure out why that case was so important to Granddad that he held on to it all these years. It's got something to do with that clock of his. Like, that's when he got it. The clock, I mean."

Pen asked, "What about the second file?"

Mama stood abruptly. "Our food is cold now, but we forgot the preserves. Let me go get them."

Just like when we were kids, she'd do this same thing when Daddy would come home, telling the three of us about what'd happened that day. If it looked like the story was going to get too grisly, Mama would end it, saying those kinds of stories were not for young girls' ears.

She went to the pantry for the preserves she'd made herself. When she returned, Pen was saying, "The other file? What's it about?"

I stifled a grin. Back then, Pen would do the same as she did now: ignore Mama's intrusion on story time, and who was Daddy to deny young, inquisitive minds? Who was I?

I happened to look up at the news, a headline flashing on the screen. "Actually, I think it's about that." I pointed to the TV, and as if on a string, Mama and Pen turned in unison to see what I was referring to.

The jar Mama was holding dropped to the floor, shattering and spilling the apricot preserves. Pen and I jumped, both of us turning to see what her problem was.

Pen was first to the storage closet, pulling out the brooms and dustpans. "Let me help you. Don't get cut." Always the doctor and caretaker.

I, on the other hand, remained seated, wondering why Mama had zoned out—she didn't even notice Pen bent in front of her, picking gingerly at the thick pieces of glass.

Mama said, "What did you say, Jac?"

I was laser focused on the lost possibilities. "Pen, don't you think we can—"

"No, Jac." Pen read my mind. "There's none of this that can be saved."

I pouted, staring disappointedly at the spreading gloppy mess at Mama's feet. I hoped she had another jar in the pantry.

Mama said, "What was that about barrels?"

Was Mama still on that old news? "Oh, the file said 'Lake Worth' on it. I looked it up and realized it's the same lake that they've been talking about on the news for the past few months. It made headlines when the lake level was receding, and all this sh—"

I sneaked a look at Mama, but she hadn't even noticed. It was like she wasn't in the room.

"—stuff surfaced. Decades-old stuff people threw in the lake. Guns, clothes, rowboats. But the biggest find was a metal barrel. They opened it up, and it had human remains in it. Soup du human, Texas-style."

"That's not funny." Pen grimaced, rinsing the dishrag clean of preserves beneath the running sink faucet.

"Your granddad had a file on that?"

I nodded. "Mm-hmm, like he's been keeping tabs on it."

Mama said, "That's all it had, information from articles about the lake and town?" She looked so serious it worried me a little.

I held up a hand. Scout's honor, though I'd only been a Girl Scout for a year before I told my dad I never wanted to sell another box of Samoas again in my life. Didn't think they were called that anymore. They were deLites or something now.

"I mean, I don't know if it was soup. The steel drum was sealed pretty tight, but there was definitely a body in it. The latest, according to what's on the screen, is that they did a DNA test, and the results might be in. We might find out who Soup du Barrel Man is."

"Lord," Mama whispered.

Pen shook her head, then handed me a wet rag and reached to pick up glass shards to drop in the trash. I made a noise as I stopped her and exchanged the rag for the glass and the trash bin.

"I'm not a kid," she muttered.

"Yeah, well, humor me," I muttered back.

I stopped when I realized Mama hadn't moved from her spot and was still out of it, staring off into space with an expression I couldn't identify—either disgust or terror. I nudged my sister to ask what was up with our mother, but Pen only shrugged and resumed wiping up the sticky mess.

"Something wrong, Mama?"

Mama startled, coming back to her senses and looking surprised as she took in the mess at her feet, like she hadn't been here the past five minutes. "Nothing," she answered, but she was lying. "That's just horrible . . . finding a body like that. Have they identified him yet?"

"I'm sure they'll do a big reveal any day now. Then the family will come out, and the story of what happened will too."

"Lord," she whispered again. Her stricken look made me second-guess talking about it. She disliked anything that wasn't Hallmark Channel. "That's horrible."

I added, "But the issue is that the lake is receding."

Pen snorted. "I think a dead body that was definitely murdered is a pretty big issue, sis."

"I mean, yeah, it is. But the barrel never would've been found if it wasn't for global warming. The environment, Pen, we're fuck—"

Mama hissed.

"We're trashing the earth. It's overheating, making water evaporate and uncovering body-disposal sites. What's a person to do if all the good locations have gone up in mist?"

Pen got into it. “Bet it was a mob hit. It’s always the mob that makes people swim with the fishes.” She swiped the last of the preserves. “Were there fish in the lake?”

I thought about it, sucking my teeth. “You know? They didn’t say.”

My fist pumped into the air when Mama returned from the pantry with another glass jar of preserves. Breakfast was saved. I held my hands out for it, worried Mama might have klutzy fingers again.

I slopped more preserve on the toast than I should have, suddenly ravenous. I dug into my plate.

“Warm it first?” Mama said, appalled, her own plate in her hand on the way to the microwave.

“No time,” I said through mouthfuls of egg and bacon. “I have a couple errands to run.”

“You have errands?” she asked dubiously, as if I’d just announced I was going to walk on the moon. What did she think I’d been doing these past six years? Not once had I asked for money because I was busy handling my business.

“I know how to adult,” I said sourly, deciding to hold off on mentioning my upcoming visit to the police station. “That includes running errands.”

“Well, stay out of trouble.”

I offered her an exaggerated salute because that’s what smart-asses like me were expected to do, especially when hiding their hurt feelings from the constant reminder that nothing they did, could ever do, would be right in their mother’s eyes.

25

I entered the Brook Haven Police Department armed with the evidence they'd need to investigate Faye. Coming to the station was weird at first. I hadn't been here since my dad died, and it was odd seeing new people (and old) and a different name engraved on the chief's nameplate. I was feeling pretty confident. The Taser wasn't irrefutable, but coupled with the marks on Granddad, that should be enough to make her seem suspicious. And as far as motive . . .

"Maybe you should wait until we get more solid evidence," Sawyer suggested from her cubicle. Her hair was now styled in one long French braid, the end of which she played with as she shot apprehensive peeks at the chief's closed door.

"Don't try and talk me out of this, Sawyer," I said. "I had to do something. She owns a Taser."

"Like probably the majority of the people in this state. And an assload of guns too."

"You weren't against this when you were distracting people and I was busy breaking into her office." Another offense to tack onto my growing list.

Sawyer put a finger to her mouth, shushing me. She looked around, waving her hand so I'd sit across from her. Around us, the station bustled, with no one paying either of us any mind.

"Oh my God. Keep it down!" she demanded, eyes like saucers.

I didn't understand what was up with Sawyer's sudden case of nerves. What was hard for her to understand? How was she not able to connect the dots like I had? It made no sense.

"You're acting hot and cold. It's not just me that thinks something weird is up." I counted on my fingers. "Mrs. Harris believes me. And Mia from the grocery store thinks the lady's got a secret room in her office."

That was two. Two people. I held up the corresponding fingers, which Sawyer grabbed and crushed in her grip. My mouth dropped open, more from surprise than pain.

"Stop that," I snapped. "We're not in middle school anymore."

"Then stop acting like a child. That's two people, and a bunch of guesses." Sawyer snorted. "A secret room? Come on now, that's Manor lore."

I couldn't believe her. We'd always had each other's backs, 100 percent. What was this? Was Sawyer turning on me too?

"Sawyer, if you're like everyone else and think I'm making shit up, I don't think I could take it. Not you too. If I went to Nick like I went to you, he wouldn't doubt me, and it's his family."

"Nick's in love with you, Jac. You're still that dense that you don't see it? Or pretending not to see it? I bet he'd cut his own father loose if it meant being with you. That's how deep into you Nick is."

Ridiculous. "It's really not that deep," I said sheepishly before getting off that topic. "You're my homegirl. My ace. We ride for each other. You know I'm not bullshitting. Just rock with me on this one, please." I pleaded with her to believe me, even if everything sounded too wild to make sense. It *was* wild. All of it.

"If there was another way, I'd be all over it. But this is all I have, and I need your help," I implored her. "Can you see if your resources can find me someone to talk to about the Colleton deaths?"

Sawyer scowled. "You're not a cop. No one has to talk to you, and I don't think I'm allowed to share what I find using work resources with nonwork people."

I groaned, stomping my feet like I was six. "Come on, Sawyerrrrr. Please. I need a win. When I show this to Chief Linwood, you'll have no excuse not to follow up about Colleton. Matter of fact, he'll ask you to."

Scratch that, another win, because in a minute the Taser would vindicate me.

Sawyer considered me for much longer than she should have before giving in with a curt nod. "Get the hell out of here. Some of us have jobs."

I nearly asked her what she'd heard before realizing she was making a crack at me lazing around for the last couple of weeks like I had no job or life motivation. Wouldn't be far from the truth.

I stood, raising my hand in mock salute, my bag with the Taser inside banging against my hip. "Yes, ma'am." I sneaked a peek at the way to the chief's closed door. "Is the chief in?"

"I think he has someone in there, but you can wait." Sawyer didn't look at me.

I nodded. "We'll get together later, yeah? With Nick?"

"What about the hot doctor? Walter."

"Weigert."

She worked it through. "I like Walter better."

I scratched my scalp.

Sawyer lifted an eyebrow. "What's up with him?"

I made a face. "So I'm supposed to screw both Nick and Weigert? You sound like Pen."

Sawyer tossed her thick braid over her shoulder, giving me a satisfied smirk. "Always knew Pen was the smarter Brodie."

"I hate you."

"I know." The smirk became knowing as she waved me away with the back of her hand. "Now go. Before you piss me off again."

I left. I couldn't afford to piss any more people off. I waved lightly and decided to give Sawyer as much space as she'd need.

With the Taser burning a hole in my bag, I approached the chief's closed door. The blinds were drawn shut over the glass-walled enclosure that made up his office. I hesitated at the door, building up the courage, running over the facts in my head so I'd sound as concise and logical as possible.

I had answers to the questions he'd ask—well, I had guesses. But those were okay. Guesses were what eventually became facts with investigation. I was giving the chief the guesses to start an investigation into the dealings of Faye. The whole breaking and entering thing would be easy to overlook.

I gave his admin assistant my name so she could call me in. I was well aware of the stares I was getting from her and everyone else. I could practically read their thoughts—the old chief's kid in to visit the new one. The old chief's daughter, who had something to do with the death of the man who used to sit in that very office, probably coming in to cause more trouble. I kept my head down, focusing on my boots and wishing Chief Linwood would hurry up.

"The chief's ready for you," the assistant finally said.

I pushed off the wall I'd been holding up, unable to sit because of nerves. I took some cleansing breaths and entered Chief Linwood's office.

Faye Arden twisted in her chair, her lipstick bright and dazzling as she smiled at me. Beyond her, the chief stared at me with an expression that nearly reduced me to a puddle on the floor.

"Close the door, Jac," Chief Linwood said, sounding uncomfortably like my father.

I closed the door. It was like I was closing my coffin. What the hell was she doing here?

"I'm glad you came in, Jac," the chief began, clearly trying to control his anger. "It prevents me from having to send a squad car to get you."

I flinched. Squad cars were for arresting. There was no need for that.

Faye continued staring at me, her eyes bouncing around my face like she was trying to memorize my reaction and getting off on it. I tried focusing anywhere but at her expectant and self-satisfied smirk. What was she doing here?

"Have a seat, Jac," the chief commanded.

I kept telling myself to stay cool and stay out of trouble, for two reasons. The first was so I wouldn't mess things up for Mama and the great night she'd had the night before. Our family name was everything to her. The second was so people would see me as something other than the troublemaker for a change. That they'd find me a help and not a harm to the town. I had proof in my bag. I had plausible evidence to connect Faye and the Taser to my granddad.

Faye turned slowly as I took my seat. Her face wiped clean like a dry-erase board and then took on an expression of quiet indignation and victimhood.

I settled in my seat, waiting for the chief to go first, with the bag on my knees.

"Is there something you want to tell us?" he asked, restraint coating his words.

I lifted my head. "Us?" I looked at her next to me—her head down, like she was so upset. "Us, as in you and her? I don't owe her any explanations."

"Chief," Faye implored him. "I have to suffer through this too? I came to you quietly because I don't want to cause any trouble, but this behavior can't go on."

My lips curled. *Behavior?* She was tripping. I clamped my mouth shut, refusing to say a word. My arms crossed over my bag.

The chief attempted another approach. "Jac, what is it you came to the station for?"

I didn't know why Faye was there, but I was going to go ahead with my plan. It would save the chief a trip, not having to drive all the way to the Manor.

"I came to give you something, Chief. I was concerned about the manner of my grandfather's death. I know you didn't look too deeply into it because he was prone to heart attacks. But I thought his position was peculiar."

"Peculiar?" The chief raised his eyebrows and shared a look with Faye. She ducked her head down, pretending to hide her smile.

I plowed on, reaching into my bag. "Peculiar," I confirmed. "The doctor said his pacemaker failed, causing the heart attack."

"Yes, I know. Move it along."

My lips twitched up into a snarl; then I told myself to calm down. "Pacemakers can fail from electrical charges administered from an outside source. Like Tasers." I pulled the Taser from my bag, then placed it on his desk and slid it toward him. I sneaked a hard look at Faye, knowing I'd gotten her now. What explanation would she have for this?

"The doctor said there was bruising on his skin where his pacemaker was located, consistent with the probes of something like a Taser. This is Faye's Taser. I think she used it on him."

There, I'd said it. I'd said the words out loud, and there was no taking them back. I waited for the chief to begin questioning Faye about her whereabouts. I hoped she was quaking in her chair, even though she looked way too calm and collected.

The chief stared at the Taser. Then he looked at me, his face inscrutable. He tapped his fingers lightly on his desk. "How'd you come across this Taser?"

My mouth dried. This was the tricky part. "I don't have the autopsy reports to show you, but I'm sure Dr. Weigert can get them to you so you can see what I'm talking about. It tracks," I said. "Because she had my granddad's clock, and you know he never left the house with it. He'd never give it to anyone, and yet she had it after he'd suffered a conveniently massive heart attack."

Faye sighed. "This again. I explained how I had the clock. I don't know how it got there."

"Right." I made a face. "You don't know how it got in your locked office that only you have the key to."

She made a noise. "Apparently not."

"What?" The room was becoming warm. I uncomfortably shifted in my seat, not liking where this was going.

"Faye came in to inform us that her Taser was missing from her office after the charity dinner she and your mother hosted at the Manor. They work together, Jac, and honestly, is this behavior becoming of a young lady?"

If we were in one of those cartoons I grew up watching, like the Road Runner and Wile E. Coyote, my bottom jaw would have dropped to the floor in astonishment with my eyes bugging out of my head. This couldn't be happening. This couldn't be happening. I had been so sure. So confident the chief would want to use this Taser to find concrete proof against Faye, out of respect for my grandfather.

Helplessness wrapped its cold, unforgiving fingers around me. I was locked in a box with no way out of it. The box was Faye Arden.

My mouth opened to speak, but the words died in it. I looked at the two of them, one angry and disappointed, the other working valiantly to hide how happy she was that she was once again playing everyone against me.

Faye's voice quivered. "I don't want to press charges. Her family has been through enough, and I'm sure it's not any easier with Jac's history here in town and that whole horrible tragedy with her father."

"Now wait a damn minute!" Sudden molten rage elevated my voice and hardened my tone. In no way would I stand for her referring to my father in any capacity. I pointed at her, shaking violently as I held on to the last vestiges of restraint. "Don't you dare bring up shit you don't know about."

I could kill her where she sat. I could—

Linwood interjected, "Jac, Jac, calm down."

"Don't tell me to calm down. Don't have me sit here and hear this woman tell me about something she doesn't know a goddamn thing about, that happened before she was even a thought in this town."

Faye's brows furrowed. "But isn't that what you're doing, Jac? Aren't you running around blaming me for something tragic that happened when you weren't here?" She appealed to my father's old friend. "You see what I mean, Chief Linwood? Why I'm concerned? This is what I'm trying to avoid. This—this—this inexplicable animosity she has toward me. I don't know what I've done to deserve it. And to be honest, I'm beginning to feel unsafe." She shuddered. "Her anger makes me feel unsafe. I'm scared of it."

And there it was.

I couldn't hold in the bark of laughter. The "angry Black woman" label, always used to deny us our power and voice. It was so demeaning, so utterly ridiculous, that all I could do was laugh.

"You!" I balked. The audacity was too much to bear. "You feel unsafe? You?"

Chief Linwood was out of his seat.

Faye implored him with big wide eyes like she was all sweet and innocent. She wrung her hands like she was lamenting bad fortune. Her voice trembled. "That's slander, Chief, what she said. That's a lawsuit if she doesn't stop, and bad press to the department for letting her harass me the way she is. And if this gets out to the media when we're opening Moor Manor to the public soon, the mayor won't stand for it."

"Then bring it," I shot back, not caring that I was practically screeching in the same office where I had found so much comfort when my dad was chief. I couldn't believe that this room, which had always been my safe place, was now my nightmare.

"Bring your lawsuit, you bitch." I was sure the people outside could hear us. But I didn't care. I'd had enough of this shit—hers and his.

"That's enough, Jac!" Chief Linwood bellowed. "I can't . . . What has gotten into you?"

Faye's hands flew to her mouth. Her eyes filled with tears—big, thick, Emmy-worthy tears—as she volleyed between staring at me, then Linwood.

If I didn't know her, the real Faye, who wasn't so sweet and beguiling when eyes weren't on her, I would have thought the way she was looking at me, wide eyed and so *persecuted*, was for real. I would have dropped all defenses and made excuses and apologies for her, like Linwood was doing, to stop her white-lady tears. I knew what Faye was doing, and yet she was so convincing that every word she said—every tear that dripped, landing in splashes on her fuchsia-colored skirt—confused me and made me hate her even more.

She calmed herself down, vacillating between the honey and a trembling flower. It sickened me. What was even more sickening was that the chief was buying the whole act.

"I don't want to compound it. I just want Jac to stay away from me. I think she has an unhealthy interest in me. Nothing sexual, mind you . . ."

I barked out a laugh. It was all I could do to withstand this complete and utter bullshit.

"No," Faye said demurely, her voice coaxing and tricking the chief into thinking this was her true self. "I don't know what it is. But it's got to stop, or I'll be forced to involve Mayor Tate and take more drastic measures to be left alone." She added a little sniffle, dabbing at her eyes to drive her act home.

The whole scene was un-fucking-believable. Apparently, in everyone's eyes—even maybe my best friend's—I was unbelievable too. But then Chief Linwood introduced the final humiliating blow—a body slam.

"Don't you have something to return to her? No charges. No more to make of this. Just return her property."

If I wasn't seated, I would have fallen from the blow.

"No charges if she promises to stay away from me. Angela and Penelope are such lovely people. I have heard so much about the former chief that I can't believe she's a part of . . ."

Chief Linwood cleared his throat, discomfort sliding over his shining brown face and *Magnum, PI* mustache I used to find so funny but now thought was hateful. And stupid.

Faye stopped herself short, likely knowing she was about to lay it on too thick.

I clutched my bag to my body, trying to protect myself from these people. Chief Linwood pushing the Taser back toward me, imploring me with his eyes to hand it over to Faye. Faye's mouth twitching as she fought to keep from reveling in my misery.

I waited another beat. And then another, both sets of their eyes on me—waiting, waiting, waiting.

Chief Linwood's voice was low. Heavy. "Go on, Jac."

Waiting, waiting, waiting. I didn't want to. I locked eyes with my father's friend, begging him not to make me do this. Don't make me supplicate this mother. Fucking. Woman.

He prodded me along with a head nod, mouthing *Please*. Like I was making things hard for him.

I threw my cross-body bag to the floor, grabbed the Taser from the desk, and whipped my arm in Faye's direction, the cool, hard plastic in my hand. I never took my eyes off the chief.

The damn woman, like she was some kind of regal queen awaiting her scepter, swept her hand out and held it in front of me, palm up, expectantly.

I wanted to vomit on that fucking hand.

Without looking at her, refusing to ever give her a damn thing, determined with the last thread of my dignity, I slammed the Taser back on Chief Linwood's cluttered desk.

I snapped my head in Faye's direction, throwing all caution to the wind, saying to her while still training my gaze on him, "Don't think this is over. Not by a long shot."

I stormed out of the chief's office, the door slamming against the wall. I didn't look at anyone as I passed all the staring eyes. All the people in black-and-gold uniforms and civilians alike, looking at me with contempt over the scene their dead Chief Brodie's daughter had made. To them, I was a disgrace to his honor and the office he'd once held. I saw Sawyer and the horror on her face at my epic fail. Her look alone was enough to last a lifetime.

26

Gotchu911: Even if the chief believed u, he can't use the taser.

JrD: Why not? He can run tests to match it to the marks on my granddad

PI Guy 39: Doesn't work that way. Wud be inadmissible in court

Gotchu911: Yeah and something I heard on Judge Judy once. Gotta have clean hands.

JrD: ???

GirlFriday022: Means you can't have done a wrong to fix a wrong. You can't commit a crime to show someone has committed one too.

Gotchu911: Yeah, you can't have any dirt on u and as bad ass as it was to break into her office, that's stealing

JrD: So what does this mean?

BlueLineCopper: Means you're up shit's creek. You're totally in her line of fire now that you went in her territory and tried to take her down. You're a problem now.

PI Guy 39: Watch your back, JrD

Mrs. CrimeofPassion: UR playing an ugly game of chicken, girl

I pulled into the parking lot of Edgemont Road's Dollar General, several blocks from the police station, with my brain feeling like it was about to explode, mulling over my exchange with the Armchairs earlier that day. The script, the scenario, the Taser. Nothing had gone as I'd envisioned, and suddenly I was feeling alone. The only other person who I could have talked to, who would have understood, was gone, and I was left with judgment and, well, persecution from nearly all sides.

Maybe I'd been going about it all wrong. Maybe the key was to be more like Granddad, who knew about solving cases, while I'd mostly been along for the ride. With nowhere else to turn to, I'd gone to the one place that might take me seriously. I'd pulled out my phone, logged in to the site, gone to the Armchair Detectives. Disappointment and shame guided my thumbs as they clumsily typed out a message. I reintroduced myself and made sure to thank them again for their sentiments before launching into my tirade. I'd closed with an update of my most recent, spectacular failure.

"Goddamnit!" I pounded the steering wheel several times, my anxiety and outrage at level ten. I sucked in quick spurts of air, unable to get enough, my chest feeling as if it were about to explode.

I tossed the phone in the passenger seat, letting out a yell. "Goddamnit!"

All the pent-up frustration and anger and grief and humiliation geysered from me. "Goddamnit!" I said repeatedly. How she'd managed to get the drop on me was beyond my understanding. With the dinner and guests and cleanup, I had figured she'd be too busy to notice that anything in her office was missing. In the chaos of party hostessing, why would she need the Taser or the extra remote?

It was when everything was out, when nothing but expelled carbon dioxide filled the car, that I remembered. I was supposed to return the remote to Mia this morning, and in my rush to get to the station first thing, I'd forgotten. I'd left Mia hanging all morning, and she was probably freaking out.

"FUCK ME!" I let out another scream, ignoring the startled mother and small child rushing their cart to a red Dodge minivan. I had to get Mia the remote before Faye realized it was missing. She could be on the way to the Manor this very moment to find out how I'd gotten to the Taser I'd shamefully had to return to her.

I pulled out of the parking lot, making a U-turn to rush to Moor Manor. "Meet me to get the remote," I said into the talk-to-text feature in my phone's Messages app. "So sorry. I'm coming now."

The sun was already cresting in its ascent to high noon, hanging brightly above the trees lining the one-lane road to Moor Manor, when I finally arrived. I parked where I thought Faye couldn't see me and got out, clutching the circular remote in my hands. Mia was already waiting for me, moving side to side nervously.

"I'm so sorry. So sorry," I gushed, trying to appease the anxious girl as I shoved the plastic thing into her hands. "I should have left it somewhere in the house for you to find."

She was near tears. "You said you'd bring it first thing. You promised."

I nodded. "I know, I know. I'm so sorry. Today was a horrible day." I shook my head. "No excuse. Take it, quickly, before she comes back. Go now. Yell at me later."

I took her by the shoulder, turning her around and propelling her up the shortcut that ran diagonally from the road to the house. I could hear her thundering through the trees. I waited a couple of beats. It didn't feel right to head back to the house and leave Mia like this. What if Faye returned before Mia had a chance to put the remote back? I was already in the doghouse. What did it matter if I got into more trouble by being at the Manor when I should have left Faye alone?

The decision made, I hopped in my car and drove the short distance up the road until it opened up to the sprawling grounds of Moor Manor. I scanned the grounds and didn't see any signs of Mia. She'd gotten in, I told myself, looking at the windows of the Manor facing me. It wasn't so bright out that I couldn't see inside from where I stood in the grounds. I tried to single out Faye's office from memory. It looked dark and empty.

I thought I should hang around until Mia had left, just to make sure she'd gotten off okay. There was no way I was going into the Manor. Matter of fact, I didn't want anyone to see me hanging around. The last thing I needed was to have a stalker charge added to my growing list of offenses.

One of the most popular places for us to go when we were young was to the bluff. I hadn't been there since the night my dad fell off it. I didn't know why, but my feet started moving toward it. Depending on your pace, it was at least a twenty-minute or so hike around the Manor and maze, which backed up to it.

My feet recalled the old paths as if they were a bicycle I hadn't ridden in years. The wind whistled through the trees, carrying echoes of my past. My head hurt—from the day's events or lack of eating, I wasn't sure. Though it could've been because I was approaching the bluff's edge. I stopped short of it, not wanting to go any closer. My feet were rooted to the ground and refused to take me farther.

The weather was perfectly calm. No mist or fog. No wind or rain. No night. I could see for miles, even where I stood. Nothing but endless bluish-gray skies. The memories of the night my dad died were not whole. They came in jittery patches that refused to run linearly. They came in bits of distorted pieces. Never enough to let me know what had happened in the moments between Daddy finding me and Nick in his car and me holding on to Daddy's hand—trying to save him as he hung off the cliff—and then letting go.

I sank down to the ground, trying to recall the events, my mind racing. But every effort of mine was like grasping at smoke—the memories intangible and evaporating between my fingertips. I gave up, disheartened. Even my memories were against me. I trudged down the path, the sun overhead as I approached the Manor. The place appeared empty. There were no groundskeepers around. No cars indicating there were workers inside the house. If Mia had a car, I didn't see it. I did see Faye's car. The black SUV she sported around was parked where it hadn't been before.

My car was still out of view. But what if she'd seen it? She could call the cops and say I was stalking her. I moved to get to it and get the hell out. Mia had to be gone by now, having returned the remote to its proper location. I hoped she'd made it look as if it had never been touched. She had to know to do that—she was smart, resourceful.

Something moved at the edge of my peripheral vision, and my body felt electrified, hairs standing on end. One of the angry ghosts. The murderous Caretaker. The terrors of my youth sprang up like a leak, flooding my mind with grotesque stories told by campfires at the bluff. Never at the Manor, which we were all smart enough to stay clear of. But now the Manor grounds weren't looking as warm and welcoming as they had at the dinner last night.

I thought I heard a tiny cry. It was so faint, a whisper on the wind or in my imagination. And then a flash of movement that made my heart jump. I turned and ran toward it, suddenly close enough to the Manor to see in properly, unsure how I'd cleared the distance so fast. My car wasn't this way—it was in the opposite direction and off the road, tucked away out of sight.

Thoughts of the car and escaping in it before I'd be forced to take a mug shot went away when I saw two figures in Faye's office window. The light was fading fast, making it easier to see. The light in the office was not on, but something dim was illuminating them inside. Their hands moved. Faye pointing, shaking. Mia waving her hands as if to say no. The air inside that room must have been charged with tension radiating from the upstairs down to me.

What should I do? Go in there, bang on the door, and say it was me? That I'd found the remote and taken it? I could say that. I could say I'd snooped the night of the gala and found the spare in her bedroom curio cabinet. I was about to do just that when Faye's rage unfurled like spewing lava. She reached around, grabbing something dark. It looked heavy. Mia was backing away until she was nearly out of view of the large bay window while Faye advanced on her, raising the object in her hand above her head.

Mia spun around to run, and the hand swooped down snakebite quick. So quick it was like a flurry of checkered tweed. Mia was no longer in view, but Faye was, or her arm and half her back was as she bent over. Her arm swung and hit. Swung and hit. Over and over as Faye unleashed a torrent of blows down on Mia, so many I lost count and turned away, unable to stomach watching her beat Mia to death.

I stumbled back, falling hard on my rear. My hands slammed over my mouth to stifle the scream that was about to tear through me. I needed the cops, but I valued myself.

Mia.

I wanted to curl up and die. My throat filled with a sob. I couldn't breathe. I couldn't swallow. I couldn't move. I couldn't force myself to look at that window again and see more of what I knew would be forever burned in my mind.

My brain began to reengage, and I fumbled with my phone, my fingers cold from the temperature and probably something else. I dialed 911.

"Come quick." My voice sounded so trembly on the line as I tried to give the operator information. I just couldn't answer right. "Please," I begged. "Come. Someone's been killed."

When the cops arrived, a cadre of black-and-yellow cars and trucks shrilling to a stop, their blue lights whirring, they found me still seated on the ground. They rushed to me, first demanding I put my hands up, and then, when they recognized me, Patrick approached, asking if I was okay and if I'd made the call. I nodded once.

Patrick said, not angrily or accusatorily, but concerned, "What are you doing here, Jac? You shouldn't be here."

Understatement of the century. I should have been home. Not here, but back with Maura. I never should have stayed in this town.

The front door opened, the light from within spilling out onto the porch. Faye stood in the doorway. Her silhouette was illuminated from the light behind her, casting an eerie glow around her. I allowed Patrick to get me to my feet. There were too many questions coming at me at once. Chief Linwood approached.

"Jac," the chief said, stopping in front of me. He gave me a look that said *Why am I seeing you twice in one day?* "You said someone's been killed? Who might that be?"

I threw off the aluminum blanket someone had tossed over me. Flashlights dotted the terrain as they searched for evidence of foul play.

"We need to go in her office," I said, charging past Patrick toward the front of the house and where Faye stood just inside, holding herself and talking to a couple of officers. "Now."

I ignored the chief's protest as I pushed through, determined to get in that house and in that office, where they'd see what Faye had done to Mia.

Mia, whose only sin was helping me.

"What—what is she doing here? Chief? What's going on? Why are you all here?" Faye was blathering on, working herself into her Faye frenzy. She was also on the line, talking to Mayor Tate.

I pointed at her. "You killed Mia. You didn't have to do that. She never did anything to you."

Faye feigned confusion. "Killed?" She looked from face to face for verification. She pulled the phone back to her ear. "Did you hear her? She says I killed my cleaner!"

Killed my cleaner. As if Mia wasn't a person but rather something Faye owned. It incensed me.

"In her office. I swear to God I saw Faye beat Mia in her office." You couldn't swear to God too many times in the South, or else they'd think you were a heathen, but I did it anyway.

Faye was so shocked, she laughed. "That's preposterous. Haven't I been put through enough accusations during the whole Taser incident?"

"The office," I insisted. "Let me show you."

The foyer was crowded with personnel, and I pushed through them all, the chief and Faye and Patrick calling my name, clamoring up the steps behind me.

"She can't do this. She can't go in there. Chief, are you really going to allow this? What about my rights?"

The chief huffed up the steps, out of shape from too much desk copping. "Jac, Jac, you need to stop."

Patrick paused at the top of the steps. "Ma'am, she says someone was murdered. We have to check it out."

That stopped me. Patrick had spoken up for me instead of disbelieving me off the bat.

"Jac!" Nick's frantic call came from down below.

"We're up here," Patrick replied over the din. He looked back at me. "I called him. Kept Sawyer out of it, though she likely knows."

I spun on my heel. "The office."

The group followed me to Faye's doorway. I grabbed the door handle, jiggling the latch, knowing it was locked. I turned to look at Faye, who'd nestled herself in between the chief and an Officer Talley. She wore a slightly amused look, head canted to the side, as if she were watching a show or movie.

"Open it," I demanded, her reaction infuriating me more. "Mia's in there. She may still be alive."

"I thought you said I killed someone," Faye said, pretending confusion. "Chief, are we really doing this?"

The chief wavered. "She seems pretty dead set on it, Faye. Something's got her worked up."

"Now!" I screamed, two seconds from jumping on her and snatching the remote.

She stared at me for a long moment, her amusement and innocence and indignation slipping. I no longer amused her. I was not fun. I had become a problem.

The door clicked, and I twisted the handle, about to go in, when Patrick stopped me. "Wait, we need to go first."

I moved next to Nick, and he pressed in close to me. I moved away, not wanting to be touched, even by him, right now.

"She killed her," I said. "She killed her, and you know she did. I wouldn't lie about this. I'm not lying. I saw her hit Mia over and over."

Patrick and his partner went in first, their hands on their service weapons. They clicked on the light, and nothing came from the office for a second while they checked it out.

The chief said, "What have we got?" He moved past Faye and the rest of us, entering the room as well.

"Good God," he exclaimed.

I shot Nick a triumphant look. "You see! I told you she killed Mia." I ran in behind the chief.

Ran right into the middle of the room. Turned in a complete 360. And saw nothing.

"Where?" I trailed off, my mind not computing what my eyes were seeing. Absolutely nothing. "Where?"

There was no body. There was no blood. Blood couldn't be the easiest to clean. And how could she have moved a whole body and left no sign?

I walked the length of the square room, muttering these questions to myself over and over.

"She killed her," I told them again. "You don't want to believe me, but she did. I watched her do it."

Faye entered the room, looking around just as the cops had. Everyone—the chief, Patrick, Talley, and Nick—was looking at me, an array of expressions and emotions on their faces. Faye watched me, too, with interest. With the air of satisfaction and authority of a person who had the upper hand. A person who was used to cleaning up her messes. She scratched the side of her neck.

"If I killed Mia, then *where* is the body?"

"You moved it," I fired back. "I don't know how you did and so fast, but you had enough time." Who knew how long I was sitting in a frozen state of horror at what I'd seen? It had felt like seconds, but it was probably longer, and then twenty minutes, minimum, for the police to get there, even if the officers used lights and sirens. It wasn't a quick drive up to the Manor.

I took a chance. Licking at my dry lips, I said, "You hid her. In your room. Your secret room."

I threw it out there for shock value, my attention trained on Faye, waiting to see her reaction. *There.* My chest swelled just a little, and I nearly cheered in celebration. To everyone else, her face remained placid. But I saw the slightest tic of her right eye. The tightening of her face as her jaw flexed, just a little. The rest of them missed it. But I saw it. And she saw that I'd caught it.

"Come on now, Jac," the chief said, exasperated. "Now there's a secret room where she hid a body?"

I said, "Everyone knows there is a secret room and hidden passageways."

"Not true," Faye replied smoothly, back on track. "I know every inch of this place. None of that is true. Unless you want to count the pathways in the hedge maze." She didn't stuff poor Mia in the hedge maze. Mia was in here. Somewhere. I looked around.

I pushed, hoping to make the little pinprick I'd managed to open wider so Chief Linwood and Patrick would see. "What's true is that you are a murderer. You killed my granddad, and you killed Mia." Then, hot tears filled my eyes, making everyone blurry. "You killed her."

Patrick asked, "Why? Why would she kill Mia?"

"Because Mia took her spare remote to the office and gave it to me. That's how I got the Taser. Faye must have known from the moment she realized the Taser was missing that I had it."

I looked around, wiping at my face, pissed that my emotion was showing while Faye was totally unfazed.

"There's a secret room in here." It came out weak, pitiful, unsure.

I went to the walls, knocking on each in various sections, listening for anything hollow. I moved to the wall-length bookshelf, running my fingers over the books. I gripped the spines of a couple, tugging on them to see if a hidden door would spring open. Just like I'd done the other night during the gala. Nothing. Mia had evaporated into thin air. I circled the room again. Where was the thing Faye had hit Mia with? Both of them gone. No body. No weapon. No hidden room. No signs of a struggle.

"How much longer will we humor her?" Faye finally asked in a bored tone. "Clearly, she's having a mental break. She needs to go home, and I need to go to my fiancé. I think you all have traumatized me enough."

I shot her a baleful look, one full of all the hate in my entire being. She merely blinked back as if she'd done nothing wrong.

I approached her, but Patrick slid in between us, taking me by the shoulders. He ushered me away from her to create space.

"Don't," he whispered.

"We'll need to take her in," Chief Linwood said, sliding his hand over his face. He sounded worn. He looked like I felt. Beaten down, with nothing left. "This has been a day."

Indeed it had.

Patrick turned to the chief. "Chief, she's been under tremendous stress. Her grandfather was very close to her. Please, let me talk to her? Get her home?"

The chief gave me a stern look as he thought it over, assessing the situation, deciding if I was a threat or not. Not realizing the threat was not me. She was standing right next to him. The saving grace was that he didn't ask her to weigh in on my fate. At least he gave me that decency.

"Don't make me regret letting you go home, Jac. You'd better stay there until we sort this all out."

Patrick gestured to Nick, who came to my other side and began leading me out. We passed Faye, who looked from me to Nick. Her irritation was evident.

"Really, Nick? After what she's put *me* through? What will your father say?"

She tried to approach him, but he stepped back, her face registering shock and hurt when he did so.

"So that's how it is?" They stared at each other, a silent communiqué passing between them.

His jaw only flexed in response.

"Nick," she implored him.

He didn't answer, instead blocking me from her view as he guided me through the doors, with the rest of them soon following. I glanced behind me. Faye was the last to leave, casting one assessing look around the room before shutting off the light and closing the door and clicking that goddamn remote of hers.

"When Mia doesn't show up at the grocery store, then you'll know I'm right," I said weakly. But I wasn't sure if I'd said it so anyone could hear, or just for me.

"Nick," Patrick started as we climbed down the stairs, a repeat of the first time with Granddad's clock. Only this time, they didn't rush, and Patrick didn't yell.

"Already done." Nick took my arm.

This time I didn't move away from his touch. I leaned in, there and not there, images of Faye's uncontrollable rage as she bludgeoned Mia to death replaying over and over in my mind.

Patrick said, unexpectedly gentle, "I'll bring her car home."

I didn't bother to ask for my bag, which was in the car. All of it seemed unimportant now.

"I'll let your mom and sister know you're on the way."

The images wouldn't be shaken—they were the only things I could see.

Maybe I really was as screwed up as everyone seemed to think. Maybe I'd imagined the whole thing. Mia was alive and well, and home. Faye was actually innocent of this one thing. I was distorting my fantasy with reality, my mind adding extreme images of a murder that didn't happen to overcompensate for the images from my past that I could not, and maybe should not, remember.

27

The Lowcountry is made up of a network of tiny one- and two-lane roads and back roads that might be paved and clear one moment, then pocked with deep gouges the next. The roads cut deep into the swamps and marshes. They can be treacherous. They are as black as the night sky will allow. They stretch endlessly, connecting one to the next. A rough web of passageways that, if unlucky, one might get lost in and never be seen again.

But it was in those backcountry roads, that network of routes cutting though the swamps, marshes, and forests, where I grew up running. I hadn't had a good run since graduating high school. I found running in the concrete jungle of DC ugly and painful. I wanted to feel the wind through my hair as I was sweating it out. I wanted to smell the scents of the swamps, woodsy and wet and animalistic. I didn't want to hear car horns or have streetlights marring the experience. I yearned for the clarity and purity from before life had become so muddled.

I had tried to do what my mother had always taught us: *Don't dwell on the bad. Bury those things deep, and forget.* But what Mama didn't tell us was that burying the truths we didn't want to face would only create a rot that would consume us from within. I'd buried the events of what had happened to my father and wasn't better for it now. Burying something meant never being able to truly move on, and so, I remained stuck.

Witnessing Mia and Faye's encounter, watching Faye attack, and knowing Mia's body had been there one moment and gone the next had unraveled me. I'd spent the next couple of days in replaying everything, trying to figure out where I had made a misstep and if I had been wrong. I even went by the IGA grocery store, praying she'd be there. Those prayers went unanswered.

I was supposed to find the secret room. I was supposed to find concrete evidence, and Mia had literally given me the key. She'd trusted me, and I'd returned the remote too late. Mia had been discovered.

Maybe everyone was right about me, and it was me who was reading everything wrong.

As if second-guessing every decision I'd made wasn't torturous enough, I'd pulled out Conrad's notes. I'd barely glanced at them since arriving in Brook Haven, keeping them out of sight and out of mind because the thought of revisiting my past made my stomach turn. But now I wanted to see myself through Conrad's words.

It was a big mistake. To say he embellished. To say Conrad made me out to be a monster, like I'd purposely and willingly taken my father's life, then moved on like nothing mattered. It didn't sound like me at all. It sounded more like Faye Arden, and I was both sickened and horrified.

Was I like Faye?

Mia had been killed because of me. Would I just move on?

The need to run, not away from all the drama but toward a solution, was so great that I had to listen to it. I laced up a pair of sneakers after finding some old running clothes I still had. I hoped they'd hold out.

I mentioned to Pen that I was going for a run.

"Oh." She was surprised. "I didn't know you still ran. Do you really think you should? I mean, after all that drama at the Manor?"

"I'll run where people can't see me," I said miserably.

"Well, be careful," she said.

She didn't stop me. Just watched me leave like I was a prisoner on my final walk to the gas chamber.

As much as I whined and was creeped out about Murder Manor, running in the woods, being on empty roads when everyone was asleep, comforted me. I liked it best when there wasn't noise.

Guilt ate at me. I couldn't run away from it. It clung to me like a gremlin on an airplane wing, one only I could see. Mia died because she had decided to be on my side. A woman was dead, and no one fucking believed me.

I barely registered the dark SUV when I ran down the drive of my house and out to the main road. The music from my AirPods mostly drowned out the sound of the engine starting up. The focus on steps and regulated breathing weakened my situational awareness.

It must have followed me for at least half a mile, until we were clear of the town lights and other cars and people. Then it inched closer.

My instincts began to tingle, and I had sense enough to keep my stride while turning off the music. That's when I noticed the car. I quickened my pace, and, of course, it kept up with me. I chanced a look back, and it was like the hounds of hell were at my back. I could feel the vibration of its engine, which wanted to overtake me.

It would inch closer, then back off, a sick, twisted game of predator and prey. I couldn't run off road when it was as dark as it was.

The SUV would not back off, chasing me with no lights on. It wouldn't pass when I motioned for it to do so. It hunted me. I tried to think of any way to get away from it as it pushed me through a series of twists and turns. Playing with me. Toying with me.

I was too terrified to scream. My phone had lost its signal. The SUV kept coming within inches and then backing off, driving me farther and farther away from any safe space.

My brain screamed for me to make a break for it and leap off into the ditch by the side of the road. Hopefully, there wasn't a hungry gator waiting, or a drop too steep, or a swamp too deep and murky down there.

My face was hot and slick from the mugginess. The moon that had once guided my way hid behind a burgeoning cloud, abandoning me.

In that instant, both of us, me and the driver behind that wheel, made a choice.

I couldn't be certain if they were trying to kill or scare me. If killing was their goal, I thought I would have already been dead. They'd had plenty of time and road to do so. If they were trying to scare me, they were doing a good job. Perhaps it was payback from Faye for breaking into her office and stealing her Taser?

Could have been Conrad, raising the stakes and trying to intimidate me into giving back his notes, angry because his incessant stream of texts, messages, and calls had gone unanswered. I could cost him his job and, if the university backed me, likely his reputation. Once the publishers got wind of that, he could kiss his six-figure deal goodbye.

Jac, consider all the probabilities. Granddad's favorite line to say to me whenever I came to him with a problem, which was often. Think of every angle, then pick the best one out of the bunch.

It was all I could do—focus on a plan to get me to safety, or else . . . I couldn't think about the "or else."

Then act.

I had one chance.

I turned at the moment the driver seemed to make their choice. Go hard or go home. I wanted to go home. The vehicle revved, its engine sounding like a roar, thundering in my ears. Its tires spun into a squeal on the unkept road, sending up a shower of dirt and rocks behind it, kicking up a windstorm.

The distance between it and me began to shrink as it bore down on me. Time stood still and sped up at the same time. My breathing was ragged as all other noise fell away, filling up my ears, taking the place of the roaring engine and the screeching tires.

As the bumper of the SUV connected with me in a glancing blow, I jumped.

I sailed through the air, tree limbs whipping against my body, then snapping from the impact. They rained down on me as my body crashed hard to the ground and began tumbling across the embankment over broken branches, rocks, and slick fallen pine needles until, finally, a thick tree trunk ended my accelerating roll, eliciting my deep grunt. The hard stop made me bounce back.

Pain shot out, multiple lightning streaks of white-hot agony reverberating out from the impact point to every part of me, known and unknown. The woods were still. The world was still. And as I hovered between being conscious and not, I was still.

The road was at the top of the embankment, making it hard to see up the incline clearly.

I couldn't see it, the imagery forming in my muddled mind, as the SUV stopped after making me jump off the road, then backed up several feet and stopped again. I needed the dark to shield me now.

Whether the driver had wanted to kill me or scare or warn me, I wasn't sure, and I didn't want to know.

Stay still, stay hidden, stay alive.

That was no life lesson taught to me in the comfort and safety of my family. That was a lesson from intrinsic survival instincts.

I heard the chimes as the driver's door opened. The interior lights marked the SUV's spot. I heard the door shut again with a muted thud.

The driver's feet crunched on the gravel and dirt, making their way to the edge of the road. The driver leaned over, peering into the dark crevasse, trying to pick me out from the vegetation.

They spoke.

"You should have left well enough alone, Jac." Faye's voice rang into the night. The sound of her voice made my blood run cold. I tried not to shiver and expose my location by rustling leaves and snapping twigs. She felt so close, as if she were right behind me.

"Now look what you made me do, Jac." And then she said, "I get rid of people in my way, so don't think this is over. Not by a long shot."

My very words flung back in my face.

I held my breath, praying that nothing would skitter or slither over my skin, which tingled with fiery sensitivity and adrenaline. Any and every touch would drive me to scream, betraying where I hid. She stood there for what seemed like an eternity until she finally gave up. I heard her crunch back to the SUV, open the door to light and chimes. She kicked the gear into drive and rolled away slowly over crackling rocks and tinder, taking the halo of light with her and tossing me into complete and utter darkness, where I remained after the vehicle was long gone, leaving tendrils of danger and warning in its wake.

28

By the time I hobbled home, it was late. I hoped the house would be dark and Mama and Pen off to sleep or out when I arrived battered, bloody, and bruised. I lucked out. Mama was asleep, her car in the garage. Pen's car was gone. Probably at Patrick's. I let myself in the house and made my way up the stairs as quickly as I could. I didn't want Mama to see me. She'd have too many questions I couldn't answer.

The mirror confirmed what I already knew. I looked horrible. I had managed to bruise just about everything but my face. Jeans and long sleeves it was.

"What are you really doing, Jac?" I asked my mirror image, standing in the bathroom, door locked in case Mama made a surprise entrance and saw that I'd been on the losing end of a fight.

"What is it you want?"

I wanted a lot of things. I wanted the truth. I wanted purpose. I had neither of those things, and it was frustrating and demoralizing. I hadn't asked for any of this, and yet I was in too deep, with a target on my head.

"You made a play with that Taser, Jac," I said to mirror me. "You drew your line in the sand, and she pushed back."

She was winning. My skin, darkening in the tender areas, was proof of that.

I'd been called many things, I thought as I dabbed my scrapes and cuts with alcohol, sucking in a cold burst of air and trying not to make sound when I hit a raw spot. *Coward* wasn't one of them.

I picked up a tube of Neosporin and applied some of its contents to my cuts and scrapes. Tomorrow was a new day.

29

The following day arrived faster than my aching body was ready for, and I forced myself out of bed, wincing in pain with each movement.

"This must be what getting old feels like," I muttered, using my hands to push myself off the mattress and to the bathroom, where I was going to prepare to take on the day. I was down, but I wasn't out. At least not yet.

I went to Main Street, thinking I'd grab one of Park Diner's famous double-decker club sandwiches and other supplies I might need at Granddad's, including a fresh box of Expo markers. I was determined to make a go at the evidence board. I thought hitting Main at eleven o'clock would be a good time because it was right before the sacred hour of noon, but I found downtown busy with people wanting to jump-start lunch or enjoy the beautifully crisp autumn day. They were already trickling out of offices and buildings with hunger on their minds.

I had just thanked Park Eun Jin, whom I was pretty friendly with in high school (a.k.a., I'd always thought he was hot growing up), for my lunch. I had left the diner with the bagged containers of food when I thought I heard my name, like a question on the wind. A quick visual sweep of the bustling street told me my mind was playing tricks on me and that there was no way the voice I'd thought I'd heard was correct. As I was getting ready to move toward my car, a hand caught my elbow.

"There you are. I actually found you in this godforsaken place."

My stomach shriveled, and I turned to face him, the white plastic bag in a death grip in my hands. My eyes darted around again, as if I thought I would be surrounded by DC Metro police or maybe the FBI, since I'd crossed state lines. It was only Conrad, in a navy blue blazer over an untucked button-down and jeans.

I took him in, and all the emotions I'd managed to bottle up and bury deep came bubbling up to the surface, threatening to break through the already thin layer of calm I'd been able to build up until this point.

The sight of him had my feelings warring. The way his dark, wavy hair hung over the right side of his forehead nearly made my hand automatically reach up to brush the strands to the side. His piercing blue eyes held a mixture of anger and impatience and relief as he looked at me. His body position was domineering, his stance like he was about to lay into one of his students because they were in deep shit.

My doubts and self-consciousness began to descend. Maybe the knife in the door had been too much. Too aggressive. Maybe if I'd given him a chance to explain why he was secretly recording everything I'd told him about my experience and why he'd written a salacious story about me. Maybe if I'd just asked why he'd told the judging committee to deny me the fellowship.

"Where is it?" Conrad barked out, straight to the point and not bothering to keep his voice down, a bit of panic saturating his question.

My hand gripped my bag tighter as I played for more time to get my thoughts together. I had to be calm and collected. I felt eyes on me. Checking out the newcomer. Checking out the wild Brodie girl. What trouble was she about to get into now?

I took a breath. "Where's what?" I tried to be as light as a feather.

"You know what I'm talking about." He stepped toward me, and his voice lowered. "The manuscript. You stole it from my house."

In an instant, any trace of affection or remorse disintegrated. How could I steal what was rightfully mine? What had been stolen from me? My story. My darkest inner thoughts about how I'd killed my dad. Things I'd never said before, not even to my family. The assumptions Conrad must have made about me to fill in the parts I couldn't. The gratuitously salacious way he'd portrayed me and the way my dad died.

"What you tricked and stole from me, you mean," I countered in measured tones. "My story. Something you have no right to tell." I fought to keep calm in the face of the person who might have betrayed me the most. Even though I'd never expected a real future for us, I'd never thought that I wasn't anything more than source material for him. I hoped he couldn't see how deep inside he had hurt me. I felt violated. I felt . . . invaded. And it couldn't go down on my home turf.

He ran his fingers through his more-salt-than-pepper hair. A Patrick Dempsey move I used to think was so sexy. It didn't hurt, either, that Conrad kind of favored the actor. That was then. When I looked at Conrad now, I felt only contempt, betrayal, and sadness.

He said, "Look, I've held off calling the cops. I haven't said a word to the department either."

Like he was doing me some kind of favor. I let out a dry laugh at his audacity. "What would you say to the department, that your TA stole your computer and the unapproved book of lies you wrote about her using the most important thing she ever told you in confidence? Go right ahead because I don't give a fuck."

"Cut the bullshit, Jac!" he snapped. It came out loud and made me jump. I'd never heard him angry like this. Not even in all the voicemails he'd left, begging me to come back so we could talk. Begging me to return his precious work. Work from material he'd stolen, though he'd conveniently left that part out. He sounded ridiculous, almost like he was two steps from breaking, confronting the person standing in the way of his salvation. Conrad would have nothing else to lose if he lost this. His words sliced through the air like thunder, and all of a sudden, everyone was watching, and the street was way too quiet, and the spotlight was on us.

He sneered. "Don't you realize the kind of money a story like that would pull? That money would have been your money too. All the crap we went through together. The Fellows thing—to hell with it. You can buy ten thousand fellowships with the money you'll make if you give me back my notes."

If only he knew about the latest chapter. How I'd watched a person being bludgeoned, and I had sent her to her death. He'd drop my father's story in half a heartbeat.

"Do you know how great a book it would be? The world that's full of true crime podcasts and detective reality shows would love to eat up a story about a woman who killed her dad and how the whole town hates her."

I stepped back. Hearing him say what I already knew was too much. It wounded me. "What you wrote was lies. You wrote that I killed him for—"

"It doesn't matter why you did it. What matters is the hook. What matters is that the reason in this *fictionalized* book"—he made a point of emphasizing the word—"is good enough for a story. Real life doesn't matter."

It was a gut punch. It was my real life, no matter how Conrad tried to spin it for his publisher and the literary world he was so desperate to get back into . . . so desperate he'd lie and steal to get there.

I steeled myself. "No, you can't use my story. You can't write the book."

His eyes went flat. What I'd thought was anger before was nothing like how he looked right now. His face flushed. His lips went into a thin white line. His jaw flexed as I watched pure murder fill him up. He took another step toward me.

"You don't want to do this, Jac," he said, so close I could smell the coffee on his breath. "Don't do this, or I will call the police and end whatever career you thought you had at the university. Give me back my manuscript. You won't win in this. And I have the knife with your prints and what you left on my door. That's evidence of stalking. That's a threat to my life. That's time and your career. You sure you want to play that game with me?"

He looked around, noticing that cars rolled by and people were openly staring at our public display. His lips parted into a smile. "Or maybe I should tell your town cops and your family what you've been doing up north? Seducing your teacher. Telling your story to a stranger when you haven't even told them. Sticking knives in doors. Killers do that, Jac. Killers threaten to harm."

"Shut up." I shoved him hard, rage directing my movements. "I didn't sedu—shut up!"

He stumbled back and regained his footing. He let out a laugh, holding his hands up as if in surrender. "Do they know you haven't changed one bit? That you're still the troublemaker you've always been? Look at how they're all crowding around. They're ready to toss you out on your ass. They're not looking at me like I'm the problem. They're looking at you like, 'What has she done now?'" He raised his voice, calling out to the crowd. "And you know what Jacinda Brodie's done? She cost me my career! She got me fired."

It was as if my rage filled my ears with an angry buzz. I could hear someone calling my name faintly in the background, but I didn't listen. I couldn't stop myself, even if I'd wanted to.

He taunted me, his voice lowering so only he and I could hear. "You can't push me like you did your dad, Jac. There's no cliff for me."

Something in me snapped.

All I could see was red. All I could think was murder. All I wanted was his throat in my hands and to squeeze it until there was no breath in his body. I didn't need the bluff. I had my hands.

I lunged at him, abandoning all attempts at self-control. "I'm going to kill you! You're dead. Don't you talk about him. Don't you ever mention his name, or I swear to God, I will fucking kill you."

The words tumbled out over and over, so fast I didn't know where one sentence ended and the other began. My fists pummeled every inch of him that I could reach. He careened backward, trying in vain to grab me and stop my hurricane of hits, but I was too quick. I was too strong. I made him bleed. There was no stopping me.

His face was right in front of me. Then it was Faye's. His again. And then the both of them melded into one hideous monster coming after me. After my family and friends. Innocents. All because of me. I couldn't stop myself. And I didn't want to. If I'd had the knife like I had weeks ago, I would have plunged it deep into his chest. Into hers. I would have twisted it and watched them bleed out. I'd have watched them die, just like I'd done with my father. But unlike with my father, I never would have given it a second thought.

Hands grabbed me around the waist, pulling me back, lifting my feet off the ground as whoever it was spun me away from him. I struggled against them, writhing, twisting, screaming for them to let me go. Trying to get at him the way I couldn't on the day I'd found his notes and story about me. Conrad had violated me, and I would kill him for it.

Don't do it, baby girl / Junior Dick.

Daddy and Granddad said it together, in one harmonious song, and the fire, the murderous rage, fizzled like water thrown on a firepit. The steam whooshed up and out of me with a hiss. All of the fight left me, stripping me clean of everything but my humiliation.

My tunnel vision expanded. It wasn't just Conrad and me. It was everyone on Main Street. It was everyone coming out of the side stores and spilling out of Park Diner. All of them looking at me with disdain and shaking their heads as if they knew I'd do something yet again. Always causing a commotion. Forever the wild Brodie girl.

The arms that had grabbed me let go as I snatched myself from them, spinning around to see who had the nerve. I huffed as realization forced its way through. Plum suit from the dinner, sans the suit but still with the boots. The cowboy hat was not around, but I bet it wasn't far. And this time there was clearly a belt.

He dipped his head, greeting me like he had the night of the charity gala. "You all right to get on?" the cowboy asked.

Get on. To leave. I didn't answer him, shoulders heaving from anger still unfurling from me. I looked around. We were surrounded, the crowd growing by the second.

Conrad was busy waving away the few townspeople who'd hurried over to his aid. He dabbed at the blood pooling at the corner of his mouth, one of the places where I'd hit him.

"I'm okay. I'm okay. No, I don't need a doctor. Thank you." He was all proper and professional now. He looked at me. "I was just asking Jac to give me back my property that she took and to implore her to return to the university before she gets in trouble there."

It was as if the group collectively turned their judgment on me. Looking at me as if I were the devil incarnate, tsking under their breath.

"I bet Chief Brodie's rolling over in his grave," someone mumbled, followed by a chorus of *mm-hmm*s.

My hands balled at my sides, and I counted down so I wouldn't use them.

Conrad said, "It's all I came for, and I don't want to cause any problems. I'll be at the Holiday Inn off the interstate when you come to your senses."

My eyes slid toward Faye. She was at the edge of the crowd in full view, watching us with that same expression she always had, like she already knew the ending before the story had begun.

"Over my dead body will you ever get my story," I told him, doubling down on him. On all of them. "And if you come near me again, you will never again see the light of day."

I turned heel, passing the cowboy and walking away from the crowd pressing in on Conrad for more salacious tea about what that girl was up to now.

I put distance between me and the scene on the street, taking myself to the liquor store to stock up on Casamigos because we were going to become real close and personal.

Once I was back in my car, Conrad's rental drove by, the man no doubt heading out to his hotel to nurse his wounds and his pride.

I exhaled, shifting my gear to reverse, then drove with all sorts of intentions guiding me behind him.

30

"Oh! Jac." My mother startled when Pen flipped on the kitchen light and the both of them found me sitting at the table, chin in hands, staring at Conrad's notebooks. "Why are you sitting here in the dark?" She moved toward me and put a hand on my forehead as Pen set down two brown bags of food. Smells of dinner wafted from them and made my stomach turn.

Mama asked, her tone slightly more panicked than before, "Are you sick? What is it?"

I almost expected her to add *now*, but she didn't.

"Jac," Pen said, coming around to my other side. "We brought dinner from the diner. Chopped steak with sautéed onions and mushrooms and the brown gravy you like so much."

Pen waited for me to reply, but when I didn't, she just looked to our mother and shrugged, having no idea what my issue was.

The only thing I could think of was the notebooks and how they had ruined my life.

"I don't know what's wrong with this child." Mama sighed. Then, "Jacinda!" She called it more firmly this time.

"Mama, just take the food out." Pen bent down next to me. I pulled myself to a sitting position and out of despair. "What is it, sis?"

I looked at Mama and then my sister, taking in both of their worried glances and how slowly Mama was unpacking the containers of food as she waited on me.

The bottom fell out. "I screwed up again." And then the dam broke.

Through my tears, I told them everything that had happened in DC with Conrad and my job, and how Conrad had shown up in town to get his work back. I'd probably have charges for theft, I added.

"Oh, Jac." Mama sat down heavily in a chair, the task of preparing our takeout immediately forgotten. I steeled myself for the inevitable comments, letting me know I'd disappointed her once again. "Jac."

My head dropped. I had done it again. I had lived up to her expectations, and this time in epic proportions. I'd committed the sin of fucking up, and now the whole town knew I'd run away from Brook Haven only to cause more trouble.

Pen took the seat next to me, rubbing circles on my back, the switching of our roles not lost on me. I was the older sibling, and yet it was my younger sister taking care of me. Again.

"I'm really sorry," I blubbered through a sheet of tears and snot. Someone pushed a paper towel under my nose. Pen, as she attempted to comfort me. Because Mama was still sitting there, watching with a look like she was unsure what to do next.

"I know I did the worst thing. Telling family business to someone who isn't family."

"Don't think about that," Pen said. "It's not your fault."

I cried harder. "It is. I shouldn't have stolen his work. I could have sued instead, or something." I peeked at Mama over the soggy paper towel. "Now everyone will be talking again."

Mama snorted. "Girl, they never stopped." She made a disgusted noise before getting out of her seat.

My chest pitched. *Here we go.* This time I had it coming. I had brought this on them.

Pen said, "Mama."

The bags rustled. "Where's the lie? They're always talking, this town. What difference does it make now?"

I couldn't look at her. Or Pen.

"We should be helping Jac. Not piling on," Pen chided. "She doesn't need that."

The rustling stopped. Mama stood there, hands on her hips, glaring at her youngest child. "You may almost be a doctor and all, but you'd better watch your mouth, talking to me. You didn't even let me get a good word in."

Pen muttered, "That's because we know you."

I squeezed Pen's hand for her to stop. "It's okay, Pen, she's right."

"What's right?" Mama said. "I haven't said anything yet." Her gaze landed on the notebooks at the center of the table. "This man . . . this writer or whatever he is. He was your boss and your teacher?" Her eyebrows furrowed.

I nodded.

"And then you were sleeping with him?"

Another nod and a side of shame with it. My stomach dropped now as I waited for her to call me a jezebel fast-tailed girl. I knew her older beliefs about proper-lady behavior would drive her to say it.

She snorted. "And while you two were sleeping together, you confided in him your story that's been troubling you for years. Am I right?" Her voice was hard, stripping away any remnants of my dignity.

All I could do was nod, a fresh wave of tears sprouting up and pouring down like hot wax against my skin.

Mama snorted. "Sounds to me like you should have cut his balls off with that knife you stuck in his door."

The room went dead silent as Pen and I stared at our mother with our mouths open. I was unsure I'd heard her correctly. Mama was on my side. Agreeing with me. For the first time I could remember.

"What?" I breathed, afraid it was a dream and this was all my imagination.

"That man lied to you. Betrayed you when you gave him a gift."

I was confused, looking at Pen. Pen shrugged back, as astonished by our mother's seeming 180 as I was.

"Gift?" I sputtered.

"You gave him your trust and your affection," Mama huffed, pulling the empty bags from the table and balling them angrily in her hands. "And he took it and betrayed you. He hurt you."

Mama's anger seethed, touching something deep, the source of which I had no idea. "You had to do what you had to do." She marched to the aluminum trash can, waving her arm over it so its top would open. She slammed the balls inside in a slam dunk. "Ain't no faulting you for that."

Pen's face mirrored my feelings. What had happened to our mother?

Mama spun on the both of us so quickly that Pen and I startled from the sudden move and the ferocity in her eyes.

"But you need to stop running now, Jacinda. You face your issues, your fears, and that bastard head on. And you solve your problem," she said. "Cuz you a Brodie, and that's what we do."

I'd never heard Mama so resolute and steadfast as she was in that moment. Never said a crass word against anyone that wasn't coated in honey. She adored my father and automatically took up for men over women. This could be problematic and often clashed with how I lived and how I felt about male/female relationships. Pen used to attribute Mama's beliefs to her old-school way of being raised—the whole "women should put their lives on the back burner for their man and their kids" way of thinking. It wasn't surprising to hear Mama ask after a boyfriend and whether we'd given him dinner or tended to his needs as if we only existed to serve our man. That old way of thinking that he was the catch and not us. Thus, the reason I never brought guys home.

Tonight, Mama was different. There was no "benefit of the doubt" or her finding ways in which I had somehow failed Conrad, driving him to do all he had to me. She didn't have a shred of doubt or compassion for him. There was only anger. An anger I didn't know she had.

I glanced at the notebooks again, thinking of where Conrad was staying that night. The Holiday Inn. I had a problem. Seemed like it was time for me to do as Mama said—face the bastard head on and put an end to at least half of my problems. But I was strangely hesitant, like the debacle earlier had drained me of any confidence I had left. I still had the Casamigos and a cabin in the woods to drink and hookah my way to self-assurance. Maybe I'd bring the notebooks and head to Conrad from there.

31

Oven-level heat and bright sunlight drove me awake the following morning. My eyes landed on the old Biggie and Tupac poster—two greats from before my time, yet timeless. They had been on my wall since junior year at Richmond Regional High. They knew everything about me.

"What did you two let me do?" I asked the two rappers as they posed, looking hard and oh so good together. RIP to them. But more pressing at the moment was how I was going to get myself out of bed. My head felt as if someone had taken a sledgehammer to it, crushing it from the outside in, and then wrapped it in a thick cotton ball of haze and fog.

I sat up too quickly, my hand rushing to prop up my head, which felt as heavy as two bowling balls, and my stomach roiling. My hand slid from my head to my mouth, balling up and pressing against my lips to keep in whatever my stomach thought was going to come out. I waited for the nausea to subside, groaning slightly. Alcohol had never been my thing because I'd always been a lightweight and hookahs were more my speed, so last night's indulgence was hitting me hard. That coupled with a serious round of hookah was not a good mix, and this morning's roller-coaster ride of head-splitting pain and nausea was a perfect example of why.

"One or the other, Junior Dick," I said aloud, the coarseness of my voice making me look up to the two rap icons in surprise. "I sound fucking horrible." I waited, like they were going to magnanimously disagree with me to spare my feelings. They did not, being paper and, well, dead for over twenty years.

The muffled noises coming from downstairs were what alerted me that the house wasn't empty. Pen wasn't at work. Mama wasn't at one of her fifty-eleven obligations that had her up at the ass crack of dawn. And Patrick was here, too, though I was pretty sure he took early shifts and worked later to avoid having to deal with me.

I could hear them, of course, talking about me and the strange white guy who'd suddenly shown up in town and accused me of stealing his shit. Mama was probably complaining about how I was upstairs sleeping off alcohol and hookah (as the partial images of my excessive drinking that had started at Granddad's cabin and ended, somehow, back here began flickering in and out of memory).

I had totally embarrassed them again in the middle of town in front of everyone, and Mama would never again be able to show her face to the ladies of all her leagues, boards, committees—you name it.

It was nothing new. I was, of course, the town pariah and had made them the talk of the town—in a bad way—for six years. My behavior yesterday was on brand. Not for the hundredth time, I wondered why I was staying in this goddamn town.

Why was I? I couldn't stop the emotions from rushing me as I struggled to my feet, from nearly making me double over and curl up into a ball on the floor because the guilt was too much of a cross to bear. I hated the way my mother pushed me to be the proper Black southern belle, and I resented the hell out of this town for never letting me forget what I'd done that night, for making my family work extra hard ever since then to remain in its good graces, while I'd escaped its wrath by running away so I wouldn't have to deal with it or look at how I'd blown up my family's life.

I thought I was finally doing the right thing . . . coming back home to see Granddad off, supporting Mama and Pen while they grieved the loss of the man who'd taken care of them after I'd cut and run. The town was mad at me for leaving, for not dealing with what I'd done and being a punk about it. Hell, I was mad at myself. I'd never forgive myself for being the coward that I was. Always the fucking coward when it came to things that mattered the most. My dad. My family. And now this.

How I'd handled Conrad, taking his work. Leaving his kitchen knife embedded in his front door, channeling my freaking Alex from *Fatal Attraction* or, better yet, Brandi from *A Thin Line between Love and Hate*—cinematic gold from the past, I knew.

I wasn't obsessed with Conrad. I never even thought he was someone who'd be in my life forever. And I certainly wasn't trying to fight for him. Erin could keep his raggedy ass. I just wanted my story back, and I wanted a little payback for the fellowship he'd denied me—the asshole.

I'd gone about it all wrong. I could get into real trouble for the knife and breaking into his condo, even though I'd had the key he'd given me to watch his house when he traveled for a collegiate conference and had just never returned it. All the decisions I'd made in the heat of the moment had made Conrad follow me here and bring more drama to my family's doorstep.

Why had I stayed after Granddad's funeral?

Because I knew Faye had had something to do with his death, and no one believed it but me. Because even though I couldn't live in Brook Haven, it was still my home, and I couldn't allow Faye to make it hers any longer.

More voices added to the noise downstairs, indicating that more than just the three of them were down there. I glanced at the clock; it was seven. Southerners were early risers, but they didn't conduct social visits at this time. I stood, holding my hands out at my sides until the room had stopped rocking back and forth. Once the room had stilled, I eased my way on unsteady feet toward the closed door.

When I opened it, Mama's voice drifted into the room. The sound of her was instantly sobering and put me on high alert. The high pitch of her voice didn't sound embarrassed or annoyed or overly polite in her attempts to explain away my misdeeds. It sounded stressed. It sounded fearful. And that drove away all the self-pity I was working up to get myself through the lecture I knew I was in for.

In socked feet, a faded Washington Nationals T-shirt, and sweats, I followed the voices to the kitchen.

I recognized the chief's voice as he apologized for coming so early. Saying this was the only way, and they had questions. I hesitated on the steps as I tried to decipher his tone. Maybe they'd found something on Faye and realized I was right. Vindication was my hangover tonic. Finally, something was going my way.

I pounded down the rest of the steps, forgetting that moments ago I'd wanted to hug the toilet, and nearly broke my neck sliding in my socks on the polished wood floors like I was Tom Cruise in *Risky Business*. My insides surged with hope at the thought that Faye was finally about to get what was coming to her and that Chief Linwood had shown up to tell me about it, maybe even apologize for not believing me when I'd tried to tell him over and over. I passed the large bay windows, barely registering the two squad cars parked out front and the chief's SUV. Odd that so many had come when they should've been at Moor Manor arresting Faye's ass.

"Just a few questions, okay, Angela? That's all I wanna ask," Chief Linwood was saying as I approached. "I'm sure there's an explanation to it all."

Mama's response came right after. "Of course there is, Weldon. It makes no sense. He's the one who came all the way down here and confronted—no, attacked—her."

"Did you arrest her? For Mia and Granddad?" I asked as I rounded the corner from the hall into the kitchen. I skidded to a stop as I hit the wall of black uniforms. Four cops turned in sync to me. Beyond them, Chief Linwood stood next to Mama, with Pen on her other side as if guarding her. They were at the center island, and everyone stood watching me. No one was offering fresh, steaming cups of coffee, the scent of French roast permeating the air. Mama always offered whoever came to our home a beverage.

Mom's hands were clasped in front of her at her waist, a kitchen towel crumpled in her fists. Her eyes were watery and wide, looking like she was telling me something, but I wasn't picking it up. She gave a barely imperceptible shake of her head. I couldn't tell what she was thinking. Pen was on her other side, in sweats, her hair pineappled in a bun atop her head. On the other side of her, standing near, was Patrick, like he was glued to her side. For once he was not glowering at me but was looking at me with . . . regret, I think. That was the moment I became afraid.

There were too many vibes coming at me all at once, from the cold hostility from the cops to the heavy judgment from Chief Linwood to my family's confusion and horror. My stomach rumbled loudly, reminding me that it still had grievances to air with me.

I took a step back, feeling vulnerable in my pajamas and with unbrushed teeth while everyone else, all dressed and knowing something I clearly didn't, stared at me, emitting the vibe that this was not a friendly space. As Granddad would say, they were raising my hackles.

My fingers went immediately to my hair, searching for the flex rods I usually used at night to twist it. There weren't any because I'd been too drunk to put them in as part of my nightly routine. My hair was free and wild. I smoothed down the wayward strands, then swiped at the sides of my mouth, hoping no drool was crusted there. Whatever this was, I had the incredible urge to look decent.

"What's going on?" I edged out, not really wanting to know. "What's happened?"

Because the way everyone was looking at me, something clearly had. This wasn't a "Jac was right" visit. This was a "Some shit has happened" visit. Only, what did it have to do with me? What did I do last night?

"Morning, Jac," Chief Linwood greeted me, stepping toward me from his spot beside Mama. "Why don't you come in? Join us for a bit?"

He asked like it was a suggestion, but it most definitely was not.

Mom's eyes flickered to him, a little fire in them, as if she were about to chastise him or ask him to stop. Her mouth opened slightly, but if she was going to speak up, nothing came out.

I frowned. Why was she so afraid? What did she not want him to say?

"Morning," I said, feeling all of ten instead of twenty-eight. I shifted a couple of baby steps into the kitchen. It was them against me. A couple of the cops broke from their line, sauntering past me as if they were sightseeing, looking around at the figurines of Mom's ducks and mounted signs like **Family Is Everything**, ending up to my side or behind me, blocking the door I'd just come through. Patrick was watching them hawkishly. His lips practically snarled.

Dread building up in me, I asked softly, "What's happened?" This wasn't good. More so, this wasn't good for me. I knew what the cops were doing. My dad and granddad used to be cops. But I didn't want to believe they were doing it to me. Not again. *What happened last night?*

I looked at Pen and then Mama to confirm they were standing in front of me, so nothing bad had happened to them. "What is it?"

Chief Linwood was closer to me now, looking grave. His jowls moving. He didn't like what he was doing. He wasn't hungry for whatever was about to go down, like his younger cops were. Not much happened in a small town . . .

"That young man you had a run-in with yesterday afternoon?"

I wouldn't consider Conrad "young," but I guess if compared to Chief Linwood . . .

The chief referred to his notebook. "A Conrad Meckleson?"

I swallowed. My stomach felt sour from last night's liquor and the growing feeling that something wasn't right. Why was he saying Conrad's name like that?

"Yes." My voice came out stronger than I really felt, surprising me. I wouldn't look at my family, a familiar feeling of resolve steeling me for what was coming next. I straightened, looking only at the man addressing me. "What about Conrad?"

Not much happened in a small town, but when it did . . .

"Well, his car was by Sugar Creek embankment, back near your granddad's place. Front end's messed up a bit, with mud on it like it was run off the road."

I became a statue. I wouldn't give Linwood anything. He'd have to spell it out for me.

"We also had a call that said they saw your car late last night out and about."

"Anonymous, I bet," I blurted out with a dry smile, because that was my luck these days.

"You remember being out?"

I'd been pretty messed up last night. I drank. I hookahed and chilled. Then I . . . the rest was *poof*, gone like hookah smoke.

I inhaled, nodding slowly as I began tracking what he was putting out. "You think I ran him off the road?"

"Well," the chief drawled out, watching me real close for any sign indicating guilt, because he surely wasn't in my kitchen looking for innocence. Why not add hitting Conrad's car to my growing list of criminal mischief?

Linwood rubbed at his voluminous mustache like it was helping him think, just like he had when he was yelling at me while kowtowing to Faye back in his office.

Linwood grimaced like he was in pain. "We're gonna need to check out your car, Jac."

My soon-to-be brother-in-law looked stricken and, for the first time, outraged, the implications dawning on him now that they were playing out before his eyes. He opened his mouth as if he was going to object, but I shook my head. I wasn't going to lie. He actually looked like he cared. I was touched, but I didn't need Patrick speaking up for me. Not because I held a grudge from the times he'd acted like an ass to me before, but because he was going to have to be the strong one and take care of Mama and Pen.

Pen could only stare, looking as horrified as I felt. I didn't dare look at my mother. If I did . . . and saw her look that had traumatized me for as long as I could remember . . . the thought was too much to deal with.

I forced myself to stay focused and present. To look at everyone else but her. To look at the kitchen floor and how spotless it was. To wonder if Linwood and his folks had wiped their feet before traipsing dirt all over Mama's spotless floors. I refused to think about any of the other stuff. I refused to consider how Mama must feel, watching me talking to cops again.

"But Conrad," I managed to get out. "He's okay?"

Chief Linwood pursed his lips like he was thinking of the best way to say it. "Well now, that's the thing," he drawled. "That young man is missing."

Big things rarely happened in small towns.

But when something actually did, it was like an explosion with the magnitude of an atomic bomb.

32

The last time I'd been at the police station, it had not been as a suspect. Seemed this was the road I had been traveling ever since returning to Brook Haven. I'd thought I was being an avenging angel. Turned out I was a murderous criminal. Laughable, since the real criminal was sitting pretty, with the whole town eating out of the palm of her hand.

I was lucky enough that the chief didn't put cuffs on me. He didn't make me sit in the back of the patrol car like a criminal. He let me get dressed and brush my teeth. He even comforted my mother when she started to cry and promised to call down to Miami to see if my cousin knew of any good criminal lawyers. If only she knew the reason *why* he knew so many.

"Don't tell them anything," she called out, with Pen attached to her side. "I'm going to call K'Shawn."

"He prefers Keigel," I muttered, not that it would matter.

They led me out the front door, polite and respectful. I may have been a suspected killer, but I was still Chief Brodie's daughter. I was thankful for the little things.

The events of the last few weeks replayed in my mind as we rode to the station. All the mistakes, when I'd underestimated people. Was Conrad so angry that he'd fake his disappearance to teach me a lesson? Could it have really been that serious? Was my story worth that much?

Maybe that was what he'd done. Maybe if the world thought I was capable of kidnapping someone, then it would believe I was capable of seducing him into an inappropriate workplace relationship, all to ruin his career. Would Conrad really have gone to those extremes?

I couldn't say. Because the person I thought I knew, I didn't. Apparently, this was the story of my life.

Instead of white privilege, I had Dad privilege. They weren't going to put me in a cell. They weren't going to book me—it was just for questioning, the chief assured my mother, while also convincing her that she didn't need to come to the station with me. That was strategic.

"I'll take her to the car," Patrick had volunteered in the kitchen of our house after the chief announced I had to go in. "While you finish up in here."

So there weren't a bunch of cops escorting me to the car with drones and helicopters circling overhead like they always showed on TV. It was all very underwhelming, to be honest, and I was a little disappointed. If I was going to be the big, bad Jacinda Brodie like everyone made me out to be, they should have pulled out all the stops.

Patrick and I stopped at the passenger's side of the chief's SUV. I'd planned to spend more time at Granddad's today, checking if the questions I'd posed to the group had yielded any new responses.

Patrick shuffled from one foot to the other, acting like he had something to say. I couldn't take another of his lectures like he'd given me after the clock incident.

"Don't say anything to the chief when you're there. Nothing to incriminate you. We'll figure something out." The second time in less than an hour that someone had told me to keep my mouth shut.

He surprised me. Could that be care and consideration Patrick was displaying toward me? I wasn't sure how to feel or what to say, so I said nothing at first.

I finally said, "Aren't you going to ask me? I mean, if I had anything to do with Conrad's disappearance?" I couldn't look at him because I didn't know what seeing the accusation in his eyes would do to my resolve.

He slipped his hands into the pockets of his black joggers, and I realized that he wasn't in his uniform. This was his day off. I cracked a smile: This was what he was doing with it?

"Why would I ask you that?" Patrick asked.

I shrugged. "Because you think I'm a screwup and that I've brought nothing but trouble to my mother and sister."

"I mean you are, and you have," he said introspectively. "But no one jumps from thinking some white lady is the bogeyman to kidnapping people just like that." He snapped his fingers, half grinning. He grew solemn. "Plus, this isn't right. I don't know who that caller was, but not sure I buy their story. Kind of convenient."

I nodded. *Convenient.* I was finding it hard to concentrate, unsure this was my real life.

Patrick continued. "But they're going to check out your car, like Chief said, since the caller said they saw it. You don't have any shit in there that might cause a problem, do you?"

I shrugged. "I hookah. You should try it sometimes. Sometimes, you're wound too tight."

He half smiled, giving me that dig. "Anyway, don't say nothing, all right? Just say you don't know shit, even if you do know."

"But I don't."

"Yeah, well . . . " He trailed off when the chief joined us.

"Ready, Jac?" He said it like we were about to go run errands.

I gave him a baleful look in response. Then turned back to Patrick, who I guess wasn't so bad after all. "Watch out for them for me."

"Already done."

The nicest thing Patrick ever did for me was to stand in the drive while we drove away, watching me leave. He stayed there until I couldn't see him anymore, like a lighthouse in the dark that I was rushing toward like a storm-blind clipper ship.

The hours ticked by. The worst part was coming in and seeing all those eyes look me over, do a double take, then stare outright, curiosity radiating from them. They weren't gonna fingerprint me or make me take a mug shot that only that one light-skinned guy on the internet—Prison Bae, I think—could look good in.

Chief Linwood sat across from me at his desk, the blinds open this time—for transparency's sake, of course. He was polite but business-like. I kept Patrick's words in mind by saying very little, waiting for the moment they were going to arrest me.

"It's only a conversation, Jac." Linwood raked a hand over his mustache again, considering me. I wondered if he realized his tell and that I knew he wasn't sure what to do with me.

"Can't we talk? We're all family here."

I gave him my most incredulous look, then snorted. Some family.

He leaned back in his chair like he was about to get comfortable and we'd be here for a bit. I settled in as well.

He considered me a long while, trying to find something in me that he could use to open me up. "What is going on with you, Jac?"

"What do you mean?"

"What would your father say? Hmm?" He motioned to the walls around us. "About all of this."

I looked around as well, taking a moment to look through the windows behind me until I found Sawyer's cubicle. She leaned against her semitransparent partition, biting the nails on one hand while holding a phone to her ear with the other. Giving the person on the other end a blow-by-blow of what was happening. "I think he'd say you're doing a fine job here. Keeping it together. Doing your job."

He suddenly found his own nails very interesting while he absorbed what I said. When he was good, he returned to me, but this time, the chief was different. Softer, maybe even apologetic. He sighed, his stocky chest rising high and falling. "You know I don't want this for you, right, Jac?" he asked imploringly. "All this mess with Ms. Arden. I really don't know what's going on there. I want to help you, I really do. But you gotta talk to me, Jac. You gotta let me know what's going on so I can help you."

"When I asked you for help about my granddad and the Taser I found—"

"That you stole."

"—that Faye owns, you kicked me out of here. What happened with Granddad's pacemaker was suspicious, especially since the clock ended up missing," I said.

It was more than I'd said at one sitting since the chief had come knocking at our door. "There was proof on his body. But no one checked. It's marked on the autopsy report, but no one will check. I called you all to Moor Manor because I watched Faye Arden beat a person to death, Mia, who worked for Faye part time at the Manor. Then the body was gone, but you never looked into it because you all think I'm . . ." I spun a finger slowly around one ear. "Or a liar. Or a troublemaker. You pick."

"Now, Jac."

"Have you checked where Mia is? Have you done a wellness check? It's been days."

"She's gone."

"Where?"

"Probably with her brother to wherever he ran off to. She left a note at her house."

I huffed a laugh. "Of course." I shook my head. "That mother*fucking* Faye."

I couldn't even get mad. It was just too damn funny.

"So, why would I believe you'll help me now, Chief? Would *you* believe you if you were in my shoes?"

Linwood and Daddy had worked closely together when Daddy was the chief. They had been friends. When Daddy died, the chief was kind and gentle. He did all that because of that friendship. But I couldn't help wondering if his help had an expiration date.

He sighed heavily, leaning forward on his elbows, preparing to lay down the law while I waited, remaining as still as possible so I wouldn't let anything show.

He was about to speak when a knock sounded. He called for them to come in, and when the door opened, one of his officers poked his head in.

"Moment?" he said, halfway in and out of the door.

Chief Linwood excused himself while I remained where I was. He was gone only a few minutes, but when he returned, the air about him was different. Colder now. He had a little paunch that hung over his belted waist. I watched it as he sat on the edge of his desk beside me, crossing his arms over his chest, looking down at me. He left his mustache alone this time.

It wasn't even lunchtime, and the day felt like the longest one ever—and about to get longer still. Finally, my eyes made their way to his beneath his thick brows. That was what was different when he'd come back in. His earlier reluctance had turned to cold judgment, all because of what he'd been told out there.

There was only one thing it could have been. Bad news he had to share. Maybe Conrad wasn't trying to frame me. Maybe he was really dead.

I steeled myself. "What is it?" I asked. "His body?"

The chief shook his head, his eyes never leaving me. "No, no, he's still unaccounted for."

I wasn't following. "Then?"

"They found blood in the trunk of your car, Jac."

"Blood? There's no way. No." The need to defend myself, to protect myself, was automatic. Instinctual. It was one thing for them to throw around accusations. It was a whole other thing to say there was evidence.

"No. I wouldn't. I couldn't." I said it before I could stop myself.

His head tilted. "Couldn't? As in you're not sure if you did or not?"

My lips clamped together. I'd said too much. I wasn't supposed to say anything at all.

He ran a hand over his face, resigned. He didn't want to do this. I shouldn't have been here. But it was his job. He was the chief.

Then he said, "Let me tell you how all of this is going to work now. Okay?"

33

The house felt like a prison. The town and the people were the guards, monitoring me always. There was nowhere I could go without hearing their whispers.

"Did you hear? They say she did something to some man from up north."

"Up north, you say? The one who she attacked on Main Street? Still can't believe she did that."

"Montavious would be rolling in his grave."

"How do you think Angela's holding up? Imagine . . . having one daughter who's been a model child and the other who's a . . ."

"A stone-blooded killer."

"Again."

It was the *again* that got me. Every time, they referenced what had happened with my dad. As if it didn't weigh on me every day.

"You know she don't talk about that night. Says she don't remember."

As if I hadn't begged for me to remember all the details instead of only snatches of images that couldn't explain how we'd gone from arguing at the bluff to my father falling. Nonsequential images that Conrad had siphoned from me and fashioned into a grotesque caricature of me as a small-town killer for his manuscript. He'd come all this way to take it back, except Conrad seemed to have left with more than he'd bargained for.

Mama and Pen, though not accusatory, walked on pins and needles around me. Pen had gone as far as to reschedule her appointments so she could be around. Both of them watched me like hawks, waiting for me to either crumble or explode.

Nick was always looking at me, always waiting for me to "just say the word." It was comforting to know he'd be there the moment I needed him. But it was also another expectation I wasn't ready to meet. To know he'd been waiting all this time was too much responsibility for me to take on. I might have screwed up, going to his house the other day after the argument with Mama. It was the second time I'd done that, the first six years ago. Even back then, Nick had been waiting for me to just say the word. And after I'd said it and we were together for that one night, I ran away and never came back.

Sawyer was always willing to put herself on the line for me. And everything I did, every ask I made of them, leveraged our friendship and loyalty, when I was the least loyal to all of them. What everyone always said about me was true . . . the town, Patrick, even Mama. They all sacrificed for me, wanted to protect me, and I just took and ran. I never gave back.

I needed to get out of here and go to what had become my safe space. Granddad's. I could check the forum and see if any leads had come up on Colleton and if they had any advice for my situation here. The Armchair Detectives were becoming as important to me as they were to Granddad, as important as the people in my real life. No judgments. No expectations. Just cold, hard facts and cases to solve.

I needed something to do so I wouldn't sit around like a shaken Coke bottle on the verge of that explosion Mama and Pen were so scared about. The time *tick*, *tick*, *tick*ed over my head. Each moment, any moment, the cops could come and say I did something I knew I hadn't done. I thought I hadn't done. Like with Daddy. That was why I needed to leave the house. Needed to figure a way out of here without Pen or Mama following me. Watching me. Wondering if I could do anything right.

I was suffocating, and the nervous energy from this shit with Faye and no one believing me was too much.

The doorbell rang, sending a bolt of electricity through me, bringing me back to life. I jumped off my bed, where I had been lying and staring at the ceiling as if I was being punished. House arrest, that's what this really was, the adult version of being grounded.

I was out of my door in a heartbeat.

"I got it!" I yelled over my shoulder, hoping to beat Mama and Pen, who was working on records in her office. My immediate thought was that it was the police. The thoughts that followed were all the probabilities. The DNA results had come in. Or Conrad had been found floating face down in the creek by some kids skipping school or had washed up onshore somewhere. Or that he'd come to my house with cops to demand his notebooks back. Or a lynch mob of townspeople was here to chase me out of Brook Haven. I wanted to buffer Mama or Pen from whatever was on the other side of that front door.

When I opened the door, it wasn't any of them. I stepped back, confused. I looked around to see if someone else was behind him to explain how the cowboy had ended up here.

"Cowboy in the plum suit," I recalled, taking in the stranger I'd seen about town over the last week.

His laugh came from the belly, accepting my label for him. "Or Carl. Carl will work."

Carl had been at the gala and then on Main Street, pulling me away from Conrad. Carl the Cowboy was always popping up everywhere I seemed to be, and now he was at my door, holding his hat in his hands and wearing those boots. I wasn't sure why he was still hanging around when he'd paid his respects for Granddad at the gala.

"What is your business, anyway?" Since I hadn't thought to ask him much at the gala, and he'd offered little, now was as good a time as any to get more information from him.

"Was family business," he said. "Tying up loose ends." Vague. He was always vague. And careful. And observing. But the vibes he gave off never felt dangerous.

I brightened. "You have family here? You never said that. Who? I probably know them."

He looked wistful, a dark shadow passing over him as my words took him somewhere I couldn't follow. "You just might."

Presently, I said, "Did I leave something behind in the street the other day?" I checked for a buckle to see if he'd completed his western look today. He had.

He hesitated, as if for the first time, he was realizing he might have made a mistake. He opened his mouth to speak, but nothing came out when he looked past me, into the house. I followed his gaze, turning to see Mama behind me, dishrag in hand.

"Jac, who's at the . . . oh." I was no longer in her thoughts. She stopped wiping her wet hands on the rag, taking Carl in, trying to place him. "Haven't I seen you somewhere?"

He nodded once, my head volleying between them as I stood on the threshold between out there and in here.

She smiled. "Around town, I think. And the gala." She pointed at him, smiling. "You were the one that bought that abstract painting."

His voice was gravelly. He cleared it. "I did."

"What brings you here? Jac?"

I shrugged, not owning this one.

She smiled. "Well, then. Can we help you with anything?"

He cleared his throat again, delving more and more into the realm of the uncomfortable. "You don't recognize me, huh? Guess not. I wasn't really around back then. Was sent upstate."

I went back to Mama. Her smile was frozen in place, her teeth showing. Her body like a statue. I did a double take between them, not understanding what was going on and why this Carl was here.

"Jac, do you want to order some pizza?" Pen asked, rounding the corner from where her office was located. She slowed to a stop, immediately sensing that the vibe in the foyer was weird and the cowboy filling up the doorway was even weirder. We made eye contact, and a silent question passed between us. I shrugged in response. I had no idea what the hell was going on here.

I spoke up. "Maybe this isn't the best time for you to show up unannounced, Mr. Carl. You know we just had a death, and some other things are going on. Okay? Okay, thanks."

I was about to ease the door closed, because I wasn't sure what had brought him here like this. Surely our occasional conversations hadn't made him think it was okay to show up at a stranger's door asking questions of my mother. And there was no way he was interested in her, and this was a miserable attempt at shooting his shot.

Mr. Carl stopped me. "How are you going to ask me to leave when you're the one who reached out to me?"

34

"Who did?" I looked left and right before pointing to my chest. "Me? I—I reached out to you?" He was crazy.

He nodded. "You did."

I was aghast and highly offended. "I did not, sir. I don't know you." I turned to Mama and Pen, who'd moved to Mama's side. "I don't know what he's talking about. I swear."

This was not going to be on me. I'd been in enough shit, and this wasn't about to be added to my plate.

"Maybe we should call the cops, huh?" I suggested, frantically trying to come up with a fix for whatever screwup was about to happen. I looked at him pointedly. "If you won't leave."

He wasn't looking at me but past me, at Mama, who remained rooted where she stood, the most horrified expression on her face. Like she had come face to face with the devil himself.

"You could call the police," Mr. Carl said simply. He was looking down at his wide-brim hat, rotating it slowly in his hands.

His vibe was not threatening, yet not welcoming either. Sad and resigned, like he was about to do something he didn't want to do but had to.

There was a slow simmer, something bubbling up. I looked around for anything I could use should he try to attack. He looked like an old US Marshal—all he needed was a five-pointed star badge.

"You could call them, but then it'd be your mama going to jail."

When bombs dropped, time didn't really stand still. It kept going and going even though it felt as if nothing was moving. But something was. We were still breathing, inhaling and exhaling. Staring at one another. Waiting for someone else to make the next move. That someone was Mama.

I expected her to tell us to call Linwood, or at least Patrick. I expected her to get anxious and try to kick the man out or break to pieces. I expected her to be frantic. But she did none of that.

"Let him in, Jac."

I must not have heard correctly. "Are you serious?"

At the same time, Pen said, "Mama, no. He's clearly dangerous or in need of help. Let me call Patrick. Jac, close the door."

I began to close it.

"You'll do no such thing," Mama said coolly, determination set. "Move aside, Jac, and let the man in. Pen, get us a few glasses of sweet tea."

~

Mama, Pen, and I sat together on the couch, Carl across from us in a wingback chair. He'd placed his hat on his knee, which was crossed over his other. He was the only one who'd taken a sip of his tea. Surprising, because I'd have thought he'd be cautious of what he drank from someone he'd just threatened. Carl was the most comfortable one of us all. Mama perched at the edge of her seat, her hands gripping her knees, waiting for him to begin.

"I been watching you for a bit." He brushed an invisible something from the top of his nose. "Yeah, been watching how you get around with your girls. How different you are from how you used to be. It's only been a week, and I got you pegged. You got this ole southern belle thing going on. I can't imagine how it's been all their life if you've been forcing that down their throats. No wonder your oldest got issues now."

I held up a hand. "I object to the 'got issues.'"

They both ignored me, immersed in their weird standoff. Carl continued.

"You thought you were leaving mess, but you just created more mess. Look at her. You got this girl thinking she can never measure up to your standards because you so afraid she may end up like someone familiar."

"Like your brother?" Mama asked, looking Carl in his eye with more fire than I'd ever seen in her before. Gone was the docile, perfect wife and mother who could do no wrong. Gone was the woman I'd known for the last twenty-eight years.

"Like you, Angela," Carl said, like he was disgusted with her. He scowled. "You afraid she's grown up like you. A stone-cold killer."

"So what are you going to do, Carl? Huh? You're holding all the cards. My husband's gone. You've hunted me down."

He held up his hands in protest. "Hey now, I didn't hunt you down. Your girl called me."

My hand raised again. "To be fair, I was just going off stuff Granddad had in his locked-up folder. I was curious about this town in Texas. Lake Worth. It was where they found a body in the barrel. You remember the body-in-the-barrel news report that we saw the other day? It aired the morning you dropped the apricot preserves. Anyway, Granddad had a folder about it all, so, I don't know, I emailed the contact listed in the article." I looked at him. "The contact person on the article was—"

"Roberta Lyken."

Carl took the name right out of my mouth.

"She's an associate of mine."

"Wow, I forgot all about that email I sent. I never heard anything back, so I assumed it was a dead end."

Carl's jaw flexed beneath his skin. "I asked her to let me reach out."

I snorted. "Some reaching out. An email would have done the trick. Coming across the country and skulking around town is weird."

Mama still watched him. "What do you want?"

"I want to know why I shouldn't turn you in to the feds right now." He looked around the house, taking it all in. "With your house—real nice, by the way—in a town that knows nothing about the real you."

"Who's the real me?" she snapped, rubbing at her collarbone.

Carl snorted. "You tell me." He gestured to me. "And her. Tell me why I shouldn't drop a dime on you right now and ruin the good name of your dearly deceased husband, Chief Montavious Brodie. Junior."

35

Angela Brodie was the only person on this planet I knew who could sit across from a person in her house and offer them refreshments after being threatened by them. I wasn't sure if that was southern hospitality or if Mama had lost it from the stress of me being carted off by Chief Linwood. But here we were, all seated—one circle of clusterfuck in her great room, the room reserved for Oprah and Obama—with a pitcher of sweet tea and four nearly untouched glasses filled with it. My mother could both terrify and amaze me.

"So why'd you reach out instead of the person I emailed?" I asked, no longer able to wait out their silent standoff.

"Because you said your grandfather had a file about a discovery made in Lake Worth over a year ago."

Beside me, Mama stiffened, her hands tightening on her knees.

"You said your grandfather had been following it. And you gave his name. Montavious Brodie."

I looked down at the rug, wanting to kick myself. Some kind of junior detective I was: continuously letting the villain one-up me, accused of getting rid of my ex-boyfriend, and now volunteering identifying information over the web that had led a stalker to my mother's front door.

From the other side of Mama, Pen said, "So what if Granddad had a file on the discovery? He liked that kind of stuff. He was probably working the case with his forum friends."

Mama said, "Because your granddad had been keeping an eye on North Brill."

"North Brill?" I repeated. I mentally flipped through the folder. "Nothing on North Brill."

Mr. Carl leaned in. "Where we're from," he said. "Your Mama and me."

I laughed. "No, Mr. Carl. Mama is from Arkansas. She grew up in foster care and has no family other than me and Pen."

"I did," she replied, looking at Carl, who was looking at her.

I stood up, unable to sit still. "And who's he?" I pointed to Carl, who sipped his tea quietly, watching, waiting for the right time. "A brother? An ex-boyfriend?"

She said, in the same monotone she'd been speaking in, "He is not either of those."

"Are you the reporter from the article I emailed about, because how'd you get the email? Talk fast, Mr. Carl, because the time clock is on you before we're calling the cops." I said that as if the cops were my best friends and not looking to slap a possible murder charge on me.

"The reporter is a friend of mine," Carl answered, finally looking at me. "If you'll take a seat, Jac, I can start from the beginning. Then maybe I can get the answers I came for, and then I'll leave."

"And leave it at that?" Mama asked.

Carl pursed his lips, offering a sly smile. "That depends on your answers."

I sank into the other armchair. I needed to see everyone clearly.

Mama asked, "What is it you want to know, Carl?"

He leaned forward, setting the glass down, becoming serious. "I want to know why you killed my cousin."

I squawked out a laugh. "Who, *my* mother? There's no way. Tell him, Mama. That's ridiculous and a stretch to connect some innocent email I sent to your cousin being killed. Do you know this woman at all? She's scared to death of guns. Pen, do you hear this?"

Pen, much more reserved than I was, eyed Mr. Carl warily. "It's unbelievable," she said slowly, turning her attention to Mom.

"It *lit-er-ally* is unbelievable," I said, becoming serious. "Look, I don't know what you want, Mr. Carl, money or to scare my mom or whatever, but this ain't the way to get it." The only person who was allowed to give my mom shit was me.

And, I suppose, Pen.

"It's true." Mama's tone was flat, her position unchanged. She was a robot with Auto-Tune coming through her lips.

Pen's hand, which had been around Mama's back, fell like a dead weight, while all I could do was watch like I was on the outside looking in. This couldn't be my reality.

Mr. Carl nodded slowly. His eyes had barely left Mama, but now he turned to me. His sudden attention made my breath catch. Whatever he was about to say, I didn't want to hear it. "Let me first apologize to you, Jac, for not being honest about my intentions the couple of times we've interacted. It was with no malicious intent."

Easy for him to say.

"And for using the information you unknowingly provided, which allowed me to look you and your family up."

"Yeah, that's gotta be illegal. Catfishing or something. Your reporter friend can get in trouble for stalking my mother," I told him, bitterness filling my pores.

I couldn't look at my mother. Just when we were getting somewhere and she was finally loosening up on me, here came Carl with his bull-shit, proving that everything I did ended up with trouble. I couldn't meet her eyes, fear hitting me like flash fire.

I was terrified to look her way. If I did and that look of hers was back . . . the fear of something in me rearing its ugly head . . . that expectation of me to disappoint . . . that nauseating wait for the other shoe to drop . . .

I would never survive if we went back to that. *We* would never survive it.

"I came to find out the truth about Ralph's disappearance."

So his cousin had a name.

"When Roberta—the reporter—mentioned she had a hit on her article, after years of not knowing, I had to check it out. When I saw your grandfather's name, it shook a memory out for me."

"Lucky you," I muttered, plopping back in my chair, settling in for the ride, which, at this point, I was glad had nothing to do with me. This was my mother's shit. My saintly, perfect mother who apparently killed a man once upon a time.

Mr. Carl gave me a long look. "I remembered Ralph mentioned the name to me one day when he'd come to visit me. I'd been locked up for burglary and was hearing all about Ralph's girlfriend, Angie, and that she was stepping out on him with some marine at Fort Worth. Said the man's name was Brodie. Jac's email comes in with that name, and I think it can't be a coincidence. Ralph was heartbroken. You broke his heart, Angie. You could have just left him. You didn't have to kill him. Then . . . then . . ." His face colored, the anger spreading through him as he pulled up memories that must have haunted him for years. "A barrel, Angie? For nearly thirty years. If the lake hadn't receded, we might have never known. How could you be that cruel? What did Ralph do to deserve that kind of treatment and disrespect?"

The pain in Mr. Carl's voice was so suffocating. It billowed from him, taking all the air, making it hot, permeating the room. But the way Mama sat there was like I'd never seen her before. No anxiety. No denials. No tears. She looked at Mr. Carl and his grief as he poured out his truth and accused her of a thing so heinous, I couldn't imagine living with it.

. . . the only case that should never get solved.

Granddad spoke to me as if he were next to me. This case. He hadn't wanted this case to ever be solved because he knew all along.

"Hmm." Mama came alive, studying Mr. Carl introspectively. "That kind of treatment and disrespect, you say?" She looked at Pen tenderly and then at me in apology. She took longer with me, holding my questioning gaze.

She tore her eyes from me to say to him, "I regret your family were left to suffer, not knowing where he was. I thought often about sending a note to let you know where to find him. You and your family certainly didn't deserve that. It is the biggest regret of my life, Carl."

She addressed Carl, but it was like she was speaking to me.

He dropped his gaze, and she returned to me.

"But what your cousin didn't tell you was what he'd been doing to me. I won't go into details because my daughters are here, I don't care to relive it, and I don't owe that to you. But your cousin was an evil and vile man. There were times I thought he'd kill me, and he would always make me think it was my fault. I would apologize to him for what he 'had to do' to me. There is that. I met MJ, my husband, when he was stationed at Fort Worth. He was out with his friends, and I was at the market for groceries." She smiled, her eyes unfocused and decades in the past. "I tripped on the sidewalk curb. My paper bag ripped, and all the groceries spilled onto the street. The eggs smashed, most of the food was ruined, and I was in a panic. I'd spent my weekly allowance on the groceries, and when your cousin found out that the food was wasted, that meant I'd be apologizing again."

She took a breath while I held mine. Even Mr. Carl listened, the rage he'd been holding on to moments ago abating as he listened to how his cousin had treated the woman he'd claimed to love.

"MJ saw how terrified I was. I didn't even have to tell him. He just knew. His friends told him to come on. They had to be back on base. But he told them he'd catch up. He walked me back in the store and bought me every single grocery item I'd lost. He never asked why I was so worried. And then he took me home. It was the nicest thing anyone had ever done for me. We began a relationship, MJ and I—a secret one when he could get off, when Ralph was at work at the garage. I tried to leave Ralph many times, even before meeting MJ. But Ralph was not . . . one to be left." She looked away, gathering herself. Continued.

"MJ got his orders. He was to move overseas, and he asked me to come with him. To be his wife. We went to the justice of the peace and eloped. We had everything planned for me to leave when Ralph was at work. But Ralph found out. Maybe someone saw us at the courthouse, I don't know, but Ralph knew. Anyway, that night MJ and I were set to leave, with MJ planning to get me later that evening once I'd finished packing. The plan was to be out and on base before Ralph came home. But Ralph came back early."

It was like Mama was traveling twenty-nine years back in time. Her eyes welled with tears, and she began speaking as if she were reliving the scene in real time.

"He sees my bags, that I'm dressed like I'm about to leave. He flies into a rage, and he tells me he'll never let me go. He'll kill me before that man can have me. That I am his and his alone. It's not the first time I've heard him stake a claim on me, but this night is different. He attacks me. It is worse than any other time. But I am different. I have a future. I finally have happiness. And then I start to realize that Ralph doesn't mean to just keep me with him. He means to kill me. I keep thinking, 'This man means to kill me.'" She swallowed. "He nearly does. But I fight back and my fight surprises him, and I manage to throw him off of me. I don't know how. But I get hold of the gun he owns as he was trying to get at me again, and—"

Mama's hands closed around an invisible gun, shaking and barely able to aim. Her eyes, streaming with tears, were wide as she saw through us, her future, as she remained in her nightmarish past.

"I aim it, and he's screaming, 'Angie, you don't got the guts. I'm gonna gut that man like a pig soon as he gets here, and I'm gonna let you watch. Then I'm gonna kill you.' I shoot him one time. He staggers back, surprised, but his rage is so hot the shot doesn't stop him. I shoot him again. Right here." She raised a shaky hand to the middle of her forehead. "And he falls back into the table, dead. It is blessedly quiet, and I am safe."

Mama blinked several times, coming back to us. She looked around, getting her bearings. She used a hand to wipe her cheeks. "I would have stayed like that until the police came to take me away. But MJ came first. He saw the mess. Saw Ralph. Saw me and the gun. We got rid of him the best we could. We weren't proud. I've thought about what I did every day since. I didn't know I was pregnant until after we moved to Germany. When the doctor told me how far along I was, I compared that to when MJ and I were first together, and the due date didn't add up."

No one spoke when she was finished. She peeked at me. That slight peek. Said everything. I shook my head. No. No, this was not where her story was going. No, she wasn't about to say what every nerve in my body was hinting at. Montavious Brodie Jr. was my father. He was the only father.

I stood, needing to move. Needing to break through the oppressiveness of this room and these people. I didn't want to hear any more. I didn't want my mother to tell me anything else.

I reared on Carl. "Are you happy now?" My voice cracked. "Did you get your revenge, or do you need her locked up too?" I couldn't see behind the wall of tears.

"I didn't want this," the cowboy said in his slow, devastated drawl, like he was trying to catch his own breath. "I only wanted to know why."

"Well, now you know. My father, MJ Brodie, is dead," I told him, towering over his seated form. "He's dead. You're trying to take him from me again."

Carl's calm broke, and he shook his head repeatedly, his mouth opening but nothing coming out. Mama crossed the room toward me. Pen came with her, ready to envelop me, but I broke away from them, not wanting to be touched or pitied.

I turned on Mama next. "That's why you've always treated me the way you did. That's why I could never do right in your eyes."

"That's not true," Mama said imploringly. She reached for me, but I pulled away. "That wasn't it. It was never about you not being right in my eyes."

My stomach twisted in knots. My throat was closing from the fight I was having not to cry here. Not in front of them. "It is. You were afraid I'd be like Ralph. I reminded you of him."

I was the product of an evil man. One who'd abused my mother. I was the product of her trauma. How could I ever live with that? "When you look at me, you see him. You hated him, and so you hated me. But my dad knew I wasn't like that man. I was MJ's child."

"No, Jac," she said over and over. She held up her hands. "I killed a man with these hands. No matter what he'd done to me, I took his life. And then I erased him from the world for nearly thirty years. There's a special place in hell for me, I think."

"Mama, don't," Pen began softly, not one to let anyone beat themselves up. I remained silent.

Mama nodded, tears dripping from her chin, making wet splotches on her skirt. I couldn't count how many times her hand reached for me, only to hover in the air, fingers straining to touch me. The kid she feared would become evil. The kid of the man she'd put in a barrel.

"You should have told me," I sobbed. "I shouldn't have found out like this, and not in front of him." I gave Carl a contemptuous glare. If I could, I'd put him in a barrel too. I would.

Pen slid her arms around me, our roles well defined. She was always the big little sis. She was the success. The one with the good temperament and good legacy. She was the real Brodie. While I was the unwanted child of an abuser and a murderer. No wonder I was so fucked up. I got it honest.

I pulled away from my sister's arms. Half sister. Sister. "So what are you gonna do, Cousin Carl?" I sneered, saying the hateful word. "Since you also lied to and played me, pretending to be one of my grandfather's friends."

He was stunned. "I . . ." The word came out in three beats. "Never said that. I just asked about him."

"Semantics," I spit. "It was still under false pretenses so I would confide in you while you manipulated."

Carl looked around for help that wouldn't come to him. "I did not intend to manipulate you. I only wanted to know you."

This was bullshit.

Carl stood, pleading his case, trying to be the calm in all this storm, the storm he had brought. "I didn't know that about Ralph. I won't ever say what was done to him after was right, but I can't fault a person for protecting herself. And I would never do anything to harm you, Jac."

I looked at him, wishing he was as dead as his cousin. "You already did." I backed out of the room. "I can't. I need to get out of here."

My cell buzzed like a beacon, saving my life.

There was a text from Sawyer.

Rachel Anderson 702-555-9289
You owe me drinks at Cog's. No a night out in Charleston.
Asshole.

After what happened at Mama's house, I needed a win. And a laugh. Sawyer was good for both, throwing me a lifeline from Colleton, Nevada.

And an escape from my imploding world.

36

I made it to Granddad's in record time. Having something to do other than think about the mess I'd left back at my mother's was invigorating. Gave me purpose. Pissed me off as I realized on my way there that a lot of shit had been done to me. I may have been better off if I'd kept my ass in DC.

I settled on the couch, the two case folders sitting on the coffee table. I pushed the Lake Worth one so it slid across the pockmarked wood and fell to the floor. Case closed. I counted down until my hands didn't shake as much and spread the contents of the Colleton folder in front of me. I looked at what I'd just scribbled on the whiteboard with my new markers.

- THREE HIGH SCHOOL SENIOR GIRLS DEAD OF CARBON MONOXIDE POISONING AT WEEKEND SLEEPOVER FROM ONE OF THE GIRLS' CARS LEFT ON IN THE CLOSED GARAGE
- IN A LATER INCIDENT, ANOTHER SENIOR, DAPHNE FRANKLIN, WAS FOUND DEAD IN HER HOME FROM A DRUG OVERDOSE. COPS NOT SURE IF DEATH WAS RELATED TO THE COL. GIRLS OR NOT
- DAPHNE OVERDOSED
- TALK TO R. ANDERSON
- WHAT DOES F KNOW?

Anxiety ticked up with each second Rachel Anderson took to answer. I could only hope she'd provide more insight into the deaths. From Granddad's notes, I knew there was another friend in the group who was connected to all the girls but had not been around when either incident occurred. Interviews with her turned up no deeper insight on any of the girls, but Rachel Anderson was related to her and might have inside information. An unsettling thought began to take hold as I went over what I knew.

At the park, Mrs. Harris had said something had riled Granddad up before his heart attack. *Colleton Girls* had been erased from the whiteboard, and the clock had ended up in Faye's office. It was a long shot . . . but could Faye be related to Colleton?

Mrs. Anderson's voice finally echoed through the line, and I introduced myself.

"Don't know why after all this time, but I have some time before my Zumba class. My stepdaughter, Faith, grew up in Colleton, and her father doted on her, probably because her mother left them when she was young and he felt guilty. Her father and I married when she was about ten, and I noticed right off the bat that something wasn't quite right with her."

I prompted. "Something like?"

"The girl had a mean streak. And she was sneaky. She would get into things and then act like it wasn't her. You know the old saying, 'Throw the rock and hide the hand'? That was Faith. She liked to play games that would turn people against others just to see how they'd react. She thought it was the funniest thing. Tried it a few times between me and her father until I caught on and put an end to it."

"How'd you do that?" I jotted down notes as Mrs. Anderson spoke.

"I flat-out told her if she left me alone, I'd leave her alone and pretend I didn't see her causing fights when her friends came over. I didn't compete with her for her father's attention, but she would play her father against me. Initially she made life a living hell for me because at first she didn't want to share him. He was very respected and Colleton's coroner, so I wasn't about to mess up a good thing for me."

I kept my judgment to myself, glad the woman couldn't see my face.

"She finally got bored messing with me, realizing that by my being around, distracting her father, she was free to do whatever she wanted unchecked. Faith was one of those people who could twist the things you say to make you look awful. It's hard to argue against a cute, lovable girl. You know what I mean? Can never win against them."

I did know all too well.

"People bought into her little schtick. Thought she was the sweetest little thing. But I knew what she was really like when no one was watching. When she ran off, her father thought she'd been kidnapped. But I knew why she left. She ran off because she had something to do with their deaths. Probably had something to do with that Daphne girl killing herself. Sweet girl. Quiet. Wanted to be a writer or poet or something."

"What about Daphne, Mrs. Anderson?"

She didn't immediately answer, and I waited, not wanting to disrupt her free flow of information.

Mrs. Anderson lowered her voice. "At Daphne's funeral, I went to her mother to offer my condolences. Her mother was in a state. Totally gone, like she'd lost her wits from the grief. She'd mutter something about her baby hating pills and how bitter they must have tasted. It wasn't until I was home later and rethinking everything that I put two and two together to make four."

"What was it?" My words came out like a horror story with the monster around the corner about to jump. I wanted to cover my eyes but still peek through my fingers.

"I think Daphne was afraid to take pills. Some people are afraid to swallow, so they'll either cut them into manageable pieces or chew them. 'How bitter they must have tasted.' Right?"

Mrs. Anderson left the rest to me, but my mind wouldn't cooperate. It didn't want to put two and two together and question how someone would choose to take pills when they were afraid to swallow them unless they were forced.

"You know that children's poem—don't know why it's a kids' poem, seeing as how it's dark as hell. But aren't most children's fairy tales and poems and chants about death and disease? Grimms' had kids eaten, stolen, and turned into things. 'Ring around the Rosie' is about dying from an epidemic."

"What's the poem?" I asked, attempting to get Mrs. Anderson back on track and keep my impatience in check.

"'The Spider and the Fly,'" the woman said easily, as if she'd been thinking about it for a long time. "Read it, and you'll know exactly what I'm talking about."

"I know it," I said, recalling the gist of the creepy poem.

"Doesn't it make your blood run cold because it sounds like her? Asking you to be friends. Sweet-talking you. She goes on until she gets what she wants, she gets bored, or you cross her. Then *bam*. If Faith ever sets her sights on you and gets you caught up in whatever she has going on, like that poor Daphne girl and those other girls, it won't end up so well for you. That's all I'm saying. She's one coldhearted bitch."

"What happened to Faith?" I asked, unsure I believed this wild story. It was too fantastical. But it filled out the gaps from the old articles I'd found when I initially searched for the Colleton Girls.

"She ran away with some of her father's money right after she graduated high school. As for Faith's father, he spent the rest of his days looking for her. He's gone now. Maybe Daphne's mother will talk to you like she did your grandfather. I didn't speak with him myself. Didn't feel quite comfortable with Faith around and always watching, but since she's gone now . . ." She trailed off, then excused herself to sip whatever she was drinking. "How do you know of her again?"

"My granddad passed away a few weeks ago, and I came across his old case notes. He had this one, and I began reading it. Took an interest and thought I'd call around and ask if this was true. It reads like a true crime mystery."

The woman scoffed. "I'd throw that case in the garbage if I were you."

It was too little, too late for that. "Do you happen to have an old picture of Faith that you could either mail or screenshot and email? The photos I have don't seem to have her in them."

Mrs. Anderson hesitated. "What do you need that for?"

"Research. I won't put it on social or do anything with it."

Mrs. Anderson humphed before finally coming around to the notion. "Don't put it up on the internet or superimpose her face on anything improper. Faith may not be right, but she's still my husband's child."

I promised, walking over to Granddad's desk, where the darkened computer awaited me. I called out my email address to Mrs. Anderson as I turned it on. I repeated the address twice more until she got it right.

"Let me offer you a piece of unsolicited advice. Take it or leave it, because I don't want you ending up like any of those girls."

It was too late for that.

"I hear you talking on this call, asking these questions, and it sounds to me a lot like you're getting swept up into something that may not end up well for you," Mrs. Anderson said, and a knot formed in my chest and started to grow.

I looked around the four corners of the room. As if the woman could see me sitting in Granddad's chair he refused to upgrade (along with his phone or computer) with the yellow stuffing coming out of the torn pleather seat.

"Just saying. Now check your email."

She disconnected before I had a chance to remind her that she didn't know me from a hole in the wall. She didn't. I snorted, my head shaking in incredulity at her assumptions. Me, obsessed with Faith Anderson? Getting sucked into that spider-and-fly shit Mrs. Anderson kept trying to compare her stepdaughter to? It all sounded like a movie that should be on Lifetime.

Obsessed. I sucked my teeth, pulling up the forum. *As if.*

I ignored the little voice in the back of my mind: the one that sounded too much like Angela Brodie; the one that said, "But Jac, you just might be."

37

Gotchu911: Her mom called her a psycho? Well damn.

I typed in the chat room, flexing my muscles of deduction: Stepmother. But basically.

After what I watched her do to Mia, all bets were on *hell yeah.* If Faith is who I'm thinking, could she be a serial killer?

PI Guy 39: Unlikely. From SrD's Colleton notes you told us about and ur call w/ step-mom, ur looking at a sociopath.

JrD: But they can be serial killers too

Gotchu911: Yeah but I don't like this lady for one. She likes to screw with ppl, sure. But if she kills, it's to either hide, to get her way, or to clear a way to whatever she wants, not bc she's compelled to kill. A difference.

No, definitely both, I concluded, blowing out a frustrated breath as I slouched into the chair. "To either hide, to get her way, or to clear a way," I repeated, my mind spinning. Of course. If I thought about all the deaths linked to her, they all fell in one of those categories.

> GirlFriday022: Have any of you geniuses considered the most blaring coincidence?

A stream of question marks and one thinking emoji followed.

> GirlFriday022: The initials.

I shot up from my seat, the chair spinning from the sudden move. She wouldn't. Needing to see GirlFriday022's response actually written out to even begin to wrap my head around it, I scribbled on a scrap piece of paper. I could have kicked myself for not making the blaringly obvious connection the moment I'd seen Faith Anderson's name. I wish I'd just thought all this through in the beginning, putting all the puzzle pieces together before showing my hand to Faye or approaching Chief Linwood with accusations I couldn't back up.

Line 'em up before you take 'em down, Granddad used to say.

No way Faye could be that—

> PI Guy 39: Stupid. No way. No way. 😒 Too obvi

> BlueLineCopper: It's audacious. In my years on the beat working confidence crimes, the easiest way to not confuse aliases is to use various iterations of your real name. Most ppl want to keep a piece of who they used to be.

> PI Guy 39: Which is whyyyy FA is a socio. And she thinks she's smarter than everyone and can manipulate anyone. Bet Brook Haven Faye never thought anyone would put it together that she's Colleton

FA. That's both genius and insulting as hell. She thinks you're an idiot JrD.

I paced in front of the blue light of the illuminated screen as the messages rolled, unable to sit still, the realization going over and over in my mind. Brook Haven's Faye was Colleton's Faith.

Somehow, she'd eventually found her way, thousands of miles and decades between them, back to my grandfather, who had only been in Colleton on consult as a favor but had never believed the story she'd told.

I grabbed Granddad's file, shifting through the loose pages until I found his latest notes on letterhead from a year ago. My finger scrolled down the list of his sporadic scribbles I'd been too careless to pay attention to earlier. So stupid, Jac. I could practically hear Granddad telling me.

**Off record and in the heat of anger I told her when she was ready, she should look me up. Killers like her always circle back to tie up loose ends.*

FA = FA w/ new face???

And then: *I am the loose ends.*

I took my phone, scrolling through all the voicemail messages, finally coming to Granddad's number and the last time he called, realizing it was the night of his heart attack. My mouth ran dry as I pulled his message up and, with trembling fingers, pressed the play button. My heartbeat palpated as his crackly voice filled the room and I finally listened.

I think . . . think I screwed up real bad.

I dropped the phone, guilt swallowing me whole. All there. It was all there, and I'd never listened. I'd never paid attention. Granddad had realized and might have tried to lay a trap for her. Not only had Faye underestimated the old, nosy cop from twenty years ago, but the cop had underestimated her as well.

My eyes went to the whiteboard where I'd retraced *Colleton.* Since then, I had added Faye Arden's name and beneath it everything I suspected about her, whether or not my suspicions were yet proved:

Murder Manor ➡ *Nightmare*

Granddad ➡ *pacer fried by Taser—why??*

Beneath Faye's name, I added: *Faith Anderson* ➡ *Faye Arden—multiple aliases, runs cons, plastic surgery, sociopath*

I surveyed the board, my face crumpling into disappointment. It was horrible. No rhyme or reason and looked nothing like the evidence boards I saw on TV or when Granddad had made them. I could go to Michaels in town for some red yarn and tie things together. Maybe then the board would make more sense, but now it looked a hot mess. I could practically hear Granddad behind me, hand on the hip that had troubled him ever since his hip replacement, his face scrunched in confusion, eyeing his precious whiteboard in disgust.

"Junior Dick, what the hell is this shit you put on my goddamn board?"

BlueLineCopper: Honestly the socios are the worst kind. Serials kill bc it is their disability or it's something they can't help.

PI Guy 39: It ain't a disability and you can't psychatize every damn thing. Some ppl are just plain evil.

Gotchu911: Here PG goes. 🙄 Psychatize . . . is that a word?

PI Guy 39: Expand your vocabulary.

Gotchu911: I bet u were the star student in class. Oooookay. 👍🙄

PI Guy 39: 🖕

Gotchu911, BlueLineCopper: 😂

GirlFriday022: So what are you gonna do, JrD?

I ignored the ongoing forum banter. If it were two weeks prior and I wasn't holed up at Granddad's waiting on pins and needles for the chief to contact me with the results of the DNA test on the blood found in my trunk, I might have joined in the poll about which Hollywood celebrity was a psycho or socio.

I pulled up my inbox on my phone while suppressing the urge to yelp when I saw a blue dot next to my newest email with an attachment from Mrs. Anderson. I clicked on the AOL link, ignoring the warning against opening attachments from unknown email senders—or the fact that there still were AOL email users.

With Granddad's Wi-Fi, it took longer than my impatience could tolerate to open and configure the grainy photo. But then it did.

My mouth dropped open, but nothing came out.

It was one thing to say someone was a killer.

It was an entirely different thing when you were looking into the eyes of one.

Because, despite the probable plastic surgery Faith had had—I was pretty sure Faith had had—she wouldn't have been able to change the eyes. Or the look in them.

Proof was an elusive beast to me, but my heart was pounding and my hands shaking as I looked at the image and connections began to *plink* in my piggy bank of clues. I was fairly certain that Faith Anderson was not dead and had once been Faye Arden.

And somehow, she'd found her way back to my grandfather, the investigator, called in as a favor, who hadn't believed the tale she'd spun. He'd given her the invitation . . . he had been the spider and she the fly that time. And she'd come calling when she was ready to tie up her loose ends from Colleton.

"I did it, Granddad," I barely managed to say, wiping at wet eyes, the loss of my grandfather hitting me unexpectedly and rendering me inconsolable. "We did it."

The magnitude of what I might be up against began to dawn on me. Faye Arden was a stone-blooded killer, with possibly four other deaths attached to her that I knew of.

Consider all the probabilities, and then pick one.

Granddad had given her an invitation . . . he thought he was the spider and she the fly, but she bided her time, came calling, and flipped the script to tie up her loose ends from Colleton. The old man hadn't been ready for her. But maybe I could be.

I sat at the keyboard again, sending a question to the group.

TechGirl99, who'd just logged in and was catching up with likes when I sent my last question, replied.

> Just got a new subscription w/ PimEyes. DM me the pic and a recent. Let's see what matches up.

38

The next day, I was on the clock, counting down, trying to keep myself busy and my mind off my troubles with the law. If the blood ended up being Conrad's, or anyone's, I would be arrested and arraigned. There was no more time for me. I'd have to make a move, but what? And how? After what went down with Mama and that Carl, even though I'd brought him here with my stupid email and opened up a new can of worms I didn't even want to think about right now, I couldn't go to them. I couldn't go to my friends either. After Mia, I now knew it wasn't safe.

Plus, neither of them was in the position to help. Patrick was right. Sawyer worked for the department, and it was enough, my getting Mrs. Anderson's phone number from her. And Nick . . . my heart double flipped, and a bout of nausea came on. Nick was going to be Faye's stepson. She'd been a part of their family—she even cared about him in an odd territorial way—for so long. How could I ask him to basically destroy his father's chance at happiness?

Everything I thought I knew about myself, about my family, had gone down the drain. I finally had the evidence Granddad had waited so long to confirm. Now, I had information that would make Chief Linwood give Faye a second look. Maybe even search Moor Manor for Mia's body.

The next dose of reality was a blow, making me sink into the worn couch with the springs that stabbed you and made it hard to sit comfortably. But I didn't feel the springs, even though I'd sat down hard. My brain waved a glaring red stop sign.

How was I about to tell anyone anything when I was currently the person of interest in the disappearance of my ex-boyfriend?

And how could I make sure that this time, when I went to the cops with Granddad's folder and what I'd learned, the chief would listen and do something and not allow Faye to spin her way out of it?

I moved back to the desk to keep an eye on the forum. I checked the time on my phone repeatedly, waiting to see if TechGirl99 had found a match between the old photo of Faith and a recent image I'd found of Faye from a story that had run in the *Charleston City Paper* about the Manor's upcoming opening and the charity Faye and Mama had held.

The chat had continued without me, everyone chiming in with the debate or discussing other things. I caught one question meant for me.

> Mighty_Judge: Did you know if SrD ever did what I suggested and checked the clock? It's important for a reason.

The clock . . . my eyes flicked to the mantel.

> Mrs. CrimeofPassion: Not trying to naysay but why couldn't SrD recognize her? She's lived there 2 yrs., right? Why didn't she go after him right away?

Fair point. But according to the stream of responses blasting Mrs. Crime for her lack of imagination, the kind of killers in it for the long haul took their time and got to know their victim. They didn't want to be caught.

> Mighty_Judge: We talked about this the other day. Go back to the newbies chat.

I read it, but my mind wasn't in it. It was over there, with the clock.

According to one of Granddad's case notes, Daphne's mother had gifted him the clock, saying it was Daphne's favorite thing and that she tinkered with it often. At first, I just thought it was a comfort item for her. But now that Armchair Guy had brought it up, had Granddad checked it?

Curiosity guided me to the mantel, where I looked at the clock that no longer told time. I picked it up, studying it. I turned it every which way. I shook it, listening for anything loose. Nothing.

I examined the seams. I pulled. I pushed. There was nothing. Why did Daphne's mother think it would help Granddad in the case?

I was so intent on the clock that when the computer dinged a notification, reverberating in the silent room, I startled, and the clock slipped from my hands.

"Oh no!" I lunged, trying to catch it before it hit the ground, but my fingers just barely grazed the smooth surface as it crashed to the floor. I dropped to the floor after it, praying I hadn't broken it.

When I picked it up, grimacing as I did, I jostled it. Something inside rattled, and my stomach dropped.

"Shit!" I stared at the crack that had formed in the seam at the bottom of the handle. It had survived all these years, just to have me break it in a matter of weeks.

I took it to the desk and plopped hard into the chair, defeated. I'd have to go to Walmart and get some superglue. See if I could glue it back together.

I shook it, and whatever piece had broken off clinked against the inner walls. Not clinked, I thought. Clunked. Something heavier.

The forum's direct message pinged. I tapped the notification box, and TechGirl99's message popped up.

Same girl.

She included a file, and when I clicked it, Faye's face popped up. Not Faye's—Faith's. Both. It took me a second longer to realize that one picture was superimposed on the other. Despite any reconstructive surgery Faye could've had done and that she was twenty years older than the high school version of herself, Armchair Dudette had pinpointed the areas on her face where the two photos matched. Tiny white dots and lines dissected the photo and intersected at the points of match. I inhaled.

The eyes—the cold look of knowing, of calculation—were the same in both photos.

What would Chief Linwood say now if I showed him this?

I exhaled. Probably that I should leave the policing to the police, little girl.

My phone rang, and I ignored it, my mind on the message from Armchair Dudette. I wanted to stop time, take a moment to breathe, because everything was coming in fast, all at once, with no time to pause, let alone process.

I groped along on the desk for the phone and pressed the green circle to accept the call.

I turned the clock so the barrel faced me, the piece inside clanging around. The only bullet it held was the picture of two shiny bullets on the clock's face. Below them was the tagline: *One Shot, One Kill.*

"I'm good. You don't have to keep checking in."

I wasn't ready to divulge any information yet. This time I had to play it right. The countdown was on for Faith.

But for me, the clock (pun intended) had just run out.

Sawyer said, "Just heard from the tech doing me a favor that the blood results came in."

I pulled at the seam slightly, closing an eye to peer in. Something dark was in there.

"What does it say?" I asked, but her tone gave me all the answers I needed. Story of my life. From highs to lows. I used a letter opener to dig into the opening, widening the gap. Definitely something in there. And small.

"It's a match," she said straight. "It's confirmed to be Conrad's blood in your trunk. The chief will get the results tomorrow morning, and then . . ." She trailed off, unable to continue. Sawyer's breath caught, and the phone rustled as she tried to hide her crying.

I paused, allowing Sawyer's words to sink in. Tomorrow, they might come for me. I'd have to go back home because I refused to be arrested in my last refuge.

I shook the clock downward, and a small black mini flash drive dropped out.

Shiiiiiiit. My heart thumped. Thumped again.

"What are you going to do, Jac? There's no body, so even with blood, the case is still circumstantial. They can still pick you up whenever they want. Maybe Nick can help?" Sawyer rambled, talking more to herself than me. "No, I think he's on his way back from Charleston for business for Mayor Tate, but I'm sure Nick knows someone good. You need someone there with you."

I didn't bother telling her Mama had already called my cousin, and he'd already texted me: And I thought I was the criminal mind. Damn girl! I got you though.

A shroud of calm settled over me, and I released all my anxiety, all the insecurity that had been strangling me my entire time here. The way forward was so clear. It was much easier to focus on other people's problems than to face my tomorrow.

"Understood." I sounded alien. Like I was there but not. My MacBook and bag were on the coffee table. I went over with the drive, anticipation growing as each second ticked by. I sat on the worn brown couch and fished out a travel-size computer dock, then plugged it into my MacBook. From there, I inserted the drive and waited for my computer to accept the new device.

There was one Word document on the drive, and I clicked it.

39
"HAVE A LITTLE FAITH," BY DAPHNE FRANKLIN

Colleton, Nevada, 2001

Las Vegas, Sin City, the City of Lights, was a city of many names, a place of dreams and hopes and aspirations. It had a famous line, "Whatever happens in Vegas, stays in Vegas."

It was a line she loved because behind all the glitz and glamor, Vegas was a place people went to get into some shit.

And Faith Anderson loved to get into some shit.

Out of all the names the city was called, Sin City was her favorite. There was a wealth of possibilities in that one word . . . "sin." It was alluring. Sexy. Tricky. Deadly.

She felt a kinship to the city, not because she was born and raised just outside of it, but because it was just like her. Beautiful and glittery on the outside. A promise of a good time and good fortune. But beneath, under the pretty packaging, the city was complete sin.

Like her.

It was ugly and hateful and could kill. Like her.

Faith knew this young, that she was different. The beautiful brunette with eyes the color of wheat, who made heads turn, young and old, any gender or none, was cold, hollow, and bored on the inside. Inside, she was deadly, and nothing was ever enough.

She held on to that thought, always attempting to go for bigger and better ways to get warm inside, fill that bottomless pit, drive away the endless boredom. And things did for a little bit. Sex with kids her age. Then sex with people not her age. Sex with people who had other people, and then threatening to tell but asking for nothing. Just leaving them spinning on a thread, caught up in her snare. That was fun. Still fun. But it was not enough. Sex and threats, mindfucks and fear, though enjoyable in every aspect, did not make her feel whole anymore. Faith wanted more.

In her junior year, she decided she was too big for Vegas. It couldn't hold her. And she planned to leave once she'd graduated. She planned to leave as soon as she crossed the stage, accepted her diploma, shook hands with all the teachers and admin who'd bored her to death during her high school career, walked down the steps of the stage, and escaped the suburbs of Sin City.

She had dubbed them the Fickle Four throughout high school, even though she was the fifth member. She, for years, screwed with them every chance she got behind their backs while smiling in their faces and making them think she was their best friend. Faith's wait time was scary long when she set her sights on someone or something she wanted. She liked to take her time with people. Liked to dig in deep and find out what they wanted the most, then take it for herself or destroy them.

When the Fickle Four unknowingly strayed into her line of fire, they were already dead meat. They had irritated her. Bethany, the lead, was studious and head cheerleader. Then, in her senior year, Bethany surpassed Faith and moved into the number one spot in their class. Faith didn't like that. She was second to no one, had never been second to anyone, and she wasn't going to start now. Just ask her stepmother.

So it was clear to Faith that Bethany had to go. And because Abby, Caitlyn, and Joss were on Bethany's team, because they were insipid creatures who were barely capable of independent thought and looked down on kids who were different than them, they had to go too.

But Faith wasn't going to get her hands dirty. The fun in this place of sin was planting the seeds and moving others around like chess pieces to do what she wanted. The fun would be to mastermind everything and see if she could get someone else to do the ultimate thing and kill. She'd let them take the heat, then slip away and melt into the world. Find a new life, and do it all over again at Faith's pleasure.

The summer before senior year, Faith quite literally bumped into Daphne Franklin. Daphne was quiet, relatively new, having moved to Colleton over the summer. She'd already had a run-in with Bethany and her crew at the pool when Bethany's boyfriend, Raul, paid a little too much attention to the strange new girl.

Faith watched them from her seat as she basked in the sun. She watched Bethany take her anger out on the innocent girl rather than on the one who really was the cheating culprit. The boyfriend. From that moment, during summer at the pool, Daphne became Bethany's target. And Bethany became Faith's.

Don't get it wrong. Faith didn't take Daphne under her wing, help build her confidence, spruce up her style, or stay by Daphne's side because she was some champion for the unpopular. Faith wasn't going after Bethany to teach her a lesson in women's empowerment and all that shit. Faith didn't give a damn about any of it. She made Daphne a tool to eliminate the girl who always made Faith feel second-rate.

Over the course of the year, Faith grew Daphne's confidence so much that she eventually convinced Daphne to go after Bethany's boyfriend herself.

"I mean," Faith said, "since Raul can't seem to leave you alone, and since you're already being blamed for his wandering eye, you might as well get some fun out of it, don't you think?"

Daphne wasn't sure. "I mean, he is gorgeous, but he'd never be into me."

"But don't you want to know what he's like?" Faith asked. "Don't you want to know how he tastes?"

Faith knew. But there was no point in letting anyone know about that.

"Do it in secret," Faith told her in Faith's large bedroom, where Daphne sat on the stool in front of Faith's vanity mirror with Faith behind her, tilting Daphne's head this way and that to see how well the makeup came out. Faith leaned over until their heads were side by side; their reflections (one wide eyed and worried, the other most assured) stared back at them.

"What do you mean, secret?" Daphne asked.

"I mean have Raul in secret. Just you and him. Bethany doesn't have to know. It'll be delicious. You kill two birds with one stone, as my dad always says. It's the perfect payback for all the shit Bethany's put you through."

"But you're like her best friend. You hang with her and the others all the time."

"Only because my dad golfs with hers, and we grew up together. I have to be her friend. But I hate how she treats people." The lies slipped from Faith like raindrops coming down harder and harder. "I tell her all the time to leave you alone. That it's Raul she should be pissed at. But I think she's dickmatized. He must be really good."

Daphne covered her face with her hand, giggling behind it. Her face flushed. "Faith! Oh my god!" She looked around like Faith's dad or stepmother would walk in at any moment. They would not. They knew better than anyone else how much Faith valued her privacy, and her room was most certainly off limits.

Faith pulled Daphne's hand from her reddened face, kissing her on her cheek. "Take him, Daphne, and enjoy it."

"What if I can't?"

"You gotta have some faith, girl." And then she laughed and laughed.

~

Faith's plan worked perfectly. Daphne and Raul were screwing every chance they got, right under Bethany's perfect upturned nose. Faith was adding fuel to the fire, implying that Daphne was out to push Bethany out and take

Raul for herself. But it didn't matter because graduation was coming up and she and Bethany would go to Harvard, just like they'd always planned.

Everything was coming to a boiling point, and Faith sat back, enjoying the show. The angst from all sides infusing her with such entertainment, she found pleasure in nothing else. But then college offers began rolling in, and Bethany called Faith with news Faith couldn't control.

"I got in! I'm in Harvard! Check your mail. What did they say?"

Faith had gotten their answer. She hadn't been accepted. Bethany was, yet again, always fucking first. Faith couldn't allow that. Even if Raul broke Bethany the Saint's heart, in a matter of months she would fly off to Massachusetts, and Faith would be left with nothing but second choices. It was time for a big finish to all of this shit.

"Are you sure he took photos?" Daphne asked between wails a week later. "Are you sure Raul would do that?"

Faith looked heartbroken. "I would never lie," she lied. "I am so sorry. I wouldn't have believed it myself if I hadn't heard Raul and Bethany talking about sending it out."

The tears refreshed. "But why? Why would he do that? I thought . . . I thought . . ."

"Love you?" Faith finished. "Is that what he told you?"

Daphne nodded, still unable to speak.

Faith patted her back. "What was it like, when he said it?"

"It was beautiful," Daphne sobbed. "It came out of the blue. We weren't even doing anything. Homework. And he just said it. He said he was going to tell Bethany that it was over between them."

But the only thing Faith heard was that he'd said he loved Daphne, and it wasn't during sex either. Those were the only times she'd ever heard anyone utter those hollow words to her.

They loved her because she screwed them, Raul included. But apparently, he was capable of loving someone with no sex involved. Someone like Daphne. What did he see in her that he hadn't seen in Faith? Faith obsessed over that question for days after she and Daphne had made the plan to stop Bethany before the photos got out.

"If you confront him first, he might send it as payback," Faith said. "Bethany surely would. So you have to stop her. Teach her a lesson not to fuck with you ever again. Teach them both a lesson because they've been planning to make you look like a complete idiot all of senior year."

Daphne agreed.

A week later, two months before graduation, Daphne and Faith waited outside of Bethany's house. Bethany's parents had gone on a weekend trip, and Faith had conveniently suggested Bethany have a sleepover. One big hurrah before graduation and their high school lives ended. Bethany agreed.

They partied hard. Raul and his friends came over, and they partied even harder, drinking, smoking weed, sex, everything. To Faith's surprise, Raul did nothing with Bethany, who was already three-sheets-to-the-wind kind of drunk and passed out on the living room couch. Eventually Raul's friends trickled out and left for home. Bethany's friends dropped one by one until it was only Raul and Faith left. Faith pretended to be sick, too sick to stay over. She wanted to go home, which was the next street over. Raul, being so kind, offered to take her and did, but not before Faith left the back door open.

When Raul drove off, Faith went in, greeted her stepmother, who was heading to bed, and went to her room, still pretending to be sick. When her father and stepmother were asleep, Faith sneaked back out through her bedroom window, which didn't have the alarm probes on it like the doors and windows on the first floor.

Daphne was waiting for her around the corner, wearing all black like Faith had instructed, a match to Faith. Together they went back to Bethany's home. They went in and to the garage, where Bethany's SUV was.

Daphne got into the driver's seat and turned the car on. "We shouldn't have the car on with the garage door closed," Daphne rushed out, her voice trembling. "It can like . . . kill."

Exactly my point, Faith thought, letting her breath out low and slow to release her annoyance. Ever since Daphne said Raul had told her he loved her, Faith could barely stand to be around her. She kept thinking, What does she, like Bethany, have that I do not?

Faith couldn't understand it. She didn't want Raul in the slightest. She found him to be a big uncouth ogre, and apparently lovesick. But not for her. She didn't like that. The way to hurt Raul, for not loving her, though she didn't want him to, or maybe she did, was to take from him the thing he did love . . .

Faith's eyes zeroed in on Daphne.

Luckily Daphne couldn't see her roll her eyes. "Don't worry. I'll turn the engine off but leave the ignition on so that way the battery runs out and Bethany will be basically stranded until her parents come home. She'll have to cab it anywhere she wants to go or just stay home. It'll fuck up her whole weekend."

"And the pictures of me and Raul?"

"I saw the camera in her bedroom. We gotta be quick though in case someone shows up. Head up the stairs to your right. Don't touch anything but the camera. Bring it out. I'm right behind you once I turn the car off."

Faith directed Daphne to the living room where the girls slept like the dead. Daphne would enter Bethany's room and find the small digital camera on the desk, the camera Faith had purchased at a CVS one town over and left there during the party. It was the camera she'd taken various pictures of Raul and Daphne on without their knowing. Only she never had any intention of distributing the photos. *That* would be disgusting, and even Faith had lines she would not cross.

Daphne hesitated only a second, casting a look at the headlights illuminating the large garage and the engine idling.

"You're turning it off, right?"

Faith made like she was heading around to the driver's side. "Right now." Another second and Daphne finally began to move her feet.

Faith slid into the SUV, humming quietly. From driver's ed class, she remembered it only took a few seconds for carbon monoxide to fill the garage, but Faith felt she could help it along for extra measure. She pushed the gas pedal a few times, hearing the engine gun, hoping it wasn't loud enough to alert Daphne. Then she got out, checking to make sure there were no signs of her or Daphne.

Faith entered the kitchen, leaving the door cracked.

She pursed her lips, locking her hands behind her back like she was some security guard on patrol as she checked the living room, right off the kitchen. The girls still slept. The others were collateral. Bethany was who she wanted. For getting into Harvard when Faith had not. For being first in class when it should have been Faith. For nothing at all. Faith tapped the door open more with her foot.

She didn't need to go upstairs because Daphne bounded down the stairs, raising the camera in her hand in victory.

"Found it," she nearly sang. Having the planted photos in hand was like a load was off her shoulders. The lucky girl.

Faith mimicked Daphne's buoyant smile. The girl looked quite pretty in this moment. It was almost regrettable how things would play out for her.

"We should go."

Daphne nodded. "Yeah. Okay."

"All right then."

Faith ushered Daphne past the door leading to the garage, talking all the while, hoping Daphne wouldn't hear the car running. Daphne sniffed, her steps slowing.

Faith pushed her out the door to the backyard. "Do you smell gas?"

"Probably from when we turned the car on initially."

Faith locked the knob from the inside, shutting the door behind them. They moved in the shadows, making their way out of the backyard. When they were safely down the street, Faith stopped, Daphne colliding with her back. Faith gritted her teeth, then plastered on a winning smile and turned to her friend.

"You don't know what you've done for me, Faith," Daphne said. She looked at Faith with so much gratitude and relief that it made Faith's eye tic. It wasn't remorse she was feeling. She wasn't sure what.

"Delete them at home, then get rid of the camera. And say nothing to Raul, okay? Better he thinks he has something and realizes it's gone than you lose your upper hand." Faith held Daphne's shoulders, ensuring the girl was paying attention.

Daphne nodded like a bobblehead. "I will. Thank you."

Faith waved her off, watching the girl leave to where she'd parked her car and drive off. "I think I should be thanking you."

~

The bodies were found late the following afternoon by the housekeeper with the car still running.

~

The funerals happened. Graduation happened, though the affair was muted and somber. The first in class still went to Bethany, which Faith hadn't accounted for. She should have thought about that, that the admin wouldn't put someone else in her place, memorializing it and her. Oh well, Faith still got to give the address. And she talked about Bethany, Abby, and Joss and how great their loss was. It was beautiful. Faith's best work, she'd say. At least there would be no Harvard. Faith wasn't the one left behind. She was doing the leaving. All in due time.

But there was still a loose thread to tie up. Daphne had been scarce since learning of the Colleton deaths. Faith had tried reaching out. Had gone to her house, but her mother said she wasn't home, even though Faith knew she was. She saw Daphne less and less. She didn't see Daphne at graduation at all.

It was unfortunate. Faith couldn't leave town until she knew what was up with Daphne. She'd actually forgiven Daphne for that whole Raul-loving-her fiasco. Faith was going to let Daphne be. But now she couldn't. Not with Daphne giving her the silent treatment, acting as if Faith had the bubonic plague.

With graduation over and the town still reeling from the loss, Faith paid Daphne a visit one night when Daphne was home alone, her mother having gone to work. Faith had taken a bus, then walked the rest of the way. Her parents thought she'd gone to bed early, depressed and heartbroken over Bethany's death. They didn't know that in Faith's room, she was listening to MTV and BET and practicing all the latest dance moves that she'd be able to perform when she finally left for the East Coast and began to live her new life.

Daphne opened the door. The shock on her face, how it morphed into unadulterated fear, was nearly as good to Faith as an orgasm. Faith smiled, then switched to sadness, her face crumpling as she smashed it in her hands and cried.

"I don't know what to do! I can't believe this has all happened."

Faith called upon her acting skills, learned from the classes her mother had made her take before skipping out on her and her father when she was ten. The selfish bitch. She almost hyperventilated. She needed to get inside the house. It was the only way she would get clear of this damned town.

Finally, after what seemed like an eternity, Daphne deflated and took a few steps backward. "Come on."

"Really?" Faith squeaked pitifully, feigning hesitation.

She peeked through her splayed fingers on her face, appearing as innocent and harmless as possible. Daphne's expression was a world of confusion. Wariness, fear, exhaustion. She looked horrible, gaunt, like she wasn't eating. Her blonde hair was greasy and matted. And her once-pristine face was at war with acne. Meanwhile, Faith ate like three grown men and her skin glowed like the sun's rays. One needed sunglasses to gaze upon her greatness.

Faith shuffled in, closing the door behind her. She wiped at her face, sniffling. She looked around the small, simple house. It smelled like old fried food, and Faith fought the urge to gag and curl her lips in distaste. She'd never been in here in the year that she'd known Daphne. Now that she was inside, she realized she'd made the right choice.

She noted the mismatched furniture. The TV playing in the background, Comedy Central, and the tiny dinner table with two chairs. Just Daphne and her mom. She smiled. Too easy.

"Are you okay?" Faith asked haltingly. "You haven't been returning my calls. Isn't what happened horrible? I still can't believe it. I can barely eat or sleep. The memorial. Their parents. Raul. Everyone is destroyed over this, Daphne."

Daphne looked at her, unsure what to say, what to do. "You said we were draining the battery. You said that was *all* we were going to do."

"I went there to help you out, Daphne. We went there to keep those pictures from getting out. Maybe one of them woke up when we left and thought she turned the car off but turned it all the way on. Who knows? They were so drunk and high."

Daphne's hands balled at her sides, her face reddening. "You let the engine run. You meant for them to die."

Faith ran a hand over her face. "But you turned the car on, Daphne." It came out calmly. She was in now, no need to continue to ham it up.

"I—I—I— You!" Daphne stuttered. Her eyes bulged, and cords in her neck strained against her throat.

"They're gone, Daphne, okay? Gone. It's too late for them. Tragic and all that shit." Her hand fluttered in the air. "But it happens. You're alive. You have free access to Raul. Life can be good."

Daphne gawked, open mouthed, at Faith, clutching her stomach as if Faith had punched her. "Are you serious? I can't . . . we can't . . . there's no way Raul and I can be together after this."

Faith's eyebrows rose. "Oh, then that is tragic." She puckered her lips. "So what do you want to do, Daphne?"

Faith waited for the sniveling girl to say what she knew Daphne would say.

"We need to tell. We need to admit we did it. That we played a horrible trick, and it went wrong."

Faith nodded. "They'd throw us in prison. That's premeditated murder, Daphne. Are you ready for that?" Faith's head tilted to the side.

"It's what we deserve, Faith. Whatever Bethany and Raul did. The teasing, the pictures, it wasn't worth her life. Her friends didn't even have anything to do with it. We totally fucked up! Shit!"

"Imagine that." Faith sighed. She reached around her back and pulled from her waistband a long hunting knife. It was from her dad's arsenal. Looked like the one from that movie her dad liked so much, *Crocodile Dundee*. She showed it to Daphne, who shrank back, her eyes glued to the glinting metal.

"We can do this the easy way, or the hard. Your choice."

"What? What? What?" She took steps back with each question, and for every step, Faith stepped forward.

"The easy way is for you to do it. Nice and neat. Your mom will be crushed. But eventually it'll ease to a dull ache. The hard way." Faith waggled the knife in Daphne's face. "The hard way is if I gut you like a fish. And believe me, I will do that. If I have to do it the hard way, your mom will come home, see your insides spread on the outside."

Daphne backed down the hall with Faith following, in lockstep, methodically.

"You can't. You couldn't. We're friends. You helped me. We're . . . friends."

Faith continued as if she hadn't heard a word. "And when your mom gets home and sees you and gets all worked up at the sight of you, then I will pop out. And I will kill her too."

Daphne was in her bedroom, having instinctually gone into her safe space. The back of her legs hit the bed, and she tumbled backward onto it, bouncing slightly from the impact.

Faith took a quick look around. The room was barely decorated. The only thing there was an ornament, a handgun with an analog clock built into the center of it. It was abhorrent.

Faith asked incredulously, "What the fuck?"

Daphne didn't comprehend. "You wouldn't kill me."

Faith made a face.

"Wouldn't I? Why do you think Bethany and her girls are dead? Does it look like I give a damn? I don't. And I won't over you and your mom. Believe me when I say this. I will kill you horribly. And then I will wait until your mom gets home and cut her throat."

Daphne sat down hard on her bed. "But if you take the easy way, then I'll leave your mother alone. And you will be at peace, since you can't live with the guilt of the deaths of the Fickles hanging over your head like a guillotine, swinging and swinging until—" Faith pantomimed the knife going across her neck. She stuck her tongue out the corner of her mouth, half closing her eyes like the dead.

"Save your mom, Daphne," Faith said. "Save yourself too."

Daphne was in such shock, she couldn't cry or say a word. She couldn't think, except that guillotines didn't swing. But she wasn't about to tell Faith that.

Daphne couldn't do much of anything else but stare at the girl who she'd once called a friend. Now, she saw Faith as she truly was, for the first time, and Daphne hoped one day, they'd take a look inside her most treasured clock.

To learn why Daphne had chosen *the easy way*.

The End

For all of them and for me

40

Once again, my plan wasn't entirely formulated, but that was okay. I was the play-it-by-ear kind of girl. I tidied up the house and signed off the forum after telling them good night. They didn't know anything about Conrad or that I was now a suspect. They'd find all of that out in the news, so a few more hours of them liking Senior Dick's granddaughter would be a blessing to me.

I put the gun clock back on the mantel and the flash drive and Colleton folder in the safe. If I failed, Faye would return to the cabin to get rid of the clock, but at least it wouldn't have the note. If I'd had enough time, I would have mailed it. Or maybe told Patrick or Sawyer to take it. I couldn't say anything to them now because that would alert them, and I didn't need that.

When I was satisfied that everything had been put away and I'd left the house neat and presentable, I closed the door behind me and began my journey through the woods.

~

I was halfway through the forest to Murder Manor with a half-cocked plan. I had to stay on brand, act out, do the most to get Faye to admit who she was. I thought it was what she wanted. I thought it was why she'd left Granddad alone for so many years, coming back to him when she was at a level where she felt she could take him. And then waiting another two years to establish herself in this town, one as closely knit as hers had been, maybe more. She liked playing with people, making them think she was a shining star, when truly, she was . . . unbelievable.

But if I was going to play Faye's game, she would need to know I was coming. She'd need to think I was coming to beg because I needed something that only she could give me. Peace. My name back. My town back. Maybe my freedom, because I knew without a shadow of a doubt that Faye had killed Conrad just to frame me, to tighten her control over me so I'd always be under her thumb. I'd bet she even had a way to exonerate me. I'd be the willing fly, entering her lair to get her to admit everything she'd done by laying out all the facts, and I'd record it. It was simple. It was stupid. It was all I could think of on the spot.

I pulled my phone from my back pocket as I trudged through the woods, making my way from Granddad's property onto the Manor's. Soon, I'd reach the fork in the road: one a shortcut leading to the bluff, where I would not go, and the other leading to the Manor. I stopped to do two things because it wasn't smart to walk and text in the woods at night.

The first was to send a text to my newest family member—which was weird to say—asking him not to blow up my mother's world and to cut her some slack for me. I added that it was nice to meet him, though I wasn't yet sure how much I meant that. I left his immediate response unread.

The second was a call to my sister. "Pen," I said when I heard her on the other end.

"Jac! Are you okay?" The concern in Pen's voice was evident, making my heart swell and forming a knot in my throat. It was all I could do to keep from breaking down in the middle of the woods, where the Caretaker could snatch me up and make me his fifteenth victim.

"I'm . . . good," I answered. "Mama okay?"

"She's good. Hey!" Her voice went high as she greeted someone in the distance.

I could hear Mama beside her and Pen's breath as she huffed.

I frowned. "Where are you?"

"Where are you? Mama got a call from Faye saying she saw you on her property, and she was going to call the cops unless we came to get you. What are you doing here, Jac?" Her voice went out, the phone rubbing against a fabric of some sort.

A scene began to form in my mind. Mama and Pen getting a frantic call from Faye about me coming after her. They'd believe her, thinking I'd lost it after all this mess with her, and especially after Conrad. The two of them would come running to keep any more police from becoming involved. They'd run unknowingly right into the spider's parlor.

Pen said, "Tell me where you are, and I'll get you. Mama is already— Hi, Faye. Where do you think you saw her?"

A woman in the background, her response unintelligible, answered back.

"What's happening?" I asked, my panic rising, terror taking over.

Something heavy thudded once and then again. Pen didn't answer. Someone screamed, the noise cutting me to my marrow, and I knew it was Mama. I stopped, bending over to heave, nausea welling up and vomit following.

There were sounds of struggle and of confusion, whimpers—whose I couldn't discern. I did an about-face, trying to determine the fastest way to the Manor.

I looked at the screen. We were still connected. Hang up and call the cops? Would they even believe me this time?

"Pen," I said into the phone, trying to get my voice to carry over the noise, but it only bounced around the trees and back at me. "Mama! Someone say something! Where's my family?"

In the background someone was crying. Someone was asking about me. Someone was walking, their footsteps clicking closer and closer, louder and louder, until the noise stopped.

She sang in my ear. "Hi there, Jac."

I was dunked in a vat of nitrogen, freezing my entire body. It took a second for my voice to unlock and for my mind to kick into gear.

"They don't have anything to do with this, Faye. I'm the one. I'm the one who's been fucking with you. They don't know anything." I gripped the phone like the only lifeline that it was. Whatever my plan had been, I couldn't remember it now.

"That's what they all say in the movies and books," she said. "I wish it were true, but people always know too much, and I can't have that."

"They don't. I promise." I pleaded for her to believe me. "Don't involve them. Your issue is with me."

"But you don't seem to listen. No matter what warning I give you. Maybe now that Pen and your dear mama are involved, you will."

I smashed the back of my hand against my mouth to hold back a cry. I leaned against a tree to keep me standing. They were not part of my plan. They were supposed to be safe back at the house.

"Leave them out of it."

"Why should I, Jac? Why should I do anything that you want when you've been fucking with me ever since you got here?"

I played the only card I had. "Because I know who you are, Faith."

She was silent on the other end, and in those seemingly endless seconds, my imagination went into double and triple time. The only sound I could hear was whimpering in the background. I imagined her assessing the situation. Listing her probabilities and going with the one for her best possible outcome.

I prayed she'd cut her losses and decide to leave, her identity discovered and confirmed.

"I could call the police," I bluffed, knowing full well the truth about that.

"I don't think so, Jac." She was calm. Much too calm. "We both know where you stand with them."

I could hear her pacing, her heels clicking on her newly renovated floor.

"But I have the evidence to prove who you are and what you made Daphne do to those girls and to herself. From Daphne's own words. It was in the clock all this time."

Faye took in a sharp intake of breath, which sounded gloriously refreshing. It felt like a tiny win. Finally, she was on the losing end.

"Bring it to me," she said.

"Let my family go and I will." I added, "And then you can leave, and I won't say a word. Go to your next location. Just leave us all alone."

There was silence as she thought over my deal. Interminable, damnable silence that followed me as I started trudging through the woods closer to the Manor.

Faye blew out an audible breath, her words coming out measured, like she was finally returning to me. "You should have left well enough alone. You, your damn grandfather . . . Mia." She sighed resignedly. "How do I know you'll give me whatever it is you think you have?"

The heels resumed on the floor. *Click. Click. Click.* As she waited.

"Well," I said, pausing my stride. "I guess you're gonna have to have a little bit of Faith."

The pacing stopped, my words cinching the deal, giving Faye irrefutable proof that I had connected her to her past, that I held the keys to her castle . . . or prison cell.

She inhaled again, deep and slow. I did the same, counting down to calm myself. Mama calling my name and telling me not to come, to call the police, was cut off midsentence, the call screen switching to my home screen, signaling the call had been disconnected.

I began to run.

I whipped through the narrow trails of the woods, cutting through paths that had long since become overgrown with shrubs from years of disuse. Old shortcuts materialized in my memory as if I'd been running them only yesterday. My singular thought was getting to Mama and Pen in time . . . before Faye decided to make a clean cut, as she had done to those girls back in Colleton.

My breaths came out in ragged spurts. I was not prepared for the strain of running on an incline through this terrain without my usual prerun conditioning. My heart rate tripled, quadrupled, from fear and exertion. I was still rusty, running on this kind of terrain, but I didn't let it slow me down. I stumbled, my toes catching on underbrush and roots protruding from the ground. I fell, the flats of my hands and my knees hitting the ground hard.

No time to think. No time to assess any injuries. No time to consider what I was running into without a plan. I jumped back up and kept going. Nothing was going to stop. Not with the fear of my family's impending deaths driving my feet forward faster than I thought was possible. Towering trees swayed and bent from the wind rushing through them and past me, whistling a warning as I charged against it, using my hands to propel me through. Branches whipped at my face and slashed every exposed part of me. I barely noticed the sting. Get to Mama. Get to Pen. Put an end to this shit!

I broke through the final line of trees, and the lit house was up ahead on the hill against a backdrop of angry ink-black sky. The forest expelled me at the back of the Manor, where Faye's newly created hedge maze, with its spiderweb of twists and turns and dead ends, greeted me. Thick dark walls of greenery yielded no light or way in. I hesitated for a moment. But going in was quicker, a way through rather than trying to circle around. My mind went back to the schematics displayed in her office, the renderings of the ways through. And without further thought, I rushed in. Like a fool. Not anticipating that Faye was one step ahead, always. And that she would be waiting. For me to step into her lair.

It was when I was nearly out, my memory for once in my goddamn life not forsaking me. *Left at the third bubble shrub—no.* I banked a hard right, the literal light at the end of the tunnel up ahead like a beacon guiding me to the maze's exit and to the back of the Manor, leading to its decadent, large sunroom.

I was laser focused on the end. On getting in that house and to my family. On exposing everyone to one of the secrets about Faye Arden that I had uncovered. On fixing my mess. I didn't see it coming. Didn't hear the *whoosh* of something rushing at me until it was too late. Until it collided with the side of my face, making the world go sideways and fuzzy. Of the dull *tiiiing* of metal-on-Jac that snatched my breath and my senses. Then, no more because it was lights out.

41

No one goes into Moor Manor because once you check in . . .

The pain hit me, sharp in the back of my head, pushing me from unconsciousness. Next was the cold, and my body shivered from it as I gingerly touched the area where the throb of pain pulsated. Someone rustled beside me, making me realize I wasn't alone. I wasn't dead . . . because pain . . . and the bright lights behind my closed eyelids weren't the gates of heaven—not that I ever had a chance of going there.

"Sleeping Beauty finally awakes."

Faye's voice held no warmth. It was the real her talking. Not the fake one she tried to present to the rest of the town. My eyes snapped open, and I tried to get up too fast. The room sloped sideways, my nausea swelling. I groaned, trying to keep from throwing up.

"Easy," she said, without any inflection in her voice. No mirth, no anger. Nothing. "You'll make yourself pass out again."

It took another couple of seconds for my eyes to focus and for my brain to catch up. I raised my hand to the side of my head for comfort as I tried to take in my surroundings. I was on a cold, hard floor in a tiny room. It didn't have much in it, resembling a sterile examination room.

The metal stretcher above me rattled. Faye's eyes lit up, and a wide grin spread across her face. "The other Sleeping Beauty's awake too. Stand up and say hi, Jac. Easy now."

I used the wall to prop myself up, sliding to my feet slowly as the room began to settle around me. I stared at the foot of the stretcher, the feet under the white sheet moving. My eyes trailed the length of the writhing body, past the hands that were balled into fists and strapped down. Anxiety grew in me, inch by inch, as my imagination ran wild. I didn't want to see who was on the table. The voice was muffled, but it was clearly a man under there. I flinched at the Rorschach image of blood smeared on the sheet covering his head. Who was underneath? Patrick? Had she taken Nick? Where were my mother and sister? Who was she about to torture me with now?

"Pull off the sheet," Faye commanded, leaning casually against the countertop on the other side of the room. A gun hung loosely in her hand by her side. Beside her, on the silver tray next to the gurney, was a long, shining butcher knife. I tried to keep calm so she wouldn't see the panic rising in me. I was glad the person under the sheet was moving around so the noise hid the thumping of my heart. If not for that, she would have definitely heard it.

The flush door was closed, blending in with rest of the eerily white walls, the seam so small you could barely see where it was. The whole thing reminded me of a padded cell. It would be as hard to find a way to leave the room as it was to find a way in.

"Let's go," she prodded, bored. "I don't have all night. I have things left to do."

Like peeling off a Band-Aid, I grabbed a handful of sheet and pulled it back in a snap of fabric.

I hopped back, my knees buckling as I came face to face with my wide-eyed, previously-thought-dead-but-suddenly-very-much-alive ex-boyfriend.

~

I jumped back as Conrad yelled at me through the ball stuffed in his mouth, held there by the rubber tie strapped around his head. His forehead was washed in blood. It dripped into his eyes, making them appear bloodshot. His eyes bulged as he strained against the straps.

I couldn't believe that he'd been here all this time. Shocked, I looked him up and down. Tentatively, I jabbed his arm, because this had to be a hallucination.

"Surprise!" She said it brightly, as if she'd given me a birthday gift and not a whole human. She pushed off the countertop, coming close to the gurney. Conrad twisted away from her, his words unintelligible through the ball.

"You're from here, so you know what this place used to be—the Manor, I mean. It was a facility for patients. And this room in particular was used to treat the extreme cases. It was kept quiet. It even has a drawer for where they kept the body of a patient who didn't make it."

I followed her gesture to the opposite wall, where a cut square that I swore hadn't been there before suddenly appeared. Conrad followed along too. If his eyes got any wider, they'd have popped out. He shook his head.

"When I purchased this property and discovered this treat, I couldn't believe my luck. Here is a secret place where no one would know about the prizes I held in it. Isn't that amazing, Jac?"

"It sounds like you've lost it, is what it sounds like," I replied.

She tsked. "Watch your words," she said. "They call words like that 'ableist terms' now. You wouldn't want people coming after you for being insensitive, would you? But I guess it wouldn't matter anymore. Depending on what you decide."

I pulled my eyes away from Conrad and the morgue box and focused on Faye. "What do you mean?"

"I mean I tried to be your friend. I thought you were the most interesting person in this backward little town—not that mine was any less, I guess. When you came back, this prodigal daughter, town social pariah, the girl who killed her daddy and everyone hated her because of that one fateful night, I thought, 'Finally, there's someone worth getting to know in this dry as nails place.'"

"Why are you here if you don't like the town or the people?"

"I never said I didn't like the town," she told me like I'd said something audacious. "I love it. I love the seclusion and how I can move in and out with no one knowing or caring as long as I keep a pretty smile plastered on my face. That is, until your grandfather. He should have left well enough alone and not been nosing around. Must have been when I wasn't thinking. I was downtown, and the high school kids had just gotten off school. Must have been spirit week or some shit, but they were dressed like the early 2000s. Called it a Blast from the Past. Imagine that, calling 2001 the past. We're still in the 2000s! I think I made some comment about how a girl was wearing her hair and these friendship bracelets like how we did in Colleton, and he heard me. Had to be then, because ever since that moment, the old bastard kept sniffing around. Asking questions. Being weird." She snorted. "Fate really has a way of fucking with you."

"People would call that karma."

"Well, karma's a bitch," Faye returned, adding, "and then, you die."

She said *die* like she was really comfortable with it, increasing my discomfort exponentially.

"You have something on me, Jac. You know about my past. Who I am and what I did in Colleton. If you want to live, if you want your family to live, you'll handle your business now."

I balked, not understanding. "Handle my business?" I repeated. "I don't know what you mean. If you think I'm going to tell anyone about Colleton, I won't. I've got everything about it that you want. I'll give it to you. Just let us go." My eyes moved to my ex. "Him too."

That caught Faith off guard. "Him too? Even after he cheated on you? Even after he ruined your chances at your fellowship and wrote a book about your father's death behind your back? You want me to let this asshole go? Oh, honey." She scowled, disgust all over her face. "You're more pitiful than I thought."

42

"You take his life, and then we're even. I have a secret you're keeping, and you'll have a secret I'll keep to my grave." Her smile made my blood run cold. "Call it a blood pact."

"So you can turn on me like you did Daphne? I'll pass."

Faye stepped back and set the gun down carefully on the countertop. Her hands balled up in front of her. She looked like she wanted to kill me with her bare hands.

"I didn't make her do that. That wasn't my fault," she floated, watching to see if I'd bite.

"It was all your fault. You thought she'd stay by your side forever. But when you killed those girls, you killed her too."

Faye snorted. "You want to talk about friends? Do you really want to have a discussion about what friends do?"

There were more words right on the cusp of her lips. Something Faye desperately wanted to say to me. Her eyes danced with enjoyment. She wanted me to know very much. But she held off. "It's not the right time," she said, calming herself. "You'll eat your words real soon, Jacinda Brodie. This right here"—she waved toward Conrad—"doesn't even compare to the real truth."

I'd had it with her. With her games. With her riddles. With the way she'd played with me like a toy ever since I'd gotten home. What had I really done to her but wonder how Granddad had died? My grandfather, whom she'd killed because he knew too much. And now I did. And she was playing with me again.

"Kill him, and we are square. I'll leave Brook Haven—I'm bored here anyway—and go somewhere else. I'll even leave Mayor Tate alone, call off the engagement. You'll have your little town back, and I'll be like a ghost that never was." She looked at Conrad lying on the gurney, his bare chest exposed and caving in as he exhaled deeply.

"All you have to do is kill the lying scumbag of a cheater."

I looked at him. He was looking at me. I tried to parcel out my feelings. I'd lived the last six years not really living, knowing this man didn't give a damn about me and that he was just using me like he was all the other women working under him. I'd let him make me feel less than because I thought it was my punishment for my father.

This man didn't care about me. He didn't care about anything. He planned to tell my story to the world, to make money off me. He'd mined me for information and used me. He'd taken advantage of other innocent women who'd looked to him as a mentor and someone they could trust. He was a leech. A predator. Scum of the earth. If he died, no one would miss him. Hell, to the world, Conrad Meckleson was already dead.

"They'll never find the body," Faye said softly as if she were reading my mind. "And the blood in your car is circumstantial. He could have broken in looking for these notebooks or whatever he's been whining about. You would never be charged because you have proof he stole your story and intended to sell it to the highest bidder. Sure, that's a reason to kill him, but with no body and with him stealing and then coming to you, they won't charge you. Kill him."

It was so easy. So simple to just kill this man. No one would know. No one would care.

"I'll get rid of him. Like Mia and everyone else who got in my way. Just. Gone." She gestured as if her victims had evaporated into thin air, emphasizing her point.

"Everything is taken care of. All you need to do is seal the deal."

Her words shrouded me like an overcoat. They were intoxicating. If I did this, killed Conrad, she'd leave my family alone. Leave me alone. And I could rebuild myself in this town, show them I wasn't the wild Brodie girl like they'd always thought. I'd show Mom that what I'd done was for her, just like what she'd done back in Fort Worth, Texas, was for me and for Dad and most of all for her, to save her life. She'd killed to protect. And I could too.

"Deal?"

Faye was the devil on my shoulder. She was the temptation in the desert, and I wanted to listen to her. I wanted to believe that what she promised was for real. That she'd leave the town and never look back, go to darken another doorstep. But Daphne's story and Granddad's note told me I couldn't trust Faye to keep her word. There was no way she'd just leave.

What happened in Colleton had haunted my grandfather all these years. I'd never understood why. He'd kept that clock that Daphne's mother had given him, and I didn't get how it could help. I doubted if Mrs. Dixon even knew, or Daphne, that the truth about Faith would finally come out.

"Granddad had all the pieces he needed about you. He just didn't know it. But one thing he knew about you was that you don't like loose ends, Faith. You didn't then, which is why you went after Daphne. I think you found Granddad, knowing he was the one person who didn't believe your innocence, and even though it was twenty years later, your ego wouldn't let it, or him, go."

Faye snorted, rolling her eyes. "Think you're some kind of detective now? You missed your calling? Do we have a deal or not?"

I held up a hand for her to wait, all the pieces formulating in my mind. "When you saw Granddad, you tested him for a while to see if he'd recognize you even after your cosmetic surgery. I think he was doing the same, testing you, waiting for you to trip up."

"He told me about a handgun clock he had from an unsolved case he was close to solving," she replied.

"And it triggered you, which is why you went after him, killed him, and took the clock, wiping the whiteboard too. You didn't account for me and that I grew up on Granddad's cases and that clock. That I'd know its significance. Then you had to deal with me."

"You're boring me, Angela Lansbury. What's it going to be?" Faye snapped. "You don't have to end up like any of them. I will leave. I value my life and freedom way too much."

Right, I thought. So she could come back and tie up my loose end?

"You kill to silence others, protect your identity, and keep your past hidden. Your whole everything is a lie. Would you really let me go? Did you let my grandfather? Or Daphne?"

Faye's expression remained blank except for the flicker of an eyebrow. "So what are you saying, Jac?"

I lifted my chin, matching her gaze, trying to pass enough time so I could think of a way out of this room. "I don't feel like being another loose end."

She stared like she was trying to drill a hole through me. And just as quick, she broke out into that smile, the disarming one, so bright yet so cold it had sent shivers down my spine since the moment I first saw it.

The smile that told me I was as good as dead.

43

"Well, all right then." Faye's face went through a gamut of emotions as she studied me in the midst of our standoff. She was unable to move me, to regroup and come back for the Final Girl takedown. And I was unable to let her get off so easily. Even if it meant my life.

She finally said, "Look at you. You came into town pitiful and broken because your boyfriend cheated on you and your town hates you. It's like you found yourself some purpose." She placed a hand daintily over her chest. "All because of little ole me?"

Then Faye's southern hospitality began to recede, curse words she'd never use in public slipping in as her true self began to emerge. Her honeyed voice lowered and lost its singsong lilt. The twinkle in her eyes extinguished, darkening her eyes, like the predator that she was.

"Now you're a regular Sherlock Holmes, aren't you? Or maybe a bumbling Columbo, playing like you're an idiot and don't know how to figure shit out."

I shrugged, feigning calm. I was afraid that if I moved, my body would betray how terrified I was. "I'm no cop. I'm just a researcher."

"What you are," she corrected, "is full of bullshit."

"And I'm not the only one."

The words flew from me before I could stop them. Faye looked at me, surprised. Then she let out a sharp laugh that echoed in the tiny room.

She pointed a finger at me. "Touché." She smirked, then began tapping the tip of the gun's barrel against the metal counter, the light clangs like pinpricks on my skin every time the gun made contact.

It was all I could do not to flinch, forcing myself to stay strong. I couldn't let her see how terrified I really was. If I acted more like her, fearless and predatory, coming forward instead of running all the time, then she'd think I was interesting enough to keep around. All I needed was a little more time to figure out how to get out of here, save my family, and for once, solve the problem instead of being the problem.

Faye was a predator. She killed for convenience. She killed to clear the way for what she wanted. One day, she'd think I was in her way. I would be the only person who had evidence to link her to her home. I was the only person standing in her way who could clearly identify the Faye from today as the Faith from twenty years ago.

No matter what she said now, she'd come for me later, once she thought I'd relaxed and let my guard down. Hell, she might not even wait, and before leaving Brook Haven would pump my house full of carbon monoxide like she did to the Colleton girls.

"Deal?" she repeated, drawing me out of my thoughts.

I looked at Conrad, his head shaking as if to say *No deal, no deal!* He pleaded with me not to agree. I looked at her. She was smiling, nodding yes. She picked up the long knife, holding it out to me over Conrad's supine body. He bucked and squealed.

"He sounds like the pigs at Schroder's Pig Farm," she joked. Then the smile fell away. "A place about thirty miles or so from the Strip. We went there on a class field trip, though I have no idea why." She took in a deep inhale. "Make him sound like the pig that he is." She thrust the knife toward me.

My fingers itched. I wanted to grab the blade. I wanted to hit it away. I wanted to stab him. I wanted to run. Faye was both very right and very wrong about everything.

"No," I breathed out.

She cocked her head. "What was that?" she barked.

"I said no. No deal. I'm not killing him."

We stayed like that, on opposite sides of Conrad, with the gurney between us. The knife hovered in the air as she continued to hold it out to me like she didn't believe I'd turned down her offer. She stared at me blankly, as if she didn't know her next step because she'd banked on her power of persuasion. The same power she'd used on countless others to get them to kill, to trust her, to make them love the most evil thing they'd probably never know they were in the presence of until it was too late.

I'd been the cause of one death. I wasn't about to be the cause of another, no matter the outcome.

I should have thought faster and taken the knife when it was held out to me. She'd put the gun down, but it was still within her reach. And there was the gurney, which screwed any good vantage I had to stab her. I could wheel the gurney into her and then maybe could gain the upper hand. I could—

But Faye was too fast and thought even faster. Before I knew it, the cart was wheeled into me, knocking the wind out of me. She drove me back into the wall, pinning me there while Conrad struggled between us, begging for his life, not mine, I was sure. I tried to suck in air, but Faye pushed and pushed while turning the knife in her palm until the blade pointed down.

She looked at Conrad, who shrank under her gaze. "If you wanted a tell-all exposé about a small-town murdering girl, you should have talked to me. At least I would have been worth you losing your life. Time for plan B."

Faye's movements were too quick. All I could catch was the glint of steel as it caught the light.

All I could hear was Conrad squeal behind the gag.

All I could watch was Faye raising the knife farther above her head as if in some ritual of sacrifice and slamming it down, plunging it deep into his chest with so much force the table shook.

All I heard was the whistle-like inhale Conrad emitted as his extremities shot out from shock and the squelch the blade made as it pierced skin, sinking deep into muscle and arteries as Conrad took his last breath. I didn't see the Taser that suddenly appeared in Faye's other hand as it swung toward me, slamming into my body and releasing volts of white-hot lightning into me.

All I remember was deep, dark blood and that I had no control of any part of me as it pitched forward with nothing but Conrad's dead body to break my fall.

Then darkness followed.

44

When I finally began to come to, there was no telling how much time had passed. I thought my eyes had opened, but it was so dark I wasn't sure if they were really open or if I was imagining they were. And my room was cold, much cooler than it usually was, so maybe I'd left the window open and the night air had dipped down to a disrespectful temperature, as it often did in South Carolina—hot, sweaty days and freezing nights. Enough to keep you having a cold, Mama would always say.

But the air in the room felt odd. Off and unnatural. The smell was different. Medicinal mixed with something metallic. My bed had lost its soft-but-firm feel and was hard and lumpy, with sharp edges I couldn't decipher. My eyes tried adjusting to the pitch black, which was also odd. There were often no streetlights in the country, the night frequently illuminated by the moon and stars. But even without them, it was never so dark that I couldn't see my hand in front of my face, not like it was now. I waved my hand in front of me, feeling the disturbed air to prove something was there but not seeing its outline. My other hand was beneath me, and I began moving it, feeling the lumps, eventually making out a shape that did not move. A human-size shape . . .

Not. Moving.

Distorted images and snatches of memory began to invade my mind. Faye's twisted face. Conrad's terror-filled eyes. The glint of the light against the knife's steel blade. The flash of it in the air. The suck of it as it dug into Conrad's chest. The expelling of breath. The jolt of electricity ripping through my body and everything going dark.

My breathing quickened to fast heaves. I tried telling myself I was asleep. This was all a nasty dream. I was really at home, in my bed, or maybe at what had become my safe haven, Granddad's cabin.

Please, don't let this be what I think. Please, don't let this be what I think!

Mama had always said I had a wild imagination. I'd barrel into her and Daddy's room at night because I'd had a bad dream, and when she grilled me, it would be because I'd been up late sneak-watching scary movies on the USA or Syfy channels. She'd say I was a glutton for punishment and not to come running to her when I scared myself to death. She was right every time. But her bedroom door was never locked. And it was like she and Daddy left that spot in the middle just for me to climb up on and wiggle into. She wouldn't say a word, but she would be awake, being the light sleeper all moms seemed to be, while Daddy continued to snore. Only he would be surprised by the additional body in the bed when he woke up early the next morning. But Mama always knew. And she always expected me.

For all the anger and betrayal and disappointment we shared, she was always there to wrap me up and chase away the bad dreams.

I had never wished for anything as much as I did in that moment to feel Mom's arms around me, protecting me and chasing away the visions of monsters and vampires and evil alien clowns from outer space. But my brain was telling me that this time, it wasn't a dream. This was a living nightmare I was in.

My fingers stopped their discovery mission, not wanting to go further and actually corroborate what might be beneath me. But my mind wouldn't be still; it had to know. I had to see and figure a way out of wherever I was. With my other hand, I dug into the pocket of my jeans, finding the lighter I still had on me from my last hookah. Thank God for small favors.

I flicked the lighter. It lit after a couple of tries. The first thing I saw was that I was surrounded by metal walls, and they were too close, too confining, like I was in a box. Metal box. The light went out.

I flicked it on again. I was close to the ceiling—closer than I should have been. I wasn't claustrophobic, but feelings like it started clawing at my throat. I had to think about my situation. I had to calm myself before I freaked the fuck out. And to do that, I had to determine where I was. I shifted, and whatever I was lying on didn't give. It wasn't a tray, wasn't hard enough. Not a cot or a bed. Not soft. The light went out again.

I twisted to my side, propping myself up against the wall and ignoring how the cold seeped through my clothes like whispers telling me what I was in. I flicked the lighter on a third time. Conrad's unseeing eyes stared up at the ceiling above us.

Something like a gasp, scream, and unintelligible words gurgled out of me as the lighter dropped, bouncing against fabric and clattering against metal. I was swallowed in black again. The image of his eyes that stared at nothing while his mouth hung open in a perpetual frozen scream was seared in. Even when my eyes snapped shut, his face filled everything.

This time the black was ominous. This time the black was full of a real-life monster coming back from the dead, a face-eating zombie that would lift itself up and devour me, with nowhere to go. I was stuck in this metal tomb with my dead ex-boyfriend, whom everyone already thought I'd killed. He was dead for real, for real, stuffed in here with me.

My hand flew up, banging into the ceiling. I barely felt the sharp sting of the impact. I just wanted to keep myself from screaming and losing it entirely. My other hand started to dive down to look for the lighter when I realized what I was doing. Thoughts of feeling around an actual dead body rather than a lumpy unknown surface made it nearly impossible to get my frozen fingers to move.

Here was a body I could show the police. I could prove Faye had taken him and killed him, tried to frame me, and made people think I was losing my mind. I forced my fingers to move, to gingerly roam over the body that I knew better than most. Only this way, I didn't know it. It wasn't warm and moving up and down with breath. I wasn't touching it while he made sounds of pleasure. This wasn't the man I knew, even when he was being an asshole. I would have gladly taken asshole Conrad over a dead one. This was an empty shell of him. A dead shell. Another one dead because of me.

No, I told myself, hard like a slap in the face. Not me. I didn't kidnap him. I didn't strap him to a gurney. I didn't barter with his life over his head like he wasn't a human being. And I certainly didn't plunge a knife into his chest.

I moaned into the back of my hand, breathing deep so I wouldn't hyperventilate. I felt a wave of heat coming over me. My throat constricted like I was losing air. *Will I run out of air in here?* The thought nearly sent me into a tailspin until I reminded myself that there was air. I could feel the cool refrigeration pumping through tiny vents. It offered a tiny bit of comfort: maybe I wouldn't suffocate to death.

I needed to steady myself because freaking out wasn't going to get me out of this. I was still alive for a reason. Faye needed me. She needed Granddad's file and the clock with the flash drive that would out her as the brains behind the deaths of her friends in Colleton.

Adrenaline began to infuse into me; a little bit of bravery too. I focused on what I needed to do, which was to get the hell out of there. I had to beat back the fear that pulled at me, trying to drag me down into the abyss. Find the lighter. Find a way out of here. And then what?

When I felt calm enough to think and realized that Conrad wasn't going to leap up and take my throat, I started to move. With shaky hands, I searched around for the lighter, trying to touch as little of him as possible.

You're all right, Jac, I kept telling myself. *You're all right.*

I searched and prayed, groped and poked and prodded until my fingers touched the plastic cylinder under Conrad's arm. I pulled it toward me gratefully, gripping it and lifting it. I let out a couple of calming breaths, telling myself I needed the light because I had to see a way out of here.

Don't focus on the body or his eyes. Could I close them? Like they did in the movies? No, don't think that worked in real life, not with rigor mortis settling in, whenever that started. *Focus on the door.*

I flicked on the lighter, forcing my eyes to look everywhere else but at his. I adjusted myself the best I could, trying to squeeze myself between the wall and his body, shoving him over as much as possible so I wasn't all the way on top of him anymore, but next to him. It was tight. The space was meant for one body at a time. Why was there a morgue-drawer thing in a bed-and-breakfast to begin with?

Then I remembered what Faye had mentioned earlier about drawers and bodies, and what Moor Manor used to be before she turned it into a country inn. It had been a facility. In facilities, sometimes people died. In this one, they definitely did. And when they did, their bodies needed a place to literally chill until the authorities came. Of course someone like Faye would keep this crypt thing up and running, hidden behind a secret door so no one would know where she kept the bodies of those she deemed no longer necessary for this world. The thought chilled me because I knew I soon was going to be one of those unnecessaries . . . like Granddad. Like Mia, whom I'd watched die before her body disappeared. Like Conrad.

The square of wall behind us wasn't a door, but at our feet, I could see hinges at the bottom and a door cut into the metal. I couldn't see a locking mechanism, and of course, the door was the farthest thing away from me. *Please God, don't let this thing be locked.* But then I rationalized, Who would expect the dead to get up and walk? Didn't mean there wasn't a lock on the outside. Dread filled me, but I beat that back too. I couldn't afford to think about that. I was going to channel my inner Angela Brodie and my inner hopefulness that Faye had been in too much of a rush to lock or block my way out.

I didn't look at Conrad. I steeled myself and began to inch my way down toward the door. I moved as quickly as I could, working by the flickering of my lighter, hoping there was enough fuel in it to last me. Once my feet were firmly planted against the door, I pushed.

The door didn't budge, and panic bubbled up.

I hadn't applied enough pressure. I needed more leverage, better positioning, and I wasn't going to be able to do it while holding the lighter. *Shit.* My hands trembled as I focused on the lighter. Tears pooled in my eyes until my vision blurred. I swallowed over and over, begging the universe not to force me to put the lighter down and be in the dark.

If the light went out. If the door didn't open. If I was stuck in here forever or until Faye got what she needed from the cabin and returned to kill me, then erased every trace of my existence like she had with Mia.

My chest tightened, the familiar pangs of anxiety wrapping their fingers around my heart and squeezing and pulling, pushing acid up my esophagus, where it sat there, burning. There wasn't enough air. And whatever air I sucked in was filled with dead Conrad, though he had yet to smell.

I don't know how long I lay there, willing myself to move, but I finally shifted my body over Conrad. I was a little less than halfway down his body, lying on him on my back. I faced the ceiling, knees bent with my feet against the door. I wiped at my nose, which was dripping with snot. My fingers flexed like I was preparing to take a leap. My breath came out in short pants like I was a dog sitting out in the heat. And then I took my thumb off the fork of the lighter, and the flame, for the third time, went out.

45

I spared not one more second. I dropped the lighter on my stomach and placed both hands on the walls on either side of me. I braced myself, trying to use as much leverage as I could to give my legs enough power. I drew my legs back and threw them out. My feet hit hard against the door.

It didn't move. And I didn't let panic kick up, though it popped its head out at my first fail. I needed a counterbrace. My arms weren't enough.

I wiggled until I was down between Conrad's legs, the back of my neck at his crotch.

If Conrad were alive, he'd scream bloody murder for what I was about to do to him.

I scooted down a little farther toward the door, locked my arms, bracing them tight against the sides again. I drew my legs up toward my chest, sent a prayer to every deity out there listening. I sucked air like I was on the diving board about to jump into Earle Lake at the pier.

One. Two . . .

My breath exploded from my lungs as my legs shot out simultaneously like a bullet, slamming my feet against the door with more force than I'd expected. My body slid up, smashing backward into Conrad, snapping the back of my head into his crotch.

They call me the ballbuster. No, no one ever called me that. But they could've now.

"So sorry," I mumbled to the dead man, thankful that he hadn't felt a thing.

The air-cushioned door blasted open with a loud bang, clanging against the outer wall, and dull yellowish light from the outer room flooded the drawer. I shimmied down toward the light.

After the heaving lump of me took a moment on the floor of the tiny examination room, sucking in deep gulps of fresher air, I took one final look at Conrad's body, now lying crooked and hunched up at the top of the drawer from my use of him as a springboard. Images of our good times together scrolled through my mind like a movie reel as I quietly closed the drawer door. Once the door was sealed shut, the images shut off like a remote control had clicked off.

I tiptoed to the secret door. From in here, the door was just barely visible, cut away from the rest of the white walls. I leaned against it, listening for any sounds from Faye's office. It was silent. I inserted my hand into a groove on the flat surface and almost pushed against it when a thought occurred to me. What if this room was soundproof? It had to be. What if Faye was right outside those doors waiting for me, and I walked right into her?

But she wouldn't be expecting me. If the room was soundproof—and I was pretty positive it was, given how she (and the past doctors of this horrid place) had been using it—that meant she couldn't hear what had gone on in here. She wouldn't have heard my escape from the box of death. And when I popped through those doors, she'd be just as surprised as me. Maybe even more so because I was expecting her to be out there. She wasn't expecting me.

She could have the gun in hand. Or the Taser. But I had the element of surprise. And I could move fast enough before she reacted to avoid a bullet or the Taser probes. I ran through all these thoughts and this reasoning before pushing against the door. It opened with a quiet pop, like a vacuum seal, and swiveled open on its axis in the center of the doorway.

I jumped out, trying to use my element of surprise, only to find the office dark, with cloudy moonlight coming through the open curtains of the large window. It took me a moment to reset and come down off defense mode for a second. Thinking about my next steps kept me focused on the physical, on things I could do, instead of obsessing over whether this night was going to be my last.

Next steps: *Get out of this office. Stay alive. Find Mama and Pen. Don't get shot. Get the hell out of here. Don't get tased or stabbed. Find help. Don't get killed.*

In that order.

A quick scan of Faye's desk and through her top middle desk drawer got me a sharp-tipped, ornate pewter letter opener. Having the letter opener in hand gave me a modicum of relief, like I could fuck up some shit if I needed to—not go down without a fight, like my cousin Kei always drilled in. I left the hidden door open so that if anyone happened to walk by, they'd see it, and so I could find it again . . . when I eventually went to find help.

I did a quick check around for a phone or something to call 911, but there wasn't one. I had no time to look deeper. Faye could return at any moment, and I had a to-do list to take care of. I light-footed to the door, doing the same routine as I had in the inner chamber.

Listen for noise. Hear none. Open door and peek, half expecting Faye to be waiting for me on the other side. The hall was empty, and I was in the clear. I let out a stabilizing breath, noticing for the first time that my knees were shaking.

I psyched myself up before slipping out into the dark hallway, letter opener pointed straight out at chest level, shadows swirling, centuries-old house creaking, and psycho lady stalking. It was a complete mindfuck, but the need to make it to my mom and sister was greater than my fear or my lack of the skills needed for this kind of shit.

The wall gave me courage, and I stayed close to it, sliding down the curved hall, glad the carpet runner padded my steps. Every part of me beeped like a heart monitor on high alert as I checked for any signs of

Faye or anyone else, friend or foe. I followed the semicircle to the top of the staircase. From up here, the staircase looked foreboding, sloping down and around in an opposite curve from where I'd come.

The Manor was empty, no guests or workers, probably because of the impending storm that was starting to kick up outside. Through the windows I could see the swaying treetops against a black backdrop. It was dark and felt like the scary abandoned mansion with a long history of both good and horrible things, most recently the subject of many a kiddie tale of ghosts, monsters, and murderous doctors experimenting on vulnerable patients.

As I made it halfway down the winding staircase, voices floated up to meet me. I could distinguish Faye's, though long gone was the melodic tone like she was a note away from breaking out in song. Then my mother's responses, low and halting. My gut twisted. If Faye no longer cared about revealing her true self, it meant she didn't plan for us to leave here alive.

I took a couple more steps down, their voices getting louder and drifting up from the parlor.

"Will you walk into my parlor?" said the spider to the fly . . .

Every molecule of my being wanted to go right instead of left, toward the front door instead of through the other one. The fight-or-flight feeling rushed me like a linebacker.

I couldn't do that. I'd done that six years ago, deserted my family when I should have stayed by their side and told them about Daddy's final moments, no matter how horrible they might have been. I'd thought only about myself back then.

So no, there was no way I was doing that again.

No matter what awaited me on the other side of that door.

"O no, no," said the little fly, "To ask me is in vain,

For who goes up your winding stair can ne'er come down again."

46

I cleared the rest of the stairs, giving the front door an extra-long glance and weighing my best options. I could try to go for help. Faye might not check on me in the death box for a while, which would give me time to get to the main road and find someone heading up here before she went after my family. But what if she went up earlier? What if the door chimed that it had been opened, alerting her? She wouldn't catch me but could take it out on my family.

My feet hit the glossy dark wood floor on the main level. I followed the muffled voices until I could make them out more clearly. They were still in the parlor, or what was probably once the intake room of the facility. The hall was dark, with barely any lights on in the house, making it look eerie and every bit as haunted as we'd grown up believing. Faye probably kept the lights off so no one would show up, thinking the Manor was open.

"Where is my daughter?" Mama was saying, her voice shaky.

"She's cooling off." Then Faye cackled like the witch she was, the only one who found herself funny. I tightened my grip on the letter opener, the urge to ram it into her arrogant face making my body vibrate from my restraint.

"Whatever you think she has, she doesn't. You can just let us go, and we won't say a word to anyone."

Faye scoffed. "You really think I believe that? That line just works in the movies. All I need is to keep you alive long enough for Jac to give me what I need, and then I'm done with you all and this damn town and the nosy-ass people in it."

I edged closer to the partially closed door with the beam of light shining through, sliding across the floor to distribute my weight so I wouldn't hit any creaky parts.

Faye continued, her voice getting near, then far, as if she was pacing back and forth.

"If that old man had left well enough alone back then and now, then we wouldn't be in this shit. Or if Jac had just minded her business and not kept buzzing around like a goddamn mosquito, we wouldn't be here right now. I'd be preparing to marry the mayor. But no. I am probably going to have to wrap it up here and move on." Then she muttered to herself, "As usual."

My mother let out a cry. My hand flew to the edge of the door, ready to shove it open, but I stopped myself. I could see a sliver of them, my mom on her knees on the floor in front of Faye, who had grabbed her hair with one hand and was pointing her gun with the other. What made my heart leap in my throat was seeing Pen in a crumpled heap on the floor beside them. She wasn't moving.

My grip tightened on the door. Any sudden moves might make Faye shoot. But I couldn't let her terrify my mother any further, and I needed to see about Pen. She had to still be alive, or Faye and my mother wouldn't be having a conversation right now because Mama would be losing it.

"You damn Brodies are making me do this. You know, I was content to just be the wife of the mayor. I cultivated this identity and a whole new life for myself, and you all aren't about to fuck up all this work." She tightened her grip on my mother's hair. Mama squealed, and I burst in, unable to hold back anymore.

Faye spun. "How?"

"Let go of my mother."

I had thundered in, holding my weapon out halfway between the doorway and where they stood near the roaring fireplace. I could only see red. Who cared what happened to me as long as they were okay? I was about to barrel into Faye, but her recovery was quick. She shoved Mama aside like a sack of potatoes and lifted the gun as I charged forward until it met with the middle of my forehead, right between my eyes.

"Uh-uh," Faye warned, shaking her head.

She had moved so freaking quick. Her eyes flickered to the letter opener between us, and she cracked a smile. "A knife to a gunfight? You *are* stupid."

I almost snapped back that apparently it wasn't politically correct to say things like *stupid*, but seeing as how my current situation was dire, I tamped down the urge to be a smart-ass.

She pressed the gun hard against my skin as encouragement to drop my weapon. I weighed my options. Did I have time to stab it in? That would take effort, and her finger was on the trigger, which I doubted had the safety on. Stab verses trigger. My mother whimpered.

Faye stared at me, pressing the muzzle into me. "Give me a reason. I'm begging you."

I complied. So much for my modicum of protection.

She gave me a killer megawatt smile, the one she laid on the townspeople that made them think they were the most important people in the world. It had always made me feel uneasy. Like a hungry lion snowing you, only to turn around and take a bite later.

"Attagirl."

She kicked the opener away. She looked at me, then Mama, then Pen, who was moving slightly. Thank God.

"I oughta kill you right now. Burn this shit down and leave."

"Then how are you going to get Daphne's clock?" I matched her deadly tone. "The information that Daphne left? You kill us, you'll never find it. Plus, I've set it up so if something happens to me, the information is going to the FBI and your town."

It was a lie. There were no such arrangements.

Faye blinked, her deadly dialing back to an unsure status. "What information?"

I bypassed Faye and dove down to Mama, where I threw my arms around her neck and pulled her toward me in an awkward hug. Faye could have shot me in the back and, in that moment, I wouldn't have cared. I'd never been as happy to see my mother, with the tear-streaked mascara running down her face. My next check was of Pen to assess her condition. She was supposed to be the healer, but this time the tables had been turned on her. *Your fault,* my mind told me. *All of it.* Seeing Pen's state because of my own overconfidence sent a fresh wave of pissed rushing through me. I would kill Faye Arden.

I thought I'd never see my mother again. Same woman I'd cursed just the day before, when Carl had blown up her world and mine with stories about bodies in barrels and missing boyfriends and big who's-the-father reveals.

"Are you okay?" I asked repeatedly, checking them for injuries like I was the mother. It was easier to check for things I could see than deal with the compounding guilt I was feeling.

If I had left well enough alone. If I hadn't antagonized Faye, trying to out her all the time—if I'd let things be, like they did so often in the South—then they wouldn't be here. I didn't want to think about what I would do if Faye had hurt them. I would kill her with my bare hands. Pen was bleeding from a cut on her head, but Mama was fine.

Mama took me in, checking me as I had her until she was sure I was okay. I tried to smile for her, to assure her that all would be well, though I knew it wouldn't. Then she looked behind me, her eyes widening. She pulled away from me, sucking in a sharp breath.

"Jac," she whispered.

"It's okay," I said, soothingly. "We're gonna get out of here and call the chief."

Mama was shaking her head, her eyes wide and scared. "No," she whispered. "No."

"What is it?" I asked, confused. Yes, Faye had the gun, but she wasn't directing it at anyone in particular. We could still get out of this. Maybe.

"You still don't get it, do you, Jac?" Faye said behind me. "You never listen. You're not even listening to your mom now."

"Shut the hell up," I snapped over my shoulder, refusing to give her any more attention than I was giving her right now. Pen's head lolled to the side, an effect of being hit. I guessed she had a concussion. We needed to get her to the doctor.

"Enough of the family reunion bullshit," Faye cut in, digging her gun muzzle into the side of my head.

I snatched my head away, forgetting it was a gun I was getting pissed at.

"What information?" Faye repeated, sounding unsure for the first time in the weeks I'd known her. It came out like the word had gotten caught up in her throat.

I hope she choked on it.

I indicated to my sister, hoping deflection would give me the upper hand. "You didn't have to hit her." I remained squatting on the floor, looking at Faye. "You could have killed her."

Pen's pulse was there, but erratic. She was out cold, and a small circle of blood pooled on the rug where her head lay.

"How did this happen?" I asked Mama more frantically as she grabbed Pen's hand, rubbing it.

"She's in and out," Mama whispered anxiously. "She hit Pen with the gun once we got to the door, and then again when we got here because Pen was giving her hell."

I couldn't help smiling a little. That was *my* little sister.

"I think she might have a concussion. But what about you? Are you okay? Are you hurt?"

My chest burned from where the Taser had hit me. The back of my head was tender from whatever she'd hit me with at the maze and then again in her secret room when Faye had come at me. There was also the likely lifelong trauma of being holed up with a dead body. But who had time to dig into that now?

"I'm okay." I gave her the most reassuring half smile I could manage.

Behind me, Faye reached down and dug her nails into my shoulder. I yelped, and Mama reached out to beat Faye's hand off, but Faye only dug in deeper, bending me to her will. She swung the gun from me to Mama.

"Back up," she barked, motioning with her gun.

"Mama!" I tried to push her out of Faye's line of fire and stand in her stead. "Me, Faye, you want me, right? Because only I can get in my grandfather's safe and get you that flash drive that will tell the world everything you and Daphne did that night. There's no hiding from it now. Granddad had the evidence connecting you now to you then. I have it now. I'll get it for you."

Faye stared at me, the gun still pointing toward my mother, making me more and more nervous. "There was really something there? The bastard really had something?"

I wasn't about to tell her Granddad was pulling a cop move and bluffing to trip the suspect up.

"You drove your friend to suicide. You made her help you kill your friends. You're sadistic and evil."

Faye faltered. "They never thought she was good enough. They thought she was beneath them and treated her like trash."

"No different than how you like everyone to stay beneath you. What they did wasn't worth a death sentence. You planned it all and made her think it was just a joke, when you were really killing them. Then when she realized what you both had done, you had to clean up your loose ends."

I thought about Granddad's notes. *I am the loose ends.*

"I bet she chose to take pills, right?"

It was conjecture. Daphne might have decided to go on her own terms, just to get the untouchable Faith in the end.

Faye's expression revealed my guess had landed. She tried to gather herself, tried to pull her usual air of confidence, but it failed her, leaving her practically speechless. "How?" she asked. "How?"

I didn't answer.

Faye huffed out a laugh. Except, this time it was a less confident one than before. "Daphne killed herself. She ate, like, a million pills."

"Daphne played you, you know?" I was doing some Emmy-level acting, pretending like I wasn't terrified that this woman was a shot away from killing me. "There's something you didn't know about her. One thing she kept from you."

Faye's face rippled into unadulterated rage. "And what the hell might that be?"

Sitting here tonight with a gun in my face after watching Conrad become a pincushion, my sister bleeding on the floor with our mother beside her, I realized there was no more hiding from the truth. This was all the reality that I needed to face.

Faye snapped her fingers in my face, jolting me back to attention. "What don't I know?"

"That if she was gonna kill herself, it wouldn't be with pills. Because she was deathly afraid of swallowing them. But you didn't know that."

Faye reeled. Pen, who I thought had been unconscious, struck out her leg, taking Faye in the ankle. I used the distraction, slamming my hand down on Faye's arm.

"Mama, move!" I yelled as Faye and I struggled. The gun went off, and Faye's knees buckled.

I launched myself at her again as she attempted to grab the closest body to her, Pen's. Faye pulled the gun up and smashed it down again, rendering Pen down for the count. Mama lunged, her fingers clawing for Faye's face.

I'd never seen Mama like this. So angry. So ferocious, a mother protecting her cubs. This must have been what it was like when my birth father attacked her, when she had to make that life-or-death decision. When Mama killed him and Daddy helped her get rid of the body.

Mama would and could do it again. But this was my fight and Faye's, my problem to handle. Mama had already taken one for the team. It was my turn.

Faye aimed, preparing to fire on purpose this time. Mama tried to get a hand around Faye's neck. Faye gagged, beating Mama back. She wheeled around on me, slamming her head into my face.

Blood poured into my mouth. I could feel its warmth dribbling down my chin. White spots flashed in my vision, but I didn't let up. We were grunting, grappling for the gun, both of us trying to gain purchase and the upper hand. Mama lunged forward, but Faye anticipated it, kicking her foot out and catching Mama directly in her gut. She fell back against Pen, who had just barely started coming to, the poor thing. I hit Faye once and then again. She raked her nails down my face. Blood created a hazy glaze over my vision. Would she kill me? Us? Without having the flash drive?

Before I got a chance to find out, light spilled down on us from the sprawling fixture on the ceiling.

"Faye, I thought you might be up here. Dad asked me to come out because the Weather Channel said the remnants of Tropical Storm Lee are about to hit. It's not good to be here alo—"

Nick's words died on his lips.

47

Nick stood in the doorway, his attention leaping from head to head as if he wasn't sure whether this was real life or a dream.

His mouth opened, but he couldn't force the words out. He cleared his throat. "What is going on?" He hovered at the door like he was considering doing an about-face.

It was another frozen moment in time before the floodgates opened and all of us, except Pen, began to speak at once.

Faye said, relieved, reaching out to him, "Finally, honey, they have lost their collective minds. I thought these women were gonna kill me! Thank God this is a stand your ground state."

We were the ones bloodied, beaten, and on the floor in a tangle of arms and legs, proof that if anyone planned on killing, it wasn't us, but she was back at it again. Playing the role that made her the victim and me the villain in my own town. I fought the urge to jump up like a child and chant, "See, I told you! I told you about Faye! Now you have to believe me."

This wasn't the time for *I told you so*s.

"She kidnapped us," I said, which sounded like a line from a movie and not my real life. From Nick's dubious expression, he thought so too.

Cautiously, he said, "What is this?"

"It's true," Mama confirmed, in the assured, meticulous way she spoke. She always sounded so rational, which was why everyone listened to her. "This woman brought us here. She called Pen and me here, claiming Jac had stormed in, and said either we come or she'd call the authorities and have them take Jac away. And you know Jac's situation with the police right now."

Faye rolled her eyes, putting on a grand show like she couldn't believe our audacity.

I added, "She told me that I'd better come if I wanted to see them alive."

Nick said, "I didn't see your car out front."

"I was at my grandfather's. I ran through the trails to get here." I had so much more to tell him but no time to do it. We needed Chief Linwood. Maybe not him. We needed SLED and the FBI. I was sure this was a case for them. We needed to get Faye before she slipped away again.

Faye wiped her face, smearing the blood rather than cleaning it off. She ran her hands down the front of her trousers and blouse to smooth them, gripping the damn gun as if it were an extension of her. Faye's appearance was no longer the picture of perfection she always presented.

"All lies," she said in a husky voice. She brushed back her tousled hair with her empty hand. "I just wanted to discuss this situation with Jac. I wanted to appeal to Angela's better senses. And they attacked me, thinking I got Jac in trouble with the police. They will support whatever Jac says to keep her out of more trouble."

"I need to think," Nick said, his eyes on me, eyebrows furrowed.

Faye gave Nick an irritated snort, stepping closer to him, and lowered her voice. "I wish you didn't have to take so much time deliberating, like your father. That's why people will always get the better of you. If you wait too long. We need to talk, Nick."

Faye spoke matter-of-factly, as if they were talking mergers and real estate closures instead of about three women in various states of distress being held at gunpoint on her parlor floor. Murder Manor still living up to its name.

Faye inclined her head toward the hall. "Out there."

I jumped up, taking a chance that she wasn't going to hurt Nick. She seemed to care about him to some degree. He hadn't worn out his usefulness yet. I ignored how my body screamed in protest, every muscle of mine yelling bloody murder. Every nerve jittering from the round with the Taser. Nothing about me was right.

I placed my bet and began my rapid-fire storytelling about the hidden room upstairs, finding Conrad, the drawer. Being tased.

"Jac, slow down?" It came out like a question. He seemed to back up, like he was distancing himself from this insanity. I couldn't blame him. "Wait a minute. What do you mean, tased?" He flicked a glance at Faye.

"I can explain," Faye said quickly.

I pulled down my shirt, abandoning all modesty to reveal my cleavage and bra and show him the darkening bruise from the Taser's points on my skin.

Nick's eyes didn't leave my body, taking in my wounds, but he spoke to her. "Faye?"

"She attacked me," she replied. She crossed her arms over her chest. "Self-defense. You can see I'm bleeding, too, because *they* came to attack *me*."

"She's lying," my mother and I said in unison.

"Like her mother would ever say otherwise against her own daughter," Faye was quick to point out.

I wanted to show Nick the hidden room in her office and Conrad's body cooling in the drawer. I approached him like she had, carefully, like he was a gazelle and we were lions on the hunt preparing to duel over a meal. But I took it a step further. I kept my hands out, showing that I held nothing.

"The gun," I whispered like it mattered.

Nick's eyes slid over to where Faye stood, zeroing in on the handgun she held, which was pointed at no one in particular. It looked more like an accessory now. Where were the threats she'd been lobbing at us a minute ago? Now, she looked old—older than Mama, who had her by more than a decade.

He asked, "Why do you have the gun, Faye?"

"I was here wanting to get some business done at the Manor."

"But the storm . . ."

She nodded. "Yes, before the storm came. I thought I had time. Sometimes it gets creepy here alone when it's dark, so I had this out for protection, like you and your father told me to do when no one was around. When they showed, I had it on me. And then things went a little sideways."

I snorted but remained quiet. The old Jacinda would have been cutting Faye off, trying to get my narrative out before she did, trying to make everyone believe me, believing that they would because I was from here and she was the outsider. I had failed every time. So this time, I was going to wait it out, see what she said, then blow it out of the fucking water. I motioned with my hand behind my back for Mama to remain quiet. I didn't want any attention on her or Pen.

Nick watched Faye with incredulity. His Adam's apple bobbed as he swallowed and rationalized everything he was hearing and seeing. I could relate and felt horrible for him.

"Nick, I'm sorry you have to find out about her like this. I know your dad loves her, and they were going to be married," I said. "But it'll all work out. She'll go to prison. She's done a lot more than what she's done here. She's killed people in her hometown. My grandfather found out all about it, and that's why she killed him!"

Faye raised her eyebrows, throwing a glance Nick's way. "Why *she* killed him." She placed her hand over her chest as she mimicked me, mocked me, pretending to look chastised. "I concede I did. I killed your dear old pappy," she said in a drawl that dripped with sarcasm and insult.

"And Mia. You tried to make it sound like I was crazy, but I watched you kill her in your office."

Faye watched Nick expectantly, as if waiting for him to say something. "Did I?" she countered, amused at the recollection. Truly, a cold-hearted bitch.

Nick stood frozen in the light, his face inscrutable, his hair flopping over his forehead, nearly covering his eyes, making him look like he did when we were teenagers sneaking up to the Manor property to hang at the bluffs and play kiss, marry, kill with the other students from Richmond Regional High.

Faye gestured with the gun toward the hallway. "Nick, we need to talk privately. You don't want to do this here."

If they went out to talk, she would convince him I was lying, crazy. She'd make Mama and Pen accessories to whatever crime she'd try to pin on me. That was the power of her words, the power of the spider in her lair. And I think Mama knew it.

Mama started to rise slowly. Faye's gun shot up like it was on a drawstring, and she pointed it. Mama froze. I yelled, "Don't. Don't!" Unable to think of more words.

Nick said, "Faye, put that shit down. What are you doing?"

Faye licked her lips, looking like she had plenty to say. "Nick, my patience is thin."

Mama raised her hands to show she was no trouble. She looked at me.

"Mama, sit," I said, more begging her than not. I needed to be the one in Faye's line of vision. I needed Mama to just be quiet.

Mama's eyes were fervent. "Jacinda, I need you to know something."

"Not now, Mama," I whispered back, never taking my eyes off Faye and Nick. "Not here." The last thing I needed was Faye knowing my family's dark deeds so she could use them against us.

Mama shook her head. "No, now is the only time I got because I don't know what's gonna happen here. I don't know if we're going to make it through, and I can't have you thinking that you were anything but the daughter I've always wanted."

I took in Mama's haggard face, from the incessant worry to the bags beneath her eyes. Me and my drama had done this. Mama had been through so much, too much. She didn't deserve this. She hadn't deserved any of this.

"I let my fears of you becoming like that man and me—people who hurt, people who could kill—make me fail you. I drove you away, wanting to mold you into this perfect young lady who would never hurt a soul. I should have taught you to be proud of whoever and whatever you were going to be. I should have had faith in the type of woman you would become. But I stifled you. Held you back. Made you think you were a failure to me, when it was me who failed you. That's what your daddy tried to make me see all these years, when you and I were always butting heads. I was so hard on you because I was terrified you would end up like him, your father, or worse, like me, the one who killed him."

"Shhh, shhh, Mama, it's okay." None of that mattered now. I only wanted to get her and Pen out of here.

"What man? The chief I've heard could walk on sainted water?" Faye guffawed. She waved her hand. "That's rich! And you had the nerve to act like I'm wrong for my past. The perfect southern belle, Angela Brodie, wife of the illustrious Chief Montavious Brodie Jr., has a bit of dust on her after all. You hear that, Nick?"

Faye was too tickled, wagging a finger on her free hand. "I know people. A killer knows a killer, and I could spot her like I did you, honey. I just couldn't figure out what." Faye coughed, blood rimming her mouth. "You never really know who you think you know. Isn't that right, Nick?" Her smile was lecherous.

"Why are you doing all of this?" I had had enough of the sound of her voice. "You didn't have to do any of this."

"I already told you why, Jac," Faye said. "Blame your grandfather. I don't like loose ends. Do I, Nick?"

Nick wouldn't look at her.

I pressed. "But why?"

"Because I can." She tucked a lock of hair behind her ear. "Because when people screw with you, like you and your grandfather did from the beginning, you need to show them who runs things."

I said, "That makes no sense."

"I don't need you to understand me," she replied. "This isn't therapy, okay?"

"You're evil," I told her, my hands fisting at my sides.

She smiled demurely, dipping her head in a thank-you. "However, I'm not the only one."

Nick remained rooted in his shock. He needed to get himself together. We needed to figure out a way out of here alive. With him here, there was no telling what Faye would do. She didn't have the same energy she'd had before he arrived. That meant she must have really cared about him and didn't want to come off to him the way she'd done to us. The phone conversation I'd had with her stepmother came back to me.

If Faith ever sets her sights on you and gets you caught up in whatever she has going on . . . it won't end up so well for you. Nick fixated his attention on the ground, refusing to acknowledge us, while a storm swirled around him; whatever he was holding in was locked tight.

"Nick," I finally said. I nearly touched his shoulder but was afraid of what Faye would do.

"Nick?" she echoed, her tone filled with expectation.

"Maybe this is all a misunderstanding," Nick said. "Maybe we just need to talk this all out. My dad—"

"Screw your dad," I said. "Conrad is dead upstairs, and she killed him!" I pointed at her. "There's no talking anything out."

Faye tutted, leaning against the cabinet. "At least we agree on something. Some of us aren't making it out of here tonight."

Forever and always Murder Manor.

"Do you hear her?" I attempted, feeling panic settling in. "She's been playing this whole town for her own perverse reasons. We're a game to her. Me. You. Mayor Tate. She's going to hurt you like she's hurt many people her whole life. It's what she does."

"God." Faye rolled her eyes, making the word a four-syllable one.

She pushed herself off the cabinet, striding toward him. She stopped close to him. Too close. I took a step back, unsure what she'd do. The gun dangled by her side.

When she spoke again, her voice had changed to honey. "I wouldn't hurt you, Nick. Haven't I protected you all this time? Your secrets? Haven't I made your father a more viable candidate for his political aspirations? And you . . . haven't I been there for you?"

She definitely cared about him in some way, maybe because he was the closest thing she'd have to a son, maybe because she needed him to firmly secure the bag with his dad. Whatever the case, she was trying to reason with him, as if he'd ignore the fact she was holding people against their will.

What? "What is she talking about?" I asked Nick.

Nick said, "I can fix this. It's not what . . . Jac, we just need to talk."

"Awww," Faye purred, slinking closer to Nick until her body was pressed against his side. "This is a tough one. Not how you imagined your reunion with her, hmm?"

Then Faye took her free hand and tenderly moved away the hair hanging over his eyes with her fingers. The act was intimate, not affectionate, as might be expected from a family member, but something different. It shocked me. It was as if the two of them were . . . revulsion hit me. I didn't want to say it. To think it. I took a step back. And another.

Behind me, Mama asked, "What is going on?"

I swallowed. Not in my right frame of mind. I was reading more into things than I should. My imagination was running wild.

"Get away from that boy," Mama demanded, looking like she wished she still had the shotgun that had put a hole in my biological father.

Faye sighed.

"I had so much hope for you, but you turned out to be such a disappointment," Faye said, ruefully. "Both of you."

"Faye," Nick warned, something simmering just below the threshold.

"What's there to help at this point?"

Faye pulled up her gun from where it had been dangling. Nick jerked back away from it. He looked at her, shocked and confused and maybe a little hurt as she turned on him too.

But I understood it all clearly.

We were all going to die tonight.

48

Faye's shoulders dropped; she was clearly dejected and disappointed that we weren't following her script.

"You all are like a damn soap opera," Faye grumbled. "Let me enlighten you, since Nick seems unwilling. You've gone all these years thinking everything was your fault. But if you knew what your bestie did—"

Nick growled, but there was something new in his eyes, panic and an alertness that wasn't there before. "Shut up, Faye."

She put her hand on her hip. "Why the hell should I? You know what I can't stand? When women beg after a goddamn man, running after him, sniveling, happy with scraps of love and attention he throws out when he feels like it, and her thinking she's won some fucking grand prize. You should thank me for Conrad. He was a real prick, you know that? He told me he'd give me a cut of his book deal about you if I let him go. How'd you get out of that drawer I stuffed you in, huh? Where's *that* Jac? When you appeared down here, I thought, 'Okay, maybe. Maybe this girl can be salvaged.' And now we're back to simpering, hoping some man will save you, even if that man is our Nick here."

Our Nick.

"Nick saved my life that night," I said. "He pulled me to safety."

"Oh, honey, if you only knew." She made an exaggerated turn toward him. "Will the real Nicolas Tate please stand up."

I was now behind Mama and Pen, who'd woken and was in a sitting position. I motioned for them to be quiet. No attention veered my way as I moved farther and farther back until I couldn't anymore, my back against the grooves of the fireplace. I searched my memory for where the poker was, trying to keep as quiet as possible. Trying to keep them talking about whatever it was they'd been doing.

"You shouldn't have touched her," Nick fumed. "You were not to touch her."

My mind screamed, my eyes riveted to him. *What, what, what is going on here?*

She pretended to think. "You know, Nick, I've held on to this long enough. And you have too. I thoroughly enjoyed the little taste you gave me. You are so good in that bed of yours."

I thought about Nick's house and how I assumed Faye had helped him design it.

Nick whispered, "Shut the fuck up." He took a step toward her. She stood her ground.

His hands flexed, and mine curled around the iron handle.

"You get so personal in bed. You tell all your little secrets."

My stomach roiled.

His body moved in time with his breathing. "It was only a moment. I wasn't thinking."

"It was enough," she snapped. "I was even okay with you renewing your relationship with her. I mean, I heard you'd been pining after her for years, but my God, Nick. You're delusional if you still think you're the good guy here. This woman will be the end of you. Again."

He took another step toward her, the shock wearing off and morphing into a rage I'd never thought possible of him. Nick's face flushed deep crimson, his eyes becoming small, dark stones. Descending into darkness.

Unbothered, Faye watched him, her smile widening as she goaded him into morphing into a whole other person. She still held her ground.

"What would Daddy Tate say if I told him that I screwed both the daddy and the son?"

He seethed. "I'm going to fucking kill you."

"Famous last words," she teased. "And yet I'm still here."

All I needed to do was bide my time. I counted down.

"Ask him, Jac." She switched up suddenly.

I held my breath, afraid they'd seen what I'd done, but Faye's eyes remained on her number one threat, Nick. I shifted, hiding the poker behind my leg.

"Ask him," she prompted, grinning again. "Come back here so you can hear this really well." She showed teeth, looking monstrous.

I looked down at Mama and Pen.

"Don't," Mama said under her breath. As in *Don't engage.* Don't follow them down this rabbit hole. We'd been down enough. And one more thing might break me completely. But I'd do whatever I needed to do to save us. Even if it meant sacrificing myself. I did as I was told by Faye.

"Nick saved my life." It came from me in a whisper, hesitant. I didn't want to hear what Faye was forcing her flies to confront.

All I knew was that Nick had been there after Dad went over—grabbing my waist, keeping me from following my dad down. He'd held on to me until the cops arrived. I owed him.

She cackled. "Saved your life," she repeated. "I don't think you'd be begging your bestie to save you if you knew what kind of 'help' he gave you at the bluff."

"You don't know what you're talking about," I said at the same time Nick barked for her to shut up.

"Ask him," she said. "Because it's about time you really knew who your friends are."

Nick said, "Stop it."

Faye bared her teeth, contorting her face into something horrible. Never had such a beautiful woman looked so hideous.

"Tell her, Nick, or I swear I will."

My body trembled. Whatever her truth was, I didn't want to hear it. I had to remain strong. I had to remain thinking. I needed to remain laser focused. But the way Nick was looking—scared and angry, wanting to strike out but holding himself back to the point he was so red he might have a stroke—gave me pause.

I turned to Nick, making eye contact, seeking clarification to the confusing web Faye was spinning.

"Ask your best friend what he did to your daddy, Jacinda Brodie."

What he did to your daddy. Her words reverberated.

"Jac." There was a desperate plea in the way Nick said my name. It broke my heart, confirming a truth that was too devastating to comprehend.

Faye was hungry for something salacious, enjoying this, drawing it all out to the point of insanity. It was traumatizing. It was all too much. It was bubbling up inside me, starting from the pit of my belly, growing and expanding. Taking on a life of its own. Pop Rocks in a bottle of Coke, fizzing, about to explode.

Faye inched closer to me, so close I could feel the heat radiating from her body. She thrummed with energy. It was like she was feeding off my and Nick's misery. At any moment, I thought she'd skyrocket to the moon.

"Tell her, or I will kill her where she stands. I swear to God."

Faye wouldn't let up. Pushing and pushing. Layering and layering. Making it impossible to tune her out. She had me on the plank with a sword's tip at my back, nudging me to walk it.

"Go on. Ask your best friend what happened that night, Jac."

"Shut up, Faye. You have no idea why I pushed—" His mouth clamped shut.

The air in the room vacuumed out, my hopes and security with it. Why should I believe anything Faye had to say? She was a verified liar, a sower of discord. I should believe my best friend, the guy I was supposed to be reinvolved with. But there was one thing missing after all the accusations Faye had hurled at him. What was missing was any denial. What he'd given instead sounded like a partial admission, but of what?

His shell shock mimicked mine. Sensible thought could not form in my mind. Images of then and now swirling in a black-and-gray mix of fog and mist. I put space between us, the room spinning on its axis. I struggled to remain clearheaded.

Nick fumed. "I said, shut the hell up, Faye."

"It's a family affair, Jac, honey. Bet you didn't know that either. You think the mayor didn't know? He protected Nick after what Nick did, and hung you out to dry. He made Nick go in the military to protect him. While you grin and giggle in our faces, you were nothing but a plaything and a scapegoat."

"It's not true," Nick said. "You were never a plaything. You were—are—everything to me."

He grabbed her hand as she started to raise the gun to level it at me. They struggled as the gun's muzzle toggled back and forth in a wretched game of tug-of-war that Nick was winning, overpowering Faye. I should have gone for the gun hand. I should have gone for the biggest threat at that moment. All this time I'd been after Faye for what she'd done to Granddad. That was believable, but Faye's words were the forgotten combination to a lock long engaged. The threat I hadn't known existed for the past six years was now the only thing in my line of vision.

I pulled out the iron rod that was hidden behind me, raising it up in the air with a speed I didn't think myself capable of. The poker came down at his head as the gun went off, to Mama's and Pen's screams in the background.

Faye grunted, reeling backward, her eyes round and filled with incredulity. Her hands clamped over her abdomen as she fell back. She landed in a heap on the floor against the liquor cabinet.

The poker's hook caught Nick in his face. He twisted away with a deep laceration along the side of the same cheek I had caressed not too long ago. He stumbled back, tripping over a piece of furniture and going over it. All the while his hand attempted to seal the two thin flaps of skin back together again.

The combined smell of gunpowder and warm blood permeated the air. Nothing and no one moved.

Faye's words repeated in my head—*Ask your best friend what he did to your daddy.*

My mind parsed Faye's revelations about Nick, giving them weight and validity. It was my fault my dad was killed. For the last six years, that was what I and everyone in Brook Haven had believed. It was why I'd left, vowing never to return. It was what had made me run and forever punish myself with bad relationships and missed career opportunities, why I'd denied myself my family except when they came up to see me, forcing themselves on me.

If I wasn't the one who was to blame, then who was? The memories came to me in spurts of night terrors. Nothing was shown seamlessly. I had never said what had happened. Why I was on the bluffs. Why Dad and I had fought and how he went over in the fog. And how Nick chased us down, finding me at the bluff's edge about to go over, trying to get to my dad in time.

Pen swayed to her feet.

Faye panted. "How could you, Nick? What about me?"

Mama and I worked to balance Pen's weight between us.

"I kept your goddamn secret, you and your father. I was here after she deserted you. I tried to give her a pass, but she just. Kept. Fucking with me!" Faye screamed.

A light switch went on in me. I left Mama to hold Pen up, staggering to the writhing woman. All I could see were all the times she'd terrorized, ridiculed, turned everyone against me. They flashed across my mind like a montage. I towered over her, panting as everything fell away and all I saw was red. Her, bathed in red.

"What are you gonna do, little Jac?" She coughed up a trickle of bloodied spit at the corner of her mouth. She barked out a laugh. "You ain't gonna do jack shit. How about that! That's why it was so easy to play you. So easy to read you. So easy to make you the pitiful bad guy this hick town wants you to be. The big baddie."

I raised the poker above my head. She watched in awe.

"What are you gonna do, huh? Kill me? Well, do it. Go ahead. Do something, Jac, for fuck's sake. Do it."

I wanted to. She'd killed Granddad, made the last few hours of his life horrible, and Mia. Those girls. Daphne. She was like a swarm of locusts, ravaging the whole town, obliterating anything and anyone in her path.

"Why?" I had to ask. "Why those girls? Why my grandfather?"

She half smirked, then looked utterly confused, as if the answer should've been obvious to me. "Why? Because I can."

"Why me?"

"You fucked with me first. You gotta take responsibility for that," she said pragmatically. "That's on you."

The poker trembled in my hands as it hovered above her.

She licked at her lips like someone in need of water. "Kill me. Death is better than being locked up like I was back home. Always having to pretend to be who everyone else wanted me to be, when all I wanted was to burn it all down. And I did!" She chuckled. "I burned it all down. Or, carbon monoxided it." She laughed and groaned. "Then kill yourself, because you fucked and found comfort in the man who killed your father."

My arms were slamming down, angling the poker to come straight at Faye's heart through the base of her neck, when they pivoted violently off course. The poker spiraled out of my hands and whipped through the air.

"No!" Faye and I screamed in unison. For the same and different reasons. Both of us wanted her to die. Me, for her to pay for her crimes. Her, to avoid them. The poker clattered loudly to the floor.

Mama held me. Her hand gripped my wrist with an immovable strength I never knew she had. Her other arm circled my waist, pulling me to her body. About to make me break in two.

"Don't," Mama said in the back of my neck. "Don't have her death on you like Ralph's has been on me. She is not worth your soul. Let her live and pay for what she's done. In prison she will see every life she took. They will haunt her for the rest of her days, locked up."

"Shut up, you old cow—"

My fist slammed into her mouth, stunning Faye into silence. She slumped over, hair curtaining her face. If I couldn't kill her, then I'd shut her the hell up. I shook my stinging fist.

Behind us, Nick stirred.

"He's coming to," Pen said, her panic increasing. "Mama, Jac!"

"Jac," Nick groaned from where he tried stabilizing himself on the ground. "I didn't mean to."

Mama spun me around. "You need to get out of here." She pushed my arm from around Pen's waist, ignoring my protests. I couldn't leave them. We had to get up and go now. We had to do it together. I wasn't going to leave them behind to face the wrath again, like I'd done before. I'd never leave them behind again.

"Come on, Mama, Pen, let's go now."

I tugged at Pen, but she was so sluggish, like dead weight. I was prepared to hoist her up and drag her, if that's what it was going to take to get us out of here. Mama tried to help, but she was unsteady and dragging us down too. I still tugged and pulled, frantic to get us out of there before Nick fully woke—the idea of him was immobilizing, the implication of Faye's words too much to consider now—and came to his senses, because he wouldn't let us, me, go.

I chanced a glance over my shoulder. Nick was on his hands and knees, swaying. He called my name, holding his face. He begged me to just listen to him. He looked at the person he'd shot, then at us as we struggled to move, still foggy. His face oozed blood. Faye remained out cold.

"It's all right, baby girl," Mama whispered to Pen, carefully placing her in one of the accent chairs and guiding Pen's head gingerly. "She won't be quick enough."

I vibrated on my toes, anxiety building. "We need to go, Mama," I pleaded, shooting glances at Faye to check her progress. Her eyelids were fluttering open and she let out a pained groan, looking down at the gut wound. Her eyes widened, bewildered, realization hitting her. Nick was both there and not.

"I won't leave you." Desperation made my heart thunder.

"Go." Mama lowered her voice. "Run as far as you can, Jac. Don't you look back. Don't you let him get you." She stared deeply into my eyes, as if we weren't in the middle of mayhem. For as long as I could remember, Mama and I had been two ships passing in the night, but in this moment, we were one. "You come back alive, no matter what you have to do."

Mama drew her shoulders back as she straightened. Determination and a ferocity I still wasn't used to shielded her like armor. "I'll hold him back as long as I can."

I was in awe of Angela Brodie's strength and bravery that she'd kept hidden for so long. I saw in her what I could also be, and it infused me with strength I needed to go on.

Pen and I shared a look, with Pen nodding her approval as if she knew the thought of my leaving them, the fear of what Nick would do to them if I left them alone, was killing me.

Nick roared from across the room. "Jacinda!"

Mama grabbed my arms. "Go, Jac, run!"

Tears slipped down my cheeks. Mama pulled me into her, hugging me quick and tight. She ran her hands, soft, warm, over my face, wiping away the tears as if I were five again. I smelled the faint baby-powder-and-lilac scent. Then she pushed me away.

Need to lead him away, before he decides to clean house. The thought dropped down, rattling in my mind like a penny. It sounded too much like Granddad.

I'd draw Nick away because I was who he wanted . . . who Nick had always wanted, and he'd come for me, and Mama and Pen could find help.

"You'll be okay," I told them, mostly for myself. If I didn't believe it, I would never be able to leave.

I gave one last look to my mom, then my sister, searing the images of them in my mind and locking them in, just in case I didn't come back.

Then, I was on the run again.

"Jac!" Nick's voice sounded like a wounded animal, like his world was ending. "Wait."

I was already running toward the back doors, spilling out in the darkness to the patio and the dark, sprawling maze below me. Beyond it, along the horizon, were the dark silhouettes of the trees cocooning us and the upward slope leading to the bluff.

Nick's frustrated and agonized screams for me chased me out of the Manor and into the windy night, into the thick blanket of fog curling around the trees and making its way down to the earth.

If I ran, he would follow me.

Now that you're back, I'm never letting you go again.

My heart broke, shattered in pieces, as I bypassed the maze to begin my ascent to the bluffs. My best friend. My lover. My father's murderer. All this time.

Ask your best friend . . .

Faye's words, and a newly upside-down world, guided me as the storm came for me. From above. From the Manor at my back.

. . . what he did to your daddy.

Said the spider. To the fly.

49

I bypassed the maze's entrance, heading up the single path through the woods instead of down, where I would have met the road and hopefully a car passing by. But the need to get away quickly, to draw Nick away from Mama and Pen, was greater than any rational thought to get help. Maybe Mama and Pen would be able to call the police, with Faye pretty much down for the count.

Nick followed behind, right on my tail. He felt so close I could practically feel his breath on the back of my neck, could feel the tips of his fingers just before they grabbed me. Terrifying thoughts went through my mind of what he might do to Mama and Pen if he was left alone with them, or if he got ahold of me in the state he was in—pissed because I'd betrayed him and physically hurt him with that poker (which had made him accidentally shoot Faye), and because I wasn't going along with whatever plan he had in store for me.

"Jac!"

Every time he called my name, my body automatically recoiled. Each call of my name came with more ferocity and urgency than the time before. I pushed on, my hands out and swatting away branches and hanging vines from my path as I moved deeper into the forest and higher into the fog.

"Jac, please stop."

I couldn't.

"Let's talk it out. Let me explain."

Explain what? That even though I was purposely, stupidly drawing Nick away from Mama and Pen while they hopefully got the unspoken message to keep Faye subdued and call the cops, I was also running to the truth?

Nick had taken something from me that night, years ago. He'd allowed me to believe I'd killed my dad—had let the town believe it, too, making me the pariah. He'd hid behind me, all the while remaining my friend, trying to get even closer, to become more again. He'd even encouraged me to apply for a Fulbright scholarship after I'd bared my soul and told him what had happened with Conrad. And he'd been intimate with me—again—even when he knew he was the one who . . . the words refused to come.

We were like that for some time. It wasn't a straight shot or an easy route to the bluff. Nick kept calling to me, and I kept driving forward, trying to think of what I'd do once we finally made it to the bluff and there was nowhere else for me to go except to double back or go down to the craggy rocks and the Atlantic's crashing waves below.

When the trees began to thin out and the sky started peeking through more clearly, I knew I was almost there, at the clearing, with Nick hot on my tail. I'd passed the glades where Nick and I had been having sex when my father caught us. And where my father and I had argued. How the whole night had been an avalanche of the effects of the fight between me and Mama. Then finding Daddy. Then Daddy finding me and Nick, and everything that went down afterward. That night, it had been me against the world, and I'd lost miserably. Tonight, it was me against something entirely different, and I couldn't . . . I wouldn't.

"Come on, Jac, don't do this," Nick pleaded, pitiful enough to nearly make me slow my step. Faye could have been lying. This could have been another one of her manipulations.

Then, in the next breath. "Let me fucking see you!" he screamed, piercing the storm-heavy air.

I froze. The quickness with which Nick's change came on him, from supplication to rage, was dizzying, and I didn't know which way was up or down. Maybe this hadn't been a good idea, traipsing in the dark with someone after me who could kill.

"Jacinda." His voice struck me like a snake. He was closer than I'd thought.

I could kick myself for letting my doubts slow me down, taking me years back instead of grounding me in the present, where I needed to be to stay alive. I had to keep moving quickly to keep away, to keep Nick from catching up to me.

I ducked in the thicket, hoping my not-as-white T-shirt wouldn't give away my location. My view of the clearing was unobstructed, but it was so dark, and there were no lights, not even from the moon because of the storm clouds, that it was hard to see more than a couple of feet in front of me. I could hear the waves crashing at the bottom of the bluff. Somewhere in that fog, so thick you could cut it, lay the edge of the bluff, and if I wasn't carefully watching my steps, I could easily just drop.

Nick sobbed into the ether. "Please, Jac. I just wanted to be with you. I just wanted us to be together. I never meant for any of it to happen. I didn't think you'd leave for so long because of it."

The *it* he was referring to was when he'd killed my father.

Déjà vu. It was just like the night Dad had gone over the cliff.

Nick crashed through the trees, coming up behind me like a train, passing me in a rush of air, his heavy breathing making him sound animalistic. He moved into the clearing, Faye's gun in hand, pointing it without much purpose. It was as if he were just holding a rag. He turned slowly in a circle, trying to peer through the mist. I watched him, regulating my breathing so I wouldn't make a sound and alert him to where I was hiding in the bushes.

My heart thumped crazy beats so loudly I just knew he could hear them. It pounded in my ears, mixed with memories of Faye saying Nick was behind my dad's death and my dad's screams on his way down, intermingled with my own as I reached and reached for him.

"Jac, please." Nick repeated it over and over, turning round and round, the gun barely hanging from his fingers. He sniffled, running the back of his hand over his nose. "Please, just give me a chance to explain."

If I waited long enough, someone would come. I could wait him out. I knew how to be quiet in the woods when waiting for the prey to come. I'd sat in blinds with Granddad and Daddy while they were hunting, writing furiously in my seventy-page one-subject wide-ruled notebook or reading any one of my library books. I didn't care how long we sat out in the hot or cold because it meant I was with them and wasn't being forced to attend some kind of etiquette class or tea with Mama. It hit me then that I'd never have the chance to share a blind with my daddy or grandfather again. Because of Nick.

My knees were strained from my position, and when they couldn't take it anymore, I sat and lost my balance. My hand reached out to break my fall, but I landed hard on the damp forest floor, snapping a skinny fallen branch. I held my breath, my body freezing like one of the deer just before Granddad took a kill shot.

When I looked back into the clearing, Nick wasn't there. I panicked. I hadn't heard him leaving. I couldn't hear him barreling through the underbrush, slapping away the Spanish moss hanging low from the branches. It was as if he'd disappeared into the now-swirling fog as it descended from the air. Shadows danced in the moonlight. The faintest outline of the bluff's edge was etched faintly beyond me. I half stood, craning my neck to see if I could make out Nick's form.

Has he?

For a second, the briefest, my heart leaped in my throat.

Gone over?

I raised myself up a little more, a prairie dog popping up out of its hole to inspect what was out there. I was alone, with nothing but dark shadows swirling in the descended fog that was dampening my clothes, coiling my flat-ironed hair back to its natural state.

Then one of the swirling black masses was moving faster than it should have. The leaves rustled, and a burst of wind kicked up around me. I spun, about to dive back into my burrow, but it was too late. Hands wrapped around my waist and pulled me from the safety of my newly created blind, yanking me out into the open while I kicked and screamed for Nick to let me go.

"Don't touch me," I said, beating at his arms. The muscles were hard and firm around my midsection, dragging me as if I weighed nothing, and I wasn't a light-as-a-feather kind of girl.

"Stop it, Jac," he grunted over my beating. "I just want to talk. Just hear me out."

"Hear what?" I seethed, whipping my arm around to catch him on the side of his head. With all his military training, he could have taken me down right there, but he didn't. He let me hit him. I owed it to him. He spun me around.

"It was an accident," he said, finally grabbing my elbows and putting pressure on my points to subdue me.

My mouth opened in a silent scream as I leaned over to ease the pressure. Tears sprang to my eyes. "You don't know how long I waited for you, Jac. How long I'd been dreaming of us being together, and when we were again, these weeks have been the best of my life."

I didn't want to hear any of that. It was bullshit. "We were together, Nick. We were together when my dad saw us down there . . . together."

"Can I explain?" Nick's eyes looked so dark in the night. I remembered telling him all the time how I loved his baby blues. We were never supposed to have hooked up with each other. Nick, the then-councilman's-now-mayor's son; me, the chief's troublemaking daughter.

"Tell me it's not true. Nick. Tell me you didn't . . . and that you didn't have me believing I killed him all this time."

"Please, Jac." His voice broke, breaking me with it.

I hated myself for caving even a millimeter. But, my God, I wanted to know. *Needed* to know why he'd taken the most important person in my life and then lied to me and everyone for years. But I didn't need him to tell me. The memories I'd repressed for so long rushed over me like a deluge.

50

I killed you, Daddy. I let you go.

"You need to clear away those thoughts and see what you've really been missing."

Was it Daddy talking? Or Granddad? My present blurred with my past, becoming one and the same—time traveling me back to that night.

Daddy had found me exactly as I had found him, in the arms of someone I shouldn't have been with. He forced me to get out, warned Nick to stay away from me, told me that boy was no good. I'd run from him. Daddy chased me, but I refused to listen, the ice-cold rain pounding, soaking my dress, which dragged in the mud and grass like a weight.

I was in the clearing with thick rolls of fog billowing around us, thick rain coming down on us. It wasn't Nick, but Daddy. Daddy holding me, grabbing my shoulders, shaking me. Trying to make me listen. But I didn't want to hear anything he had to say.

"Why, Daddy, why? Don't you love Mama anymore?"

Shame filled his face. "Of course I do, Jac. I would—have done—anything for her. It was a mistake."

I didn't want to hear it. "She loves you. She gives you the world, and you just . . . betray her? I'm leaving here, and you don't ever have to worry about me again. Me and Nick."

Daddy hesitated. "Tate's boy? You can't go off with him. His father wouldn't allow it. *I* won't allow it."

"Don't bring Nick into this."

Daddy looked away, struggling with whatever was going on in his mind. "He's just not right for you, baby girl. What he's got is unhealthy. I see it in him. And I can't let you . . . he's not safe."

"You're crazy."

"Even if he tried, it will be over my goddamned dead body. You can hate me all you want, Jac, but I will not let you be with that boy."

The wind whipped the fog around us. The moon was obliterated, pitching us in complete darkness. I could barely see my father in front of me. I could not believe what he was saying. Not Nick. We'd been best friends since high school. College. And tonight, we'd sealed the deal between us. Why shouldn't I have someone who'd love me as much as Mama loved Daddy? Nick would never hurt me.

"You can't tell me anything after what you just did."

"You will see that boy over my goddamned dead body," he bellowed. Angrier than I'd ever seen him. Fearful too.

I was twenty-two but feeling thirteen and under the thumb of my parents, who'd pretended to be a perfect couple when my father was nothing but a cheat and a liar.

Daddy had caught up to Nick and me after I'd seen him in the storage shed. We were in Nick's car having sex. We'd snagged some bottles of Councilman Tate's whiskey and had finished a bottle between us. It could have been an act of rebellion, doing something I knew would hurt my father as much as he'd hurt me and our family.

Daddy was so angry, pulling us apart like we were weightless paper dolls. He threatened to kill Nick if he ever laid a hand on me again, saying we'd never see each other again. I broke away from them. I was humiliated, angry, and confused. Nothing I did was right, first in my mother's eyes and now in my father's. Daddy's disappointment in me drove me toward the bluff.

"Jac—"

"Don't." I snatched my hand away from him.

Daddy reached for me again. "Careful, Jac, the edge—the fog. Watch out."

I didn't care. "I wish you'd just die!"

He tried grabbing at me. I fought back. Alcohol, anguish, embarrassment, confusion, fear all fueling my actions.

I growled, "I'd rather you die than Mama ever having to know how you betrayed her. I wish you were dead!"

I screamed for him to die over and over, getting louder and louder. Daddy grabbed me and his touch felt corrosive, burning me. I flung him off, not wanting the smell of him and the woman from the shed—whoever she was, not that it would matter—on me. I shoved my father hard. Too hard, wanting him to heed my words and just die, but also not. My world had imploded. The very best man I knew, a man my mother idolized, was not that. I needed some space, but he kept coming. Kept trying to explain. Kept telling me he was sorry. That I couldn't be with Nick. Just kept talking, when I just wanted him to stay away and not touch me. Let me breathe as I tried to figure out what—how—to tell Mama. If I should tell Mama. Knowing this would kill her. It simply would. She would blame me. To Mama, Daddy was a god. To me, in this moment, he was the devil. With all my alcohol-infused strength, I shoved him hard.

He grunted, not expecting the force. He staggered back, grunting from the impact. Daddy was a big, brawny man, and it wasn't normal for his significantly smaller daughter to move him.

I spun on my heel, not waiting to see if he righted himself and got back on solid footing. The air whirled, shadows with substantial mass moving around me, lightly feathering my skin. Even in my fugue state, I remember thinking that the fog and mist were so thick they felt like they had solid mass.

There was no moon or stars. I imagined that this was what being in a black hole was like, dense and heavy and dangerous. I lost all sense of direction, unsure if I was facing the woods or facing the bluff. If I walked on, I could go over the cliff. I was taking a hesitant step forward when a mass of wind and fog and rain whirled by me. I heard my father speak.

"What are you—" His sentence cut off, and he grunted hard, like the breath had whooshed from his body. Daddy's voice bounced off the thick fogbank, echoed, then nothing else.

I spun in a complete circle, searching for Daddy's outline.

"Dad?" I called out, working through the haze both in my head and all around me. I slid a foot forward, toeing the ground. The edge could be anywhere. It was so dark. So foggy.

I heard another grunt of struggle.

"Daddy?" I moved toward it, the alcohol burning away as if I were directly facing the sun. Point-toe-slide-shuffle. Point-toe-slide-shuffle. I continued that until the waves got louder at the bluff's edge.

"Dad."

I dropped to my knees. I didn't hesitate a moment longer. I didn't let the fear of what I'd see stop me because I wasn't in control of myself anymore.

I leaned over the edge and through the mist and fog, which had thinned without a surface to cling to, and I could see him. My dad. He was hanging on to a root or something that was jutting out, stopping his fall.

He was grunting. His feet kicking a little, trying to find purchase and slipping on the slick surface.

"Daddy," I said, my voice coming out in a squeal. I was barely able to comprehend what I was seeing. This couldn't possibly be real life. That couldn't be my father down there.

I threw myself on the ground, stretching my arm out. I used my toes to push myself forward, inching myself over the edge bit by bit, my hand reaching, reaching for his.

I cried out, "Daddy, grab. Can you grab?"

My fingers strained toward him, trembling, locking up from the strain of me trying to get to him. I inched and inched, elongating my body, wishing I was taller so I could reach him.

My other hand propped me up, but my upper body was well over the edge, and I was teetering. Stretching. Daddy was shaking his head. "No. Stop. Don't come any farther. Stop, Jac. Before you fall too."

But I couldn't. Couldn't let him go. He was my daddy. He'd come up here to get me, to bring me home. He'd never once given up on me. And I couldn't give up on him.

"Take my hand, Daddy, please," I pleaded. I stretched farther. My toes digging into the rock I lay on. My left hand shaking from trying to hold my weight and keep me from keeling over. My back spasmed from the effort. But I ignored it all.

"Take it." I could pull him up. I could save him. I could do this thing.

He dug his feet into whatever foothold he could find. His fingers found mine, and I grabbed on. Our hands were wet from sweat and from the misting rain with its intermittent downpours. We couldn't get a firm grip. The rock was slimy and so slick with rain. My father's weight and gravity combated mine, and I was no match. My body started to slide forward. My toes dug in deeper, cramping, bending. The pain was so intense. But none of that stopped me from pitching forward.

Until something grabbed me from behind, stopping my forward momentum with a jerk.

"Jac, no!" It was Nick, who'd reached us finally, grabbing onto me to keep me from sliding.

"Forget about me, Nick," I said. "Get my dad. He's down there."

"I'm sorry, Jac. I'm so sorry," Nick said. He wouldn't let go of me. He held me around my waist, his muscles tightening like a boa constrictor. I couldn't breathe. I couldn't let go. I couldn't look back. I wouldn't take my eyes off my father.

Then my father lost his footing, and the only thing holding him up was me. My arm wrenched in its socket, forcing me to cry out in pain.

Gravity kicked in, and we—Daddy, me, Nick—began to slide forward again.

That's when Daddy looked at me, wide eyed. Terrified but resolute. I shook my head, knowing what he was thinking before he said the words. I shook my head again frantically, my exposed stomach grinding into the gravel, tearing my skin.

Love you, he mouthed.

I shook my head. "Don't," I said. "Don't you do it. Hold on. Nick."

Love you.

"Daddy, I got you."

But I didn't have him. Because he was prying my cold locked-up fingers from his. He was looking at me, telling me I was okay. I was okay, even while he twisted the tips of his fingers from mine. Even when the final two were undone, and for a second we were frozen in time, in midair, eyes locked.

You're. Okay.

Time unfroze, the distance between us suddenly stretching as he moved away from me.

I lurched forward, but Nick held on tight, not letting me go. I bucked. Tried to kick. Watched my dad grow farther and farther away.

My last vision was of my dad, Montavious Brodie Jr., his round, terrified eyes accepting death to keep me from coming with him. I watched him get swallowed by the swirling mass of fog and mist with the waves crashing against the jagged boulders below.

His arm remained extended, reaching out to me and mine to him. I screamed for him, over and over, as if my screams would reverse his course and float him back to me. I would have gone down with him willingly. I couldn't imagine life without my father. Life with my mother and sister, knowing how I'd robbed them of a full life with him. And all because of my selfishness. My hooking up with Nick. My going against my father's word.

All of that had cost my father his life.

I watched the black and fog swallow my father up. Heard the sound of him as he slammed into the jumble of boulders below. Was pulled back onto the bluff and enveloped by Nick's arms as he rocked me, murmuring "I'm so sorry. I didn't mean it. I didn't mean to" over and over.

The sound of my father slamming into the jagged boulders below was what I remembered, what had driven me awake from nightmares nearly every night of my life since. Was what had consumed me, blotting out other parts of that night so I never had a complete picture. The sound of him silenced me, and I couldn't speak of it until I had with Conrad.

Nick's words hadn't registered. I never recalled them. Never added it all up together. I had believed Nick was apologizing for pulling me up, for saving my life and being unable to save my father.

What I hadn't realized then was that Nick wasn't apologizing because my father was gone. He was apologizing because he was the one who'd killed him.

51

"Why?" I croaked out the question. Rain pelted lightly on my forehead as I looked up at Nick. There were too many thoughts fighting each other to be in the forefront. It was the question I had been asking myself for years.

He held me in a firm grip, his mouth clamped tight, his lips forming a thin line. He begged me with his eyes to understand something that I couldn't.

"Why?" I said it louder because the wind was picking up. The weather reports were spot on; remnants of the tropical storm were about to hit land. Thin ribbons of white light started outlining the clouds hanging heavily overhead, about to split open.

I repeated myself.

Nick swallowed and refused to say anything.

"Just say it!" I screamed, unable to control myself any longer. His hands on my arms burned through my skin. I just wanted him off me. I wanted him away. I wanted him to be my friend. I wanted him to say he didn't do it, that I was remembering it wrong. That the swirling mass of shadow and fog that passed me and rushed at my dad wasn't him.

Inside my chest, heat as hot as the lightning stretching across the sky started forming. At first it was a tiny little marble, sparked when I came to on the cliff and realized Nick was standing in front of me, not my father. It pulsated, growing.

"Say it."

Thunder cracked above, reverberating around us, sounding like a sonic boom. My ears picked up another sound beneath it, tiny and seemingly far away. A high-pitched sound, like someone calling. It was hard to tell if that was real or imagined. It had been nearly impossible to tell fantasy from reality for too long.

"Jac." Before, when Nick would say my name, it meant comfort. It meant safety and friendship. Now, it meant confusion and anger. It meant death.

The high-pitched noises were coming closer. Others, calling my name.

"Tell me."

Before they came. Before they stopped us and he never admitted to anything. I needed him to admit it to me. Before they came and took me away for things I didn't do, for running around, acting like the wild Brodie girl they swore I was, he had to admit it. I stopped struggling, my hands flat against his sides, feeling the fight slipping out of me. I had to know.

"Because I wanted you."

The answer was too simple. In another world, in another kind of story, this answer would have made me swoon. It would be the kind of confession that anyone would wait a lifetime to hear. It was the kind of answer that formed a union between families instead of a crevice. In another kind of story, this kind of answer would mean the beginning instead of the end.

"You killed him."

"He said he wouldn't let us be together," Nick continued, raising his voice over the crack of thunder. The wind whipped furiously, so hard we were forced to brace ourselves against it. We should've been taking cover. It wasn't safe to be out here in the clearing with the edge just nearby. It wasn't safe anywhere.

"You let the town hate me, blame me," I said.

The sounds grew closer. Tiny circles of light dotted the thick, dense trees.

"It had taken me eight years—all through high school, all through college—to finally get a chance to be with you. That night," Nick said, holding me by my arms still. "That night was the beginning of something between you and me. When Chief Brodie said we couldn't . . . because of my dad's shit, I couldn't let yours keep us apart. I couldn't let yours destroy my family either. I got angry."

Nick stopped, struggling with himself. "Suddenly he was grabbing you. Yelling at you. I don't know, I ran at him and—and—" He swallowed. "I pushed him. I knew the edge was close, but I pushed. I just wanted him to leave so he wouldn't convince you to leave me. You always ended up listening to your dad."

Nick let me go when I pulled myself from him.

"You killed my father." The words were foreign, like they hadn't come from me.

Nick searched my eyes. There was no more explanation he could provide. No excuses. Only acceptance. Only accountability.

The air left his body, and it deflated, his shoulders hunching. "I killed him."

His admission was so simple. Anticlimactic, after all the years I'd spent blaming myself. In one act, in three words, Nick Tate had altered the course for the both of us.

We looked down, seeing the gun in my hand that I'd pulled from the waistband of his jeans, its muzzle pointed at his stomach, heavy in my hand. I couldn't even say when my hand had made contact. When my finger wrapped around it. When I pulled it free.

"Jac," he whispered, resignation setting in. "He said we couldn't . . ." He couldn't finish.

The irony of blaming my father. The audacity.

"Thing is," I began, looking into Nick's ruined face, "I would have chosen you."

Nick's eyes widened, turning to horror as the realization of my words set in.

The clearing exploded with light from all sides. From above, an earsplitting crack, from beneath, an earth-shaking rumble. From all around, spotlights burst through the trees. A cacophony of noise, of demands to put our hands up. A scattering of calls of my name and his, demanding we back away from the edge. But none of that registered. It was just me and Nick. Nick had punished us both—and lost any chance for him and me—for nothing. Nick had always been filled with good intentions to protect me and what he and I could be. Instead, he'd chosen the road to hell.

The intrusion of people and noise, the surprise from the storm right above us, startled us. Nick lunged for me, unable to give up, still trying to make a way when everything between us was dead.

He grabbed me, crushing the gun in between us, twisting my hand in the process. Someone who was coming into the clearing screamed my name, and it carried on the increasing wind.

Thunder cracked again at the same time the gun did, the heat building between Nick and me. There was wind. And pain as we stumbled from the impact.

Then there was misty air as we went over the edge of the bluff at Moor Manor.

52

Nick took me with him as he toppled over, the weight of his body with gravity making him slide down the length of me. The gun fell away, and the world went sideways. Suddenly, I was pitching forward into the abyss, unable to find any purchase. My hands flailed uselessly in the heavy air. I twisted, grasping at anything that could stop my momentum.

My hands shot out, finding a jutting ridge of rock, and I grabbed it with both hands, pain ripping through my arms from the hard stop. Below me, Nick held on to my ankle. I managed to look down at him. My fingers trembled as I strained to keep my hold on the slippery rock. My weight, and Nick's weight, seemed to amplify. There was no way I could hang on any longer.

My fingers slipped off the rock, and gravity took over. But from the dark, a pair of hands grabbed my still-outstretched ones, stopping my fall with a hard jerk. I looked up to the face of my father overhead, our positions reversed. He hovered over the edge, his hands firm around my wrist, strain evident in his face.

I nearly let go from the shock at seeing him, but he held on firmly, there, when he'd been long gone for six years.

You're okay, Jac, Daddy said.

"Don't you give up." Daddy's voice was changing, lightening, becoming feminine. Becoming my mother.

His face changed, and there was my mother, holding on to me with both hands. Half her body was over the edge, and just like I did six years ago, she was sliding toward me, not away. My weight and Nick's were pulling her down.

And just like that, I understood why my father had forced me to let go. His love for me was worth more to him than his life. And my love for my mother was the same. I wouldn't take her down with me. And just as my father had, I tried to pull away to save her from being another victim of Nicolas Tate.

I sobbed. "Mama."

She held on tight. "Girl, don't you dare. Don't you even think about it. You give yourself a chance."

I looked down at Nick, still holding on, holding his side where the bullet had hit him when I fired the shot.

"Jac."

I wouldn't let Nick take one more thing from me. I wouldn't let him take my life.

I kicked at him, shaking my leg to get him off. He grabbed at it, trying to hang on. We made eye contact, a whole conversation transpiring in seconds. It was enough. Nick had done enough. He stopped fighting. He stopped wanting and finally gave me up. He let go, falling wordlessly into the nothingness that swallowed him whole.

Mama was no longer sliding toward me but away, and I was moving with her. I crested the bluff's edge, able to see the mass of people in the clearing. Behind Mama was Pen, my beautiful, courageous little sister, her head bandaged, arms around Mama's waist. Behind Pen was Sawyer, and then Carl, who I thought I wouldn't see again but was so relieved I did.

Chief Linwood and more cops arrived, hands reaching to grab a part of me from the edge, from the world of the dead, and pull me back to the world of the living . . . to safety.

All of them there not to condemn me this time but to save me.

EPILOGUE

Pen and Patrick's wedding was the mark of a new day, a celebration of love and of new beginnings. The air buzzed with excitement as I stood proudly as Pen's maid of honor beside her, newly married, in a barrage of wedding photos. When my maid of honor picture duties were complete, I lagged behind the rest of the wedding party to await the couple finishing up so the reception could get started. Then we made our way to the sprawling back of Moor Manor.

I watched Mama tutting around, welcoming everyone and making sure they had what they needed. I plucked a glass of champagne from a server moving past me. The ceremony was a testimony to the resilience of the Brodie women. We gathered, had weathered the storms of betrayal and tragedy. We were still standing.

"Jac." Mama came from the side, having finished buzzing about. She slid an arm around my waist, squeezing me to her. She leaned forward, looking at my nose. It twitched, and I waited for her to say something annoying.

"When you and Pen go, I'll be alone for the first time in a long while. I think I'll get one of those things too." She touched the base of her nose lightly, smiling as she gazed out at the maze, pretending I wasn't gawking at her.

"You're going to get a septum ring?"

"Hmm," she said mysteriously, her smile coy, leaving me to wonder if the woman wasn't actually considering it. Her happiness, the relaxed way she hung back as the wedding, minor hiccups and all, played out without her trying to control it all, or me, was infectious, and I joined her, appreciating Mama's new easy humor that had flourished ever since her truth was laid bare when Carl came visiting.

"Heard anything about that woman?" Her voice hardened, and I immediately knew whom she was referring to.

Sadness squeezed my heart, thinking back to when I'd said the same things earlier that day at the cemetery, where I visited our family.

"Senior Dick, Chief Dick, Junior Dick reporting for duty," I announced, taking out a small bouquet of lilies and placing them atop one of the center stones. "For you, Grandma, because I know you don't drink. But for the rest of the fellas . . ."

I had poured a shot for my uncle Jack, Daddy, Granddad, and lastly, for myself. After the year I'd had, I definitely needed it. I sat facing my Brodie family, allowing myself to feel the weight of being there with some of the people I loved the most, who should've been preparing for Pen's afternoon wedding, here with me and Mama instead of below the ground.

"Faith Anderson, a.k.a. Faye Arden, was found guilty here for attacking you, Granddad, and for killing Mia. A few hunters found Mia's body about a month after Faye was arrested, rolled in a tarp two counties away, dumped in the woods. GPS tracked Faye's SUV traveling that way at a high speed, stopping in the area where the body was found for about thirty minutes, and then racing back to town. She's been extradited to Nevada for the deaths of the Colleton girls and Daphne Franklin. But check this out. Don't know if you heard, but the professor, Conrad? His death made national headlines. I guess because he was embroiled in the whole sex scandal with me and other staff at the university, plus stealing my story was such good drama it was on the Today *show and* Good Morning America. CBS Mornings *too. And guess what? His publisher—the one that bought my story from him—they want to work with me. They want me to write my story and everything about Faye, the whole deal with you, Daddy, and Nick . . . Think I should?"*

I poured a shot of bourbon at each grave, dribbling out a little bit from the glasses for each fallen Brodie.

Poured one out for Daddy. One for Granddad. One for Uncle Jack because I owed that to Cousin K'Shawn, who was somewhere traveling internationally with the best friend / sister he couldn't tell me about yet, or so he'd said when I'd thanked him for the lawyer.

"Would make a great book, don't you think? Apparently, all the big publishers want my story. And some production companies have been sniffing around for a movie or TV series. How's that for being on the come up?"

Guess I had Conrad beat there.

"Patrick and Sawyer will take care of the cabin for us while I'm gone," I'd assured Granddad in case he was worried. *"I've already told the Armchairs so they won't worry either."*

The FBI was investigating if any more victims had been left in Faye's wake for the twenty years she'd been on the run and reinventing herself over and over to achieve the happiness and satisfaction that was always elusive to her. Sitting cross-legged in front of them, I lifted up my fifth of bourbon in the air.

"To closing cases and setting things back right."

I honored each headstone: Daddy, Granddad, and Uncle Jack on Grandma's other side. Then I'd tossed the drink back, grimacing and blowing out breath loudly through my teeth to assuage the burning trail it made down my insides.

I relayed all that to Mama.

Mama said, her eyes filling with tears, "Mia, poor child."

I should have poured one out for Mia too. Her death was on me. Would stay on me for the rest of my life.

Mama squeezed me again, hard, like she was making up for so much lost time. If she didn't stop, she would break me, both inside and out.

"I love you, Jac."

My chest swelled until I thought it would explode from my chest like in that *Alien* movie as I luxuriated in the warmness of her. "Love you too, Mama."

We stood wordless as we watched Pen's special day shift from wedding to reception and the guests got themselves comfortable while waiting for the happy couple. I was still unable to fully believe that Murder Manor had been exorcised of its infamous past. Too much had happened there, as recently as a few months ago. But the Manor was the most beautiful venue Brook Haven had to offer, and Pen was determined not to let Faye Arden, the Tates, or the ghost stories of Murder Manor mar her dream wedding.

"The wedding will be the beginning of a new leaf for the Manor and for all of us," Pen had said, interlacing her fingers with Patrick's as she reaffirmed her resolve to have the wedding she envisioned, damn what anyone else thought.

I asked Mama, "What about Carl? You think he'll keep it secret about his cousin?"

"I think he cares about the newest secret member of his family. That is, until you're ready to meet them. But as for me, I think he'll let me be. For you, not for me."

I disagreed. "No, Mama, I think Carl realizes you're owed for how Ralph hurt you. You're owed most of all."

Carl had chosen to protect Mama and me, opting for a fractured family unit rather than his initial pursuit of justice.

"Jac, I never meant to let my fear dictate the kind of mother I would be to you. I couldn't see beyond the need to not let him show up in you. He didn't have the right to any part of you. You're MJ's daughter. Always."

Always a Brodie.

"I know, Mama. I know you had the best intentions."

Mama said, "You know what they say, 'The road to hell is paved with good intentions.'" She arched her eyebrow as she looked at me. "Wouldn't you agree?"

I thought about everyone who'd had the best intentions, which had led to disastrous results—me included. Even Nick. As much as I wanted to, I couldn't hate Nick, despite what he'd done. I thought about how I still kept the secret of Daddy's infidelity from my mother, knowing I'd never tell, despite what hell that road had led me to. Carl's family weren't the only ones who owed her. I owed her the belief that the man she'd fought and killed for had never betrayed her, not even once.

My understanding and acceptance of my complex past and even more complex relationship with my mother meant growth for the both of us. We were getting better. Slowly. Surely.

Mama let out a breath, satisfied she'd somewhat cleared the air. She prepared to head back to the party. "Pen and Patrick will be back soon. Don't be too long."

I nodded that I'd heard her, wanting to enjoy the last few moments of quiet before the festivities began and I would celebrate my sister long into the night.

I looked down the sloping hills with the garden maze below, the hedges and shrubs clipped and cultivated to perfection.

It had been seven months since Faye. Seven months since Nick. Seven months since I'd come back home and fought for my right to stay. And yet tomorrow, when Pen and Patrick were readying to go on their Virgin Islands honeymoon, I'd be on my way to South Korea, Fulbright scholarship in hand, to teach. It was a ticket that had unlocked the shackles that once held me. It would be an experience of a lifetime, and I was more than ready for it.

The sun began to dip low, casting a warm glow over Moor Manor and the world that surrounded it. From my perch, I could see the bluff that had once been my nightmare and was the place of my rebirth. The memories that were once locked in the recesses of my mind now played vividly before my eyes. I remembered the strained voices. How Daddy begged for me to understand. To not use his mistake to make one of my own in being with Nick. I remembered the push that sent Daddy over the edge. Nick's misguided attempt to keep us together was what had torn our world apart, fating us to never be together in this life or any other.

With all truths laid bare, I felt a sense of closure and an odd sense of happiness. I felt light, like I could float away with nothing to hold me down.

"There's my beautiful date for the evening."

I turned as Dr. Weigert—Chris—joined me, bringing with him a flute of champagne. I showed him I already had one, and he grinned. "Sorry, just needed a minute to catch my breath," I said.

"I get it. I'll leave you to it then. But I'm glad we got to have the date." He pulled a face. "Even if it is for a wedding and only for one night because you're going away for like a year. Next time, you're not slipping away. We're having a real date."

But for now, I was having a date with destiny. I laughed. "Yes, Dr. Weigert."

He returned a sheepish grin. "I like that," he said. "A lot."

He swapped out my nearly empty flute for one of the full ones he'd brought and left with my promise of joining him soon. There probably wouldn't be anything for the good doctor and me. I couldn't think of anything near a relationship after Nick, whom I still cared about, despite what he'd done and what I'd ended up doing to him. It wasn't something I'd get over easily, but I had time. And a new lease on life.

Brook Haven, once a labyrinth of secrets like the garden maze below, had released me of its bonds. My newfound purpose was to live for me. I was and could only be me. Not for Mama, or a guy, or a town.

But for Jacinda Brodie.

ACKNOWLEDGMENTS

I have many people to thank for helping me through this process, providing insight and expertise, and especially their listening ear, their shoulder to lean on, their patience while I worked, their eyes to review. And most of all for telling me I didn't suck as a writer, even when I never believed a single word they said.

To Megha Parekh, my editor who supported me in writing a different kind of thriller and backed me entirely. I love your style and how you give me space and trust me to do my work. Thanks to the fantastic team at Thomas & Mercer, including the editorial and marketing teams. Special thanks to developmental editor Charlotte Herscher, who helped cobble my hot mess of a story together, and copyeditors Elyse L. and Megan W., with a special shout-out to Megan, who reminded me that "guillotines don't swing." I loved her note so much that I had to include it in the story.

Melissa Edwards, my agent and friend. Thank you for your guidance and frankness and comfort when my feelings are hurt. You're always looking out for me, and that means the most.

To my family, who give up their time with me so I can work and do this thing that I love. I owe you a few nights of board games, where I will win.

Honestly, I don't know if I ever could have written this story if not for Jess Lourey and Rachel Howzell Hall, my sounding boards, brainstormers, and early conceptual readers. Most importantly, they're my friends.

To my writing family, thank you for providing community, being inspiring, and pushing me to do and be better. Oh, and for always answering my questions. You know who you are.

To my friend Medina Boggs and my husband, Vincent, who helped with research as I created a fictional coastal Lowcountry town near Charleston that had a cliff high enough for someone to fall from and die. And thanks to Dr. Dan Bouknight and Dr. Cynthia Pridgen for allowing me to pick their brains about pacemakers and their paths to becoming doctors.

To the readers, booksellers, librarians, podcasters, bloggers, et cetera: If not for you all, where would our stories be?

Special shout-out to my cousin Santrese Washington, who inspired Jac's love of a good hookah. You are an absolute joy, San, but can we go on that trip now? And to my friend Irene Stephens, thank you for having that crazy handgun clock displayed in your shop. It's the star of this story.

Lastly, I had a great boss and even better friend who was supportive from the moment he learned I was about to be published. Stephen Sutusky passed last year way too young, leaving behind a wife and three kids. He fought hard until he just couldn't anymore. In his last texts in our group chat right before, he said, "Keep Writing I Love it."

So I'll do just that.

ABOUT THE AUTHOR

Photo © 2021 Rodney Williams Creative Images Photography

Yasmin Angoe is the author of *Her Name Is Knight* and a first-generation Ghanaian American currently residing in South Carolina with her family. She's been an educator for nearly twenty years and works as a developmental editor. Yasmin received the 2020 Eleanor Taylor Bland Crime Fiction Writers of Color Award from Sisters in Crime and is a member of numerous crime, mystery, and thriller organizations, including Sisters in Crime, Crime Writers of Color, and International Thriller Writers. You can find her at www.yasminangoe.com, on X at @yasawriter, and on Instagram at @author_yas.